OF BROTHERHOODS

Sumit Agarwal, Managing Director of the MLA Group of Industries, Kanpur, was born in 1975. After completing a five-year integrated course in Chemistry and a minor in management from IIT Kanpur, he is now managing a group of chemical manufacturing industries in Kanpur (www.mlagroup.com).

His first book *Four Patriots*, a bestseller, is a fast-paced patriotic action thriller published by Rupa Publications. It was endorsed by over a dozen celebrities and public figures. The author's stories subtly convey a message, inspiring people to work towards a better tomorrow.

Sumit also runs PRERNA (www.prernaa.org), a non-governmental organization dedicated to developing a stronger India. He is also a music composer, lyricist, singer, actor and writer.. His music videos can be viewed on his YouTube Channel, Sumit Agarwal, or on his website (www.sumitagarwal.net), Spotify, Gaana and Jio.

You can also connect with the author via
Facebook: sumitsvoice
Twitter: TheFourPatriots
Email: md@mlagroup.com

'Despite being deeply informative and thought-provoking, the book is a hardcore page turner.'
—*The Times of India*

'A thrilling and spine-chilling story!'
—*Mid-Day*

'The book analyses the origin and growth of terrorism in the world in a very interesting way. I hope this will reach out to a large section of people, especially the youth, who need to understand the threat of terrorism.'
—**Anandiben Patel**, Governor of Uttar Pradesh

'Very well-written.'
—**Jitendra**, famous movie star

'The subject of terrorism has been woven into a very interesting story.'
—**Brajesh Pathak**, Deputy Chief Minister of Uttar Pradesh

'The story has been presented very effectively.'
—**Dinesh Sharma**, Former Deputy Chief Minister of Uttar Pradesh

'Fabulous read.'
—**Tushar Kapoor**, movie star

'A cliffhanger all the way through. Truly impressive!'
—**Pulkit Trivedi**, Director, Google Pay-India

'This book deftly weaves a very important topic—international terrorism—into a spellbinding story.'
—**Satish Mahana**, Speaker, Uttar Pradesh Vidhan Sabha

'The writer has drawn attention to a very important and sensitive subject in an engrossing and entertaining way. An amazing read!'
—**Rajendra Trivedi**, Minister of Law and Justice, Legislative and Parliamentary Affairs, Government of Gujarat

'A hair-raising thriller on international terrorism. The twists in the tale will blow your mind. A wonderful read!'
—**Avtar Gill**, veteran film actor

'It's a great read.'
—**Mona Singh**, renowned film and television star

'The thing I love about Sumit's writing is that he writes with a purpose. It's real, deep stuff and yet very entertaining. Kudos!'
—**Ashwani Agarwal**, Chief Supply Chain Officer, Lenskart

'Meticulously researched, professionally written and a deeply engrossing tale of one man's battle against organized international terrorism. A book that you just wouldn't want to put down before you reach its last page. An edgy thriller with tons of tense moments, from the first page to the last. Really enjoyed it!'
—**Dr Sanjay Kapoor**, President, All India Chess Federation

'Very fast-paced, gripping and thought-provoking. A good read.'
—**Bhuwan Chaturvedi**, Chief Executive Officer, Paharpur Cooling Towers Group

'From the streets of Cairo to the hills of Tajikistan... a very eclectic setting and an equally thrilling tale.'
—**Sanjiv Chatterji**, Head of Supply Chain (Africa, Middle East and Turkey), ekaterra

'Loved the content and writing style.'
—**Shashikant Kekare**, Joint Commissioner (Greater Mumbai), Food and Drug Administration

OF BROTHERHOODS

SUMIT AGARWAL

Published by
Rupa Publications India Pvt. Ltd 2023
7/16, Ansari Road, Daryaganj
New Delhi 110002

Sales centres:
Prayagraj Bengaluru Chennai
Hyderabad Jaipur Kathmandu
Kolkata Mumbai

Copyright © Sumit Agarwal 2023

This is a work of fiction. Names, characters, places and incidents are either
the product of the author's imagination or are used fictitiously
and any resemblance to any actual person,
living or dead, events or locales is entirely coincidental.

All rights reserved.
No part of this publication may be reproduced, transmitted,
or stored in a retrieval system, in any form or by any means,
electronic, mechanical, photocopying, recording or otherwise,
without the prior permission of the publisher.

P-ISBN: 978-93-5520-854-5
E-ISBN: 978-93-5520-855-2

First impression 2023

10 9 8 7 6 5 4 3 2 1

The moral right of the author has been asserted.

Printed in India

This book is sold subject to the condition that it shall not,
by way of trade or otherwise, be lent, resold, hired out, or otherwise
circulated, without the publisher's prior consent, in any form of binding or
cover other than that in which it is published.

Dedicated to my father,
Mr Murari Lal Agarwal, a living legend...

Contents

Prologue		*xi*
1	Mokthar and Adel	1
2	Kabir and His MH470 Obsession	8
3	The Shattering Betrayal	18
4	Chased By a Shadow	24
5	Mokhtar Meets Ghassan	33
6	Kabir Meets Keira	39
7	The Flute Player	44
8	The Man Must Live!	51
9	The Tiff	56
10	The Black Spider	62
11	The Black Moth	66
12	Mokhtar Meets Nouran	79
13	The Untraceable Rendezvous	89
14	The Grand Carnival	99
15	The Protettori	111
16	The First Taqiya	115
17	Life In a War-torn Country	119
18	Islam Is the Solution!	134
19	The Desert Hostages	140
20	The Nazi Bankroll	148
21	Olaf: the X-man	156
22	Trouble In the Mediterranean	164
23	Murshid: the Conjurer	176
24	The Palimpsest, Double Eagle and LSD	187
25	The Mission Falls Apart	192

26	The Sheepdogs and the Eliminators	204
27	Village of the Gypsy Women	210
28	Hanif, the Saviour	228
29	Brotherhood and Air-Bee: the Baffling Connection	231
30	The King's Secret Army	238
31	Off To Nowhere	243
32	The Caliphate Dream	246
33	The Lost World	250
34	The Face-off	254
35	Kabir Strikes Gold	262
36	A Parallel Headquarter	265
37	Green Dots All Over the Map	268
38	Bilal Sows His Seed	271
39	The Chinese Engineers	274
40	Hanif's Grief	282
41	Hell Breaks Loose	288
42	The World Forces Collude	293
43	The Countdown Begins	299
44	The Earthquake	302
45	Something's Off!	305
46	Enter the Cove!	307
47	The Armageddon Begins	309
48	You Are a Girl…	330
49	A Face-off Between Titans	332
50	The Surreal Experience	335
51	Keira Deciphered	339
52	The Final Skydive	344
53	Religion: a Convenient Vehicle	351
Epilogue		358
Acknowledgements		367

Prologue

8 March 2014
Inside an aircraft

Danish woke up with a jolt and found himself rooted to a seat. He was sandwiched between two passengers, both of whom seemed to be in deep slumber; even the frightful turbulence wouldn't perturb them. He had a fuzzy memory of having requested the fat lady next to him for the aisle seat, and of how she wouldn't budge. Soon after that, he had quickly slipped into a power nap, keeping his tray table open for the hostesses to leave his meal there. A glance at his watch revealed almost four hours had passed! His power nap usually lasted only twenty-five minutes.

Four hours? Danish wiped the heavy droplets of sweat clinging to his brow before examining his watch again. *H ... how?*

His head was pounding within the stifling air of the cabin; the cramp in his leg was becoming unbearable. As the horizon of his sight widened, he was horrified to note how everybody in the cabin seemed fast asleep, their heads rolling to one side or the other as the television screens in front of them continued to paint their faces in different shades. Some of the flight attendants and guests lay sprawled on the floor. Had it not been for his plummeting blood sugar levels, he wouldn't have woken up either.

We've been doped!

8 March 2014
Somewhere on an island, inside a technology centre

Robert Gray splashed water over his face in the dimly lit washroom and ran his wet hands through his hair, putting back restless curls in their place. *Wait…had a shadow just flown past the mirror?* He spun around only to find the same soothing ambience and the citrus fragrance of the air freshener lingering in the air. *Febreze!*

Anyhow, he had to get back to the action inside. He had to be quick or his supervisor would get mad. Whistling his favourite Coldplay number, Robert hurried towards the exit. He stopped for a moment to snatch one last peek at himself in the full-length mirror on a rear wall. Suddenly, something fell on him. In a flash of pain, his neck was twisted till it snapped. He fell down to the ground, his body a limp heap.

∽

What the hell is going on? Pulling himself out of the seat with great effort, Danish stumbled over the fat lady and stepped out into the aisle. His low blood sugar levels had blurred his vision and were now triggering dreadful palpitations. He reached for some sugar sachets from the remnants of a half-eaten meal lying on a tray table nearby and gulped their contents down with some water. He stood there for a while, waiting for the effect to kick in.

Once his vision began to clear, Danish trudged to the front, staring at the orange-purple hue of dawn through the tiny airplane window.

This has to be a hijacking!

But there were no traces of blood anywhere—that much he was certain of. So where were the hijackers? And how had all the passengers been sedated?

He reached the curtains that separated the announcement cubicle from the first-class cabin. Three air hostesses lay collapsed in their seats, their heads slumped forward. Breathlessness was catching up with him again. 'Oxy... oxygen?'

Wrestling with the reeling, debilitating effects, he glimpsed around for an oxygen mask and grabbed it. *Nothing.* It seemed as if the flight's pressurization system had either malfunctioned or been tampered with, depleting oxygen reserves and rendering everyone unconscious. *Hypoxemia leading to syncope!* He recalled its medical terminology from his days at commando training.

The hijackers must be in the cockpit. They must be holding the two pilots captive at gunpoint.

With great effort, Danish reached for the sole of his shoe, flipped it open and assembled the plastic-alloy mini pistol. He then crouched and crawled—more out of weakness than choice—till he reached the door of the cockpit. Raising his hand, he threw the door open and immediately dropped to his stomach, pointing his pistol straight ahead.

∽

The assaulter walked through the corridor that led to an area of restricted entry, the main control room. His gait exuded confidence. Dressed in his victim's clothes, he looked the part—his height, frame and features now a perfect match. Even his hair swayed around the centre partition in a fashion similar to Robert's.

Dipping a hand into his coat pocket, he took out Robert's index finger, neatly wrapped in a plastic sheet and placed it on the biometric sensor. *Stupid design!* If he were to ever design a biometric device, he would ensure it sensed not just the patterns on the skin, but also the thermal energy radiating from a living body part.

He entered the busy main hall and quietly strode to Robert's workstation. Fortunately, no one had noticed anything amiss.

'Hurry up, guys! We are in the middle of a ground-breaking project here,' the supervisor barked from a distance. 'That was a rather long one, Robert. You ought to shorten your breaks.'

He nodded and quickly plucked out a hard drive from his pocket, connected it to the USB port on his terminal and started clattering at the keys at remarkable speed, all while keeping his head low. He switched windows as the supervisor passed by, a short distance from his cubicle. Within twenty-five minutes, he had managed to gain access to the central server and was downloading the programs and data hidden in its deepest dungeons.

Highly classified cutting-edge technology that would be practically priceless in the international markets!

For a decade and a half, he'd trained for this hour, and now, he was in the moment.

80%. His gleaming eyes studied the progress bar. So far, the feat had been easy to pull off, far smoother than he had expected.

*Wait... wh...*he looked up. *Damn!* It was Robert's colleague and girlfriend, Brenda, strutting towards his cubicle.

∽

Danish was petrified upon witnessing the scene inside the cockpit. There was no one in there, except for the two pilots who lay unconscious in their seats. It was bizarre!

'Am I in some kind of a nightmare?'

The Air Bee 777-300GR suddenly jolted, tossing the slumped bodies around, forcing some of them to roll off their seats. The plane jittered and trembled for a good minute as Danish lay on his back, staring blankly at the low ceiling, getting ready to embrace his fate.

'Did it have to end like this?' he spared a prayer as the aircraft whirred to stability.

He tore off the seamless mask clinging to his face, revealing his wheatish complexion—a stark contrast to the pale-skinned Chinese features etched on the mask he'd been sporting so long.

'No...' gasped Danish, clawing onto the sides as he felt the floor dip. The aircraft was losing altitude fast, and the giddiness would not allow him to come up with anything remotely helpful. Mustering all his willpower, he took out a battery-powered device and switched it on. Following a torturous five-second wait, he pressed "**" just before his oxygen-starved brain caved in and he lapsed into unconsciousness.

∽

The assassin ducked to avoid eye contact with Brenda, his eyes frantically skimming over the moving bar. '82%,' he cursed under his breath, 'bad timing'.

'Robert.' She placed her coffee mug next to his keyboard and wrapped her arms around his shoulder while he continued to engage in a round of poker on his system. 'What the heck? When did my darling become so naughty?' she scoffed, lurking closer for a better look at the screen, amazed to find him playing amidst all the tension.

Strange, actually!

His hair did not smell typical; no musk emanated from the Playboy shampoo she had gotten addicted to. Another unfamiliar and slightly disturbing sign! And then she saw it! A big port-wine birthmark on his neck, like the archipelago on the Russian ex-President Gorbachev's head. Shaped like an eagle in flight, the red predator was quite lucid. Almost too perfect to be a birthmark.

This is not Robert!

Brenda moved aside and took two steps for a better glimpse of his face. 'Who are you…?' she queried in a low, frightened tone. But, before she could utter another word, his right hand subtly swung forward.

'Wh…' She felt something pierce her thigh. The next second, a dizzy spell held her thoughts hostage, and she landed on the floor with a soft thud. The assaulter quickly disposed of the small needle in the dustbin below the desk, unnoticed. The bar was at 96%.

He watched as a couple of engineers from adjacent cabins

moved towards his workstation to check on the unconscious woman. Buying himself a few extra minutes, he crouched over her body and patted her cheek lightly, his gaze glued onto the bar at the bottom of the screen.

99%.

'What's going on?' The bald supervisor was beginning to make his way towards the commotion, his team following suit.

'*100! Yes!*' The transfer was complete.

With his left hand, the assaulter yanked the drive out. He quickly pocketed it, while still patting Brenda's cheek with the other palm.

'What happened?' The supervisor bent over her as they gathered around.

'Goddamn it!' He paused, noticing the colourful display on the screen. 'No wonder the lady fainted. Who plays poker amidst such turmoil!'

'I'll fetch her some water,' the assassin croaked and dashed away. Before anyone could make sense of the chaos, the assaulter was out of the restricted area and sprinting through empty corridors. Exiting the main lobby, he found his way to a car. He drove the stolen vehicle for a few miles towards a crowded tourist spot—ferries plied between the various archipelago islands from this site. With the wig, the mask and the suit long gone, he now wore a different persona, sporting a buzz cut.

'*Yes!*' He flashed an exuberant grin at his reflection in a car window while flipping Robert's finger into a heavy haulage dump truck. 'Bye-bye, USA!'

The Brotherhood would be mightily pleased and he would be remembered a long, long time for his contribution in establishing a new world order.

1

Mokthar and Adel

Mokhtar peeped out of the window as the tram swerved along Muski, the bustling thoroughfare that ran across the entire breadth of the old town in Cairo city.

Cairo—a Western piece of furniture placed on an Eastern rug. Paris on the Nile. The view outside reflected the vivid contrast of cultures. On the one hand were men dressed in traditional Arabic attire and on the other, those donning Western suits. Women covered from head to toe in traditional Islamic dresses walked the streets alongside women sporting retro rolls, short skirts and high heels. Camel caravans of the past mingled with the Rolls-Royces of the present. A man with a turban sat at a shop selling water pipes, his goods spilling out of the shop and covering part of the footpath. In the vicinity was a classy apparel store with glass windows and mannequins displaying expensive British dresses. A cocktail of extremes!

Early twentieth-century Cairo, the largest city of Africa with a population of one million, sustained a curious blend of religious influences, both Islamic and Christian. The British had colonised Egypt till it gained independence in 1922, and their forces still continued to be stationed in Egypt, dominating local politics and governance.

With a sigh, Mokhtar took a long sip of water and placed the bottle back into his school bag. He then reverted to the sketch he had been making, his pencil moving in quick strokes.

Adel, his friend, sat right next to him. 'Show me!' He beamed. 'What have you sketched today?'

'It's nothing.' Mokhtar tried to shut the drawing book, but he was too late. Adel had already stolen a glimpse. Two pyramids set on large logs were being hauled by hundreds of frail men with ropes tied around their bodies; a few armed men in uniform whisked their whips at these labourers as they dragged the pyramids towards a river, where a large ship was docked. One of the pyramids had been loaded onto it, occupying almost a third of its vast open deck, leaving hardly enough space for the other two.

'What's this, Mokhtar?' He shook his head in disbelief. 'You and your eerie sketches. Didn't our history teacher tell us that each of those pyramids weighs six million tonnes? Only God could transport them from Giza!'

Adel took out a metallic candy box from his bag and delicately placed it on his lap. He was tall, well-built and fair; with curly hair and blue eyes, he was the heart-throb of the girls at St Andrew's High School. A dynamo at academics, sports, photography and public speaking, the fourteen-year-old was an all-rounder, popular amongst teachers and students alike. He undid the lid of the box and took out a bunch of black-and-white pictures.

Mokhtar, his sharp-featured friend with dark skin and a frail frame, peeked in. Mokhtar was nothing like Adel. He was shy and reserved, barely scraped through his examinations and had no friends. Except Adel. They were about the same age and were always seen together, since their childhood.

Mokhtar's family were employed by Adel's. They lived within their mansion grounds in a separate block housing the servant quarters. Mokhtar's father worked as a driver for Adel's father, Mr Kamaal, a revenue officer in the government of King Faoud, while his mother was a personal assistant to Mrs Kamaal. Mr Kamaal was of royal descent himself, with a sizeable inheritance to his name. He was short-tempered and formidable, but kind at heart. He was the one who had decided that Mokhtar would attend the same school as Adel. Adel, on his part, treated Mokhtar as a brother and never let him feel otherwise.

'Hmm...' Adel shuffled through the pictures, mostly of girls from school and their neighbourhood.

'What's that? Show me!' Mokhtar exclaimed, having noticed something unusual.

Hidden amongst the mundane black and white photos, he'd spotted a colour photograph of Adel holding hands with a beautiful girl on a snow-covered mountain peak. Both the setting and the colours in the picture were a novelty to him.

'A Lumiere autochrome!' Adel brandished the picture as several eyes turned towards them. 'It's a common thing in Paris, you know... they have been using colour photography for ages. And that's Cindy, my new friend.'

Mokhtar took the picture from him, wondering how many romantic venues Adel might have explored with this supposed 'friend' of his. Of course, he couldn't voice his thoughts. It would be sacrilege!

'Nice!' He ran his fingers across the grainy textured paper. Stopping just short of Cindy's hair, he handed the picture back to Adel.

'Come on, Mokhtar! You can touch her. Touching a girl in a picture would not count as a sin, I suppose.' Adel chuckled.

Mokhtar turned away, a deep grimace contorting his face. He could have bashed Adel up to airborne fluff over such blasphemy. *'Ugh!'* How could a true Muslim mingle with women so defiantly? But he refrained from saying anything, as always. *'One's beliefs and ways of life are his personal choice. We must not interfere,'* his pious father often told him.

'What happened?' Adel stared at his silent mate, his eyelids drooping. 'I am sorry. I guess my words didn't come off very well.'

'It's nothing,' sighed Mokhtar a few seconds later, deciding to change the subject. 'It's my pathetic grades. I have to get the report card signed by Baba today. It feels bad to let him down.'

'Come on… even Abraham Lincoln got poor grades,' guffawed Adel. 'You can't let anybody down with bad grades!'

'I just wish I make him proud someday. I am neither good at academics… nor sports…' Mokhtar threw his hands up in the air. 'I am not good at anything! I envy you when you carry home those shields and medals. There must be *something* I can do well!'

'Of course, there is. Some people bloom late, but when they do, they are unbeatable.'

As Adel attempted to cheer his friend, his attention was drawn towards the spectacle on the other side of the window. 'Wallah! How elegant and powerful!' He pointed to a small troop of British soldiers on horseback, smartly dressed in long black coats. In the middle of these men was a horse cart carrying a British officer and his wife.

Elegant? Powerful? Even the choice of words made Mokhtar's limbs recoil from disgust. How could someone find their oppressors impressive? He darted a harsh glare at Adel, finding it impossible to wrestle down his feelings anymore. And before he knew it, he was fuming aloud. 'It's not right, brother! What right do they have to be here, on our land?'

'Why? They belong here as much as we do. Remember our great king, Ismail Pasha? Remember what he said fifty years back when he built this great city after coming back from his long stay in Paris? We are no longer an African country. We are part of Europe. Had it not been for him, we would have had none of this—the beautiful boulevards, the Opera House and that…' Adel pointed towards an impressive building. 'The Shepheard's Hotel!'

Shepheard's, one of the most famous hotels in the world, was located precisely at the spot where Napoleon had had his headquarters after the battle of Kremlin. Men and women sporting a colourful array of Western attire crowded its famous terrace, set with wicker chairs and tables, commanding a lofty shaded view of the unfolding scenes on Ibrahim Pasha Street below. It was a playground for the international aristocracy, where every person of social standing made it a point to stop by for tea—to see and to be seen.

'We didn't need any of this!' Mokhtar scowled. 'A stupid man Pasha was... drove his realm into bankruptcy with his crazy plans! Brought these white pests over to our land in the name of development. There! See those men hanging out there? That's who we really are!' Hordes of dark-skinned Arabs in long robes crowded the footpath opposite the Shepheard's Hotel. They lingered across the street from dawn to dusk, waiting for potential customers. And when a tourist would eventually pass by, they scampered all together, falling over one another to offer their services, hoping to get lucky for once. Just as he finished his statement, a white policeman barged through the group of hawkers and grabbed one by his collar, shouting at him for pestering a tourist.

'See! They treat us like trash!' Mokhtar gnashed his teeth, watching how the policeman shook the man with such force that the old Arab eventually lost his balance and stumbled upon the footpath. The policeman then kicked and stamped on the man with his boot, over and over, while the local curled himself into a ball, howling in agony. The other guides had gathered around, but no one would dare to stop the white man.

'No! That's not who we really are. We are a progressive society, unlike these walking landmines of misinformation who spin ridiculous tales and swindle gullible tourists. He must have picked a pocket, or done something *really* awful. Those people are uncouth.'

'Uncouth? Those poor men are only trying to earn their bread to feed their families.' Mokhtar felt a sickening knot tighten in his stomach. Was Adel really so indifferent to what was going on around them? Or was it the veil of luxury that had turned him blind? 'You'll realize very soon!'

'We'll see, Mokhtar! No need to hyperventilate.'

The two unlikely friends stared out of the window until silence prevailed, a kind of truce they often resorted to. A few seconds into it, they saw a wasp buzz its way in through the window. It flew across Adel's face making its way towards Mokhtar.

'Ugh... no.' Ducking to avoid its path, Mokhtar tried to shoo it away with a notebook.

'Hyperventilating again!' Adel mocked the antics of his friend.

'It hurts like hell!' grumbled Mokhtar. 'You would panic too if you'd been stung before.'

'Relax! The poor thing will find its way back.' Adel burst out into a sharp chuckle. But barely a second after he'd closed his lips, the wasp perched itself right over them. Numbed by terror, he held his breath. His pupils rolled downwards, trying to survey the crisis. 'Damn it,' he cursed—if only this perpetrator would abort its exploration and take off.

To his horror, though, the insect seemed to have other plans. It was preparing to inject its venom. *'No!'* With his lips sealed between the wasp's legs, he couldn't call out for help. And with his companion equally petrified, he barely expected any help from that quarter either! Adel was about to close his eyes, bracing himself to embrace the pain that was to come when he saw a hand dart by. In a flash, the wasp was gone!

Mokhtar! He had very neatly plucked the wasp between his thumb and middle finger, crushed it and flung it outside.

'Woah!' Adel whispered, still in shock. 'How did you do that? A moment ago, you were freaking out!'

'You're my friend... my only friend.' Mokhtar's lips cracked into an innocent smile as he tucked his skilled hands beneath his thighs. His right thumb, all red and swollen, was smarting from the sting.

'Thanks!' Adel managed to say, a lump rising in his throat.

A silence fell over the two of them, a poignant quiet, until Adel spotted something that spread a broad smile across his face.

'Look! A Cadillac!' Adel guided his friend's attention towards a convertible passing by. Two couples were seated, one in the front seat and the other in the rear. The men were European, and the women had their faces covered with hijabs. The couple in the back seat were holding hands.

As the car drove off, Adel began his usual banter about its model and make, but his friend wasn't paying heed. Instead, Mokhtar had turned around, as much as he could, his glare closely following the Cadillac. 'Allah! The bastard kissed her...' he squealed and held Adel's arm tightly, his nails digging into the boy's skin. A gust of wind had nudged the hijab off the woman in the back seat, and the European had taken advantage of the opportunity to plant a quick peck on her lips.

Adel flinched in pain from the abrupt grip. But the very next moment, he found his gaze transfixed on a portion of Mokhtar's neck—now exposed from his shuffling around in panic—a red figure embossed on his dark skin like an emblem. A birthmark that resembled an eagle in flight! Every time Adel spotted it, it had a bewitching effect, filling him with awe.

'Stop worrying, old man.' Adel yanked off his arm, recovering from the hypnotism of the red eagle. 'Since when did you start to take such an interest in strangers?' He spun around to observe the Cadillac, but it had disappeared into the traffic. 'Relax!' He shouted at his friend, but the seat was empty. Mokhtar was missing.

Where is Mokhtar?

Adel peered ahead, only to notice a scrawny figure dashing towards the door, tugging at the bell and jumping off the tram as soon as the driver applied the brakes. Off balance, Mokhtar floundered onto the concrete road, but that wouldn't stop him. In a beat, he was up on his feet again like an acrobat, chasing after the car wildly, a slingshot tucked into his back pocket.

'Lunatic,' Adel cursed under his breath.

His friend's unpredictable aggression was going to cause big trouble someday. Little did he realize they were already headed into one!

2

Kabir and His MH470 Obsession

Kabir closed the pages of the journal and tucked it underneath the pillow with a sigh. Even if he wished to continue writing, his bloodshot eyes would not cooperate. Stretching his hand through the painful rotator cuff, he swivelled it thrice, forwards and backwards. Then, he pressed a button on the remote sitting within a silver holder. The headrest was automatically elevated to a comfortable angle.

This secluded wing of the medical facility, specially reserved for him, had not only spotless interiors but half dozen armed security personnel stationed in the corridors outside at any given time. So much so that the slightest stray whisper bounced off its minimalist décor. This was why he'd instantly caught the faint echoes of the clickety-clacks coming closer. And thus, onto the imminent arrival of the all-too familiar owner of those brown Burberry four-inch heels.

'*Six... five... four... three... two... one...*' he counted down. And a knock later, the door to his room was flung wide open.

'Kabir Rathore,' his visitor walked up to his bed, 'why am I not surprised to find you here? In this facility in Kuala Lumpur?'

'And I am fine. Thank you for asking.' A grin briefly sharpened Kabir's otherwise dulled features.

Her lovely face was a welcome sight for his sore eyes. Sarah Kinley. A young BBC reporter he'd met in Nigeria nine years ago. A journalist who'd been following his story ever since. Above all, a confidante and a friend on whom he could count on for support, wherever he was. 'Kabir...' Noticing the journal tucked underneath the pillow, she dropped her head to one side in disapproval. 'Still working, I see. Anyway, how's the shoulder?'

'The same.'

Aware of what was to come, Kabir immediately summoned his charms with a smile. But to no avail.

'Tch!' Sarah clicked her tongue. 'Not going to work on me. I've been immune to those tricks for a while. In fact,' her glare hardened, 'seeing the ghastly state you've reduced yourself to, I doubt they'll work on any girl now.'

A soft blanket of silence enveloped the pair as Sarah studied her friend. On any other day, this tall Indian officer would have made any lady's heart flutter with a mere look of his piercing grey eyes. With dark hair, a handsome face, and a sinewy frame—thanks to a decade of rigorous service as a commando—he exuded more charisma than most men in their thirties. Today, however, he looked half the man he otherwise was, weak and ashen-faced.

'Don't do it, Kabir! It's sheer madness. You are chasing a ghost...a memory.'

At the start, the story—an Indian commando desperately searching for the MH470 wreckage long after every other individual and nation had long given up the search for this lost aircraft—had left her fascinated. After all, Kabir Rathore had commandeered several impossible overseas missions to success in the past, and his determination had inspired headlines. However, unlike all other missions, this was a 'personal' quest. And she watched as his determination spiralled into an obsession that threw him into the clutches of death, several times—his latest form proof of this madness! He had undertaken a search across a terrain far less forgiving than ice-capped mountains or thick forests—the uncharted seabed of the Indian Ocean.

'Contrary to popular belief, working undersea was not as

exciting as the scuba diving flicks made it seem. While the safe diving depth for human beings was just around 40 metres beneath the sea surface, the hunt for the wreckage had to be carried out 4,000 metres undersea. A high-risk zone most would not dare to venture into.

'Searching for a needle in a haystack would be easier, Kabir. It's been nine years, and yet you come back to Kuala Lumpur every year, despite your gruelling schedule back in India.'

'As they say, objects in the rear-view mirror may appear closer than they are! Nine years seem like nine days to me!' Kabir paused. 'He … was not only my best friend, Sarah, but I also owed him… in many ways!'

His voice trailed off as a blur of memories flashed before his eyes. The face of his best mate. The days spent together with Jayant at the National Defence Academy, till Kabir's lumbar tuberculosis had forced him to quit. Jayant, his buddy, went on to join military intelligence alone, a wing of the Indian army they had planned to be together in. Kabir vividly recalled their days at the NDA… and the nights spent devising assignment strategies to cripple the enemy. Jayant had been on board the MH470 that fateful night on an undercover operation. Travelling as Danish, a Malaysian citizen.

Sarah sealed her lips with an empathetic smile. She knew of their past. She knew of how Kabir had completed his NDA training soon after his health recovered, and then joined the military intelligence wing to be able to work with Jayant. He had still been training in the field when news of the Malaysian Airlines plane crash arrived. Tragically, a decade later, the MH470 was still a missing chapter from the chronicles of human history, a disturbing and humbling reminder for mankind. Theories abounded about what might have happened. Yet, none of them could explain why a plane that took off for Beijing from Kuala Lumpur, ended up deviating down south, nearly 1,800 km west of Perth in the Indian Ocean, before vanishing into thin air.

'I know the feeling, Kabir,' Sarah said, 'but all the other teams gave up several years ago. And those teams did rake thousands of miles of seabed around the spot that the aircraft was suspected to have gone down.'

'Raked the seabed?' His eyes flashed with annoyance. 'With what exactly?'

'Come on, I don't have to tell you that! Sonar radiations, autonomous underwater drones and satellite imaging—all of it based on satellite data of the last locations of the MH470.' She snapped her fingers. 'But not a trace was found!'

'Not a trace? Sarah, we've played golf on the moon, we've glimpsed parts of the universe fifteen billion light years afar—thanks to the Hubble telescope—and when it comes to three miles under our own sea, we become lost pups in a pond?'

'When you put it that way, I admit it is troubling. Our deepest depths still remain in a kind of twilight zone!' Her pupils slowly glazed over. 'That said, there have been similar crashes above similarly deep oceans before, and all those wreckages were discovered sooner or later, as you've often pointed out. This is the only Air-Bee passenger flight in several decades whose wreckage has not been traced.'

'And if they could locate the Titanic's wreckage, decades ago, when technology was still in its infancy… why not now?'

'So, you suspect they did not try hard enough?'

'Of course, I do!' He smirked. 'Following the accident, all that was carried out were standard sonar searches across the ocean surface—regular drills. Can you believe that no special submarines were sent out? James Cameroon's passion for movie-making led him to the Mariana Trench—the deepest point undersea—in a private submarine. Why wouldn't the modern world come together to undertake a similar mission? 239 people of fourteen different nationalities were lost. The motive and desperation to unravel the truth was clearly missing.'

'Yeah! I agree,' said Sarah. 'The world seems to have given up on them. No one seems to be willing to make the investment needed to carry out such a mission. And yet, I think there's more to it than meets the eye!' Sarah knew what being given up on meant to her friend. He had spent most of his childhood in an orphanage, working his way up through crippling deprivation and adversity.

'Just think how horrifying it must have been for the passengers on board. The pilot, after flying the aircraft three thousand miles off its planned course—south, towards the Indian Ocean—quietly landed the plane on seawater and just *allowed* it to sink. I wonder how Jayant would have fought. He was not one to give in easily. Apart from the supposedly defected pilot, were there other hijackers in disguise on the flight... Did he have to brave them alone?' Kabir wondered aloud.

Apart from the fact that Kabir and Sarah had a synergistic professional relationship, both being on the side of light in the fight against terrorism, they both knew they could trust each other blindly. In fact, that was how they'd first met, when a spontaneous pursuit of his had led to the rescue of two BBC reporters from a terrorist camp in Nigeria. One of those rescued reporters, a close friend of Sarah's, had introduced Kabir as her 'saviour'; the rest was history.

'Fine! I see your point,' said Sarah, 'but these are facts well known to the concerned parties all over the world. You feel there is a conspiracy. Agreed! But hundreds of close relatives of the victims know that too. They have moved on and so should you. Look at you! You look moribund...'

'Jayant was alone, Sarah!' Kabir cut her off. 'Fearless but alone! He had barely been three years in the force. He was everything to me: friend, family, soulmate! He would call me in the middle of a chase sometimes and joke "You left me alone, partner. We would have made an invincible team. What if these buggers get hold of me someday?"' His eyes turned moist.

'And what was your reply?' she asked curiously.

'They'd better not touch you. Tell them your friend will hunt them down...to the bottom of the ocean!' replied Kabir grimly.

'How prophetic!' Sarah thought, making sense of the melancholy that shrouded Kabir. *'He had made a promise.'* It was just a figure of speech that Kabir had used. No sane man would actually go looking for clues in the fathomless depths of the ocean.

A deep breath later she decided it best to air out the gloom. 'But how did you get so gravely ill? From what I've heard, you've been in the hospital for a while.'

The obvious shift in subject prompted him to glance at her. He studied her expressions. 'I know what you are thinking, Sarah! But it's neither seasickness nor sentiment that did me in. You couldn't possibly expect me just to issue instructions from the surface. I *had* to go down there myself.' He shrugged. 'Well, as you are aware, we suspect that the cords of the MH470 crash are somehow tied to global terrorist activity, and I've been granted special authorization to untangle these knots. So as part of this assignment, every few weeks, I travelled on a special search vessel, equipped with a submarine, into the ocean. The submarine would take me as far beneath the surface as safely possible, and from there I'd dispatch unmanned robotic vehicles to scan the subaqueous depths with underwater cameras.'

'Interesting.' Sarah's frown eased. 'I've always wondered what it must feel like to stay underwater for weeks and months together. It must have broken you down... physically... emotionally?'

'No, it didn't! I am trained for much harsher conditions. The submarines are really cramped and stinky, true! You can actually feel the walls closing in on you as the submarine goes down and the pressure builds up. The oxygen levels are maintained low to minimize the risk of fire. A simple cut can take weeks to heal. I got severely infected.'

'Oh. But have you actually been scouring 10,000 square miles from within a submarine?'

'No, not 10,000 square miles,' he stalled and considered the facts he was allowed to disclose. 'We had a much smaller range to cover. A more defined area.'

'A more "defined" area? That's information I'm unaware of.'

Actually, it wasn't just her. It was a nugget of news that the world was unaware of. The reason Kabir and his team had a more specific area to comb through was simply because of a device that Jayant had been equipped with. A device with an advanced communication system designed by ISDO, the agency for space defence in India. Just before the plane went down, an SOS signal "**" had been relayed from it. Kabir's searches were therefore restricted to the coordinates based around the SOS signal.

'If you have known this for over eight years, why haven't you divulged it to the international community for better and faster results?'

'Well, that would be a stupid thing to do, wouldn't it? Someone very powerful wants this aviation debacle to remain under wraps—and has managed to do so very well thus far.'

'True that.' She briefly slipped into deep thought. 'Anyway, has this mission revealed anything?'

'No, nothing came up from the previous two searches. But my work's not done yet. Anyhow...' His smile gradually turned into a stifled yawn. 'I think I might need to catch up on some sleep now. The nurse administered a sedative just before you came in. A day or two of rest and once I'm discharged, I'll be able to return to—'

'Work? You'll have barely recovered! And how long will you be out at sea?' She grew agitated. 'Besides, you just said two of your search missions revealed nothing!'

'Exactly—'

'Wait... I'm confused now,' Sarah stepped an inch closer, still trying to process what he was getting at. 'Stop being a tease. Tell me. That's what you called me here for, didn't you?'

Kabir stared at her, the fatigue in his eyes briefly erased by a glimmer of hope. 'My ship will be scouring an entirely new locale in search of clues. Quite far from the current one, actually.' He put a palm up in the air. 'That is all I can say for now.'

'Entirely new locale? Did the surveillance system make a mistake?'

'No.'

'Wait, if no mistake was made… do you mean this was intentional? Hold on a second…' Her eyelids slowly widened, 'Does someone want us to believe that the aircraft crashed where the world thinks it did? That is what you've been hinting at all this while, haven't you? Bloody hell, this is breaking news!'

A half-grin was the only response he could offer, but that was enough to tell her she was onto his theory.

In fact, Sarah Kinley had come quite close.

Kabir had recently begun collaborating with a team of engineers investigating an alternative approach. *'What if the absence of wreckage meant the aircraft had not crashed at all?'* Everyone was aware that it took a low dip at one spot. Based on the assumption that the aircraft had plunged after that, the site of the crash had been triangulated around those coordinates. Every exploration over the past eight years had been undertaken thereabout. *But what if the plane had only taken a dip to avoid military radars on the ground? What if it had then gone into stealth mode by switching on an inbuilt radiation-shield to avoid detection? Everyone knew that Air-Bee, the second largest aircraft manufacturer in the world, had a repertoire of hidden features on their planes. What if this Malaysian Airlines plane had then flown off a thousand miles? Someplace else? To an entirely new destination?*

Kabir had many ideas.

As bizarre as the theory had sounded at first, it was gaining acceptance. Especially now that they were working with fresh eyes and had fresher calculations based on wave patterns and the most advanced 3D marine-imaging and GIS mapping.

'Now,' she said, pointing to his forehead in jest, 'are you going to tell me what's going on in that head of yours, or am I meant to mind-read?'

'You'll be the first one to know when the time's right. We might be very close to solving the MH470 mystery. But if any of this is leaked, the world may never discover the truth. So I trust you to keep it all hush-hush.'

'Oh ... all right.' Despite being an ardent believer in the potency of the press, when it came to Kabir, Sarah followed a different set of ethics. Not a word of what they spoke ever found its way to a third person—a pact that was always understood and honoured both ways.

'Fine, I'll let you catch up on your slee—'

'Wait...' Kabir abruptly pressed a finger against his lips.

She took the cue and fell silent.

Footsteps... The faint click-clack on the granite floor was a reasonable distance away. It was moving through the corridors. Nothing unusual about the sound of footsteps in a hospital wing. But with this one...something felt amiss. There was a distinct urgency, an unusual pace, which was unwarranted seeing how Kabir's condition was rather stable.

And then he heard it—a snap—and then a grunt. The sound of a neck being broken!

Hurrying out of his bed, he caught Sarah by her wrist and led her towards the narrow closet in the corner of his room. Opening its louvre door, he shoved her inside the closet and shut the door. Through the gap in the door, he saw her face for a fleeting second. The shock had turned her pale, but there was no time to explain. She would just have to trust him on this one.

Damn it. He suddenly felt a few ounces lighter, and he had to hold on to the sides of his head to keep still. The painkillers and sedatives were taking effect.

'Agh!'Another sound echoed from outside—a man's muffled

cry of horror cut short. The sound of his throat being slashed.

Kabir's first instinct was to dash out of the door to his room and face the killer head-on. But in this weakened condition—that too, unarmed—he wouldn't last long. So he locked the door instead. His adversary, whoever it was, was good at his game. Too good!

A hitman? Who could've sent him? Reaching for a glass of water kept on a side table, he splashed its contents on his face to wake himself up. *A terrorist organization? People with clout who want the MH470 secret eternally buried?*

Well, whoever it was, they'd chosen the perfect spot and hour to bury his research—lock, stock and barrel. His eyes hastily considered the door. The hitman could tear it down any minute.

Wait… I almost forgot…

Raising up the sleeve of his robe, he yanked at a black cord tied around his right arm. An amulet—a rectangular silver pellet—was threaded through its middle.

Kabir made his way towards the closet quickly, keeping step as he moved.

Sarah's eyes grew wide with terror as she watched his grim silhouette closing in. Would this be her last glimpse of Kabir Rathore?

'This!' he whispered, sliding the talisman through the closed door, 'this is why I called you down here. Hide it carefully.'

3

The Shattering Betrayal

Mokhtar sat on the cemented base of a lamppost on the pavement opposite the Shepheard's Hotel, sobbing with his head between his knees. His white shirt had blotch marks on the back, and the right sleeve was ripped along its seam. Sensing a familiar hand rest on his head, he looked up.

Adel was standing beside him, both their school bags on his broad shoulders. Mokhtar's eyes fell upon the indents that his nails had left on his fragile white skin only a little while ago.

'You scared me!' Dropping the bags to his side, Adel spoke into his face. 'What was your plan? To chase after those men in the car and shoot them down with your pebbles? Why?'

Mokhtar remained silent, his fingers tugging at the rubber of his slingshot and letting it go, over and over, making a pinging sound. He couldn't even bear to look his friend in the eye.

Adel propped Mokhtar's chin up to coax a reply. 'You can tell me what's on your mind. You know how dear you are to me. More than a friend, Mokhtar, you are a brother.'

Mokhtar shook his head and glanced aside.

'Mokhtar!' Adel's patience was already worn thin and he could feel its threads beginning to snap. 'Tell me, what is it that you want? Why are you sitting here? Why are you crying?'

An empty beat passed. Then, Mokhtar pointed a finger towards the Shepheard's entrance. 'They went in there—'

'So…?' Adel's looked surprised. 'It's their life! Who are you to interfere? Let's go!' he tried pulling his friend up.

'It was Ummi... with that European man.'

'What? Your mother?' Adel stood stunned for a good few moments before he could get his act together for the sake of his friend. 'Let's get home quickly,' he embraced his mate in an attempt to comfort him, 'and get Mom to call her back to the house.'

'We can't.' Mokhtar yanked himself free from the embrace.

'Why?'

'Your mother's in there too, with the other man.'

'Wh—' Adel's face blanched, even as he tried convincing himself that there had to be a mistake. 'M... maybe they went to the terrace for coffee. Some kind of meeting.'

'Maybe...let's go check.'

At the Shepheard's lobby, everyone was intrigued by the sight of the two schoolboys—one of them dressed in tatters—as they scurried along between the tables, their blank eyes searching for something.

To the two boys, men and women seemed to be mingling here in an environment of gaiety—over coffee, water pipes and exquisite snacks. It was a rendezvous for affluent tourists, business tycoons, lovelorn couples and leisure seekers alike. But the two women in hijabs and their escorts were nowhere to be seen.

'Sorry ...sir?' the receptionist flashed them a curt smile. 'We are not permitted to disclose any details about our guests.' Her 'please leave' expression did nothing to faze the boys' determination. The security had to be called. Their journey back home was filled with a numbing silence. The cheap taxi—a jolting mule cart—dropped them off at the mansion's entrance.

They saw the Bugatti parked in the portico and knew that their fathers would be in their respective rooms. Mr Kamaal was home for an afternoon siesta today.

Mokhtar was seething with anger, ready to pour everything out in front of his father. He deserved to know. His mother had embraced the corrupt Western culture and betrayed them. As soon as the door flew open, he hugged him tightly, his tears wetting his father's thin grey Thawb.

'Son, are you, all right?' Abdul, his father, caressed Mokhtar's brown hair, nestling him close to his chest. However, Mokhtar would not let go. Abdul gently broke the embrace and looked into his son's eyes inquisitively. 'What happened?'

'Nothing. It's nothing, Baba! Just had a fight with a good friend at school.' He could not bring himself to tell his father. It would break him. How could he hurt his pious, loving and dedicated father with news like this?

'It's okay. Don't take life too seriously.' Abdul patted him on the shoulder with affection. 'Allah will take care of everything. Let's go to the mosque, we still have an hour.'

∽

Even through the crowded bazaar streets, Mokhtar could see the mosque of Muhammed Ali Pasha loom tall. Built on the summit of a citadel, this alabaster mosque was the most imposing structure in a city of minarets, a landmark one could not miss. He loved the sights that the top of the citadel afforded its visitors. A vista of the city sprawled out below, a skyline dotted with thousands of minarets, the river Nile in the distance, and the dim outline of the three pyramids. It was spellbinding!

Alas, the mosque was falling apart. The alabaster panels of its ceilings, along with their exquisite murals, had been stolen for the king's palace, reducing the mosque to a state of ruin. Quite similar to how Arab-Muslim identity was being compromised by the greedy kings. Sycophants of the West! Thank the Lord for men such as Mokhtar's father, the Salafiyas, who upheld the values of Islam. The very notion gave him a sense of reassurance as warm as the presence of his father's hand on his shoulder!

'When did you learn to drive, Baba?' Mokhtar asked on their

way back, well aware that the subject would light up a smile on his father's face.

'Not very long ago, son! I came to Cairo from a village some twenty years back. I never rode a two-wheeler till then, and driving a car was nothing short of a fantasy. So when Mr Kamaal offered me this job, it was a dream come true. His driver, who was about to retire, trained me. Driving left me elated, it satiated my soul. A man like me who had never dreamt of using anything but his two feet had suddenly become a powerful charioteer. The wind whizzing through my mane would make me feel powerful and complete. It still does!'

Mokhtar giggled and patted his father's arm. His father was a simple man.

∽

As they returned home, Mr Kamaal was ready to leave after his siesta. Standing in the portico, Mokhtar waved at his father as the Bugatti drove off. He wondered how his father put up with the smoke from the cigars that Mr Kamaal kept at all the time. He saw Adel walking down the broad stairs connecting the main palace building with the portico. Grabbing the pair of bicycles that were parked along the sidewall, the boys sped out, ignoring the typical words of caution mumbled by the guard at the gate.

Their race would end at the spot where tourists usually mounted camels to trek towards the pyramids. It was a pastime that the two loved, and one that they indulged in every day—Adel the usual winner, while Mokhtar would reach a few minutes later, panting for breath. Today, however, the results were oddly reversed. Despite his frail body, Mokhtar made it first, the fury pumping through him as he pushed his feet on the pedals with the pace of a madman.

Once at the spot, they typically sat on their bicycle seats and watched rows of camels alongside the last stretches of road before the desert took over. Climbing onto the saddle tied atop a camel's back was no mean feat—given the height of the animal even when it was seated. And most tourists struggled. They would clamber, they would falter and then somehow make it atop after umpteen attempts, with generous assistance from the camel owner. Yet, that was not all. The real fun would begin after that. As the camel rose, with its forelegs going up first, the tourist would be thrown back to the point of rolling off. That was followed by the camel raising its hind legs, hurling the tourist all the way forward, before it'd finally attain balance on all fours. Most of the older tourists would hold onto the saddle, fearing for their lives.

And watching their frightened expressions—accompanied by a string of colourful curses—would send the boys into fits of laughter.

But mockery was the last thing on their mind today. 'Did you say anything to Abdul?' Adel asked Mokhtar.

Mokhtar shook his head in the negative. 'And you? What did Mr Kamaal say?'

'I did not bring it up. You know how my father is! He would kill my mother.'

'So? Our mothers don't deserve any better,' retorted Mokhtar loudly. Noticing a few heads turn their way, he restrained his tone. 'Mr Kamaal is a strong man. He would have done the right thing.'

'The right thing?' Adel felt his gut squirm. 'I actually care for my mother. Well, if it is so, why didn't you tell Abdul?'

'Because I care for my Baba!'

'What now?'

'I will kill her,' Mokhtar murmured, his voice turning feeble as he sank into an abyss of emotions.

'Are you mad?' Adel wondered whether he had heard his friend correctly.

'No!' Mokhtar hissed. 'I can't let this happen to Baba.'

'Let what happen?' retorted Adel, when he abruptly noticed a drawing sheet tucked into Mokhtar's front pocket. 'Show me,' he pulled it out and unfolded it.

A woman in a hijab was kissing a dapper European man dressed in a three-piece suit. They were standing below a tree in a mangrove. A Cadillac was parked nearby. Barely discernible, amongst the vegetation in a swamp in the background, was a bearded man, whose torso was buried in the bog. His hands were up in the air as he shouted for help. It was Abdul! His eyes looked real, reflecting the shock and horror at the betrayal.

'My God!' Adel felt a shudder run down his spine.

4

Chased By a Shadow

Kabir stood still, listening to the approaching footsteps, his tranquillized mind unable to pull out a response plan from the vaults of his memory. And then it occurred to him. It was right there. The open window! The classic escape route! He seized the bed sheets and looked down the window that overlooked an unkempt woodland style garden with a thick undergrowth. Just two floors to terra firma and his vertigo made it seem like he was peeping into a chasm. He heard the footsteps coming closer and knew he barely had time. He felt a severe cramp forming in his right calf muscle and slumped to the floor. Helplessly, he stared towards the ceiling, listening to the footfalls of approaching death.

A ward boy dressed in grey scrubs turned into the heavily guarded hospital corridor leading to Kabir's room, pushing a gurney ahead of him. He saw three guards, all holding their positions in a combat formation, their guns aimed towards him. Shocked, he left the gurney unattended and raised his hands above his shoulder in surrender.

'Don't move an inch!' said one of the guards, holding his position near the door, while the other two edged closer to the ward boy. The ward boy stood dumbfounded; his face pale.

One of the guards stepped beyond the ward boy to peek into the perpendicular corridor. He felt an urge to throw up, horrified by what he saw. There was no one in sight—except his two team mates lying motionless on the floor! One on his stomach with his head twisted upwards, facing the ceiling, and the other lying in a pool of blood flowing from a gaping wound in his neck.

'He killed Ahmed and Harris! *Pukimakcau!*' he cursed, as he rushed towards them, hoping against hope, to get a pulse.

The ward boy's expression changed and he started to say something, bringing his hands down. A bullet went past his thigh and he fell to the ground, screaming in pain.

'*Lakhanat! Lakhanat! Jo tuomo lo!*'

The sound of the bullet startled the skeletal eighty-year-old man lying on the gurney, an oxygen mask fixed to his face. He fell off the gurney, his scrawny frame writhing in fear and pain. Afflicted with some terminal disease, his skin was parched, with red patches all over. He gasped for breath, clearly in a state of ataxia.

The three guards frowned at each other.

'I'll hold my position.' The guard standing by the room gestured at the door he was safeguarding, before pointing to the gurney. 'You both help the patient up.'

'Baik.' They nodded in unison.

Very carefully, they held the gasping man by the legs and shoulders and started to lift him back. In a split second, the old man's left hand swung back and lacerated the neck of the guard on his rear, cutting clean through his jugular vein. The guard holding his legs was stupefied for a second as he watched the blood spray the old man's face. He let go of the old man's legs and reached for his holster.

Too late! He felt a piercing pain in his thigh. He looked down to see a syringe sticking out from his leg. He moved his hand to remove it, but his vision grew blurry and he dropped dead.

The third guard, the one near the door, unable to believe what he had just seen, aimed his gun, the forehead of the old man sprinting towards him clearly visible from the sight on the muzzle. He was still a good thirty feet away. *He would get the wretched bastard.* His finger started to bear down on the trigger, but the forehead suddenly vanished. He looked down to see the old man skidding on the floor on his knees and the next moment, he was right there between his legs, smiling up at him wickedly. Just like his agility, his tooth-line was much too perfect for his age. He pressed the gun to the old man's forehead and pressed the trigger. But something went wrong! The bullet had gone through his own groin! He could barely feel the pain in his broken wrist, twisted backwards by the killer in a split second.

The old man sprang to his feet and unflinchingly put a bullet into the last man standing. The ward boy's forehead bloomed. Then the old man began sprinting towards Kabir's room. *Two gun shots! No time to waste! The secluded wing would be teeming with backup security in no time.*

He threw the door open and gazed around sharply. The room was empty. But the window at the rear end was wide open. He looked down from the window to find the twisted bedsheets hanging down. His target couldn't have reached too far in his medical condition. He quickly slipped out of his hospital apparel to avoid being identified by the chasing security guards and the police. Quickly peeling off the artificial skin affixed to his hands, neck and feet, he removed the mask from his face to reveal a sharply chiselled face with an aquiline nose, fair complexion and blonde hair—a stark contrast to his earlier appearance.

'Oh my...' Sarah clamped down her lips tight to muffle a raspy breath as she watched the emerging persona of a frail assassin through the louvres of the closet door—the assassin who'd compelled one of the world's toughest commandos to jump out of the window for dear life. Rendered a terrified onlooker to all that followed, she saw him disappear into the bathroom for a bit, resurfacing in Kabir's joggers. Returning to the window, he furrowed his brows at a rustle in the bushes below. His hurried search seemed to reveal nothing. Sarah prayed that the bushes were dense enough to hide a man lying low.

Just as he was about to make the descent, she noticed an oddity on him. She peered harder for a better look. It was a significant red mark sitting low on the right side of his neck, resembling a tattoo of a flying eagle. *A logo of some sort? A symbol of the organization this man works for?* Whatever it was, the information would be a useful clue if she got out of this alive.

Luckily for Sarah, he descended using the makeshift vine of bedsheets set up by his prey. His supple frame made his movements seem effortless. He ducked, and keeping low, moved to a position from where he could see his surroundings clearly without revealing his own location. The assassin scanned the area, waiting for movement or sound. And then he saw his target. The tall muscular man in a crew cut hiding in the high bushes near the wire fence adjacent to the parking lot, crawling slowly on all fours towards it.

Stupid Indian! Once out in the open area on the other side of the fence, he would be a sitting duck. He started running towards Kabir. *I will shoot him point blank. Why attract attention by taking several shots?* Kabir saw him closing in and tried desperately to speed up. He was about to reach the fence when he felt a bullet graze his waist. The searing pain disabled him further. The killer was now sprinting towards him. The gun in the killer's hand had caught some attention and a few drivers in the parking were peeping out of their windows.

Kabir rolled under the fence, the wires tearing his hospital gown and scratching his skin. He had no strength to get up. The killer was barely twenty yards away now. Kabir lay on his back, spreadeagled on the concrete floor, right next to a van's tyre and exhaust pipe. Loud heavy metal blared from the driver's window. The driver bobbed his head to it, oblivious to all that was going on outside. A sitting duck indeed!

His eyes met the killer's cold eyes, his long blonde hair flowing in the wind, his face devoid of any expression. He saw the killer raise his gun.

Kabir gathered all his energy and instinctively rolled below the van.

The killer shot another two rounds, which hit the van's frame, burning bullet holes in the thin metal sheet. He put his gun back, preparing to cross the fence. It was too high to jump over. He slid below it nimbly. Lying there on the ground, his eyes once again met Kabir's. Kabir could see through those hazel eyes, the stone-cold eyes of a man on a mission, unafraid of death.

The killer calmly took out his gun and aimed it between Kabir's eyes. But he was taken aback by the thick smoke that lashed out at his face as the van's engine roared to life. He coughed and opened his eyes, only to see Kabir no longer in sight. The van had moved. The sound of the bullets had startled the driver, dragging him out of his paradise. The killer sprang to his feet and took a shot at the moving tyres, but the metallic clank told him he had missed. The scared van driver was speeding for his life. Kabir was hanging on to the chassis below, the off-road model fortunately having a good ground clearance.

The killer raised his left hand in the air and gestured. A steel grey Land Rover pulled up right next to him. He took the seat next to the driver. There were three other well-built, armed men in the back.

'Quick!' the killer barked and the Land Rover shot behind the van. They saw the van drive around the parked vehicles towards the opening in the barricade, a signboard marked *KELUAR* hanging over the exit.

The van driver could see the Rover chasing him in his rear-view mirror. He had no idea why in the world these men would want to kill him. Down below, Kabir's adrenaline was running out, the overbearing pain in his biceps and calf muscles urging him to let go.

He let out a titter to himself. *Give up? After all the training! Even at the age of nine, I didn't.* Flashes of his past flickered before his eyes as he remembered how the pain in his shoulder had originated!

Aman, the biggest bully at the orphanage, a strapping boy around twice his age was holding Kabir with his right arm twisted behind his back. He also happened to be the head boy. The warden had wrapped up the morning prayer session and left, handing Aman the charge for the physical training routine.

'Tell me, which one of them reported about the smoking?' screamed Aman. 'You little imps! How dare you?' He pulled Kabir's hair with the other hand, enabling eye contact with the other five boys who shared the dormitory with Kabir. He could see sheer horror in their eyes. With a slow consoling blink, Kabir signalled for them to hold on.

Aman twisted his arm a degree further, making him wince in pain. Kabir took in a deep breath. He barely stood a chance against his persecutor. But something inside him wouldn't let him give up. Not yet! He had heard through the din in the prayer hall, fishing for something useful. Nothing! Just the usual remarks about Aman and the warden's closeness and how the warden would turn a blind eye to everything. Kabir's mind was processing the murmurous babel, separating each strand...waiting.

Aman rendered a final malicious jerk and Kabir let out an agonized scream. He heard his muscles rupturing with a crack. But that didn't stop him from processing the information that had just resonated within his head. 'Stop! Aman! I will tell you.' Grimacing with pain, he gestured for Aman to bend down and bring his ear closer. 'I know about the lady with the mole on her left thigh,' Kabir whispered.

'About Ruhani? C'mon dude! It's the twenty-first century,' Aman snickered. 'The warden knows his daughter and I are fond of each other.'

'No! You've got me wrong.' Kabir gestured for him to bend forward again. 'I'm talking about her mother. I bet he has no idea you did his wife too.'

Aman stared hard at Kabir, not certain how to react. It was strange that the mother and daughter shared the same gene signature. He remembered how he had bragged about it to his two best friends yesterday. 'Have you guys ever had sex with an animal?' Aman had asked them.

'No!' Their jaws had dropped. 'Have you...'

'Yes, I just did. Mrs Gulshan...' He whispered. 'No less than a wild tigress she was. And guess what? Just like her daughter, she too has a mole on her left thigh, same to same!'

And these idiots had been drooling over it since! I should never have told them.

'I'll kill you!' Aman pushed Kabir hard, making him fall. 'Go to the front row... and... and never try to poke your nose in my affairs again.'

No one understood what had happened, how Aman had let go of Kabir so easily. But after that day, Aman never bullied Kabir and his friends again.

A bump on the road brought Kabir back from his flashback, the jerk to his shoulder sending a fresh wave of pain through his torso. The digital watch on his right wrist beeped right next to his face. Using his chin, he pushed a button on the watch. Kabir saw the ticket collector at the exit jumping out of their way to avoid being trampled by the speeding van.

Outside the parking lot was a circle with a fountain in the centre and then, a single road straight ahead that connected to the highway. The driver stared in shock. A Wrangler jeep was coming at full speed from the other side of the fountain. It was headed towards his van. The impact would surely send him rolling off the road. He pressed the accelerator hard but only to come straight into the collision path. He momentarily closed his eyes, ready to brace the impact. Nothing happened!

The van driver heard a deafening screech and looked back to see the Land Rover skidding towards the jeep parked across the road behind him. The jeep had slowed down, letting the van pass and blocking the way just in time for the Rover! In the rear-view mirror, he saw three men in black uniforms and caps step out, aiming their guns at the Land Rover. Hung in his precarious position, with an inverted view of the world, Kabir could see only the legs of his saviours. Indian para-commandos who had been positioned there—alerted by the signal from his watch! The van driver slowed down, peering in the rear-view mirror to catch a glimpse of the drama unfolding behind him. The driver's euphoria was short-lived. There was a deafening explosion that sent the Wrangler flying up in the air. The Land Rover was headed towards them at full speed once again.

The driver pressed down on the gas as hard as he could, casting anxious glances at the rear-view mirror every other second. *Come on... come on... come on...*

He reached the highway, found a brief clearing in the traffic and seized the opportunity. Dodging cars and vans, he veered onto the third lane, merging with the flow of vehicles.

Argh! Kabir winced while fighting to stay conscious—every skid and every swerve tearing his limbs apart.

Gradually, the vehicles on all the three lanes started slowing down due to a signal ahead. '*Lakhanat!*' The driver banged his head against the steering. The traffic ahead was thick, as clogged as a drain pipe, and here he was, like dead meat, trapped. That too on a lane adjacent to a footpath. *I'm done for!* The van eventually rolled to a halt, with the Land Rover gaining mileage, less than a dozen cars stranded between them.

'Move, dumb head!' He heard a biker shout at him, banging hard on the metallic body. The white tourist was trying to come between his van and the car behind them.

'*Maa hai!*' he cursed back, determined not to be pushed around by every darned asshole today. He was the last person to want to be stranded here, what with death chasing him like a mad hound.

But that didn't mean every passer-by could rub dirt in his face. The biker kept banging on the car, but he did not budge.

'What the hell?' he gasped as he saw the biker draw out a gun and aim it at his rear-view mirror. *Was it an overdose of the X-box GTA games he had been playing these days, short circuiting within his brain?* He promptly obliged, pulling forward a few feet, almost kissing the bumper of the hatchback parked ahead. The biker whizzed by and disappeared into a side lane.

Kabir closed his eyes and took a deep breath. His heart pounded against his ribcage at the loud sound of bullets clanking on his bonnet. He saw his tormentor-in-chief, the lean white man, running towards the van, flanked by his armed aides.

'That's it!' The driver fell back against the headrest, the last sputter of steam fizzling off. *Just shoot me and be done with it!*

He heard a volley of bullets fired at the van, puncturing his tyres.

Great! Whose arse are these guys after? Mine or the van's?

'He's not here,' one of them shouted, peeping under the van.

They spread around, frantically looking for their target amidst the stranded traffic.

5

Mokhtar Meets Ghassan

Mokhtar looked at his mother's wrist as she continued to serve him one dish after another. An expensive watch glittered in the light from an oil lamp.

Gifted by her European friend? He guessed, wincing from the acidic sickness rising in his gut.

How could she do this to his father...to him! Was it Mrs Kamaal's company that drove her to it or was it her own weak character? She had been a docile, gentle and caring mother all these years, and suddenly he had discovered that she was not the person he used to know. He felt nauseated. He ran outside, his mother at his heels.

'What happened? Should I call a doctor?' She rubbed his back to comfort him.

'No, I'm okay. I think I need some rest.' He walked back in and slumped into his bed on the floor, covering himself with a sheet.

She caressed his hair, but he turned his head away. 'I'm trying to sleep!'

'What's wrong with him,' he heard her whisper to Abdul. He fumed inside.

'Let him be. We ate outside this afternoon, maybe it's messing with him. He'll be fine with some rest,' Abdul whispered back.

After having spent tiresome hours pondering and drenching his pillow with tears, Mokhtar had eventually fallen asleep. It was true. Sleep could heal. It aided not just his aching body, but his mind too. When he awoke next morning, he had greater clarity than he did a day ago. *If fate showed me a woman I cannot recognize, she is no better than a stranger to me, isn't she?* he asked himself. Why, then, must he shed tears for a stranger? Why not get on with his life as if she did not exist? It was the most effective way to bury his pain.

That was precisely what he did thereafter.

'You scared the hell out of me, buddy,' Adel whispered, sitting next to him on the tram seat as they were returning from school. 'Did the thought of killing your own mother really occur to you?'

'I was angry,' Mokhtar mumbled, his head lowering.

The tram rolled to a stop at Midtown, the elite commercial centre of Cairo.

'What do you say?' Adel winked at Mokhtar. 'Shall we?'

A second later, they had scuttled out of the tram and were strolling on the cobbled pavements.

5

Located on a side road, amidst the stores and offices, was their favourite hangout: Cafe Memphis. The place was always abuzz with college students and young executives who would stop by for a puff and a variety of exotic coffees.

'Have you heard about this hidden power fighting for world control?' Mokhtar whispered to Adel as they waited for their coffee to arrive.

'No... who? The Europeans? The Western world? Come on, Mokhtar! You've got to come out of your world of comics!'

'No, no! Not them. These people are subtler. They are all around us, living with us.'

Adel raised a quizzical brow. 'Who?'

'The Jews,' Mokhtar whispered.

'You must be crazy! They are the most peaceful community around—progressive, business-minded. And they don't even have a country of their own. How could they...?'

'That's exactly the point. Do you know that they were the only community who fought from every side in the world war—the Russian, the British, the German, the American and the Hungarian army! They are surrounding the world from all sides, dreaming of making it one single country, the one they never had!'

'And where exactly is their headquarter supposed to be?' Adel shook his head in disbelief. 'You and your crazy theories!'

Mokhtar was about to retort when the door opened. Twenty men, dressed in traditional Arab attire, stormed in. While some of them stood guard outside, their leader—a young man in his mid-twenties—greeted everybody with an affable smile.

'All of you brothers and sisters,' said one of his fellowmen, 'stay where you are, and listen in silence.'

Adel and Mokhtar remained in their seats, terrified in part by this seemingly friendly siege.

'I come here today, friends...' the leader stepped forth, his hands majestically crossed across his chest, '...to know your views about the future of us, Muslimeen, in this country. We have been ruled by colonial forces for half a century. Their influence is visible everywhere. Their culture is very alluring. It has no boundaries. But, tell me, how many of you have read the Quran?'

More than a dozen hands gradually went up. Mokhtar joined them. His father was a Salafiya—one of those who believed in the fundamentalist reading of the Quran and in emulating the lifestyle of the early descendants of the Prophet.

'Then tell me, my gentle and noble friends, does Allah allow us to walk *their* path?'

Some people bobbed their heads in understanding. The man continued. 'Tell me, a few years down the line, would you like your children to lose their Arab identity? Be engaged in all kinds of immoral deeds and debauchery?'

'That is the future that these people are leading us towards!

Inshallah, the colonial forces will have to leave our country very soon. But before that, they will cripple us morally, make us their cultural slaves.'

'Excuse me!' A youth dressed in silk formals stood up. 'Who the hell do you think you are? And what is your point? Enough of this nonsense. I would like to leave.'

Two security personnel began approaching the youth with an aggressive stance, but the speaker signalled for them to stay put.

'My name is Ghassan!' he smiled, his expression a sea of calmness, 'I understand your anger. We have neither the authority nor the might to stop you. This man standing here with me, my deputy, is a carpenter by profession. That man standing next to you is a bicycle fitter. We are not a militant group out for a coup. We are poor people, united to help the poor. Eighty per cent of our population is uneducated. People like you and me have been taught the verses of the Quran since childhood. And as true Muslims, it is our duty to educate these people and enable them to walk the holy path.'

The angry youth walked out. Adel got up to follow him, but Mokhtar pulled him back. The rest of the crowd continued to listen intently.

'We are independent and yet not! Our king, Faoud, is a puppet in the hands of the British monarchy. He makes a mockery of the parliamentary system by dissolving it at his will, every now and again, at the behest of his masters. Be honest, how many of you are untouched by the evils of his corruption? Rampant poverty, illicit relationships, unrestricted mingling of men and women, the curse of alcohol—the list goes on!'

He established eye contact with each one there, sensing the extent to which he had been able to sow his seed in their minds. It was not easy to reform the elite non-religious youth, but it was core to his strategy.

'We are here to implore you to stand strong, to fight for the values of Islam, because Islam is the solution. The only solution! We must be governed by the Sharia, the only law acceptable to true Muslimeen. The law of Allah!'

Once he had finished, his men started handing out forms. Adel folded his form and tucked it into his pocket, but Mokhtar was already busy filling it. He was the first to walk up to Ghassan with the completed form.

'What's your name, young man?' Ghassan put his hand on Mokhtar's shoulder. The ease and warmth in his manner was endearing, almost brotherly.

'Mokhtar, sir! Hearing your speech, I felt like my muffled inner voice had found resonance. I am glad I could meet you today.'

'I am happy to hear that.' Ghassan nodded, impressed. 'We need people like you to work for the cause. Can you give us a few hours of your time every week?'

'Sure, I can!'

After the group left, a commotion ensued in the cafe.

'He is no ordinary man...'

'Ghassan Al Banna has hundreds of followers in Cairo alone...'

'He has a point...'

'He is winning hearts with compassion...'

'Bollocks!' Adel rebuffed the remarks as the duo walked out. 'It's ridiculous. That "Path of Allah" spiel. Well, by that theory, Jesus and Allah must be firing cannonballs at each other in the heavens right now. What a convenient interpretation to fool the illiterate!'

'How can you say that,' Mokhtar said, his frown deepening, 'after what happened to us recently? To our families?'

'Are you really going to work for them?' Adel stalled in his tracks. 'You do remember that my father works for the royal family, right?'

'Whose side are you on?' Mokhtar countered, 'King Faoud or Islam?'

'That's utter nonsense. There are no such sides. That man is beguiling youngsters like you to further his political ambitions.'

'If running dispensaries and schools amount to beguiling, then so be it! They are doing what the king should be doing and without taking a single penny from the state!'

Adel studied the growing fury in his friend's eyes. He knew Mokhtar was not entirely wrong. Kings had been indifferent to the suffering of the people. However, something about Ghassan's manner told him that there was more on his mind than just social welfare. And the king was not someone to mess with! He commanded a secret army that was trained to hunt down and kill.

6

Kabir Meets Keira

Kabir heard the heated argument between the van driver and the biker; then there was a loud and violent bang on the van's metal body. He lay on his back on the road beneath the van, the lactic acid in his muscles causing an unbearable burning sensation, though the wound on his waist had clotted and stopped bleeding. Death was finally knocking at his door. A few seconds and they would be around. Suddenly the banging stopped, the engine roared to life and he clung back to the chassis. The van stopped again, barely moving forward a few feet. He let go and lay on his back, his mind racing to explore his options. None! Checkmate, under the van! Even if he so much as stuck his head out, they would send a bullet through it.

He heard the sound of footsteps approaching the van. Suddenly, a metallic sound rang out behind him—a cover being swung open on a latch. He felt hands on his shoulders, pulling him towards the open manhole. He turned back to find an angelic face looking up from the open sewer manhole.

'Quick!' she implored.

He wriggled head first into the manhole. She held him tight, supporting his descent, pulling him inside, while she crawled backward into the square four feet tunnel connected sideways to the manhole pit. Soon he was sitting squat inside the pit. The sound of bullets hitting the van's trunk was amplified in the sound box the sewerage tunnel seemed to create.

'Quick! The lid!' she whispered loudly.

He pulled back the cover just in time to hear one of them shout. 'He's not here.' And then the footsteps fanned out.

A flashlight in the tunnel came on, finally allowing Kabir a proper look at the mysterious stranger. 'Oh!' He briefly stumbled for words, his eyes running a second trail over the set of exquisite features facing him. 'Who are you?'

'Later!' She pointed her finger to the tunnel ahead. 'Now follow me.'

Squirming through a pitch-dark shaft for nearly thirty feet, drowning in the overpowering stench, they reached an interconnecting duct. The walkie-talkie fastened to the back of her vest crackled. Holding the PTT button down, she murmured into it. 'All good. We'll be there in a few minutes. Over!'

After plodding on their elbows for another 200 metres, they entered a side duct. It led to another manhole pit similar to the one they'd first clambered down into.

The lady pushed open the sewer lid, her slender frame gliding out of the hole in a jiffy. She then offered Kabir her hand for a boost—the spanners and pliers tucked in her vest making her look like a sanitation worker.

A black van, parked a couple of feet away was their final stop, whose doors were slammed shut as soon as they took their seats.

'Here you go,' she said, handing him a box of sanitizing wipes.

Kabir sat on the leather seat in silence, scrubbing the grime off his face and hands. He was still reeling from how his world had flipped upside down and straightened back up—all within an hour!

He was feeling much better now after the adrenaline rush the chase had caused, minimizing the pain from the grazing bullet wound and the effect of the sedative.

His rescuer removed her helmet and took her worker's vest off. She dropped it aside, revealing a form-fitting black shirt that accentuated her lissom frame. Her hair was tied up in a bun, but a few stray curls had come loose—their blazing brown offsetting her flawlessly fair skin. Above all, she had the most striking pair of emerald eyes, finishing off that exotic look to perfection.

Opening a bag, she plucked out a strip of medicine. 'Should make the rest of the journey bearable.'

Her lips cracked a smile upon seeing his caution. 'Don't worry, it's a simple muscle relaxant.' Rolling the stray ringlet around a finger, she tucked it behind her ear before offering him the pill.

'Thanks,' Kabir said, popping the pill, 'for saving my life. You came in the nick of time. Agent Kabir Rathore, IMI.' He held out his hand.

'I saw that! The pill went right behind your shoulder.' She shook his hand. 'Keira Brooks, US Secret Service.'

Are you serious? His brows shot up. While he did admire her insight and skill, he was finding it difficult to trust the words coming from her lips. She was stunning too—a shade too stunning for an agent, perhaps? 'Secret service, did you say?' he inquired.

Her half-smile lingered for a while. 'You have a strange way of expressing your gratitude, Mr Rathore.'

'Oh, make no mistake, I am extremely grateful, Miss Brooks,' he quipped unapologetically. 'So the US secret service came swooshing through sewer lines, amidst traffic jams to rush to my aid? To what do I owe the pleasure of such a daring rescue?'

Keira Brooks was not one to be fazed by quips. 'Common enemies. Something has come up. And we realized it'd benefit one and all if the forces fighting evil banded together.'

'Common enemies?' Kabir watched her eyes once again, on the lookout for anything amiss. But there was nothing. 'All right, common enemies it is. Yet, I cannot get over the unbelievably impeccable timing of your entry.'

'Elementary that!' Her brows shot up in a tit-for-tat comeback. 'A tiny wafer chip—the size of a thumbnail—placed behind the hospital logo stitched onto the pocket of your gown, a GPS receptor.'

'But how could you have been sure that the van would come to a stop just above the manhole …'

Kabir knew the answer to that question even before he'd completed it. The biker, of course! All of that banging and ruckus was to ensure perfect alignment of the van and the manhole underneath it.

A quick scan around revealed five men working in a makeshift control room inside the van, coordinating with other agents on the ground. Their screen displayed a labyrinthine map with a dozen red dots moving about. 'That's a lot of agents they have working out there! So, the traffic jam…did they orchestrate that too?' Kabir continued.

'Yes,' she said, smirking, having read his thoughts right down to the last word. 'Traffic was stranded at the signal because of a trailer that broke down at the crossroads. The trailer was manned by one of our men. As well as most of the cars in that lane. And our IT experts here made sure the traffic signal stayed red all that while.' She shrugged with flair. 'We figured you might have a few more questions so…'

Kabir let his guard down a notch. 'Impressive!'

'No bugs. He's clean!' A man scanned him with a handheld gadget and quickly announced. Keira heaved a sigh of relief. The killer would not be at their heels.

'So, what is it that you want from me in particular?'

'Let's proceed to my hotel first to disinfect, clean up and shower. The exposure to the sewer's toxic effluents could lead to serious trouble—especially for your gaping wounds.' She spoke with disarming ease and conviction. 'We can then discuss everything comfortably over a cup of coffee. All right?'

'All right.' With an intrigued frown he leaned back against his seat. He needed to explore the synergies that could arise here, learn more about what was going on.

As the van moved along in the heavy evening traffic, the day's events played in his mind. *'Sarah!'* Did she make it out of there, unhurt? The hollow-cheeked, cadaverous face of the killer, his skin-and-bones physique and the evil confidence he had emanated. Why did this man want him dead? He had to be a commissary!

And what did the US Secret Service want with him so much as to warrant his rescue? He would soon find out.

7

The Flute Player

The killer sat on a small carpet laid on the floor of a deserted factory on the outskirts of Kuala Lumpur, unperturbed by the screams that echoed around him. Memories of his younger days flashed before him as he closed his eyes to pray.

He had just passed out of high school when training began. His father was waiting for him outside the gates of his fashionable school in London on the last day of the session.

First came strength training. Apart from extended bouts of running, swimming and isostatic postures, there were long hours of kick-boxing, mountain climbing and pumping metal. By the end of the first year, he had metamorphosed from a high school kid to a hunk. The eight-hour-long training session took its toll on his grades, which plummeted at the same rate as his popularity rose at school. He scored a clean sweep in the interschool boxing championship. He would look in the mirror for hours. *I am ready to take on the deadliest fighter. Dad must be proud of me!* He stopped attending the training sessions organized by his father and joined a much-touted gym.

One night, as he was returning from a late-night club hangout, he was intercepted by two black muggers in a dark by-lane. The confrontation lasted only a minute. He tried to punch one of them in the nose, but the guy ducked and landed an upper cut on his mouth; his lip burst open and let out a spurt of blood. Undaunted, he stepped back to regain his balance and got ready for the counterattack. The dark man didn't give him the chance; he stepped forward and punched him hard below the ribs. He reeled in pain as he felt a rib or two crumble. Still on his feet, he launched a volley of punches, none of them hitting their mark. The other dark mugger, in no mood to watch the duel further, took out his silencer-throttled pistol and shot him in the foot. He blacked out.

Lying on the hospital bed, he begged his father for help. His ego had been badly bruised. 'Where did I fall short in your training, Father?' he asked.

'We had just got you warmed up. The real training was yet to begin. Never mind! Let's start as soon as you get out of here,' his father replied. He was the one who had deployed the muggers.

His father took him to their house in the woods. He leaned on the fence in the backyard, appreciating the valley-view, when he felt something moving towards him with massive momentum. He turned around to find a bear charging at him. Bear wrestling became a daily phenomenon thereafter. Much like the wild grizzlies that were declawed and rendered toothless for professional championships in the southern states of America, the one that his father had acquired was bred for wrestling against humans. The bites were thus a tad less malicious; the bear's claws left shallower wounds. Yet, it was a violent beast, trained to fight, and the matches were gruesome. For hours he would wrestle with the creature until his body was drained of every shred of strength.

And then his father would announce round two.

The training that followed was reflex training. Muscle mass was a fad, more suited for those who fought under spotlights, within the luxurious confines of a stage. In the real world, where enemies battled to death and where there was no defined form or style of fighting, speed and deceit were what he would need. He trained to develop the reflexes of a trap-jaw ant, to camouflage like a chameleon and to handle weapons like extensions of his limbs.

'You're doing good, getting there!' his father told him as they walked a frozen lake one night after dinner. His father's mood was grim. He wondered what secret his father wanted to share with him. Or maybe this was to be his new training arena.

'What is it now? Skiing or ice skating?' he asked.

His father smiled at him. 'Watch your step!' he warned, trying to grab his son's arm, but it was too late. He had stepped on a segment of thin ice. It broke and he fell into the freezing water. He felt a thousand knives piercing his body as the freezing water engulfed him. He held his breath as he started sinking downwards, unable to move his limbs, paralysed by the freezing liquid.

'Hold on, push the water…!' He heard the smothered voice of his father through the water. He mustered all his willpower and paddled. His head hit a layer of hardened ice, sending a reinforced wave of searing pain through his torso. His lungs burned, out of oxygen. He fought hard to ignore the message his entire body seemed to be sending his brain. *Breathe!* It was pitch dark. He groped for the surface with his hands, but could not find the crack. He closed his eyes and looked inward, sure of approaching death. And then something unbelievable happened!

He felt a wave of warmth coursing through his body. His lungs no longer burnt. The craving to breathe was gone. He hung there, suspended in a state of equilibrium as his feet paddled lightly, levitating calmly in the still water. Suddenly, the darkness outside his closed eyes turned to light. He opened his eyes and saw his father kneeling near the opening, pointing a torch at him. He swam to the crack and emerged, breathing deeply but calmly. His father extended a hand to pull him out.

On the way back, he narrated the experience to his father, excited at how some unknown force had saved his life just when he was about to give up. He had lasted a good minute underwater after submission. This should otherwise have been humanly impossible!

'You saved yourself,' his father told him. 'The near-death experience made you consciously trigger your adrenaline response.

It is an old forgotten technique you will have to master. You have made a wonderful beginning!'

He realized the ice manhole was man-made. How could he have missed the almost round shape of the hole and the two-inch-thick face of the opening when he had climbed out! His father had intentionally delayed switching on the torch he was carrying in his felt overcoat. Fortunately, the ice axe and the rope he was carrying just in case his son really started drowning, didn't need to be used.

Over the next few months, he learnt how to make the cold his warm friend. The cold built up the brown adipose tissue under his skin, fortified his immune system, balanced hormone levels and generated loads of endorphins—those feel-good chemicals in the brain that elevate one's mood. This went hand in hand with breathing techniques and meditation, the remote controls to the mysterious defence system hidden inside the human body. The immune system trigger was so strong that he could will off the most dangerous infections without ever needing an antibiotic again.

'How does it feel, son?' his father asked him one night after treating him at his favourite restaurant. They were both dressed in white suits with matching white ties and shoes, looking like agents on a mission.

'I feel ready!' he replied zealously. He really needed to put his abilities and training to use now. The stories his father had narrated to him since childhood had filled him with deep hatred for the enemy. He wanted to make the entire community of perpetrators tremble at his name. And then he would break them, subdue them to dhimmis begging for mercy. *Today I graduate from dad's university. His only student. The best and most lethal in the world. He must have fancied this white graduation dress for the two of us on this special day.*

'That's not all...' His father wiped his fingers on a napkin at the end of their meal. 'I have another surprise for you!'

His father drove him to a bungalow in the suburbs.

'Your new accommodation!' He smiled, handing him the keys. He showed him around the ancestral house inherited from his dying bachelor uncle. But he did not want to live alone. He told his father how attached he was to him and it would be emotional torture.

'I am training you to be a lone wolf. You must overcome your need for companionship,' his father told him.

They went down into the basement. It was an expansive hall, tiled wall to wall with white ceramic. White painted walls, white sofa, a small white kitchen with just a white pan on a painted white gas cylinder. The white bathroom had white sanitary fittings and white powder-coated fixtures. In a corner, a few bags of white rice in white plastic bags leaned against a white wall. There were some bags with white sugar and white iodized salt too. His father's mobile rang and he climbed upstairs to find a signal. He looked in amazement at his uncle's fascination with white. He was a rice trader, true! But what was this crazy obsession?

He walked upto the sack of rice and picked up a handful. As the long, polished grains slipped out of his hand back into the sack, it reminded him of the rice grain clock that adorned the mantle above the fireplace at home. The walls here were stark naked, no art, no photographs, no wall clock, nothing. Just a warehouse with bare amenities for the storekeeper. The overdose of white was unnerving.

He walked up the stairs that led to the basement's exit and pushed the door. But it wouldn't open. He nudged, and then shoved it again. Alas, it seemed to be locked from outside. He called out to his father. Twice. Thrice. But there was no response. What emergency could have forced his father to leave without informing him?

He went back and slumped on the sofa. He did not have a cell phone. He went to sleep. When he woke up, he had no way of knowing how long he had slept. He rushed up the stairs and banged hard on the doors. All still…!

Little did he realize that the next level of training had begun—

torture! Beginning with white torture, the ultimate form of sensory deprivation designed to break the victim emotionally.

∽

As the killer finished his prayer, his thoughts turned to the day's events. Luck had been unfairly kind to the Indian officer today. And someone from outside his radar's reach seemed to be helping this guy. Someone unknown to even his omnipresent organization! Whoever it was, was bound for trouble.

He turned to his masked accomplices who had been torturing the van driver. Several fingernails had been pulled, thumb-pins pushed into delicate parts of the body, his face and arms gnashed as he bled all over.

'I swear on my children I didn't even know there was a man down there, under my van,' he cried.

'Let him go!' the killer instructed. He could see the man was telling the truth.

Indifferently, he then took out a small flute and started playing a haunting melody. The driver fell to his feet, sobbing, thanking him profusely for sparing his life. He would earn his children's blessings, he told the killer. The killer smiled at him kindly and waved his hand, signalling him to go.

The driver limped away, still uttering kind words about the killer.

As he reached the exit, he collapsed to the floor with a thud. A fine poisoned dart from the flute had pierced his neck.

The killer put down the flute and took out his cell phone. He had a lot of explaining to do. The man he worked for trusted him like no other. His failure today bothered him greatly. He hated Indians. A few years back, on a mission in Varanasi in northern India, he had been apprehended by the local police. They resorted to the regular forms of torture to make him confess. He lay on his stomach with his hands tied behind his back, a sly smile on his face as they caned his haunches. These guys' third degree was like a warm-up to him. He had experienced the rack, the judas chair, the nail ripper, the horse ropes, the cradle donkey and much more. He wouldn't have smiled if he had known what was coming next.

He was taken to an interrogation cell. Men in the control room watched his every movement and expression as they grilled him through the two-way sound system. For each of his seniors' unanswered questions, the infuriated inspector thrashed him harder. Tired, finally he ordered his men to shove a two-inch-thick unpolished cane up his balloon knot. He screamed in pain as the bastards played it around till his sphincter tore. He was carried back and dumped in a cell.

He cried for the first time as an adult when he realized its aftermath. Lying on the floor, his trousers caked on the inside with dried blood and faeces, he felt shattered and helpless. At night, when a constable unlocked the prison cell to deliver food, he escaped, killing each and every man posted there. But his body could never be the same thereafter. His sphincter had been permanently damaged, rendering his physique frailer as he suffered from all of its ungainly effects thereon. Forced to resort to the embarrassing assistance of faecal incontinence pads for life, the pervading dampness below became a constant reminder of the first tears he'd shed. *'My tormentors will suffer!'* It was the one line he unfailingly ended his daily prayers with since. That's why when his mentor had mentioned this mission, he had negotiated special plans for the country's subjugation.

8

The Man Must Live!

'What's this?' Mokhtar asked the man behind the counter, looking at the bag he had just been handed. He had walked all the way from home to attend the evening session mentioned in the form he had filled yesterday. He had mulled over Adel's warning all night. The fact that his family worked for and lived in shelter provided by a king's accomplice only added to the humiliation he felt inside. He had never liked the fact that they were being ruled by a handful of pretentious, profane white men from thousands of miles away. But he and his family were content within their limited means. After all, it was their own people, like king Faoud, who betrayed them and shared the loot with the British, leaving them to starve.

But now it was going too far. These white men had started toying with them, making them lose their self-respect. That was all that poor families like his had been left with and now they wanted to take that away too, leaving them standing naked! He would rather fight back.

What Ghassan was doing may not amount to revolt, but it was anti-establishment in some sense. It felt like the beginning of a chain reaction binding the poor together, something he had never seen happen in his country before.

'Your joining kit,' the man replied with a smile. 'It has your Rover Scouts uniform, a banner and the book of hymns. Welcome to the society of Muslim Brothers.'

Mokhtar walked past the shaded entrance to an open field, a huge stadium where he could see scores of young men training. Towards his right he could see a small troop of around thirty volunteers standing at attention and chanting hymns energetically. This was a far cry from his imagination of the society. 'What has this got to do with religious reform?' he wondered.

'What's your favourite sport?' asked a middle-aged man dressed in a robe, probably one of the trainers.

'I am not sure,' Mokhtar replied. 'But I think I can run.'

Mokhtar looked at the tall and well-built recruits in the other lanes. There were around seven of them. He looked frail and out of place; all of them had athletic physiques. He was nervous. More so because of the trainees who stood on either side of the tracks, cheering the contenders. The runners heard the gunshot and took off.

Closing his eyes tightly, Mokhtar began running a second later, his pulse booming against his ears. Having never participated in such races before, he had to force his legs to fly as fast as they could, till there came a point when his feet could barely feel the ground. At some point, he heard a loud burst of noise from the spectators. The crowds were driven crazy. So crazy that the sound of their racket was hurting his eardrums. *Had someone won?* He had no idea who but Mokhtar was certain he was hobbling along behind them. *Please Allah... let me not be the last!*

Suddenly a shrill whistle cut short the revelry.

'Stop... that's enough. New recruit—open your eyes. Stop boy!' Confused Mokhtar slowed down and gradually opened his eyes. He was standing way outside the parallel white lines, having come off track. He turned back to see the other runners were just reaching the finish line behind him.

'That's around eleven seconds. You're the fastest I have seen so far. Why did you close your eyes? You could have won,' the bearded trainer who had stopped him asked.

'Oh. Sorry!' Mokhtar said, trying to conceal a triumphant smile.

He would never again let the world scare him into closing his eyes again. He could beat them all! Many trainees came up to congratulate him and get introduced. There was a warmth in the air that made him feel secure and happy, quite different from his world outside. He had never even participated in a sports event at St Andrew's, let alone winning one. The society was already bringing out the best in him.

The sports session was followed by religious briefings inside a spacious mosque located at one end of the ground. Around a hundred volunteers sat in the centrum as Mr Umar, a gardener by profession and one of the founding members of the society, addressed them.

'Reform has to begin with individuals, then the family, the society, the state and finally, the world. Islam has the power to rid humans of their sufferings. Muslims and Arabs have forgotten their pride and dignity. As our leader Ghassan-al-Banna says, it is we who must help the ones without learning and without the will for it. So you my young and noble friends, must reach out to every nook and corner and teach our people. Spread the history and teachings of Islam amongst them! We have to renew the broken links between tradition and modernity.

'You can volunteer for any of the work areas like teaching, collection and distribution of zakat, helping run our dispensaries and so on.'

Mokhtar wondered what he would do. Certainly not teaching or organization! Collecting donations? No! What he was sure of, however, was that he had to be here. He would have to find some way to become useful. He would have to talk to Ghassan himself!

ග

'Where from?' Adel intercepted his bicycle a few yards outside the mansion gates.

'You know, I told you, right?'

'You don't understand what these people are up to, Mokhtar!' Adel grunted in exasperation.

'Why don't you enlighten me then, Adel Kamaal?'

'Mutiny. Against the king! I am warning you because I care.'

'That's not true.' Mokhtar shook his head.

'All that crap about walking the path of Allah...it all leads to one thing. They want to pull us back into the dark ages. Get the Sharia law implemented! This is the modern age. Why should we live our life the way our nomadic Prophet and his first disciples lived centuries ago?'

'Mind it, brother. I am a Salafiya...you dare to disgrace our faith?' Mokhtar stared at him angrily.

'I refuse to be conned. You tell me, isn't the Sharia regressive? It sets restrictions on what you are supposed to eat and drink and even allows men to punish women. That's sick, man! I agree that the king does not care for the poor, but neither does this man.'

'Like I said...you are no longer a true Muslim. Forget it, get out of my way,' Mokhtar said, nudging his friend aside, pushing his bicycle wildly towards his quarter. Adel stood there watching him fade away, his face contorted with concern. Despite their differences, Mokhtar had never been so rude to him before.

His mother opened the door, cheerful and exuberant. 'My dear son...'

'Wh...' Mokhtar stood stock-still in the doorway as he glimpsed the scene inside, a ghostly white paling the furious red on his cheeks. And then, on an impulse, he turned right around and sprinted off towards his parked bicycle. It was a full moon night. He left on his bicycle, pedalling as fast as he could. He dropped his bicycle where nature drew the first dunes of the sand.

Lurking by the shadowed side so that the guards would not notice him in case they woke up, he slapped a palm against a protruding edge of the pyramid.

I can't believe it! I... I... I can't... He battled his tears.

Sitting on the specially laid out carpet, he had seen his father accompanied by a white man in a formal suit. The same man he had sighted in the back seat of the Cadillac. They were having dinner together! It was a strange sight. A dapper European aristocrat sharing a poor man's food, from the poor man's plate, in the poor man's house. *No reason at all, unless...* and the possibility made him sick. *Baba is a weak man!* He no longer wanted to be like his father, he realized.

He gripped the protruding edges and gaps between the stone blocks, worn out by centuries of weathering, with the dexterity of a mountaineer. Just that there was no safety belt that would break his fall in case he faltered. The adrenaline was a good antidote for the storm inside, driving him insane. Soon he was sitting atop one of the blocks on the summit of the Khufu pyramid, the tallest of the trio. Curled up against the winds at the wuthering height, he looked at the ocean of lights in the distance below, and then towards the moon above. *What do I do with this wretched life of mine! I can't live in that house anymore. I don't know how to make myself useful to Ghassan. What am I living for?*

The moon cast its reflection on his dull pupils as he sat there, his knees huddled within his arms. He tried to shut out the memory of the encounters—of him having caught the foreigner kissing his mother, and of him watching the adulterer enjoying dinner with Baba. But to no avail. The scenes swirled in his mind relentlessly, tearing him apart at the seams. And then, he thought of Ghassan. How he had walked into the cafe with his humble aides and validated his vexations against what was going on around them. The whole scene played on loop in his mind. And then it struck him. The perilous task this man had set out to accomplish...his guileless retinue...his unsecured forays...the king's secret army! He was extremely vulnerable!

Nothing should happen to Ghassan! This man must live! Our only hope...

9

The Tiff

Keira looked stunning in the formal evening dress—grey pleated flannel pants and a light blue blouse with a plunging neckline, offset by a mother-of-pearl pendant. Her auburn locks fell right to her shoulders! She walked to the table with elegant poise, her chin raised ever so slightly. As she took her seat opposite Kabir, her beautiful face glowed in the light from the candles on the table.

Kabir was wearing a white Lacoste t-shirt and fawn cargoes, his glossy black hair combed back meticulously. A hot bath followed by a good sleep had nullified the effect of the sedative. He felt fully rejuvenated, his lean and muscular physique now showing. He had bought a new mobile and sim card and contacted the command centre.

'Thanks again, Keira.' He cleared his throat. 'I don't know if I can make it up to you... but,' he gestured towards the menu in style, 'buying you a drink could be a start.'

'I figured you might be too exhausted to make it here earlier for coffee, anyway.'

'Some wine, then? Before we begin?'

'If you say so.' She slowly leaned in to pick up the menu card. 'Merlot?'

His jaw grew taut with a grin. 'Very well, then.'

Kabir nodded towards the waiter. Soon, he was pouring them a drink from a bottle of the coveted Cabernet Sauvignon.

'So...' remarked Kabir, observing her hands as she picked up her goblet to join him. Unlike the rest of her glamorous outfit, her fingernails were trimmed short and kept plain—another sign that corroborated with her claim of being an active agent in service.

'To enigmatic rescues and extraordinary encounters!'

'To saving good men!'

They clinked goblets.

Kabir shook his head. 'That reminds me of the question that led to our rendezvous.' His voice dropped to a steady murmur. 'So what common enemy could have possibly compelled the US intelligence to track an Indian intelligence officer? Even while he was admitted in a hospital?'

Keira was silent for a few seconds, trying to frame her thoughts. Finally, she spoke, as if on resolve, looking straight at him. 'Look, Kabir, just like the Indian intelligence, the US intelligence is a moral force. You are amongst the top twenty commandos fighting against global terrorism today. We know who our friends are.'

'Our countries have been coordinating very closely in the upper echelons on this front for the past several years. I was in Kuala Lumpur for this man, your attacker. This mysterious man has been on our "most wanted" list for a while. Our people were on high alert around the hospital area when we learned that he was there to get you. When he was chasing you in the hospital parking, we thought we almost had him. But we were wrong. We did not know he had backup.

'So, when I was informed you were hanging on below that van, I shifted our priorities to saving you first. He had quite a reckless task force in place and it would have been impossible for you or anyone to resist his onslaught without assistance. A confrontation on the streets of Kuala Lumpur in a crossfire wouldn't have been a wise thing to do either. So, he once again, managed to escape. We still don't know which organization he works for...the ISIS, Al Qaeda, Lashkar, Al Shabaab or some new outfit, but they are for sure very well connected and dangerous.'

Kabir slid into deep thought. *An international terrorist, one at the top of the US intelligence's hit-list, wants me dead? But, why go to such an extent, and why single me out in Kuala Lumpur?* He had to learn more.

'Oh. So, this guy is already on your "most wanted" list? A terrorist, I assume! His details must already be in your database, I take it...'

'If you mean details of his shadows and aliases, then, yes. There have been several crimes of terror, which we are almost certain that this man is responsible for, but we don't have any identification on record.'

'No name. No identification. No fingerprints. No hard DNA evidences. How, then, do you surmise that these aliases, these shadows, all belong to the same man?'

'From his height, physical structure, methodology, capabilities and a ton of other factual and circumstantial evidence.'

'Unbelievable!' It meant the assassin hunting him down was essentially a ghost. 'So he exists on no database—yours or your allies, and is invisible to the radar of US intelligence stationed the world over!'

'Sadly, yes. That's why we are having such a tough time with him. Besides, he is a killing machine, his training and strength a notch higher than that of best commandos.'

'True! I faced him. He did not leave behind any eyewitnesses at the hospital. He blew up my security jeep which tried to intercept him with a bazooka. Fortunately, my men were outside the vehicle, but they were severely injured. My colleagues, who carried out investigations at the hospital earlier today, discovered that he was admitted as an eighty-two-year-old patient with anal incontinence. He used to wear nappies and they had to clean him several times a day. The nursing staff still can't believe the same person could have been a dangerous assassin. At one point, I was face to face with him and he looked extremely familiar. We found a face mask and artificial skin in the hospital room. So for all we know, he may have put on another mask when he left this one behind.'

'Yeah! We got a sketch made too, based on descriptions from our agents who saw him during the chase, but it did not match with his earlier appearances in our database or with the old man the hospital staff recognized. Kind of goofy! The same structure with a different face every time,' Keira added.

'Actually!' Kabir nodded. He remembered he had to talk to Sarah. Her phone had been unreachable when he had called her before going for a nap.

'I'll have to leave.' He got up and extended his hand. 'It was a pleasure meeting you, Keira.'

'Same here! See you around soon.' She smiled at him and shook his hand.

'One small request. I hope you won't mind,' Kabir said in a low voice, unsure of himself.

'Sure, tell me.'

'Can I see your identity card, please?'

'What? Yes, of course! But I'm not carrying it with me right now.'

'Agents never forget to carry their I-cards,' he said softly.

'I know, my bad!' she said. 'I'll get it from my room if it's so important,' she said, embarrassed by the sudden change in the demeanour of the person whose life she had saved just a few hours ago.

'It's okay, forget it. Just a quirk! I'm sorry,' Kabir remarked with a smirk, observing how her emerald eyes sparkled alive. They had a lulling quality, reminding him of the oceans and its mysteries he'd spend time exploring. Almost tempting him to wonder about the mysteries that might lie in these emerald depths of hers. *Agent Keira Brooks.* Could he trust her? Part of him did. He had seen the paraphernalia around her, the hi-tech van, her workforce and everything. It seemed a bit too much to fake. *Just seeing is not believing! Not in our undercover world of deceit and espionage.*

He turned around and walked away, putting thoughts of her behind. He had a lot of catching up to do. And it wasn't as if he was going to see her every other day. He took out his cell phone and called Sarah as the cab drove him to his hotel.

'Where have you been?' she asked, sounding relieved to hear his voice.

'I had a narrow escape. What about you, what happened?'

Sarah narrated the entire scene that had unfolded in front of her through the louvres in the closet. The killer's frail figure, his taking off the mask and skin, shedding the hospital scrub, putting on Kabir's tracksuit and finally climbing out of the window.

'Did you see his face?' he asked.

'Yes, for sure, I did.'

'Just get it sketched and mail it to me, stat.'

'All right, doctor, stat it shall be!' she said mirthfully. 'What about the amulet you threw in?'

'Keep it very safe. It's extremely important. I'll tell you what to do with it soon,' he said. 'Goodnight. Take care.'

'Wait! There's something important I forgot to tell you.'

'Yeah, tell me.'

'I am not sure how important this is, but when he removed his clothes, I saw a red mark, quite low on his neck. It looked something like an eagle in flight.'

'Thanks, this could be vital. Put that on the sketch as well. Organizations often get their logos tattooed or stamped on their members. Given that we don't have this man's identity, this logo, in one big leap, could lead us to his organization.'

5

Standing in front of the mirror, Keira gave herself a once over as she began removing her makeup. She wondered if Agent Kabir would have behaved in a similar fashion had she not been the weaker sex. '*Weaker!*' she scoffed. How could he suspect her and behave in such an ungracious way? Just because she was a woman? And this was not her first time. Right from her childhood, she had had to make innumerable sacrifices to prove her worth. Her mother had died while she was a kid and her own father would not trust her capabilities. They used to live in a lush mansion, but comfort was not what she craved. She clearly remembered the day her grandfather had made his last visit to their house. He was the one who had seen her potential and placed his trust in her. And soon after, her father had followed suit.

Had it not been for the mettle she had inherited from her grandfather and her determination to play this role she had aspired for since childhood, she would have given up long ago. After her father's death, she had sold off the luxurious mansion and dedicated her life completely to qualifying for the secret service. Whenever she had a weak moment she would think of what her grandfather had prophesized about her and it filled her with renewed vigour!

10

The Black Spider

Ghassan looked up from the book he had been reading and saw the boy standing at his office door. 'What can I do for you, young man?'

'I have quit school. Run away from home. Can I stay here?' Mokhtar asked.

'Yes, of course! We have a full-time boarding school. Which service have you finally decided to join, my dear?'

'I'm no good at any of them!'

'Then what?' Ghassan stared at him. 'All volunteers have to serve the community.'

Mokhtar was standing with his head down. He put his weight off his heels, rising on his toes, repeating this movement as he stood in place.

'Okay! Maybe you can help with cooking or housekeeping then. I will instruct Hamza.' Ghassan smiled, signalling for him to leave and got back to the book he had been reading.

'Can I be your personal security officer?'

'What?' Ghassan scanned his frail figure, amused. 'I don't need security. Allah will protect me.'

'Sure, he will. That's why he sent me! Just give me a few months, I will prove my worth. I will be your shadow.'

'Fine!' Ghassan smiled. 'But who would I need protection from? I don't have any enemies.'

'From the ones closest to you, usually,' Mokhtar ventured.

'Well, I am not sure how this will work, but I'll give you a try,' Ghassan shrugged, the usual pleasant smile on his face. 'I liked you the very first day you came up to me at Cafe Memphis.'

'Thank you! 'Mokhtar bowed, delighted.

'I said I'll try you. You have to show me now, give me a practical demonstration of some skill or capability that qualifies you.'

'Now?'

Ghassan grew amused as the boy stood there motionless, his head drooping, his eyes shuttling about in frantic search for a means to prove himself. It was not the first time that a young man had come running up to his door, fascinated by his speeches, thoughts and personality. But he knew how to deal with such requests diplomatically, like he was doing now—the only way to make this scraggy young man realize his limitations.

All of a sudden, Mokhtar took out a slingshot from his robe pocket and aimed it right at the leader's face. Ghassan could see a big round black pebble. It was aimed between his eyes. The boy's posture told him he was good at this.

'What are you doing? Put that away, young man,' Ghassan said steadily, his voice a shade drier and louder.

Mokhtar continued to stare at him, his right hand pulling the rubber strap further back, making it tauter and the pebble more lethal. He held the slingshot high above his shoulders, aiming it down at his face. And Ghassan realized how vulnerable he was just then. If he dared shout or raise an alarm, it would barely take a second for the pebble to dislodge his eyeball from its socket.

And then to his terror, the boy let go. The black pebble zoomed large. He quickly ducked in reflex. The pebble, however, was already past him—its trajectory just over his head. It crashed into the book-rack right behind him, shattering its glass into a thousand shards.

'Ali! Zafer! Aamir!' Ghassan shouted out to his attendants. They stormed in and held Mokhtar by his arms and neck, waiting for Ghassan's command.

'Why did you do that, young man? I trusted you!'

'You asked me to demonstrate…you left me with no option!'

'Are you crazy? That thing could have killed me.' The usually benign Ghassan was outraged. 'Throw him out and make sure he never steps inside the premises again.' The three men began to drag him out, eager to move out of their benevolent leader's sight and teach the audacious boy a lesson.

'Can I have my pebble back?' Mokhtar spoke up calmly, not resisting the force of his three captors.

'What? Did I hear you right?' Ghassan stood up and walked towards him. 'I must say, you have some guts, boy. Or maybe, you are simply insane!'

'Please! I need to show you something.'

A pause later, Ghassan glanced at Ali who walked up to the book-rack. The man groped through the broken glass amongst the pile of books, till he finally located the pebble.

'Tell me now, what is it?' Ghassan said as Ali held the pebble out towards the boy.

Mokhtar flipped the pebble around and peeled two black pulpy strands off it. He placed them in his palm and held it out for Ghassan. 'Legs of the black widow spider. The impact of the pebble must have crushed it completely. You'll find the rest of it inside the cupboard. Its bite can be fatal.'

Ali rushed to the cupboard and returned with a red hard-bound book, fragments of the spider's annihilated body still stuck to it.

'Unbelievable! How did you know it was there?'

'From its web! It builds a peculiarly uneven and tangled web, very different from the usual house spider's… and hangs upside down from it.'

'A small beginning indeed!' Ghassan brightened up and patted him on the back. 'But never do this again. You could have given me a seizure.'

'I promise, Master!' Mokhtar fell to his knees. He kissed Ghassan's hand and gently brought it to his closed eyes, its warmth healing his aching soul.

11

The Black Moth

The Murshid walked down the corridors in the 'Cove', the central command of an Islamic secret society. The Cove was a sizeable workplace, fitted with modern facilities. He badly needed to smoke…smoke in fresh air. The air-conditioning in the Cove was state-of-the-art, but he needed to step out once in a while… especially when his blood pressure was high.

The Murshid was around sixty-two, a postgraduate in political science from Harvard. He had travelled the globe more than any man alive, doing brick-and-mortar work for the mission. He was tall and well built, an Egyptian with a pleasant face, impeccable grooming and amazing interpersonal skills.

He passed through the centrum, where hundreds of operators worked on their terminals, busy coordinating the worldwide operations of the society. But they also had a larger task at hand. Preparing for judgement day! It was inching closer. Their best skills would be put to test very soon. The Cove would take control of the world on that very day. It would be the nerve centre of the mission.

Their workstations were arranged in concentric circles, with several radial partitioning alleys. He could sense his volunteers' pride and dedication at being part of this sublime mission. He gently acknowledged their greetings as he walked past the central alley. He continued for a few hundred yards till he reached his suite located at the farthest end of the Cove.

He unlocked it, and picking up a cigar, walked towards the

far wall and pressed a button. The hydraulic cylinders that held a block in place—the size of a door—creaked and pushed it outwards. The exterior of the 18-inch thick door matched exactly the stone surface of the cave outside. The Murshid stepped into the cave and walked about twenty metres to the opening through which sunlight came in. He stood at the edge and looked outside. It was all white and grey as far as he could see. The same sight always! The snow-capped peaks, the rugged mountains and the ice-cold wind. The Cove lay encapsulated in the stomach of a 7,500-metre-high mountain! Thus neutering the enemy's brigade of surveillance and spy satellites.

This was the only portion of the Cove that connected to the face of the mountain. Located at a height of around 5,000 metres on this desolate peak, the Cove did not exist for the world. The workforce was brought into the Cove blindfolded and anaesthetized. None except the five governing council members knew the real location of the Cove.

The Murshid let out rings of smoke as he puffed at his cigar. Zain, his most trusted commando, had just called in with some bad news. Another failed operation! Time was running out. The big day was so close! Everything had to be perfectly timed. The society had worked hard for the last hundred years, just to reach this day. Zain was the cover name for Khabib, his most reliable protégé. He had mentored and taken care of Khabib, and he had proven worthy of nothing less. Without Khabib, this mission would have been impossible. He had pulled off unimaginable, almost superhuman tasks for the society.

He wondered whether the Cove would need to exist once the mission was accomplished.

His pager beeped an emergency message. He rushed back to the command area, closing the door behind him. The governing council members were waiting for him in the conference room.

'Agent Sherif working at Suncor Energy, Canada, was arrested by the local police,' said Sami, a bald and lanky man is his late fifties.

'On what grounds?' asked the Murshid.

'For unauthorized entry in the central stores of the company.'

'Was he able to reach the drilling fluid storage tank or...?'

'Probably. They did not find anything on him.'

'That's good. What is our worry then?'

'The Canadian intelligence has taken over custody of Agent Sherif from the local police. He's on remand. We can't take any chances.'

'We'll need to depute Zain then. Inform him of all the details and arrange fast passage for him into Canada.'

'How much of the map is still left? 'The Murshid looked at Ibrahim, another bearded governing council member from Saudi, in charge of this operation.

Ibrahim switched to the projector slide that showed the world map speckled with mostly green dots, a few red ones in between. 'Almost 97 per cent… and 287 agents are working round the clock to ensure that the remaining red dots turn green,' replied Ibrahim.

'Great! Let's get back to work then, gentlemen, and let Zain handle this emergency,' said the Murshid, clearly proud of his mentee, his panacea for every ailment. Zain had eliminated every threat that came in their way—all except Shaytan. A name as mysterious and ominous as their own! The 'Shaytan', supposedly an insider gone rogue, was determined to stop them. He had been a menace till a few years back. He had even risked intruding into the Murshid's house, trying to steal vital information. Of late, he had been missing from the scene.

He rushed through the corridors to return to his suite, his expressions steadily turning graver. It was about time to receive a call from the master, the 'Sayyid'. And while the updates he had to give were encouraging, there were a few niggling doubts. Something the Sayyid did not go easy on. The Murshid felt an evident discomfort brooding inside him. He had no reason to fear, he convinced himself, especially not after a lifetime of service to the society!

∽

Kabir woke up with a start. It was a call on his mobile phone. He looked at the red digits glowing in the dark, it was 5.30 a.m.

Mr Menon, at this hour?

'Good morning, sir,' he said, trying his best to not sound drowsy.

'Good morning, Rathore. Are you all right now?' the Director General of military intelligence said. Kabir was one of the few agents he called directly in hours of crisis and concern.

'Yes, sir.'

'I heard about the attack. We must get those bastards! You will get all the backup and support,' he bellowed, his usual self, simmering with energy. He was a notoriously early riser, hence these near-peak energy levels. But Kabir knew he was serious about the backup. He was the one who had negotiated for the submarine for Kabir to work on Jayant's case.

'Will do, sir! And I will call you in case I hit a wall at any point.'

'What's the status on Project Jayant? Where's the flying bird's trail leading you now?' Menon chuckled.

'I've got the data, just have to decode it to know the terminal location. We are missing a piece of software. My friend is at it. Had it not been for my long illness, I would have been in Sri Lanka, working with him right now.'

The phone beeped. There was another call waiting from an unknown international number. *Pretty surprising. Maybe a mistake, a wrong number!* Kabir thought, glancing at it.

'Remember, Kabir, whenever you pull the curtain, it will be a proud moment for the entire country.'

'Absolutely, sir.'

He took the waiting call as Mr Menon hung up, groggily

pushing the sheets off his bare legs. A dull pain spread down to his arm. *Damned shoulder...*

'Mr Rathore.'

'Yes?'

'Good morning, I'm aware it's rather early, but this is an emergency. Before I introduce myself, I must inform you that this relates to the group that attacked you yesterday. We know who they are,' came a baritone voice in a posh accent.

Deferential. Sophisticated. British. Kabir surmised straightaway, 'And...'

'We have information that would be of help to you,' the voice continued, 'But we will have to give you the details in person.'

Odd! First, the US secret service. And now, a private caller. This was the second time in twenty-four hours that someone was offering unsolicited help! 'Before anything else, I'd need to know who's on the line,' Kabir said as he continued stretching his shoulder with the routine his physio had prescribed.

'I am Victor Turner. I work for an international organization called the Protettori, which tracks down and fights terrorism.' His words dragged to a halt. 'In fact, I must insist that we meet right away.'

'I have your number now, Mr Turner. I will call you back soon and let you know,' Kabir said. He'd need to research into this informer's organization first and then seek permission from higher command.

'One moment...' the man said just before Kabir was about to disconnect. 'All right, I admit I might not have been entirely forthcoming with my information. But you must trust me when I say that there is more to our meeting than merely revealing the identity of your attacker. The world is under threat. Your world... our world is headed for an Armageddon of sorts. The clock is ticking. We have it all worked out, and you are indispensable to the plan.'

Kabir could tell that the caller was perturbed despite his attempts to feign calmness. 'I am not a mercenary, sir,' he reminded the man warily. 'I work under instructions from the Indian defence forces. There's protocol to follow. You will need to speak to Mr Menon, our director general.'

'We will. But didn't he just grant you permission to go after the attackers?' He let the gravity of his words sink in. 'Mr Rathore, we have a car waiting for you outside the hotel.'

What? They have my mobile tapped? Kabir remembered having bought the local sim and cursed himself for using an unsecured line. 'You have a car waiting to escort me to a meeting now? Is your organization based in Kuala Lumpur, then?'

'No, Mr Rathore, the car will take you to our private hangar at Aziz Shah airport. A chartered plane shall fly you to our headquarters.'

Chartered plane? This was getting crazier by the second. 'Hold on a sec... a private organization that fights terrorism? Never come across the name before. Protettori, did you say?'

'We work quite discreetly. We have countered countless terror attacks, some of which could have decimated entire cities. We have infiltrated every major terrorist outfit.'

Countless attacks? Kabir could not bring himself to believe most of the man's claims. 'Mr Turner, I'm afraid I must stop you there. I have to go. You may contact Mr Menon if you want my presence at this meeting.'

'Well, all right. I have someone here who might convince you otherwise.'

A second later, there was a low shuffling sound. 'Hello, Kabir. Colonel Bakshi here.'

A familiar voice greeted him. He'd had the privilege of hearing it for years. He'd heard the voice right until the man's retirement two years ago. Colonel Bakshi was an upright and honest officer, respected throughout the ranks, and Kabir had briefly served under him as well. 'Colonel Bakshi?' he sat up, surprised, 'you're aware of this organization?'

'I work with them! Victor is right. This meeting starts a few hours from now. We have people coming in from all over the world. There's no time for clearances. I'm aware of the powers vested in you by the Indian intelligence—you are free to travel wherever your work takes you in hours of crisis. And trust me, we are facing a major one now!'

'All right, Colonel, if you say so!' Kabir relented, trying not to let his uncertainty show. 'Where exactly are we meeting? Okay, at least tell me which part of the world!'

'Europe!' came a reluctant reply as the line went dead.

Within the next twenty minutes, Kabir had gotten out of his bed, showered and slipped on a pair of combats. In an overnighter rucksack, he stuffed his laptop, journal and a couple of personal belongings. As he was zipping it shut, he noticed the red dot of an email notification on his mobile screen. He saw an email from Sarah.

The assassin's sketch! It was the same face that he'd seen from below the truck in the parking lot. And he was now doubly certain what the killer looked like.

And there's the raptor. He peered at the mark on the assassin's neck, studying it closely, when he noticed something else—something eerie that made his hair stand on end. The preying bird seemed to be holding a large silhouette in its claws, bigger than its own size. A human being!

∽

'Good morning, sir! We were waiting for you,' a man in a black jumpsuit greeted Kabir as he stepped out of the chauffeured car at the airport. Dressed in his specially designed combats, he was now prepared for any emergency.

The morning breeze was soothing as ever. Kabir remembered how crazy the day before had been, as he took a deep breath and started walking towards the hangar, the man in the jumpsuit leading the way. Especially the unknown call and then Colonel Bakshi coming on the line.

Suddenly, Kabir stopped in his tracks.

It had just struck him that Colonel Bakshi had lied to him. They were not going to Europe. They couldn't be! He had said that the meeting would begin in a few hours. And it had taken around an hour for the car to bring him here. The journey to Europe would take anywhere between ten and eleven hours. Was this a trap!

'What's the problem, sir? You look ruffled!' the man asked.

'Where's the pilot. I need to speak to the pilot.'

'I'm your pilot, sir!' the man said with a smile.

'Really?' His brows shot up. 'Where are we headed for, then?' His instincts were on high alert, having already made a mental note of the surroundings. The car had left. Not a single accomplice could be spotted at the airbase, nor a single sound heard anywhere. His fingers were pulsing, ready to grab his Glock in a split second if he noticed anything awry. 'How many of you are around?'

'It's just me, sir. No one else…'

'Then I guess you'll be the one telling me which European city we're meant to be flying to?'

'I'm sure Mr Turner must have already told you. We are not allowed to disclose this information! You'll get your answers at the hangar… This way, sir.'

When Kabir saw the hangar, he immediately reached for his holster, scanning its ramps twice. There wasn't a single aircraft parked in the large expanse. Eight blocks were marked on its grey floor with white paint, but all of them were vacant. 'Where's the aircraft?' he demanded.

'One minute, sir,' the pilot held his palms up in a truce and fished out a small remote from his jumpsuit. The click of a button later, a shutter at the far end creaked as it started rolling upwards, revealing an unusual shadow.

'Are we meant to be riding that?' Kabir peered. 'Is that a miniature B-2 Spirit bomber?'

'It's a Xssault Black Moth,' the pilot's tone held a tint of pride, 'a box-wing three-seater that flies at four times the speed of sound. We'll be at our destination in less than three hours.'

You must be kidding! Kabir found it hard to mask his surprise. 'Even Mach 3 aircraft haven't made their way out of R&D centres of NASA yet!' And here was this curious-looking aircraft that resembled a moth—just a set of flying wings, no fuselage! It reminded him of an origami plane.

'No, they haven't. Not for the world! Cutting-edge technology is not publicized. Not till it can be commercialized … and that's still a few years ahead. They wouldn't want the Chinese or the Soviets to get a whiff of such path-breaking developments.'

'I see…' Some of the facts did add up, that meant! With his curiosity piqued, Kabir continued to check out the jet. 'And they've handed the controls to you now?'

'Well, they couldn't have found a better purpose for it!' the pilot explained fervently. 'Normally it is ejected from a bigger aircraft to keep it from being sighted during take-off, but the circumstances today warrant bringing it out into the open.'

Kabir suddenly heard the muffled footfall of boots from behind him. Pulling out his firearm, he wheeled around, aiming its muzzle at the source of the footsteps. *What th…* He scoffed in disbelief at the sight of a familiar figure walking towards them.

'Keira Brooks!' his greeting came a second later. 'Imagine meeting you here!'

'Kabir Rathore! I could be saying the same thing.' She narrowed her eyes, 'I am disoriented… I am guessing you must be too… so…' She glanced at the barrel of his Glock. 'Careful with that.'

'Caught me off guard. Apologies.' He lowered his pistol and slipped it back into his holster. Somehow, he found her presence here as perturbingly strange as it was pleasantly surprising. 'I presumed you were meant to be in Kuala Lumpur, to chase an assassin.'

'Like how I presumed you were here on a personal mission!'

'All right!' The pilot cleared his throat. 'Seems we can skip the introductions then. Sir, Agent Brooks is the third passenger who'll be joining us today.'

'Third passenger?' Kabir darted the man a wry stare. 'And you couldn't have mentioned this detail before?'

As the duo resumed their trek towards the jet, with the pilot in the lead, Kabir murmured to her 'So have you worked with this organization earlier? I was hoping you could give me some insight into this "save the world" crisis.'

'Well, we'll know soon, won't we? Woah!' She tilted her head as the black jet came into view. 'That is a neat ride!'

'I agree! It's a new-age supersonic jet that is going to get us to Europe in three hours, or so claims the pilot.'

Keira wandered close to the aircraft, studying its design intently. It was a stunner on all counts—with an unconventional 'flying wings' form, a glossy jet-black exterior and a zero figure. The cockpit was a hatched cabin spread horizontally atop the centre of the wings, its compact interiors allowing for no more than three seats. The Xssault logo—an aerodynamic Alfa with a three leaf clover within—sat proudly on its wing.

Unclipping the straps of her Decathlon backpack, she cast a glance over a shoulder, watching the man who'd been watching her in silence while she examined the Xssault. 'Agent Rathore,' Keira said in a whisper just as she crossed him to make her way towards the cockpit canopy, 'why do I get the strange feeling that you have your guard up around me always?'

His eyes ran over her face hovering not far from his own. 'Let's see...' he whispered back, 'apart from the after-effects of a rather strange twenty-four hours, maybe it's the simple fact that you know too much about me... and I know very little about you.'

She broke into a smirk. 'Keira Brooks. Come from a typical American family in suburbia. Lived in Connecticut most of my life. I'm a serving US secret service officer, who put my life on the line for you.' She paused, then said, 'Would that do? Or do I need to give you my Woodhaven drive address in Hartford too?'

There was that tell-tale sparkle in her eyes again!

'I guess that'll do for now.' He rounded off his tongue-in-cheek remark by biting back a grin. In her black uniform, and hair tied up into a neat bun, she gave off a vibe that spelt *business*. But there was honesty in her green eyes. He could not shake off her gaze.

They climbed into the jet and it was airborne in a matter of minutes, the three of them securely belted inside the cockpit with the transparent polycarbonate hatch materializing as they were inside the airtight enclosure, oxygen masks secured over their faces. The pilot provided them with headphones with built-in mics for easy communication amidst the roaring engine noise. The vertical take-off made them feel woozy and then, when the aircraft reached cruising altitude, it began to gain momentum. The sonic boom was nothing more than a soft rumble and a gentle thump.

'Hope you are comfortable.' The pilot turned his head to look at each of them, seated on either side of him. 'Like I told you, the sickness bag is in the pocket right below your seat in case you need it. And in the interest of safety, I advise you to keep your seat belts on, all through the duration of this flight,' he added with a titter. 'I will now jam your voices from my headphone so that the two of you can chat in private and I can focus on the controls.'

The agents were quiet for a while, their heads against the headrests. Finally, Kabir spoke. 'Let's ponder over our impending tryst with the Protettori. Our departure is unannounced and we were told to leave all communication equipment behind. What if this turns out to be a trap?'

'Doesn't look like it from this special vehicle they sent to fetch us. And just in case it is, I have for company an undefeated champion of handling adversities—on land, air and water. Say, if something went wrong with this plane, for instance, you are probably the only person on earth who would still find a way to survive.'

Kabir knew she was right. He thought about the two pocket parachutes developed by RDOB that he was carrying in his combats. That, coupled with his tracking skills, the best in the world, made him a survivor against the worst odds. Tracking! The technique of moving sideways during free fall. While a normal person would fall face-to-earth at 120 miles per hour, Kabir could de-arch, using his body to cut the air as a means of providing greater lift, causing a much slower fall. He could travel as much of a horizontal distance in whichever direction he wanted, to find a waterbody or other safe ground to cushion his landing. He had achieved a horizontal to vertical glide ratio as high as 1.5, unheard of amongst trackers, the highest in the world.

'You seem to know a lot about me, Miss Brooks.'

'We keep track of our friends.' She shrugged.

'And what are your special skills, if I may ask?' Kabir raised an inquisitive brow.

'The tenacity of a good agent,' she said, smiling. 'And foresight.'

For most of the flight thereon, Kabir could see nothing but the ocean below them. He drifted off into a nap as they still had around two hours to go, and he could do with some sleep. Keira, who was still adjusting to the effects of supersonic travel, found it difficult to do the same.

Sometime later, Kabir woke up to the sound of her anxious query.

'Where are you going to land us?' She was asking the pilot. She looked worried. The plane was in a state of vertical descent and it was just the ocean below, as far as he could see. Was this another sabotage? The two agents exchanged worried frowns.

'All is fine. We'll be landing soon,' the pilot said reassuringly.

'Landing where?' asked Kabir. They were fairly low now, maybe just 10,000 feet.

'There! See?' He pointed towards a grey patch now beginning to emerge below them. Like a whale surfacing, white froth formed around it as the water cascaded down its back. As they zoomed in, Kabir could see that it was sizeable, a kind of mini landing strip, fit for even conventional small planes.

'What is that?' Keira asked, relieved.

'That's SOB, a submersible offshore base, with Japanese PSP, or pneumatic stabilized platform, technology. It can move around in the ocean and surface when needed. Our organization has been using this for a while,' the pilot replied curtly.

This was turning out to be more thrilling than Kabir had imagined. He had read about the VLFS—very large floating structure—during his training, but this was unheard of. Anything submersible, as large as this, was supposed to be cutting-edge technology used by the naval forces of the likes of the US and Russia. A private organization using it spoke about their size and muscle.

Able to see the SOB clearly now, Kabir wondered where the meeting would take place, as there was no discernible movement or shelter on the grey patch.

'Apparently not our final meeting venue...'. He was about to bring his observations to her attention when he realized his fellow passenger was in no mood to share in his enthusiasm of submersibles. She'd closed her eyes and was holding her breath. It appeared the 'tenacious' special agent, Ms Brooks, was battling nerves, thanks to the unusually sharp descent. So much so that her fingers had mistakenly clutched at the adjacent seatbelt retractor— the one attached to his seat. His eyes slid down, stealing a glimpse of her whitened knuckles. And then he looked ahead, a gentle smile thawing his staid expressions while Keira continued to brace herself for the impact of landing. One that would never come!

12

Mokhtar Meets Nouran

It had been over six months working with Ghassan. Mokhtar's day started at 7 a.m. His work went on late into the night, and he was free only after Ghassan's public discourses ended. He did not let Ghassan out of his sight, not even for a minute, not till he dropped him to the safety of his well-guarded house. He trained in the night, focusing his every muscle to follow his instructions and instincts. He educated himself on unconventional weapons and combat techniques, learning both through books which Ghassan would arrange for him as well as from the vast variety of warriors and tribals the both of them got to interact with. The walls of his room were adorned with every kind of armament a medieval warrior would have possessed.

'Can I do something to ease your worries, Master?' Mokhtar asked as he stood behind Ghassan, who was signing the last set of documents on his table.

'I have nothing to lose, my dear! It just worries me that the movement may get into the wrong hands. They want to open the society to the elite and the powerful. Bring in popular faces to increase our reach.'

'No! They want to kill the movement, hijack it! You have built the society with your sweat and blood. You have become the voice of the downtrodden. Now our own board members, like Ahmad, want to stifle that voice.'

'Just give me your consent, Master. Such traitors need persecution.'

'Hold it, Mokhtar! These are trying times. Organizations like ours are run with patience, and besides, we strictly condemn violence.'

Mokhtar had never seen Ghassan so worried before and it pained him. He had never felt so helpless in years, not since he had run away from home.

5

It was a breezy night, four months later, when Mokhtar was jogging his way through the suburban boulevards of the newly developed Heliopolis area; home to the Europeans and the aristocratic classes, affluence was evident in its broad avenues, terraced villas and modern apartment buildings. That said, it was a sparsely populated locale. And during such late hours, the place appeared deserted—apart from the occasional hum of an automobile breaking the silence on the streets.

A jeep veered past him. He cursed at them—four boys, brandishing beer bottles and carolling Cliff Edwards' hit single 'Singin' in the Rain'. The kind of elite youth disgracing Islam these days. In the dimly lit distance, he saw them slow down behind a pedestrian wearing a long overcoat. One of the boys got down and started to pull the pedestrian towards the jeep. Mokhtar doubled up. A part of him told him to stay away as he could not afford any aimless tussles, Ghassan's security being his prime focus. As he drew closer, he realized it was a girl with a black scarf. Her screams pierced his conscience, and he found himself sprinting towards them.

'Let the lady go!' He panted, coming to a halt behind the jeep.

'Get lost. None of your business!' one of the boys shouted, hurling abuses at him. He tried to punch Mokhtar in the face, but Mokhtar ducked and landed a full punch in his stomach. The boy withdrew in pain, holding on to his stomach. Mokhtar heard another one of them approach him from his rear left. He waited for the right moment, and when this boy was close enough, he thrust his elbow backwards. It tore the boy's lips, sending him into a panic as he spat blood. The third one retraced his steps to the jeep, watching his friends' fate. Their friend sitting in the driving seat had already turned on the ignition.

Mokhtar held the girl's hand and started to walk away. He would escort her to the safety of her house and get on with this jog.

They had barely walked a few yards when he heard something whizzing towards his right ear. He raised his hand in defence, but an object was coming at his left too. Before he could make sense of it, there were multiple missiles in the air, all headed for his face. Confused, he tried to spin away, but it was too late. A bottle crashed against his head, shattering to pieces and douching him with alcohol. Before he could recover from the impact, another one hit his head hard, some splinters piercing his body. The concussion from the repeated impacts made him feel giddy immediately.

C... can't lose to a bunch of spoiled college brats! Mokhtar desperately tried to hold himself together, but lost his balance and crashed on to the road. He saw the boys standing near the hind seat of the jeep, still shooting beer bottles at him from a crate. His vision was a dim blur, the prominent crimson in it being his own blood, trickling down his line of vision.

He had learnt his first lesson in real-life combat. *Knock your enemy out before you walk away!* The boys forced the girl into the jeep and drove away. Mokhtar lay there helpless, watching them fade out of sight. The girl's innocent face and the glint of hope in her eyes on seeing him flashed in his mind intermittently.

He lay there for a while, waiting for the concussions to recede. He then dragged himself on to his feet and started trudging along. He was now walking down the motorable road that connected the new township of Heliopolis to main Cairo city, surrounded by desert on both sides. He could see the city lights in the far distance beyond this empty road.

He was halfway to Cairo when he saw the jeep again.

It was parked at a distance from the road in the middle of the desert. That was the farthest the Jeep could have gone into the desert before the mounds rose in an incline. He walked up to the jeep and pocketed the keys. He then dragged his injured body, crawling on his elbows to the top of a mound. It was all calm and cool. A tiny piece of moon hung in the sky, its light dim. He had no way of knowing how far they would have taken the girl. Maybe beyond the next row of mounds, or the next. It was time for Isha'a, the night Salah. He never skipped the five daily prayers. His body hurt but he could not turn his back on this girl.

'Thanks for giving me this second chance,' he prayed. 'Your believer would rather die than lose. Give me strength to fight, and die, like an honourable Salafiya, if need be.'

He warmed his eyes with his palms and opened them. The dimly lit desert was serene as ever. A strong wind blew the sand and shook the acacia trees located in a clump towards his far right. He spotted a plume of white smoke and a light as dim as a firefly between the swaying trees. God had answered his prayer.

He wriggled his way to the thicket like a dangerous reptile. Hiding behind a tree, he pulled out the slingshot, but on second thought, tucked it back in. It was time to put to test his new deadly weapons! He had already made the mistake of taking the boys' strength for granted in the first fight. Never again!

He saw the girl lying curled up in the sand, her mouth gagged and her hands and feet tied. Her dress was torn and her hair splayed about. The boys were getting ready to ravish their prey, enjoying their last round of beer with sheesha. They let out smoke rings and the drags they took made the charcoal tips in the stained-glass bowl glow like fireflies.

They did not get a chance to react. Mokhtar was like a wild animal, biting into the neck of one of them and lacerating the chest of another with the 'Bagh Nakh', a tiger-claw style dagger of

Indian origin that could be worn around the fist. The 'karambit' in his other hand, drawn from his socks, tore through the thigh of the third one and he crashed his head against the fourth, sending him down instantly. They lay there like fallen dominoes, writhing in pain.

'Bastards!' He spat at them. 'I should castrate you. Leave you to bleed to death!' The boys recoiled in fear, trying to drag their wounded bodies away in the cold sand.

'Just remember two things,' he said. 'Never touch a lady against her will.' He untied their victim and removed her gag. 'And stop aping the West. Islam is the solution.'

'What kept you out so late, girl?' Mokhtar asked her firmly as they got into the jeep, handing her an overcoat from the backseat.

'I was visiting my aunt, she insisted I stay for dinner,' she said through her tears. 'This has always been a safe neighbourhood.'

'The times are a-changing. You'd better be careful. Come, I'll drop you home,' Mokhtar said gently as he turned the key in the ignition, realizing the girl must already be scared from the trauma she had been through.

'Thank you!' he heard her say softly as he drove. 'Who risks his life for strangers?'

'We Salafiyas do!' he replied, his glare fixed on the road ahead. They were in the township now and she guided him through the maze of apartments.

'I'll be in your debt forever,' she said as they pulled up outside her house. 'Please come up. My father would be glad to meet you.'

'Some other day,' he replied curtly, not wanting to appear friendly. He saw her face properly for the first time in the light from the pole outside her house. Only rich neighbourhoods, like in Heliopolis, could afford electricity distributed by private British companies. Another vice that helped the foreigners keep the affluent and influential locals in their evil clutches, he pondered.

'Shukran,' she bent forward courteously, bringing her left palm to her face.

'Ma'a al salama,' he replied, not letting their eyes meet and drove away. He parked the jeep outside a police station and jogged his way back to his room, unaware of the Pandora's box he had just let open.

5

'I am proud of you, my son! Look at you! It has hardly been a year and my little Mokhtar has turned into such a handsome young man.' Abdul gripped Mokhtar's muscular arms with both his hands and looked into his eyes. At six feet, one inch, Mokhtar stood taller than his father. They were meeting after a long time. Mokhtar used to see him outside Mr Kamaal's office once in a while but visiting him in the palace was out of the question. He would feel the emptiness in his father's eyes and how much he missed him. But the proud Salafiya was a stoic, just like his son.

He hugged his father and whispered in his ear, 'I am what you made me, Baba. You should be proud of yourself!'

'Why don't you leave this wretched job? You should come and live with me. Serve Islam like you always wanted to,' Mokhtar continued. What he really wanted to refer to was not his father's job, but Nazma, his mother. How could he bear to live with her? But the veil of propriety prevailed between father and son.

'I owe too much to Mr Kamaal, son. More than I can repay in this lifetime.'

Mokhtar nodded, reflecting over the irony of loyalties. The English officer Mokhtar had seen his mother with, the one who had later landed up at their quarter, had been transferred back to London.

'Did other English officers come to taste our food after that day, Baba?'

Abdul looked at him for a few seconds. Mokhtar was not sure

whether his father understood. Or maybe he did. If he did, why did he put up with it?

'Why do you get so mad at them, son?' Abdul said. 'Mr Harrison used to write about local culture and cuisine. He loved your mother's food and even invited us to his farewell party.'

Mokhtar tried to read between the lines—'at them'. *So there had been more of them!* He felt sick and helpless.

'I have to go. Just remembered some urgent work!' Mokhtar turned around and ran as fast as he could.

'What do I do with these?' Abdul called out after him, holding out a tiffin box of freshly prepared mahshis. 'Your mother sent these for you.'

Flashes of moments spent with his mother came to him as his eyes grew moist. She had been a good mother all those years. And now this! He could not stand betrayal. He would never betray someone he loved. The face of the girl from yesterday, glowing in the street light, flashed right in front of him. This was ridiculous. He slapped himself—again and yet again. He would never get into a relationship with a female. No one would disgrace him like his mother disgraced his father!

∽

Mokhtar was jogging through his usual route, past the residential flats in Heliopolis. A stone fell right in front of him from nowhere. He looked around, but there was no one in sight. He could see something tied to the stone. It was a papyrus, the traditional bamboo paper of Egypt. It read: 'I tried, but can't get you off my mind. Will wait for you at the Mozart Pastry Shop, 7 p.m. tomorrow.'

He looked around again, but it was all desolate. He put the papyrus in his pocket and jogged away. There was no way he would get into this. He changed his jogging route to avoid that particular suburb the next day.

As he climbed up the stairs and began unlocking his room, he saw a paper peeping from beneath the gap in the door. He pulled it out. It was a handmade greeting card with beautiful, dried blue and purple tulips neatly glued inside a heart-shaped pink background, laced and decorated with sparkling sequins. No names, though. *She followed me to my room?* This was unexpected.

The notes became a daily ritual and he would find a pretty greeting card waiting for him as he arrived at his room from the society. The colours and execution were delicate and ethereal and they always bore the fragrance of jasmine. It was an altogether different feeling. That of being wanted! But then he would realize where this was headed, and an anger would simmer within him. *I will allow no such thing!*

It had been almost a week. The new way was closed due to construction work and he had to take the old route. He had reached the place where the boys in the jeep had stopped the lady, when he saw her in the same long coat, this time in a floral headscarf.

'Stop!' She raised her hand as he approached closer to her. 'I need to talk to you, Ahmad!'

'Mokhtar,' he corrected, and immediately realized his mistake.

'Sorry! You didn't even tell me your name that day.' She smiled apologetically.

'It's not that I dislike you or something, gentle lady. Just that I am not your kind. All your painstakingly made cards had to go to the dustbin.'

'Why do you say that, Mokhtar? What is it that you do?' She was dejected.

'It doesn't matter. The thing is, there's no place for a woman in my life. You seem to be from a good family. Go back!' He swerved around her and started jogging ahead. She followed him. He peeked back at her jogging behind him and shook his head in amazement. *These modern girls!*

'Look, I wore jogging shoes. I knew this was coming.'

'I told you I am not interested,' he said, increasing his speed.

'I can see that. You didn't even ask my name. Nouran, by the way,' she said, gasping for breath, unable to keep up.

Suddenly, he heard a thud. He looked back and saw her on all fours. She had tripped over a protruding brick. Her knees and hands were bruised and blood had already begun to ooze from the wounds. He felt a strange shudder, the kind one feels when they see a near and dear one in trouble.

Sitting there on the road, with her knees folded to her stomach, she gazed at him blankly.

'You are bleeding, Nouran! You should go see a doctor, get those wounds dressed,' he said firmly, retracing his steps and extending his hand to help her up.

She took his hand and held it, not moving. She looked into his eyes and said, 'You bled for me that day, Mokhtar. I bleed for you today. I guess we are even now. Can't we be friends?' She wore an expression that would have melted the most unfeeling heart. The same inebriating fragrance of jasmine hung in the air. Mokhtar was still looking at her soft hand holding his. He stole a glance at her beautiful face and then back to her milky-fair fragile hand holding his rough brown one. It felt good. *But sensation was only skin deep*, he reminded himself. He pulled his hand away.

'What's wrong with me, Mokhtar? Why are you so harsh with me?'

'Nothing is wrong with you. I don't trust women. Besides, I am a Salafiya. There is no love before marriage for us,' he said grimly.

'Love! Marriage! Where did all that come from? I was only asking for some time together. See, I got you again!' she said perkily.

'Being alone with a woman before marriage is also evil. That's what we are doing right now, incurring Allah's wrath. Have you not studied the Sharia?' He stood there with a blank look on his face.

'Ya Allah!' She rolled her eyes. 'Okay, I will bring Fatima, my friend, with me next time. That way you won't be alone with me.'

'Bring her? Where?'

'There's a grand carnival at the Central Park. Just one day, that's all I ask of you. If by the end of the day, you think I am good for you, you can meet my father and ask for my hand in marriage, the proper Salafiya style. If not, have it your way.'

'I won't get a day off.' He flinched with annoyance. 'It's simply impossible.'

'Everybody gets a day off on Eid-al-Adha. I will see you there at nine in the morning, near the ticket counter.'

13

The Untraceable Rendezvous

A motor yacht tore through the turquoise ocean waters, leaving behind a white foamy trail. The Black Moth's vertical landing, contrary to Keira's expectation, had been exceptionally gentle.

'Where are we?' She had asked on exiting the aircraft.

'Half an hour to your destination, Ma'am,' the pilot bowed courteously, introducing them to the captain of the boat, a Caucasian man.

Soon, Kabir and Keira were standing atop its viewing deck, eager to discover their location. But there was no sign of a shore. The boat appeared to be heading for the horizon.

Leaning against the balustrade of the boat, Kabir relaxed and thought of his past. His early childhood at the orphanage was all a blurry mess. No remarkable incidents. Just some fuzzy images of the dining room, prayer hall and the dorm where he lived with the other kids. He didn't even remember the name he had been given by the orphanage. His humdrum life had been broken one morning, when he was summoned to the warden's office. He had been dressed in a white kurta-pyjama, turned ivory with overuse. A plush middle-aged couple had come in to adopt him. 'Kabir!' The man had picked him up in his arms and caressed his hair lovingly. It was almost as if he could see the remorse in the man's eyes for not having arrived earlier. As if he was the one who had abandoned him! And had now returned with the determination to give him his new name and identity—Kabir.

His life took an unexpected turn from this point on. Normally, a child from this orphanage would graduate into becoming a self-earner like a laundryman, a puncture repairer, cobbler, hairdresser, cook, etc. Things that the children would learn during their stay at the orphanage. But Kabir's foster parents gave him the best. They were a working couple with senior-level jobs that required a lot of travel, which turned out to be a blessing for Kabir who did not have to give up on his friends at the orphanage. He would stay there when they were travelling, with upgraded facilities paid for by his parents. When they were in town, they would dedicate themselves to him, taking him on outings, teaching him and motivating him to excel in life. They had once gifted him a journal, about a year after his adoption, and he preserved it like a treasure. Kabir hoped that the journal, his dearest possession, had reached safe hands; he had been reading it when Sarah had arrived at the hospital room and had tucked it under his pillow.

With his new-found family, Kabir's life moved as if in a trance. He was on top of the world, enjoying the love and affection he had heard of only in fairy tales.

Time flew and he qualified for the defence academy exams. Barely a month after his joining, he got the news that his foster parents had died in a car crash. He didn't even get a chance to attend their last rites as they had been abroad. Once again, he was alone in the world. That's when he had met Jayant.

'What waters are these? You might have an inkling.'

Kabir was shaken out of his thoughts by Keira's question. She had noticed the wistful expression on his face.

'The Mediterranean Sea would be my calculated bet. But I can't tell which country we are headed for.'

'Probably none...' She pointed at a cargo ship beginning to emerge in the distant horizon.

Before long, they were walking down the alleyway of a container ship. It was surrounded by thousands of shipping containers, stacked on top of each other, which loomed high above them. The containers were painted in mundane colours, prominently displaying the names of the shipping lines they belonged to. A well-built man of African descent, who greeted them on arrival, was the only person on board they'd seen so far. After frisking them thoroughly, he confiscated their rucksacks and firearms. Their weapons were categorised and dropped into sealed packets. 'You'll get them back later.' He signalled before ushering them into an empty storage container.

Any questions they asked thereafter were met with chuckles and sniggers, making it apparent that the man did not understand English. The doors to the container were then shut and bolted, rendering it pitch dark inside.

'A rather peculiar rendezvous, I would say.' Keira sighed softly and her warm breath brushed past Kabir's neck, drawing him out of his thoughts.

'True,' Kabir said, clearing his throat, 'but not any more peculiar than our host.'

'I admit, he did seem quite pleased by the prospect of locking us up.'

Keira began to say something else, but the container suddenly see-sawed. It was lifted off the deck. 'Woah,' they both said, clutching the hooks along the walls while it moved up, sideways and then, down. There was a loud clank as the container hit metal from both sides. With a loud screech, it started descending, as if held in place between guide-rails.

'Quite an unusual elevator!'

'The container is moving down a hold,' Kabir said. He could tell from the sound. 'We're entering the chamber beneath the deck, where the containers are stored.'

'I just hope we are not going to be stored here for too long.'

The container hit base after a long descent. The doors were unlatched from outside—opening into another long container.

The only difference was that this one was well lit.

'I hope the journey was comfortable, my boy!' Colonel Bakshi stood there with his arms open.

'Yeah,' Kabir said, finding it difficult to keep a straight face, 'quite a shuttle you've got there.'

'Welcome to the Protettori!'

A well-built man of five feet, nine inches, in a grey business suit, Colonel Bakshi had wavy grey hair; he wore a neat salt-and-pepper beard over his fair Punjabi complexion. He bore the endearing air of a jolly man enjoying his job. Following an affable reunion with his agent, he turned his attention to Keira, 'Welcome on board, Agent Brooks. Sergeant Smith is inside, waiting for you.'

This one was a 40-foot-long container, with air conditioning. There were seats fixed to the entire length of one wall, which was occupied by soldiers in camouflage uniform. There were around thirty of them, Kabir observed. The other wall had around a dozen workstations. Busy operators wearing headphones clattered away on their systems.

'Our mobile headquarters!' Colonel Bakshi explained. 'Best for international operations. No visas, no immigration checks required! There are a thousand-odd container ships that belong to the two shipping lines our organization is allied with. There are on an average 15,000 containers per ship. You may see where that would put us in terms of traceability.'

'Only if I cared to look for the particular containers and not to sink the entire ship,' Kabir quipped.

They reached the end of the container they were in, and found that it was connected to yet another one. The face recognition system granted them access through the soundproof door. There was along conference table with seats for around fifteen people.

'Meet our directors,' Colonel Bakshi said. 'Mr George from Britain, Mr Smith from the US, Mr Dominik from Germany,

Mr Ricardo from Italy and Mr Victor from France, the gentleman who called you, Kabir.'

Kabir and Keira walked around the table and shook hands with the directors.

'Also meet your colleagues for the mission,' Colonel Bakshi said, pointing to the agents on the other side, 'Agent Olaf Adler from Germany, Agent Bruce Wilson from Britain and Agent Vladimir Agapov from Russia. You will be briefed on further details about each other later.' Once Keira and Kabir had finished introducing themselves and shaking hands, Colonel Bakshi took the vacant seat next to Victor, halfway along the span of the table. 'All of you have arrived here on very short notice. Now, since the quorum is complete, I will request my colleague, Mr Turner, to brief you about the emergency at hand straightaway.'

'Good afternoon, friends!' Victor, the bespectacled man with the characteristic nervous mannerisms that accompany many a brilliant academician, got up and moved towards the projector screen fixed at the far end of the box.

But before he could start, Agent Bruce rose from his seat. A WWE fan could easily have mistaken him for John Cena—medium height, high cheekbones, lean athletic physique and a crew cut. 'Excuse me for interrupting, but I have been waiting for like almost two hours. Before you start, I want to ask this very basic question, which I am sure is on every agent's mind. If your organization is really so potent, why do you need us at all? You must have your own private army with the best talent on your rolls. Or do you work through collaborations with government agencies? In either case, calling five random agents from different corners of the world to attend the biggest emergency on your list ever... It just doesn't add up.'

'A fair question! We intended to come to this later, but now that you have brought it up, let's get to it now. The five of you have been selected for this operation by our artificial intelligence-based software that has been keeping track of the top agents worldwide for several years. It picks up data from the web—classified records of intelligence agencies across the world through spyware, our moles inside those agencies and so on. The skill sets you have, when put together, add up to something money cannot buy,' Victor replied.

'Yeah, please go on, elaborate on that a bit more. What skill sets?' said Bruce.

'Oh, that list is too long and complex to discuss now, but let me tell you that the software has simulated millions of complex situation patterns and evaluated your individual and collective responses in those situations vis-á-vis all other permutations and combinations of agents, and found this group to be the best. Each one of you is a one-man army by old-school terminology, and put together, you are the smartest and most lethal task force on the planet.'

'Sounds exciting,' Bruce said looking around with a smile at the other agents. 'It should be fun working with you guys.' Then turning to Victor, he said, 'I will buy that for the time being. Please go on with what you were about to tell us. I mean, if it's okay with the others too.'

'Okay, here we go! If anyone has a question, feel free to stop me and ask,' said Victor. 'It is said that religion is like opium! Self-administered! Overpowering! Clouds our judgement! Makes some human beings justify inflicting pain and suffering intentionally on others. It has been the major driver for terrorism in this century too, killing millions across the world. The last few years have seen exponential growth in terror attacks while hundreds of new outfits have emerged, making terror a cult in itself. But all that is being countered by respective governments and alliances of nations at the regional and world level.' Victor paused to make eye contact with each agent.

'Our concern today is much graver!' he continued. 'It seems that there is a mother organization of all these outfits that has remained hidden from the world's eyes so far. Like a secret society! It has been infiltrating governments and institutions for the last seventy-odd years, working towards its self-defined judgement day. A day on which it plans to show the world its power. By taking control of it! They plan to establish a much larger caliphate than the one that was wiped out in 1928, the Ottoman Empire.'

'A secret society? You mean something like your organization, the Protettori? The good guys vs the bad guys, right? What's this, a war of secret societies or something!' chuckled Agent Olaf from Germany, a burly man with blonde hair, short boxed beard and green eyes.

'Yeah, sort of! You could say that. We too work somewhat like a secret society, just that we are a more legitimate organization, supported by the intelligence and security wings of certain developed nations concerned about world peace and safety. An international mother OGA—other government agency!' Mr Dominik, the German director answered for his agent.

'Do they have a name?' asked Keira. The atmosphere was beginning to get charged.

'Ikhwan-al-Jihadiya. Or the Jehad Brotherhood. We have limited information about them, but recently got a lead that could expose them totally. Bring them to the surface in a fair war.'

'So what's their plan?' asked Kabir. 'The threat to the planet thing?'

'We are not fully certain of their entire plan yet. But whatever we have learnt so far is terrible enough to send shivers down the spines of the toughest men and women,' explained Mr George, the British director. 'A concerted terror attack at hundreds of places across the world! The same modus operandi as 9/11. In consonance with their policy of "death by a thousand cuts"—an ancient Chinese torture technique of slow slicing in which the victim gradually bleeds to death without feeling any sudden pain. The final plan is known only to the person making the cuts. They have made 999 cuts, and now it's time for the final one. The terror attacks are just a treacherous veil—their aftermath is meant to give their brethren in various countries much-needed cover to play their real game. We still don't know how they will pull it off, but in case they do, there will be a panic strong enough to topple governments, helping an easy takeover.'

'That's a crazy plan! I don't think it would be possible to outsmart the defence and intelligence forces of so many different countries,' said Kabir. 'At best, it will kill thousands, maybe lakhs and well, spread more hatred.'

'That's the scary part! Imagine countries blowing up planes flying over their air territories with missiles, suspecting them to be terror vehicles. In a panic situation, thousands of airplanes maybe shot down, exceeding the Ikhwan's terror target. A bonus for them! But that's one part of it. Their real plan is something much more bizarre. The terror attacks will just bring about the turmoil needed to give their sleeper cells in various countries the cover to play their real game,' clarified Ricardo, the Italian director.

'So this could be like World War Three. If this is so big, what we need is not a covert operation but the world coming together to fight this, isn't it? You should have raised the alarm long back,' Kabir said.

Victor looked at Ricardo and smiled knowingly. 'Good question. There are several reasons as to why we cannot do that. But the most important one is that once the bell is rung, the mission will no longer remain secret. First the intelligence units will know, then the media and then the people. As I said earlier, imagine the panic! Not only at the governmental level, but amongst the people. The Jehad Brotherhood will know their plan is out and they may either go into hibernation again or make some desperate attempt to pull their plan through. In either case: tons of bloodshed! An even bigger repercussion shall be the outrage against Islam—the religion followed by the second-largest population on the planet.

We don't want them to be massacred on the streets just because of a few maniacs. We have to secretly cripple the Ikhwan, as discreetly as they have been operating. That's the difficult part. And that's why we need you.'

Kabir looked at Keira, who seemed worried, as did Bruce. Olaf's expression wouldn't give away much, and the fourth agent had hardly uttered a word yet.

'So is the Jehad Brotherhood related in some way to the Muslim Brotherhood of Egypt,' asked Bruce, 'the transnational Sunni Islamist organization that even had a president in power around 2012, Mohamed Morsi, if I'm right? They are a big sociopolitical force in that region.'

'Quite possible, but we have no solid evidence. The Muslim Brotherhood has been denying their ties with any terrorist organization for years.'

'Do we have any idea *when* they plan to accomplish this?' Bruce drummed a finger against the table restlessly. 'Do they have a fixed date?'

'It should be soon; they have orchestrated everything to mark some kind of an anniversary for their organization,' replied Colonel Bakshi.

'Oh? How far then?' asked Keira, her eyes reflecting the horror within.

'Maybe three days or less...' said Victor.

'Are you serious!' Bruce exclaimed. 'You guys expect us to sabotage seventy-odd years of work in three days?'

Disorder erupted in the room as the agents exchanged a string of agitated murmurs. It grew until a deep voice boomed, drowning the clamour. 'What's your plan, Mr Turner?' It was Vladimir, the Russian agent; he'd finally decided to voice his opinion. At seven feet, two inches, and weighing four hundred pounds—most of it muscle—the reticent Siberian from the KGB was a distinctive cut above the pack when it came to strength. 'You told me over the phone that you have it all worked out. What do you want me to do?'

Bruce cast a quick peep at the rest of his colleagues—they'd all noticed the 'me' in place of 'us'.

'Relax, agents. As I said, the clue that we have could be the key. The one who makes the poison always has the antidote. We could very well be holding the winning card in our hands,' Victor turned towards the projector screen and pressed a button on the remote.

14

The Grand Carnival

It was Eid-al-Adha. Festivity was in the air and the society had also declared a two-day holiday. The volunteers and trainees were allowed to visit their homes. Mokhtar had taken the day off as Ghassan would be staying at his residence with the usual security. *Would it be right to go out with Nouran?* He had been thinking about it the entire week. But wasn't this the only way to escape this mess? Hadn't she said that he would have the final word, once they were done with their time at the Grand Carnival?

He reached the ticket counter and was looking for her when a woman in a burkha waved at him. She removed the niqab and smiled at him. It was Nouran. Another lady was standing with her, plump and shorter.

'Sabah, Mokhtar. Mokhtar, Sabah,' Nouran introduced them.

'Are you the same Mokhtar from St Andrew's? Adel's friend?' Sabah asked, pleasantly surprised.

'Yes,' Mokhtar nodded, 'Adel's friend.'

'You've changed completely, I must say. Handsome hunk!' she smiled, her braces showing.

'Oh! Time changes everything!' he blushed. 'You were the topper of our class, Sabah. I remember clearly now. Your memory is sharp as ever.'

'You know each other! Okay! Let's go.' Nouran was bubbling with energy.

The Grand Cairo Carnival was a sea of entertainment shows,

rides, games, shopping and everything else. Once inside, the ladies promptly removed their black cloaks and came out of the ladies' room donning jeans, fancy blouses and sunglasses.

'Do I look so awful?' Nouran pouted as Mokhtar stood there wearing an uncomfortable expression.

'Why would I care?' He scowled.

'Don't be like that, Mokhtar. We only have a day, let me make the most of it. Come…' She held his hand and pulled him through the crowd to their right. At the centre was a raised platform with a small table and two chairs placed on it. A well-built local contestant was arm-wrestling a white man as the crowd cheered. Half a dozen men collected wagers from the spectators. It was a one-to-ten bet in favour of the white man. They watched for a while cheering the local contestants, but the white man was too strong. He bulldozed through them, one after the other, all in a matter of seconds. Mokhtar stood there studying their techniques, looking for a useful move to add to his kitty.

'Let's move on.' Nouran took a step back. 'Our men are no match for this albino. I hate it… the way he is disgracing us!'

'Let me try,' she suddenly heard Mokhtar say. She turned around to stop him, but he had left. She looked around to see that he was already inside the ring, seated in front of the burly, bald white man, with arms the size of Mokhtar's thighs.

'Adam versus Mokhtar in a freestyle arm battle,' the referee announced. 'Let the game beginnnnn!'

'That's suicide,' exclaimed Sabah. 'Is he that desperate to impress you?'

'I wish he was,' whispered Nouran.

The white man did take a good thirty seconds to get Mokhtar's hand tilting. Nouran could see Mokhtar's face, all flushed, as he applied every muscle of his body to hold his hand in place. Both men were leaning forward on the table, their heads almost butting, their right hands interlocked and their left hands below the table on their thighs. Mokhtar was bending forward, as far as he could, struggling not to be knocked out. His hand was hardly a few inches from being crushed flat.

'That's him!' Nouran said to Sabah. 'Wouldn't give up without a fight. He did better than the rest.'

'Um… hmm.' Sabah patted her comfortingly. Suddenly, there was an uproar. They heard the crowd cheering for Mokhtar. The entangled arms were moving back up to a vertical position as Mokhtar reclaimed the game, the sweat glistening on his biceps. The white man's face was contorted in an expression of disbelief. He stretched out his left hand, trying to reach for Mokhtar's throat, but it was too late. Mokhtar had knocked him down with a final thrust. As the white man's hand was smashed down onto the table, his eyes were shut in pain, his body frozen in shock. The frenzied crowd cheered for Mokhtar and snatched their money from the bookies.

Mokhtar plucked his share of Egyptian Pounds, rushed to the ladies and pulled them through the crowd, moving as fast as he could. Nouran looked back and saw the white man wriggling on the floor in pain. *Probably a torn muscle!*

'That was amazing, Mokhtar, totally unexpected! What did you do?' Nouran screamed ecstatically as they ran towards the joyrides.

'Nothing. I guess he must have gotten his second wind,' Sabah winked at Mokhtar. While Nouran had been busy admiring his glistening biceps, Sabah had noticed his other hand move below the table and grab the white man's weak spot. It had been a cakewalk thereafter.

They bought tickets for the carousel. As the ride gained full momentum, Nouran stretched out her hand towards Mokhtar, who was sitting on the horseback in the adjacent row. In that moment, as Mokhtar looked at her enchanting face and quivering lips, he was prompted to extend his hand and touch hers. *Don't get sucked into this*, he reminded himself. Sabah, who was observing all of it from a horse behind them, felt pity for her friend. She prayed Mokhtar would find a way around his own walls.

After the carousel, they watched a belly dance show, a ballet performance, had cotton candy, slurped on a date milkshake, and shopped for some artificial jewellery. The hours just flew by! The more Mokhtar observed her, the sorrier he felt for her. She was genuinely enjoying his company despite the uptight arse that he was. All this, while he made sure that Sabah was between the two of them so that their hands and shoulders would not brush.

'Let's see the fortune teller,' she said, pointing to a fakir sitting in a small tent in a distant corner of the fete grounds.

'What for? It's such a waste of time,' Mokhtar began to say, but she was already pulling Sabah with her towards the tent. 'Only one question, I promise, Mokhtar.' He relented.

'Will he meet my father or will we part ways from here?' she asked the fakir immediately, gazing at the boy who was standing by the entrance with evident disinterest.

'Yes, he will,' the ascetic replied, a grave expression on his face. 'Is that all you want to ask?'

'Yes, yes!' She placed a currency note in his collection box and jumped to her feet, hugging Sabah and moving round in circles like a child.

Mokhtar smiled wryly and muttered, 'What a fraud!' He had had fleeting moments of attraction but it was never going to go that far. His priorities were clear.

'Beware of this man,' the fakir continued, 'he is very dangerous. You are a nice girl. Downfall awaits you.'

'Now he's telling you the truth!' Mokhtar brightened. 'Isn't this exactly what I have been telling you?'

'Dangerous you are! Agreed. And fallen for you, I already have!' she chirped. 'Let's go!' They walked out, leaving the ascetic chanting to a bored audience. It was already evening.

'He was a charlatan, Nouran! Look, I don't mean to hurt you

and that's why I don't want you to develop any false hopes that would break your heart. I won't be seeing you after today.'

'Don't say that, Mokhtar,' Sabah shouted at him. 'Why are you being such a nut? Why did you come at all then?'

'Ask her! I'm only being nice. I'm doing my best,' he shouted back.

'Cool down, guys. I'm okay with it.' Nouran sighed. 'He's right. I pleaded with him to come. Let's finish with this final ride and be on our way home.' They reached the giant ferris wheel near the exit.

Nouran and Sabah sat opposite Mokhtar in the grilled iron trolley, with seats on both sides. It swung into equilibrium as the weight on opposite seats was balanced. The seats had bars on the top and sides for safety, and the entry was secured with a lock bar. Nouran closed her eyes and put her head on Sabah's shoulder as their trolley reached the top, the spinning motion making her feel nauseous. Mokhtar's impatience was growing—his workout time was fast approaching. He needed some rest before getting on with the gruelling three-hour session.

'Can I sit next to you?' Nouran watched Mokhtar as their cabin started its descent, in its fifth round.

'No.' His tone was stern. 'We can't sit next to each other.'

'Please, this is my last request.'

Before he could utter another word, she was up on her feet. She paused midway to look at him. With the sudden shift in weight, the dangling trolley rocked slightly in her direction, but she held onto the grille to maintain her balance. Light-headed, she took another step towards Mokhtar's seat and was about to sit down next to him, when in a flash, he moved to the seat diagonally opposite to him. It upset the equilibrium and the trolley swung wildly to her side like a see-saw. The next moment, Mokhtar saw her tripping over the lock bar and she was outside the ferris wheel. He extended his hand, but it was too late. She screamed and within a moment, hit the ground on her back.

There was commotion as people surrounded her motionless body. Mokhtar and Sabah tore through the crowd, horrified. Someone checked her and announced, 'No breath! She's dead.'

Mokhtar felt that familiar horrible shudder, the one he had felt when he had seen her bleed in the knees, so intense this time that it tore down his shield. Her hair was splayed; it was similar to how it had looked when she had been lying in the desert. Even as she lay there lifeless, she looked unhappy. He wished he hadn't been such a fool inside the trolley. Outside the trolley! He had been a fool all along—every single moment that she had spent with him! He was even willing to take on the sin of sitting next to her and letting her hold his hand, if only it would bring her back. That's all she had wanted and he had made her pay for it with her life. He prayed to Allah to bring her back. The crowd began to disperse.

Some paramedical staff rushed to the site soon, two men holding a stretcher with a doctor at their heels. The doctor bent down and checked her breath and pulse. He inspected her for blood or signs of fatal injury but found none. 'Heart seizure by trauma.' He shook his head in despair. 'She needs CPR, that's our last hope,' he announced before leaning atop her.

'I can do that,' Mokhtar pulled him back. He had been trained in basic life-saving skills at the society. How could he let anyone else touch her? He sat down beside her and gently pushed on the centre of her chest. He did this five times. No reaction! He tried again. Nothing. Bending over, he opened her mouth and locked his lips upon hers. He blew a strong breath, trying to pump his life force into her. Nothing yet! 'Oh, come on, Nouran... you are the most stubborn girl I know... a go-getter... you can't give up so easily.' He repeated the procedure for several rounds, continuing to push her chest intermittently. But she showed no sign of recovery. She was gone. All because of him! 'Come on... open your eyes... open... come on!' Desperate, he grew aggressive in his attempts to breathe some life into her, kissing her parched lips while his hands seized her silky hair.

'Stop that! What are you doing?' the doctor yelled. 'She's no more.'

They pulled him back, but he clung to her, his embrace too strong for the three of them to break. Sabah who'd been sobbing all along, walked up to Mokhtar and put her hand on his shoulder gently, 'Let her go.'

Police sirens howled in the background.

Suddenly, as if by a streak of miracle, Nouran coughed and her eyes opened. Wearily, she looked at Mokhtar and closed her eyelids again, breathing slowly. The crowd clapped and cheered in a frenzy. This had been the best show of the day. The paramedics put her on the stretcher and she was carried to a nearby hospital. The hospital was short-staffed and overcrowded following the outbreak of an epidemic. So although she was shocked and silent, Nouran was discharged that night after a routine examination and some medication.

'What now?' Sabah whispered to Mokhtar as she peeped around worriedly at the dim streets outside the hospital. 'We can't take her home in this condition. She needs some time to recover. Let's take her to your room. I will tell her parents she was with me at another friend's place.'

They boarded the tram back to the downtown area. Sabah and Mokhtar supported Nouran the entire way and up the stairs to Mokhtar's room. Sabah sat her down by the bed, before turning to Mokhtar. 'I can't stay longer, take care of her. Bye.'

Nouran was incoherent. The fortune-teller's words were echoing in her mind. So, this was what he had meant—the fall from the ferris wheel. True, the ascetic's concern had been genuine and the fall could have been fatal. But here she was: alone with her beau, in his room. Ironically, it was the 'downfall' that had brought them close. He had kissed her, shedding all inhibitions. Or else they would've been walking their separate ways that evening.

Mokhtar brought her a cup of warm moghat, a drink that'd help restore some strength in her frail body, and held it so she could sip on it. Taking off her shoes, he helped her lie straight on the bed, placing her head in his lap. Her forehead was cold and her face was pale. He caressed her hair. He held her closer to keep her warm.

He had made up his mind!

A few serene minutes thus and he felt her body stir. Mokhtar bent over to place a gentle kiss on her lips, his body and mind responding like never before. Stunned by his own reactions to the intimacy, he brought the intense moment to a pause, about to rise. But he was stopped. Her palm held on to his face and drew him near, closing her lips on his again. That gesture was all it took to snap his last thread of resolve. The very next breath, they were locked in a passionate kiss. One that would unite their lives from that moment onwards. The warmth of their bodies and the overpowering joy of having survived the crisis, melted the barriers between them. And they made passionate love throughout the night, until she drifted off peacefully on his chest, their arms entangled like they would never let go of one another. As he lay with her, spent, he reminisced about how the last few hours had made him cast aside all that he believed in. He had no regrets!

The night went by fast.

∽

'Your ways are becoming increasingly autocratic, my friend,' said Ahmad Shaban, one of the senior-most members of the society, staring at Ghassan. Shaban was a lawyer, and he took care of the legal matters of the society. Aged fifty-four and as one of the most learned amongst the lot, he drew respect from all board members.

The society's monthly board meeting was in progress. There were fifteen members on the board—Ghassan, the six poor workers who had initially approached him to form the society and eight other members, including Ahmad—all of them having risen to become board members through their dedicated service and commitment.

'You know how important it is to set up the printing press!' Shaban was emphatic. 'There is no other way to spread our message. We have eight hundred members. That's hardly sufficient to run this organization, let aside to make it into a movement.'

Ghassan exhaled calmly in response to the tirade. 'I will figure a way out. We have to seek internal sources of funding. We can't start taking members like Shawky on our board. He may be rich and respected, but he is in bed with the corrupt establishment. We will lose our identity.'

'I totally disagree. We can't be so rigid if we have to grow and achieve our goal,' Shaban looked around at the remaining board members. Several nodded in agreement. 'I think this calls for a vote,' Shaban resumed with an emboldened frown. 'It has been a long time. I would prefer invoking this provision in view of the deadlock here. How many of you support me on the call to vote?'

Eight hands went up.

'All right!' Ghassan sighed. 'We go for a vote in the next board meeting. I'll try my best to muster up funds for this project internally. But in case I cannot do so within a month, we'll open up the society, if that is what you vote for, of course.'

Mokhtar saw the agony on Ghassan's face as he was guarding the board room entrance. It was the first time that he had seen Ghassan being outnumbered.

∽

'Still use the slingshot?' Adel gaped at his old catapult hanging humbly amidst the display of weaponry on the walls of Mokhtar's room. They had rarely met after Mokhtar had left the mansion and joined the society. Today, Adel was a guest at Mokhtar's home, sitting on the charpoy as his friend made tea for him.

Mokhtar was wearing a black vest, his back turned to him, and Adel couldn't help but notice his brawny physique and the changed mannerisms. The reclusive boy now exuded confidence and maturity. An impressive transformation.

'Not as much, though it's still my favourite,' replied Mokhtar, continuing to add ingredients to the tea.

'What's this?' Adel said, picking up a quaint wooden box from a shelf and flipping the lid. It contained a thin bamboo pipe placed meticulously inside a box full of small phials and some straw. 'And what's this viscous purple liquid?' He held up a vial for inspection against the light from the window.

'Put it back! It's highly poisonous!' Mokhtar took the phial and the box from him. 'It is used by the natives of the Amazonian rainforests; the poisoned straw and the blowgun is their first line of defence.'

'What's in the other phials then?'

'Different types of venoms, with different effects—fainting, paralysis, slow death, painful death.' Mokhtar returned to the stove. 'My research isn't complete yet.'

'Why do you need all this, Mokhtar?' Adel sighed. 'What kind of service to the society requires this?'

'I am not into service, the society is. My job is to protect Ghassan and I want to be fully equipped,' he replied as he continued to stir the brew. 'What about you? Still using your killer charms in college?'

'Wallah! What's that?' Adel said, bending to pick up an earring from under the charpoy. 'Looks like our killer found female company!'

'Give that to me!' Mokhtar rushed across to grab it from him. 'I don't like the way you make a joke out of everything.'

'Whoa! Easy man.' Adel grinned, raising his hands. 'So, this is serious stuff, right? Won't you tell me who it is?'

'Never!' Mokhtar replied. 'You will get to meet her at our marriage anyway!'

'Marriage? How long have you known her? Is she the first girl in your life?'

'Of course, she is! I am not the kind of man to fall in and out of love.' Mokhtar didn't realize it, but his cheeks had turned a shade pinker. 'I met her about a month ago.'

'You can't jump into marriage with the first girl you meet. Have some patience. And when is the marriage? You've got to stop giving me shocks, Mokhtar.' Adel smiled, recalling how impulsive Mokhtar could be.

'I'm not sure,' Mokhtar shrugged, pouring the tea into two cups.

'Let's go on a double date. Remember the girl in the Lumiere autochrome, the one I visited in France. She's here on a sabbatical.'

Mokhtar was instantly irked by his friend's proposition. 'Thanks. I don't believe in these Western ways. This is what I am fighting against.'

'Come on brother! I thought the lady would have made you less self-inflicting.' Adel had a gentle smile on his face as he accepted the tea. They sipped on it through the truce that followed. Adel felt the dejá vu. It was like they were frozen in time—two children looking out of the tram window! Mokhtar's reactions were still the same. However, there was a change too. A remarkable one! To his personality. From a meek boy who would see the inside when the world inflicted pain on him, to one who could give it back. Indomitable and relentless!

'I have to go now, but you take care… and give this new relationship some time.' Adel got up and hugged Mokhtar, before grabbing his backpack and heading for the door.

He was about to unlatch the door when there was a knock. As he opened it, he saw the face of a girl who was beginning to flip open her hijab. 'Oh!' She covered her face abruptly on noticing that it was not Mokhtar. There was a strange fear in her eyes.

'Wallah! God is merciful on me today,' Adel chuckled. 'I had just expressed my desire to meet you and look who's here.' He stepped back, allowing the girl to come in.

'You two have fun.' He winked and scurried down the flight of stairs before either of them could say anything.

He was glad he had not let the girl realize that he had recognized her. Nouran was his cousin. Her embarrassment on seeing him there was quite understandable. In most circumstances, a brother would react differently. Adel, however, was happy for her. Mokhtar might be a bit crazy at times, but he was good husband material—strong, sensitive, loyal and without vices.

He had never forgotten that day in the bus when Mokhtar had taken the bee sting upon himself to protect his best friend. The lone boy always had it in him. It was a trait that their teachers—those responsible for identifying the children's best skills—had missed. Protective instinct! Mokhtar would have scored a ten on that. And this was what had led him to choose his current assignment of protecting Ghassan too. Who would be a better suitor to have his cousin's back for life? And the two would make a beautiful couple!

Adel had no idea of the approaching tornado that was about to wreak havoc in the couple's life.

15

The Protettori

Victor switched on the projector. The image of a tall, gracefully matured, fair man in a three-piece suit appeared on screen. He was leaning against his Jaguar, wearing an affable expression and smoking a cigar.

'That's Neel Weigers, as his British passport claims. Just one of this man's many identities. His real name is Syed Abu Bakr. Also known as the Murshid in the Brotherhood, he is the second in command. A staunch disciple of Syed Qutb, the radical Islamic theorist from the last century. Abu Bakr is the kingpin in the scheme. We get him and we have everything.' Victor's eyes gleamed. 'He will lead us to Fatih or the Sayyid, the head of the Ikhwan-al-Jihadiya.'

'Fortunately, we have a cue that the Murshid is going to be in Libya tomorrow,' Victor resumed after a pause. 'He is going there to swear in the last lot of boys trained by Iqrar al-Sharia, the terrorist group that is providing them trained pilots to hijack the suicide planes. This organization has enrolled the likes of Suleyman, the deadly fighter pilot from Liberation Leapords of Tamil Eelam's air wing, the Sky Leapords. It's the only air force any terrorist organization has had till date. He was the man responsible for the air attacks on Sri Lankan forces back in 2007, killing scores of their men. They tried everything they could, but they never managed to strike down his planes.'

Olaf broke the silence, scoffing. 'Does the Murshid really need to travel himself?'

'This man is a perfectionist. More importantly, he is a great motivator. It is said that once a volunteer interacts with him, his loyalty becomes unshakeable.'

'And how do you know it's him?' Kabir pointed to the screen. 'What's your source?'

'The Protettori may not be as old and insidious as the Brotherhood, but we have our own web. We have corroborative evidence on this one.'

'What about the terrorist who attacked Agent Rathore yesterday?'

Kabir exchanged a brief glance with Keira, in acknowledgement, for bringing it up. 'Yes, you did mention that you had information about him.'

Victor pressed the remote and another image appeared on screen: the silhouette of a lanky figure. Kabir immediately recognized the frame and shook his head. At the bottom of the screen were a dozen portraits, all ranging from an adolescent to that of a wizened old man. Surprisingly, the sketch made by Keira's team yesterday was not there. Nor the one Sarah had sent Kabir.

'Zain... real name Khabib, the man without a face,' announced Victor. 'The deadliest fighter of the Ikhwan and the right hand of Abu Bakr—this man is a killing machine. Agile like a cheetah...he has a knack for using futuristic weapons and the latest technology. Although he has access to the vast resources of the Brotherhood, he seldom uses them. He works in isolation, like a raptor. That, coupled with his ability to blend in with his surroundings, makes him virtually impossible to trace.'

Kabir and Keira shared a grave look. The pieces were beginning to fall into place. It was fitting that an unidentified international terrorist should belong to an equally iniquitous and mysterious organization. His attack against a prized anti-terrorist commando was probably an attempt at advance insurance. But what did not add up was the timing. If their big day was so close, why would he care about Kabir at this point in time?

'Where exactly in Libya are we headed then?' asked Bruce, breaking the lull.

Victor's expression turned a tad grimmer. 'Al Kufra deserts in southeast Libya. A Chinook helicopter equipped with a Wiesel tank shall take you to the site. It shall be your transport, base and shelter for this operation.'

'What about recon? We can't land in a militant-infested territory equipped with a mini tank!' Keira rubbed her forehead, 'They use tanks bigger than that, even for local transport. We will be like a Chihuahua barking at a Doberman.'

'The Wiesel is being sent just in case! I don't think you will need it. We are not going to war. This is intended to be a covert operation. As for local intelligence, Tareq shall help you with that.' Victor gestured at the man seated at the far end of the table. 'He knows every inch of that area.'

Kabir observed the man being introduced as their chaperone with apprehension. *But he doesn't speak English. How will he communicate with us?*

The black man who'd escorted them down the creaky container hold stood up and greeted them, reserving a special smile for Kabir. 'Professional compulsions!' he said, shrugging as he looked at the other agents, who had been through a similar first acquaintance with him.

'I will be at your service 24x7. You can trust me with every bit of help you will need.'

∽

Khabib performed the strength training routine in the privacy of his hotel room. Every time he practised, his incontinence pad would get fully soaked, reminding him of why he hated Indians so much. Thus, when the Murshid had asked him to hunt down the Indian intelligence officer, he had gone in guns blazing.

But right now, he was flummoxed. Stuck between two critical choices. Their agent in Canada, who had been arrested for trespassing the Suncor energy warehouse by the local police, had been silenced already. But a major threat was still on the loose. With the final day here, the Shaytan would definitely do something. Try to throw a spanner in their plans! He wanted to be in the Cove to make sure everything went right. On the other hand, he wanted desperately to chase and bring down the Indian agent who had escaped his clutches yesterday. He hated failure!

He clearly remembered the day the Shaytan had broken into the Murshid's house. He had taken the Murshid at gunpoint, demanding to talk to the Sayyid. Khabib had arrived just in time. As he had chased the Shaytan over the old town roofs of clustered sandstone buildings in Alexandria, he had realized the masked man was no easy prey. With the distance between them growing, the Shaytan had turned to face him. The hooded jacket and his eerie hollow-eyed mask concealed his face completely. It was as if he was challenging Khabib to come get him, unafraid of the waning distance between them. And just as he was within a few metres of him, Shaytan had jumped off the edge of the roof. By the time Khabib had reached the parapet to look down, the Shaytan had vanished!

Torn between reason and vengeance, he decided to wait for the Murshid's signal.

16

The First Taqiya

'You'll be proud of me, Baba,' Nouran chirped in excitement. Finally! Mokhtar was coming to their house to ask for her hand. She had laid out the table herself—hummus, ghanoush, falafel, kibbeh, kofta, smoked vegetables and saffron milk, all of Mokhtar's favourites.

Her parents enjoyed watching her exhilaration as she rushed to the door upon hearing the bell. Mokhtar stood there, dressed in a white thawb with an embroidered high neck. He wore a keffiyeh, a white headdress, and a black cloak that flowed with the wind, making him look like a prince. Her heart skipped a beat and she stood there for a moment, mesmerized. Her family was not conservative, so she had never been worried on that front. However, getting Mokhtar here to meet her father had been an impossible challenge. Now that the moment was finally here, he was no longer the orthodox moralist she had initially met and she was curious to see how he would get along with her family.

'Dressed to impress?' She winked.

'I had to! I'm about to ask your father for a favour that he has never been asked before.' His smile wore a hint of innocence. That tranquillizing smile! She would never fear anything in the world as long as it was hers to behold.

'Mokhtar!' She heard her father exclaim from behind her. 'Alhamdulillah!'

'Oh! So you both know each other?'

'Of course! He works for our society.' Her father offered Mokhtar a seat.

Nouran sensed something amiss. Her father was being courteous, but there was discomfiture in his voice. He called Nouran aside to the adjoining room.

'You cannot marry him. I can't believe that out of all the boys in Cairo, you had to find this one.'

'Why, Baba? What's wrong with him?' She held her father's hand in hers, trying to pacify him.

'He's a barbarian. The way he glares at me during board meetings, it's scary. Imagine what his presence in the family would do to me.'

'He's a changed person, Baba. He is no longer the pitiless person he used to be.' Nouran pleaded with dewy eyes. 'You tell me what you want and he will do it for me.'

'It's too late to try and convince your daughter now, father-in-law,' Mokhtar's voice echoed from behind them. He had walked into the room as they had been speaking. 'She's missed a cycle already.'

Ahmad turned around, unable to believe what he had just heard.

'I'm not joking, Mr Ahmad, ask her!' He gestured towards Nouran. 'And by the way, she did not find me, I found her. I had to. I couldn't let you have your way.'

'Get out of my house, you scoundrel!' Ahmad glowered at the boy standing by the door.

'Should I, Ms Nouran Shaban? Is that what you want too?' He looked at her with a roguish grin. 'What will you do with the child, then? Your father is a respectable man. What will he tell the society?'

Nouran felt giddy. She was suddenly seeing a totally different side of Mokhtar—one which showed no concern for her. And it was unnerving. 'What's going on, Mokhtar?' she mumbled, 'Don't you love me?'

'No!' he uttered without batting an eyelid.

Ya Allah! Nouran began figuring out the scenario. Mokhtar had used her as a weapon against her father. It had been a set-up from the very first day, starting right from the loafers in the jeep, whom he must've hired anonymously. The whole story played out before her eyes, scene by scene.

'Did you not love me for a single moment, Mokhtar? Not even when I fell off the ferris wheel and almost died? The way you cried, kissed me, brought me back to life. All of that couldn't have been an act...' she sobbed, suddenly terrified.

'Clumsy girl. What were you trying to do? Asking the fortune teller about my feelings! He warned you. But you wouldn't listen. And yes, you did scare the hell out of me when you fell off that wheel...jeopardized my entire plan.' He laughed nastily.

'What do you want?' Ahmad charged forward.

'Simply step out of Ghassan's way and focus on the legal work you have been given.'

'What if I don't?'

'Now what kind of a question is that, father-in-law? You have seen what I can do—and believe me, this is merely the tip of the iceberg. I will go to any extent to protect my Master.'

'Bastard!' Nouran suddenly reached out and grabbed the collar of his cloak. 'I'll kill myself. Kill the child. I will not allow any harm to come to my father. I hate myself for having loved you.'

'Don't be rash, Nouran! Let the men decide this.' Mokhtar calmly removed her hand from his person. 'Let's evaluate your options here, father-in-law. One—you abort the child, an illegal act which will incur wrath from Allah and the society when they learn of it. Besides, it may endanger Nouran's life. I will ensure this does not remain a secret and your family will be disgraced and ostracized. Is that fine with you?'

Ahmad looked at him with blood-red eyes, overwhelmed with anger.

'Okay, that does not seem agreeable.' Mokhtar raised a second finger. 'Option two—you expose me. I will deny your charges and say that I love Nouran. That I am ready to wed her. You can imagine how people will react and what I will make of her life after the wedding.'

'I will do what you say ... Mokhtar,' Ahmad grumbled. 'Just get out of our lives.'

'Fair enough, Mr Shaban. That's all I expect from you.' Mokhtar was turning to leave when he stopped midway. 'One more point. In case you do not find a groom prepared to accept your daughter and her child, I can ask a nice and pious boy from the society to marry her. You can live your life out peacefully. Not a soul will hear a word, I promise!'

'Does Ghassan know?' Ahmad gritted his teeth, even as tears rolled from his eyes. 'He will throw you out when he learns what you have done.'

'You really don't want to see me off the leash, Mr Shaban, do you?' Mokhtar tut-tutted. 'I thought you loved your family.'

'How can a devout Muslim act so immorally? You have destroyed my daughter's life!'

'Refer to verse 3.28 of the Quran, sir. Taqiyya! The circumstances under which a true Muslim can resort to deception—when his life, property or religious beliefs come under threat. Your actions had put Islam under threat. I was left with no other option.'

17

Life In a War-torn Country

The Chinook CH-47 was an oldie that would blend in well with the copters in the fleets of the Libyan militia and jihadists. Old but sturdy, it was a vulture that had helped the US air force pounce upon its prey in the Vietnam war. The long roomy interiors had an air portable Wiesel tank strapped on to its front end, and towards the rear was a rusty minibus, parked alongside trunks full of ammunition.

The task force comprised the five agents, Tareq, and his team of eight men—all of them strapped securely to seats lined along the walls. The agents were dressed in worn-out dirty casuals, their faces disguised to look haggard. Tareq's team wore Woodland camouflage fatigues, giving them the appearance of local fighters. They chatted along in Arabic while the agents dozed off—taking their pre-action forty winks. Kabir, however, was wide awake.

The day's events had been playing over in his mind. He'd been asked to lead the team. No one had displayed any form of objection. Except Agent Wilson! Bruce hadn't said anything, but scepticism was written all over his face. *It will pass with time.* Kabir had reconciled himself with the situation. This was not the first time someone had underestimated his abilities. His thoughts drifted back to his schooldays.

His foster parents had insisted that he join a much-touted private school. It was a totally new ecosystem. This school had several large playing fields and the students excelled in sports like squash, lawn tennis, football and basketball, all of which Kabir had only occasionally watched on the community television in the orphanage.

He recalled the games period on a pleasant winter afternoon. The batch had split into various sports fields, choosing their pick. Kabir was in the lawn tennis field, occupying the linesman chair, while the other non-players volunteered as ball boy, umpire and audience. Pushkar, the fittest of the batch, was destroying one player after another with his angle game, forcing his opponents wide off the court.

Pushkar served a powerful ace that whizzed past his opponent's head as he ducked to avoid being hurt. The audience applauded in awe, making Pushkar close his eyes to bask in the ambience. The sound of claps suddenly died as Kabir declared a foot fault. Pushkar opened his eyes and stared at him, shaking his head in disapproval. 'You're up next!' He quickly finished his opponent.

'I'm no good,' Kabir admitted as he walked into the court, holding the heavy racket clumsily.

'But you certainly seem to know a lot about the game,' Pushkar spat scornfully.

Each serve thence was bodyline, making Kabir jump around in defence. The few times that he actually made contact with the ball, it either went wide off the court or hit the net. His serves never made it to the other side, mostly ending up in double faults. Exhausted, he sat squat, huffing for breath, his weight propped against the racket.

'Come on! Get up, champ!' Pushkar taunted, as his cronies whistled and cheered for him, enjoying the savagery.

Kabir got up, determined, but the oncoming serve swerved and hit him right in the chest with full force, giving him no time to steer clear. He crouched down in pain, gasping for breath. The other students crowded around him, offering water from their bottles, advising him to breathe deep. His vision was foggy. He saw Pushkar walk up to him and extend his hand with a smile. 'Get up, buddy, I've been through this before. It's nothing!'

Later as all the students gathered to return the equipment and gear, the sports teacher noted the preference of each student in his register. He announced, 'It's time to appoint the sports captain for this session.'

Everyone's attention was glued to the teacher's lips. The new coach was known for his offbeat ways. But even he could not afford to displease Pushkar, who usually captained most of the school teams.

'Kabir!'

His words swept through the batch like a tsunami, raising a furore amongst the lined students. The coach hadn't seen Kabir play, but he had an eye for talent. Besides, he had heard about the boy's background and thought this would boost his confidence.

A hand went up and Puskhar stepped aside, making himself visible.

'Yes, what is it, Pushkar?'

'Sir, I have no objection to anyone's appointment, but the student should at least be a sportsman. What does a guy right out of an orphanage school know about these sports? You will be pushing the benchmark several notches down.'

'He's new. I am sure he will pick up,' the coach replied, sounding a bit unsure now. He didn't want to make an outrightly controversial decision.

'I don't want to demean anyone,' Pushkar continued, 'but he can't even hold a racket decently. Everyone saw it.'

'Hmm...what do you suggest? You can't be the captain every time.'

'Fine, then! We go by your judgement. Let's assume he is a rare find, and shall pick up the game in no time,' Pushkar continued snarkily. 'Why don't we go back to the court, and if he can get back a few balls across the net, we let him be. I'll step down my game and give him a fair chance.'

The batch braced themselves for another round of butchery.

Pushkar served a fast pacer, which whirred past the net, coming straight into Kabir's face. He raised his racket just in time to intercept it. Pushkar had positioned himself forward, expecting a short return, which he would snub if it ever happened to cross the nets. But the ball lobbed, landing far behind him, just inside the baseline and bounced out.

A confused murmur went up as the chair umpire called the point out in favour of Kabir.

'Lucky bugger!' Pushkar cursed under his breath. 'Love fifteen,' he called out, lofting the ball above his head as his racket came cracking down.

Kabir's stance changed as he moved sideways and swung his hand into a full-strength return. The crowd gasped as the ball zoomed past the net to the deuce court, leaving a stunned Pushkar still standing on the ad side.

'Something's off!' He groaned. 'Love thirty,' he said and launched another serve, intending to give the coach no time to intervene. He quickly centred himself a little behind the service line. The ball once again zoomed towards Kabir, this time spinning in the air.

Kabir, in a sudden awkward reaction, held the racket with both hands above his head and hit the spinning ball in a pat-a-cake style, typical of novices. All eyes were fixed on the spinning ball, which lofted clear off the net and landed right in front of Pushkar's racket, as he swung it like a pro for a full-strength smash.

'Woooohhh!' Came another full-throated sigh from the crowd as Pushkar's racket missed contact with the ball. They really could not believe what was happening. The ball, after making contact with the ground, had not moved on to Pushkar's racket. It had instead spun backwards towards the net, making Pushkar's racket sweep through clean air.

'That was an underspin!' the coach was darting towards Kabir. 'Even I couldn't have played that shot.'

'What in the hell just happened?' a baffled Pushkar mumbled, shaking hands with his unexpected subjugator.

'I wanted to make friends, not make you swallow your pride. Besides everyone was having a good time, so I just played along. But you mistook it as my weakness!'

Kabir, with a 172 IQ and a fitness level to match, could learn physical moves and copy them faster than most men on the planet. But he never bragged about it. It would be like letting his guard down. And he couldn't let that happen. Not until his life's mission was accomplished!

∽

Olaf's loud snores pulled Kabir back from the reminiscing. He looked at his watch. It was 1.15 p.m. The cargo ship had been just off the Libyan shore. Abu Bakr would be in the Al Sharia camps in approximately four hours. The agents' strategy was that Tareq's team, posing as separatist Daisht fighters, would escort all of them to the Al Sharia leadership, presenting them as Red Cross volunteers taken hostage at Al Taj. Al Taj was a small town at the highest point in the Kufra oasis. Abduction and ransom of foreign visitors was a very lucrative business in the area. While smaller offshoot terrorist organizations ran the risk of being obliterated by NATO, Al Sharia with its network and muscle, was better placed to negotiate deals. So it would all make sense. From there on, the agents would have to use their acumen and devise a plan to reach Abu Bakr. The leader would be needed alive to breach the Ikhwan's full plan.

The Chinook was parked around a hundred kilometres from Kufra in an isolated forest clearing. The way thereafter was an undulating drive through the desert on potholed roads. The agents sat amidst the armed locals with their hands tied, as the minibus cruised its way along the blazing skyline.

There were a few villages with rundown brick houses and

cottages on the way. They also passed through a dilapidated town with crumbled buildings. At one point, their transport vehicle slackened to the speed of a crawl, as the van's wheels grated against the wreckage. While larger rubble had been cleared off this town's streets, it was still a challenge to manoeuvre through the debris—what had once been homes and places of livelihood.

Kabir woke up to the sound of grinding gears, and straightened himself as his eyes took in the fresh scenes of pathos surrounding him. And then his attention shifted towards Keira. She was looking at a pillar sticking out of a broken window. A faded red dress had been secured to the tip, its frayed ends flapping in the desert winds. Obviously, a family's desperate cry for help that had gone unnoticed. A mellow haze softened her features as Keira looked over her shoulder to exchange a silent glance with him, his thoughts mirroring hers.

'This town's been bombed several times by the NATO forces in the past few months,' Tareq said on having noticed the pair, 'suspecting ISIL terrorist activity.'

'I can still spot a few civilians around,' Kabir said. He pointed to an old woman sitting by the roadside. She was holding someone's single shoe, using it as a begging bowl. Huddled beside her was the seemingly peaceful profile of a child. It was difficult to tell if the child was hers. In fact, it wasn't even possible to tell if the child was asleep, unconscious or dead. Kabir had visited a hundred war-torn cities in the past on his missions. While such scenes had hardened him, every single one of them had taken away a part of his soul too.

'Yes. Most left! Migrated to safer places. But there are others who have nowhere to go. The desert is an unfriendly habitat! One can't just pitch a tent anywhere in this hostile arid terrain,' Tareq clarified.

'Heart-rending!' Bruce clicked his tongue softly, 'it's hard to believe this used to be one of the richest countries in the region just a few decades back, during Gaddafi's times.'

'They overthrew their dictator, dreaming of a much better future under the new democratic regime.'

'Only for the Islamic militancy to snatch that dream away. Today they are a failed state being torn apart in a power struggle between the political alliance, the military, independent militias and terrorist groups,' Bruce said.

'Sometimes…I imagine the world coming together and crushing all of these terrorist organizations in one go,' Bruce said, scratching the worry lines on his temple. 'None of them have nuclear weapons anyhow. Would save everyone a lot of money and heartache in the long run.'

'If only it were that simple!' quipped Keira. 'The world is a very complicated place now. First there are sovereignty issues. No one wants outside powers to meddle in their affairs. Then how do you draw the line between a terrorist organization and freedom fighters? Most of them work under that garb, claiming to be fighting an oppressive rule with good reason. Add to that the lobbying amongst world powers. And there you have it…a tangled web!'

'Not to forget that most of them are funded by powerful economies that want to further their Islamic agendas. Saudi and Iran, the Shia-Sunni game and all that,' added Kabir.

Keira looked at Vladimir, who sat there with a sardonic smile on his face. 'What?' she raised an eyebrow.

'Come on, lady, we are agents on commission!' he said. 'Right now you guys sound like a bunch of college students gorging on trivia! We all know these theories, so what's the…'

'All right. We stop here for a break,' Tareq said, interrupting the awkwardness. They had reached an isolated building in the middle of the desert. 'Let's freshen up. The camp is an hour's drive from here,' Tareq added.

The bus was parked in a blind corner behind a building—from where they got off and furtively approached the front door. An old man opened the door slightly and peeped through the gap. On seeing the armed men in fatigues, he yelled out to the residents inside the house and opened the door without hesitation. He knew what armed men stopped by at his house for.

Tareq conversed in the local language. His tone was polite. The old man nodded in compliance. He then led them into the house that appeared to be empty. It was a duplex with rooms arranged around a central courtyard—both, on the ground and on the first floor.

'Bathroom.' He signalled towards an adjacent corridor.

The captives were allowed the use of the facilities, while the locals kept guard.

A short while later, the agents were seated on a sofa with their hands tied, waiting for the last men to finish freshening up, when a little girl rushed in from an opposite room. She approached Keira, and stood in front of the lone lady, gazing at her with her kohl-rimmed eyes.

The girl pointed a finger to her own chest. 'Ayesha.'

Keira nodded. 'And I'm Keira. K-e-i-r-a.'

The old man scolded her, asking her to go back inside. A man and a woman, clearly her parents, stepped out from the same room and held her hand, asking her to come back. They mumbled apologies to the men with arms. The girl shook her hand free, rushed back to the room and returned with a comic book in her hand. She pointed at Keira and then the white girl in the book, bubbling with excitement on seeing her favourite Captain Marvel sitting in her house. She punched and kicked in the air, reminding the superhero girl what she was expected to do with her captors.

Keira exchanged looks with Tareq and Kabir. Within a split second, they decided to play along with the little girl's wishes. Keira sprang to action and in a few moments the captors lay on the floor, writhing in pain, their weapons lying helter-skelter. The agents were free of their disguises. Keira high-fived the little girl and picked her up in her arms. The little girl hesitated for a moment and then kissed Keira on her cheek. Keira returned her kiss with affection and handed her to her parents, who quickly retreated to the safety of their room, surprised by the strange dynamics between the kidnappers and the kidnapped. The locals quickly picked up their weapons.

'Good job!' Kabir smiled at her. Everyone seemed pleased, except for Bruce. His smirk spoke of his disapproval.

'Let's do the afternoon Salah and get moving,' Tareq told his men. The old man pointed to the prayer room upstairs. The agents accompanied them too.

As the locals kneeled down on prayer mats, their hands held out to the Almighty, the agents stood outside leaning against the railing of the duplex balcony overhanging the living hall below.

'What's wrong, Bruce?' Kabir said. 'A kind act brings no harm.'

'You don't understand,' he said angrily. 'One small mistake, one thing overdone, could lead to disastrous consequences.'

Kabir gave him a cold look, turning around to join the men inside in prayer.

Keira looked at him in surprise as he kneeled down and stretched both his hands out in prayer. 'We could do with some divine intervention…in fact, a lot of it!'

An inward smile lit her up.

∽

The silence dissolved with the noise of an approaching vehicle in the distance, probably a truck with a ripped silencer. Hollering a few loud words of caution, the old man hurried towards the door.

Tareq hustled the taskforce inside the prayer room and quickly locked the door. 'Gotta drop the charade for now,' he pressed a firm finger to his lips, before untying their wrists. The intruders could be from the militia or from the national army. In either case, there would be trouble, unless these men decided to leave peacefully after getting what they came for.

The perforated stone window of the prayer room offered them a clear view of the living area below. Six men, all sporting khaki bulletproof jackets and flat black caps barged in through the main door, each of them wielding Kalashnikovs.

'The national army! Shit...' Tareq shuddered.

Their irate leader started interrogating the old man at gun point straightaway. Kabir could not understand their conversation, nor could he afford to ask Tareq. But the mounting tension was palpable. From the surprised expression on the old man's face it was evident that even he had no idea what was going on. But he would have to eventually reveal their presence—it was only a matter of time. Suddenly, the officer pointed towards the room on the ground floor, the one in the far corner where the little girl and her parents were hiding.

'*Yallahamihami!*' His boisterous yells deafened all the other voices.

Within the next minute, the soldiers were hauling a pair of screaming prisoners out. While the girl's father was restrained and compelled to watch, they dragged the mother and daughter into the centre of the courtyard. The little girl's eyes darted around in all directions, unable to figure out where her superhero idol had disappeared. Two soldiers grabbed the mother and daughter by their hair, so tight that they almost ripped the roots from the scalp as they shoved them down on to the floor. With their boot-heels, they then held the girl and the woman down, muffling both of their ear-piercing howls.

I can't stand this. Keira grimaced, about to drop her discreet position, until Bruce intensified his glare, warning her against it.

The girl's father and grandfather begged repeatedly, folding their hands in desperation. But the leader was deaf to their pleas and continued to brandish the muzzle of his gun from the forehead of the daughter, to the mother, and back to the daughter—playing an eerie game of eeny-meeny-miny-moe.

The terrified eyes of the little girl met her mother's eyes through a gap in the heel of the soldier's dirty boots that had pressed her face flat. *So much for Captain Marvel throwing punches in the air and thrashing the villains.* The tears on her pink cheeks had begun to dry.

'*Aikhtarataljanibalkhata!*'

Bang!

A trigger had been pressed. The little girl was a headless mass, pieces of her brain splattered over her mother.

Noooo...

Keira lowered her head, her eyes clenched shut.

'Fucking barbarians!' Kabir grimaced, as did the rest of his men. His fingers had tightened around his weapon, when Tareq waved his palm asking him to keep calm.

Keira, however, couldn't keep it lidded a second longer. 'I'm done hiding.' She grabbed her gun, battling away a tear.

'Don't,' Bruce hissed, 'that's suicidal.'

'And let them get away? After what they just did?' Her lips were trembling with a rage that Kabir had never seen on her before.

'There are six of them with Kalashnikovs downstairs. It'll be carnage.' Bruce blocked her way. 'You will get everyone killed.'

'Back off, Agent Wilson!'

Kabir stepped in to diffuse the escalating argument. 'Bruce, the holes in these windows will give you men a good shot. Aim for their heads. Take a few of them down.' He surveyed their positions, rushing towards the rear window of the prayer room. 'We'll take the rest.'

Bang!

Keira fired the first shot that went right through the head of the soldier who had killed the girl, instantly calming some of that pent-up rage.

Bang! Vladimir got the second one.

'*Ya Ibn el sharmouta*!' Their leader rushed towards the stairs with three others, unleashing their ammunition blindly in the direction that the bullets had come from.

The agents and Tareq's men attempted to retaliate with crossfire to hold them back, but were forced to lie flat to escape the blitz of death coming their way. So they kept count of the rounds, waiting for the five-second breather when the assailants would have to reload fresh magazines.

But that gap never came. The shower of bullets continued to blow debris off the prayer room window, carving big holes in it. They heard the frenzied thud of boots ascending the stairs. It was impossible now that everyone in the room would make it alive. Olaf reached for his backpack, staring at a foot-long hole in the centre of the perforated stone window. He looked at Vladimir as he brought the grenade to his teeth, preparing to unpin and fling it out. Vladimir reached out to stop him on impulse. The explosion would bring sure death to the nearest assaulters, but the weak slab of the duplex would give in too, sending them all down with the rubble.

Olaf froze midway as they heard another volley of bullets and then, everything fell silent. His hand traced its way back to his backpack as Vladimir shot him a knowing grin.

Kabir's arrival had taken a bit longer than expected. As he had made his stealthy entry through the main door, he had encountered two guards waiting for him. He had adeptly brought down both guards before they could react, then made a stealthy entry that had caught the three men on the staircase unawares.

∽

The soldiers were buried in shallow graves a short distance away. And the agents stood by, in respect, as little Ayesha was laid to rest too in a humble ceremony. As the ceremony drew to a close,

Kabir realized Keira was not to be seen. He saw Tareq approach him and he broke his silence, his voice sombre. 'What actually happened?'

'That's how it is here. The common man is bullied by the outlaws on the one hand and the military on the other,' explained Tareq.

'But why did the old man not tell them about us?'

'Because they never asked for us. They didn't even know we were here.' Tareq shrugged. 'They were just trying to find which side the old man was loyal to—the military or the outlaws. The old man swore his loyalty to them. And to prove it, informed them about some terrorists who had stopped by at his house two days back. That's where he went wrong. These men actually belonged to that very group, disguised in military uniforms. "You chose the wrong side!" their leader had yelled before shooting the girl.'

'But what else could he have done… in such a situation?'

'Welcome to Libya.' Tareq patted the man's shoulder before walking off.

∽

'Could've been one of us with them, Agent Rathore… six feet underground!' Bruce paused. 'Still think Agent Brooks should have meddled? Or, does she get a free pass because… she's your… "friend?"'

The quip was low. But Olaf and Vladimir did catch the drift.

'Agent Wilson.' Kabir flicked his palm to the left with a hard frown, asking that the agent step aside. 'Care for a talk? In private?'

'Aye aye, captain.' Bruce mocked him with a salute. He didn't approve of how it had all gone down. And he was not willing to risk his life working in a team with such emotional freaks.

The remaining members watched on, while the two officers paced off towards the jeep that the terrorists had parked outside the main gate. They saw the discussion heating up. It seemed that the five-member task force commissioned to fend off the holocaust was already disintegrating!

∽

'Keira…' Kabir walked up to the agent standing by herself, shoulders hunched, leaning by a ransacked shed.

'Maybe Bruce was right,' she muttered, her hollow stare fixed on the ground where the outline of his shadow loomed closer. 'None of this would have happened had we left a few minutes earlier.'

His palm went up, as Kabir felt the need to show her support. But decided against it at the last moment, and retracted his fingers to let her be. 'Keira…that is not true…'

'What was I waiting for? Why couldn't I have stepped out a minute earlier? I failed her!'

'You did not.'

'Yes, I did! How will I ever get over those eyes? She kept waiting for me till her last breath…her Captain Marvel!' Keira sighed, her eyes moistening. 'And why did it have to be the little girl? You saw how they treated Ayesha and her mother?'

'Keira!' Kabir held her shoulders with a firm clasp and turned her around to face him, to stop the self-blame once and for all. 'Tareq told me these men were terrorists…out for the old man's life. They would have spared none. Our silence or our early departure wouldn't have stopped them. If anything, your story gave the girl one final memory to cherish, before she died. And her soul can now rest in peace after the instant karma you brought to her killers.'

Her lips parted, about to make a comeback, but she ended up looking at his eyes instead. A piercing gaze. There was honesty in his eyes. Probably the only bit of honesty she had come across in a long while. 'You… you might be right.'

'I know I am.' The mellow smile tugging at his lips dissolved when he felt his heart skip a beat. Wary of how this moment was messing with his resolve, he was about to withdraw his hand from hers. However, for some inexplicable reason, he didn't. Instead, his palm trailed up to her face, allowing him to delve deeper into the emerald eyes. The eyes that had caught his fancy from their very first encounter. They read each other's pulse—the spark that they had shared over every look, every smile, a hundred times more profound now after having witnessed death.

On an impulse, he slowly leaned in, wishing all along that she would put an end to this. But she did no such thing. An intense spell later, their lips met, his arms sensing her body melting into his clasp as she ran her fingers through his hair. Kabir gave in to the feeling as their breaths became one. It was a taste of chastity…it felt so right! A voice in the back of his head, however, kept telling him that the other agents would be waiting for them.

'We shouldn't.' Keira abruptly broke it off, her voice raspy, her emotions unsettled, still catching up on her breath. She had placed a palm against his chest, holding them apart.

'We shouldn't.' Kabir nodded in agreement, realizing how they had both succumbed to the heat of the moment. But her expressions showed little sign of regret. If anything, she was fighting temptation herself.

18

Islam Is the Solution!

'From a mere eight hundred members, to over three million in three years. Three hundred branches across Egypt and eighteen in other countries across the Arab world. The fastest growth ever! Our society is on its way to becoming global. It all started just three years back when we developed our own internal funding system and started publishing our newsletter, Al-Nadhir. We didn't have enough money to buy the printing press. Those were tough times. Then brothers came forward with their sadaqah. Poor men, labourers, craftsmen—working-class citizens contributed to form a seed capital. Saved the society from falling into the hands of capitalists.' Ghassan was addressing thousands of members of the Brotherhood who had gathered from different parts of Egypt and neighbouring countries for the annual convention. His charisma was at its peak.

'And today, we have hundreds of schools, hospitals and factories running to support our charitable and religious activities.' Mokhtar and his team were on alert, keeping the crowd under surveillance.

'And none of this would have been possible without the Ummah—we, the Muslim brothers, unified by the tenets of our Holy Prophet! Hence, I must remind you of our worldview. It has four basic propositions, which I expect every Muslim brother to remember. First: Islam is a complete and perfect way of life, making it inevitable that Muslims do not separate politics and religion. If someone should ask you "to what end is your appeal made?" say the truth, "we are calling you to Islam." If someone should say to you "this is politics!" say "this is Islam, and we do not recognize such divisions."'

The crowd cheered and clapped. Even now, Mokhtar could identify with these young men, who quite like him had found purpose and self-respect in working with the society. There was a mood of festivity as volunteers swayed the flags of the Brotherhood and displayed banners zealously. It was no less than a fete. There were numerous food and shopping stalls dotting the periphery of the ground.

'Second: Islam must be the basis of all legislation. The Islamic sacred law was drawn from the noble Quran and the Sunnah, and the decisions of the Islamic jurists are all-encompassing, covering every contingency. If the hudud punishments prescribed by God were carried out—for instance, stoning, crucifixion, amputations, lashing, etc., for crimes such as illicit intercourse, alcohol consumption, theft or highway robbery—they will be a deterrent against even the hardened criminal. We have sent out letters to King Faoud, and to other rulers of Islamic countries, to reform to Sharia law and pave the way for the restoration of the caliphate.'

'We call for prohibition of gambling, drinking of alcohol, playing improper music, dancing and fornication. Theatre, cinema, plays, cafes, provocative stories and books—all of these distractions must be kept under surveillance and confiscated if they disseminate immorality. Primary schools must be attached to mosques with imperatives to memorize the Quran. It is the communal obligation of us Ummah to command the right and forbid the wrong. To police the behaviour of our community, intervening verbally and even physically—if we see a violation of God's law.'

Ghassan paused. He had struck a chord with the downtrodden as their modern messiah. The crowd swayed and chanted slogans.

'Islam is the solution!'

'Believers are brothers!'

'Third,' he resumed, silencing the cheer. 'Western societies are decadent and corrupt. European life and culture rest upon the principle of elimination of religion from all aspects of social life. Their society is inherently materialistic, retaining Christianity only as a historical heirloom. The defining marks of their civilization are licentiousness, with an unseemly dedication to base instincts and self-indulgence—thus gratifying desires of the belly and the genitals, equipping women with the power of provocation and seduction. What is worse, the entire Muslim world is being corrupted by Western decadence. Our countries are being flooded with Western capital, banks and companies. Westerners have invaded Muslim lands with their half-naked women, their liquor, their dance halls, newspapers and novels. This cultural shift is even more dangerous than the political and military imperialism of the West. Hence we have two fundamental goals—that our Islamic fatherland be freed from all foreign domination and a free Islamic state may arise acting on the precepts of Islam.'

The crowd cheered again. Mokhtar continued to scan them with his sharp eyes. He was happy he had played his part in this phenomenal success story. Ahmad Shaban had stepped aside. Ghassan had a unilateral say in matters of the society now, and this was in the best interest of the organization. And Islam!

'Fourth, and most importantly, God has commanded Muslims to engage in jihad to spread Islam. Our divine law is superior to any man-made one. The Holy Quran appoints Muslims as guardians of humanity and grants them the right to suzerainty over the world in order to guide the rest towards the sound precepts of Islam and to its teachings, without which mankind will continue to be miserable. Today, Muslims, as you are aware, are compelled to humble themselves before non-Muslims, ruled by unbelievers. Hence, it has become obligatory that every Muslim makes up his mind to engage in jihad, prepares his equipment and readies himself.'

The night sky seemed to resound from a host of fiery slogans.

'Egypt for Egyptians!'

'Down with the Jews!'

'Victory for Islam!'

Mokhtar observed some unusual activity at the left entrance. A group of policemen were making their way to the podium. Commanding half of his team to stay around Ghassan, he promptly walked down the podium with six of his men, intercepting them midway.

'Adel! When did you join the police? Nice to see you like this, all fit and toned.' He beamed, trying to conceal his amazement.

On the contrary, Adel didn't seem too pleased to be meeting him. He stopped his men on seeing Mokhtar. His response was matter-of-fact. 'You did not turn up at your mother's funeral last week, Mokhtar?'

'Why would I? She meant nothing to me. I never once met her after I left home.'

'You should have seen the pain on her face. She kept waiting for you till her last moment. By the way, she died of heart seizure. Strange, isn't it? Seeing how she didn't have any cardiac history.' Adel inched closer, trying to read Mokhtar's body language. 'She was at the Shepheard's, delivering some important documents to Sir Geoffrey Philip, Second Lieutenant, in his room.'

'So? Why are you telling me these details?'

'Because you had the motive and the means. We also found a red inflamed patch on her spine in the post-mortem, which reminded me of your blowgun.'

'You're cooking up weird stories, officer. The red mark could be anything—an allergy, an insect bite! Why, did they find a weapon? A dart? A needle? Was it anywhere on her during the post mortem?'

'No, it wasn't. Or, I would have had the arrest warrant in my hands. Now where were you last Thursday, between 2 and 4 p.m.?'

Mokhtar stared into space for a moment, rubbing his chin.

'Oh yes, I was visiting the madrasa of Sarghatmish outside Cairo.'

'How did you go there? Who was with you?'

'Akram. Would you like to meet him?'

'Yes, right now. Can you take us to him?'

'But he can't speak!'

'Why?'

'He's my horse!' Mokhtar and his aides broke into hysterical laughter.

'Be very careful, Mokhtar. I'm warning you!' Adel squared his shoulders against his former friend. 'I know what you did to my cousin. To Nouran, remember her? I won't let you get away with your criminal acts. I'll make sure you are behind bars… very soon!'

Mokhtar was for a moment taken aback by the aggression in those otherwise genial eyes. This was not the Adel he had met in his room three years ago. Inside, he was happy for his friend. The wanton years were gone! Adel finally had purpose. But it was a pity their paths had to cross in such a manner.

'It seems Allah just can't bear to keep us apart!' He chuckled, an undeterred expression on his face.

'Let's go!' Adel ordered his men, his eyes still locked with Mokhtar's till he turned and broke the gaze.

As Adel made his way back through the ocean of volunteers, he could feel the storm approaching. Mokhtar was in the eye of the storm, but he was no longer worried for his friend. He had gone too far to be redeemed. He was worried about his country. The confrontation between the two poles—the liberals and the radicals—was imminent.

∽

Back at his dorm in the society, Mokhtar sat at his table. He was proudly inspecting his invention that had saved him today. He opened a vial and poured out its contents on a paper: micro-hypodermic needles. Inspired and developed from the potent venom delivery system of bee stingers, the biodegradable needles dissolved in the tissue soon after penetration! That's why surgeons couldn't find a straw-dart or other foreign object below the skin.

His mother hadn't noticed him standing around the turn in the corridor. Covered in a black abaya, she was proceeding towards the lieutenant's room. The little needle penetrating her back had felt no worse than a mosquito bite.

Mokhtar was surprised he didn't feel any pangs of guilt.

'I never will.' He promised himself. *'Not when punishing a kafir!'*

19

The Desert Hostages

'Kafir? What's that?' asked Olaf. 'Sounds familiar.' 'Kafir is the term they use to legitimize killing people in the name of God. Mostly our own people. Innocent people!' explained Tareq.

'How? Doesn't kafir mean infidel?' countered Kabir.

'Yes, it does,' Tareq clarified. 'But the problem is in the way one interprets the Holy Quran. The Quran, the Hadiths and the Sunnahs, like many other religious texts, are interpreted in different ways. Some Islamic scholars quote the texts when they allege that killing even a single innocent person is the worst crime, and then there are others who use the same text to justify killing hundreds.'

'Statistics say that 90 per cent of people killed in terror attacks by Islamic hardliners are Muslims themselves,' said Keira. 'The terrorists from this group that we are headed towards, Al Sharia, killed thirty-four people in a mall recently. A few days later, their spokesperson was justifying their stand to a television reporter. He said that the people shopping in the mall were pro-government, and the government is not for Sharia law, so in effect, they were infidels. Later, he admitted that such exercises also serve as practical sessions for their new recruits...to keep their morale high.'

'The pits!' spat Olaf. 'Killing innocent people for practice? And how can people live in such conditions? Families, children?'

'No one lives here by choice, I guess.' Keira shrugged.

'You are sadly mistaken,' Kabir laughed. 'In the most populated

Muslim countries, like Pakistan, Bangladesh as well as almost the entire Middle East, 80 to 90 per cent of the people are in favour of Sharia law and would like to live under it. Even developed countries like Malaysia! And I am quoting the PEW Research Centre here. Muslims living in these countries explicitly voted in favour of gender-based separation, punishments like stoning for adultery and the death penalty for leaving Islam.'

'Shocking! By the way, Kabir, sending Bruce back was a mistake!' said Olaf. 'Differences of opinion happen...doesn't mean you break the team.'

'He was meant for bigger and better stuff...I had no option,' Kabir said sarcastically.

They could see the camps in the distance now, a huge area cordoned off with poles and barbed wires. An out-of-bounds zone, where none could enter without authorization from the jihadi organization. It was the size of a small township. Visible from a distance were hordes of tents, the dome of a mosque, scaffolded watchtowers and large black flags with white Arabic text inscribed on it. The text seemed sharp and fearsome, like a set of daggers and serpents entwined in some special formation.

Our point of no return! Keira thought. Once inside, they would only come back with Abu Bakr or not come out at all!

'What's written on that black flag?' she asked.

'The Shahada. The Muslim profession of faith, expressing the two simple, fundamental beliefs that make one a Muslim: There is no God but Allah, and Muhammad is the messenger of Allah,' said Kabir. He had learnt about it during his mission against the Boko Haram, when he had rescued the BBC reporter, Sarah's friend.

'Wow! So every Muslim believes this?' Keira asked.

'Of course! There is nothing wrong with believing in a single God, that's monotheism. There is no problem with wanting to live under the Sharia law either,' Tareq defended, 'It's a matter of personal choice. The problem starts when you want to force others to follow it. Start killing for it! That's where these people have gone overboard.'

'Absolutely! You want to live with a stick up your arse, no problem. But when you bleed, it shows...and it's terrifying!' Olaf sniggered.

'Whatever! We'll continue this discussion later. Now get back to your miserable mood, captives,' Tareq grinned back.

Kabir smiled at Tareq, hoping he was not offended.

A short ride later, they reached the gates of the camp. An armed guard waved at them to stop. Tareq jumped off the bus and walked up to him. Following a small conversation, the guard left, only to return with two others, and the three of them took their seats at the front to guide the agents and Tareq to their destination. It seemed that the guards had been pre-informed about their arrival.

The camp was brimming with energy. Hundreds of young men were busy training in different enclosures—martial arts, archery, resistance training, driving and more. Kabir recognized the equipment as sophisticated and that the boys were apparently enjoying the drills. *It's not a normal terror training camp. It's a fidayeen camp.* These were suicide bombers. The elite amongst the community! The ones who shaved their pubic hair before embarking upon the final act. There was a long waiting list to get into this band, to render the ultimate selfless service to Allah by laying down one's life. And the competition to be chosen for a mission was even more intense; now, with an opportunity for a hundred of them to explode planes in one go, they had to be toppling over each other to make it!

After another kilometre deep into the camps, the bus was parked outside a big tent, heavily guarded. The message about their arrival was sent ahead by the guards who had accompanied them. Half an hour later, a hefty man with a long black beard, wearing a black cloak and a matching Islamic cap, walked out. He looked like a cleric. Walking up to the back door that had been kept open for his inspection, he took a quick look at the hostages and then turned around, signalling for Tareq to follow him inside.

'Water!' Keira cried all of a sudden. Holding her throat, she dropped to her knees in distress. The Al Sharia cleric glanced over his shoulder and checked her out. *Nubile!* He snapped his fingers at his men, ordering them to take care of her and then left for the tent.

Keira's face was blanched and she appeared dehydrated. She tried to speak, but before she could utter a word, fell down to the floor, unconscious. The guards sprinkled water over her face, but they could not revive her. So they carried her on a stretcher to the chief's large air-conditioned tent, with Kabir worriedly looking on.

∽

'These men don't look like Red Cross workers,' the chief snarled. 'The gigantic white one—look at him! What are you up to?' They were seated in the chief's tent for negotiation.

Tareq shrugged and pulled out their identification cards from his pocket and handed them over. The chief studied them carefully, stealing glances at Keira intermittently.

'Half a million Libyan dinar,' Tareq said, sniggering, having sensed what was going on in the chief's mind.

'Have you lost it?' The cleric was infuriated.

'Each,' Tareq added.

The chief stood up, vexed. 'Get out!'

'You can easily make ten million.' Tareq paused. 'Ten million dollars—not dinars. And you get to keep her as a bonus.'

The chief ran his hand over his beard. 'How can you be so sure?'

'The Russian you saw there, he's the only son of Mr Agapov, a conglomerate from Vladivostok.' He held out his passport. Vladimir Agapov. He then googled an article on his mobile about the Agapov Group—having diversified interests in hospitality, publishing, iron and steel and real estate. It had the picture of Mr Igor Agapov—its founder—sitting in his majestic office. And Vladimir was standing right behind him, the heir apparent!

The chief was deep in thought. This man did make sense. *But, messing with the Russians? Besides, the price was too high. Ten times what one would ask for the usual desert hostages!*

'Lock the hostages in one of the underground cells,' he instructed his guards. 'Let this man and his troop stay in the guest tent,' he pointed towards Tareq, 'and keep watch over them too.' Walking up to Keira, he gently ran his hand over her hair. 'Take her to the special care chamber. She is not well, let her rest there. I'll be back soon.'

'Sidi Yusuf, this is not fair!' Tareq protested. 'We haven't finalized a deal yet and you are taking my ransom in your custody. And us too?'

'I know what's best for everyone here!' Yusuf sported a cunning expression that made Tareq wonder if the cleric was onto their plan. *How were the agents ever going to make it out of the subterranean dungeons?*

∽

The large tent had several chambers along its periphery, partitioned with curtains. The one that Keira was taken to was located at the far end, furnished with exquisite wall-to-wall carpets. It also had a king-size carved wooden bed in the centre. There were two sets of embroidered curtain screens that could be secured for privacy. A pot of steaming kahwa and some nuts were placed on a small table next to the bed.

The chief sat down beside her and took off his cap and overcoat. He poured some tea into a cup, its aroma filling the air. He sprinkled some scented water on Keira's face, but she didn't respond. He bent over and kissed the tiny droplets off her face, one by one. The longer he saw her, the more he found himself falling for her. If only she would come to her senses soon. He wanted to taste her. It would help remove that iota of doubt in his mind about the deal. He started to unbutton her shirt, his entire focus on those shapely mounds.

'Uffff!' He was startled out of his dream by the sudden sound of a guard calling for him. He heard the throttled sound of a truck engine approaching the tent and shook his head in despair. He didn't know whether to be happy or angry. He was aroused beyond control, but he couldn't make the Murshid wait either. He was about to get his highest pay-off.

'Keep a watch over her,' he commanded his men as he rushed out of his special room.

Keira heard the loud truck engine roar back to life and fade off into the distance—a sign that the chief had left. The rest of her team was under detainment. She knew she would have to act fast, otherwise the Murshid would finish his task and leave the camps. She was glad she had gone through with the fainting act. *It is never wise to stay huddled up in such operations.* Despite her rigorous training to master the act of appearing unconscious or dead, the day's episode had been an acid test. The lecherous bearded beast had made her want to puke! His stink still hung in the room. The Murshid had arrived just in time. Had Yusuf opened a few more buttons, it would have been 'game over'!

She opened her eyelids slightly. Two guards were entering the room. In accordance with a plan that was beginning to take shape in her mind, she began shivering vigorously. Noticing her condition, the guards rushed to fetch her a quilt. She covered herself from head to toe and indicated that they leave to let her rest.

Keira knew she had very little time before they would come in again to check on her. She would have to be quick. With dozens of them outside, confrontation was not an option. So she peeked around for another means of escape.

Against her expectation, the walls of this special chamber, as it turned out, were made of bulletproof metallic sheets lined with fabric. She looked around desperately, unsure of her next move.

There! She spotted a vertical iron truss on one side of the room. She reckoned the gigantic tent had to be supported with these trusses along the periphery. Quickly arranging the pillows on the bed, she covered them up with the quilt so that it resembled a sleeping figure.

Slipping on her shoes, she then drew out a thin steel blade from the hem of her jeans. She climbed up the truss, cut the thick layer of tent fabric around the top and peeped up. Adjoining the vertical truss was a rafter truss—a radial hollow shaft made from round pipes that ran all the way up to the centre of the tent— overlapped by a second layer of fabric. She carved out a hole in the upper canvas layer, for access. *Yesss!* Both the flaps flopped down limply. She popped her head up for a glimpse of the scene outside.

In the dim light, Keira could spot a group of guards not far from where the tent ended. Too many of them. She couldn't risk climbing straight down that way, amidst the patrolling guards. Nor could she return to the room with a gaping hole in its roof.

Shit... only one way to go! The two-feet of space between the two layers of fabric on the roof! Of course, that could be a blind alley leading to nowhere—but it would have to do for now. She pushed herself further up, wormed into the space headfirst and lay there gasping for breath. She realized that although the canvas was strong enough to take her weight, a bulge would be clearly discernible through the fabric. Which meant she would have to support her weight inside the hollow metallic beam to get around discreetly.

Wriggling her way on her back through the rafter, she hung on to its pipes. She crawled up, one inch at a time, towards the centre of the structure into the dense matrix of undisturbed cobwebs proliferating the dark space. *Ugh.* She shuddered from an unpleasant tingle. The webs were wrapping themselves around her face and ears. Even getting caught in the ringlets of her hair. Her fingers itched to brush them aside, but she couldn't let go of the iron pipes. *No... no...just go on.*

She shut her eyes and mouth tight and kept moving.

Ouch. Her head hit a dead end. Keira opened her eyes that had gotten used to the dark by now. A quick feel around let her know that she had reached the top of the tent. She squinted and looked around. It seemed like the rafters on all four sides of the tent were connected to this central structure. The grid of round pipes from this point was too narrow, too complex to squirm through. Apparently, she had reached a dead end, and was stranded right at the top! A few torches flashing their beams upwards was all that would be needed for the guards to find her!

Suddenly, the wind howled and a strong gust of sand blew in from the holes that she had cut open. So strong, that even the structure of the tent swayed slightly.

A sandstorm?

Hues and cries burst out below—the guards had noticed the opening in the roof of her room. They would climb in any moment. *Shit!* And her position made for an extremely inconvenient and a highly-visible spot to be hanging off.

Have to move!

Keira tried to edge deeper into the network of pipes, flexing her shoulders. However, a quarter way in and she was stuck. It was as tight as it could be; the ordeal was made worse by the dense webs that had tangled in her hair. The strands were now obstructing her vision. Suddenly, she heard someone climbing up. Through the gap, she could see a guard's face appear as he tried to peek through the dark expanse between the two layers of fabric engulfing the iron structure of the roof. He climbed down a step and shouted out a few orders.

Probably asking a fellow guard to fetch him a torch. She held her breath. A matter of seconds—and they would find her!

20

The Nazi Bankroll

'What now, Ghassan? We've come a long way from where we started,' said Umar, one of the co-founders. 'Our paramilitary squads are growing in number and strength, thanks to our sports camps. The boys are more than ready!'

The expectations of the populace were growing and Ghassan was slowly but surely outnumbering King Faoud in support. The core team of the society was brainstorming means to counter King Faoud's possible backlash against them.

'Our military capabilities are only for self-defence. We are a non-violent movement and there should be no compromising on that,' Ghassan reiterated calmly.

'But we must be ready!'

'For what?' asked Nebi, another founding member.

'For a direct confrontation with the royal army,' replied Umar. 'Faoud will want to crush us as soon as he finds an excuse. All our funds are committed to social work. We need money to buy the latest arms and ammunition.'

'Let's be realistic,' Nebi folded his arms across his chest sternly. 'They have the British empire on their side after all!'

'So what? There must be someone equally powerful, someone who hates the British just as much. Why can't we side with them?'

'Well, of course, there is! And we all know this group. But it might sound far-fetched,' Fahim chipped in, an older member of the organization who now looked after the legal affairs of the society. Ahmed Shaban had recently resigned from the society and left the city.

'And exactly whom did you have in mind, Fahim?'

'The Nazis!' Fahim had a sinister smile on his face. The word rang through the hall like a fire bell. There was a short silence as the members tried to come to terms with the demented suggestion.

'But the Second World War is on now. What would they care about a religious group fighting a tyrant in some distant land.' Nebi sneered, expecting to close the suggestion and move to more meaningful options.

'That's exactly why! An enemy's enemy is a friend.' Fahim remained unfazed. 'Hitler has just formed the Axis alliance with Italy and Japan. He has attacked Poland and is all set to conquer Europe. The Allied forces led by Britain aren't able to do much to stop him.'

'So how would that put us in a position to bargain? Hitler's men wouldn't go around exchanging friendship bracelets with everyone who hates the British.'

'What exactly is your plan?' Umar appeared interested. 'How do we reach the Führer and what do we tell him?'

'Well...eh... I haven't thought about that,' Fahim stuttered with a shrug.

'Brilliant!' exclaimed Ghassan, who had been listening in silence all along. 'Why didn't I think about this earlier? Fahim is right.'

Everyone turned to Ghassan, surprised by his unexpected reaction to such a seemingly naive suggestion.

'We share another common enemy. Even more obnoxious than the British. One that Hitler despises from his core.' Ghassan continued, 'I have been writing him letters since I was twenty-two, admiring his hatred for the Jews and expressing my desire to work with the Nazi party.'

'Pen pals?' gasped Umar. 'My son is all into it.'

'Not exactly pen pals!' Ghassan smiled. 'The Führer never wrote back.'

'How, then?'

'Our common friend, the Grand Mufti of Jerusalem! Al-Husseini is visiting Berlin next week.' Ghassan paused, 'Hitler never says no to him. The mufti is even helping him recruit a wing of Bosnian Muslims into the German army.'

'What sort of assistance can we expect from them?' asked Umar.

'Hitler is known for his generosity towards his *friends*,' said Ghassan. 'After all, it takes deep coffers to run the kind of parallel government we are here.'

'And what do we offer them in return?'

'The British in 1917, through the Balfour Declaration, gave away a piece of Arabian land to the Jews, to make it the Hebrew homeland. The Arabs vehemently opposed it while the Jews were determined not to let go of this opportunity to have a country of their own. Although the British later withdrew their stand, countless Jews facing Nazi execution have migrated to this land already. And so have the Arabs, determined to hold on to our native lands. We'll send in our fighters to help the Arabs. Hitler would rather have every Jew terminated in his concentration camps than allow them a glorified existence. Ousting the British from Egypt and having a powerful ally in the Arab world would only be a bonus for the Nazis!'

'Mashallah! Seems like a plan!' Umar beamed, his face aglow.

∽

Mokhtar instructed his trusted security commanders to keep strict vigil as he left the headquarters. It was a calling he couldn't resist. The boys he had trained were competent and he could trust them for a while. The meeting had ended and Ghassan would leave for his quarters shortly.

He hopped into a taxi that took him to the nearest mosque

and picked up the maulvi who had been waiting for him. They drove several blocks to a house and knocked. An old lady opened the door and greeted them warmly. She led them to a brightly lit room with ceremonial decorations. A beautiful girl, wearing a white satin bridal outfit and gold ornaments sat across a stool with white drapery. Mokhtar promptly took his seat next to her. The maulvi sat opposite them. He placed the Holy Quran and his prayer beads on the stool. Mokhtar took out a bundle of cash and kept it next to the prayer beads.

'*An Kah'tunafsakaa'lalmah'rilma' loom...,*' the bride uttered shyly, giving herself away in nikah at the agreed meher Mokhtar had just placed on the table. Though the amount was hardly enough security and wouldn't last long, it was a handsome 'dower' in comparison to the prevailing practice.

'*QabiltunNikaha*,' Mokhtar said, accepting the proposal. With this pronouncement they became husband and wife. The bride smiled coyly at Mokhtar as their gazes met. After all, she was now with one of the most feared men in Cairo, a warrior fighting from the shadows.

The old lady led them to their room and closed the doors from outside.

Mokhtar relinquished all control on his hunger. He grabbed the girl and kissed her passionately, unhooking her dress. They were on the bed and he pounded hard, making her moan in sheer joy. He was an unstoppable beast and the girl gave in to the orgasmic tornado she was caught up in. He flipped and tossed her about as if she were a toy, taking her to the heights of ecstasy, one round after another.

Suddenly, Mokhtar slowed down and his movements turned gentle and caring. He caressed her hair and lowered his body over her, letting his breath mingle with hers. The girl opened her eyes, surprised by this sudden change in demeanour.

His eyelids were shut and there was a childlike innocence on his face she had never seen before. 'Nouran!' he whispered, and continued to make love to her, gentler than ever before.

They were soon back at the nikah table.

'You are haram for me,' Mokhtar pronounced the talaq al bid'ah, a short and simple divorce that acquitted him of his marital responsibilities. The girl looked at him wistfully. She had been through this before. She did not know when her turn would come again. Mokhtar visited their brothel only a few times a year. The old lady escorted Mokhtar and the maulvi out, thanking him profusely for the generous tip he placed in her hands.

'Are you sure this is not a sin?' Mokhtar asked as he gazed blankly through the taxi window.

'Outside of marriage it would be.' The maulvi smiled, 'But I make sure you follow the Sharia—word for word.'

∾

Two months later
The Brotherhood Headquarters

'I have just received news from the Mufti,' Ghassan announced. 'Our proposal has received a reply from Hitler himself. I will read it out to you.'

He began, the paper in his hands, '"I am delighted to hear from you after a long time, my friend. I acknowledge with a nostalgic spirit all the letters you wrote to me during the yesteryear. Some of those came as a ray of light, helping me through my worst days. The verses you quoted in your letters had a deep impact on my intellect and lifted the mist from my thoughts, like reinforcement to a troop surrounded by enemies."'

'Oh...so the Führer did read your letters, after all!' Umar exclaimed. There was an air of joy in the conference hall.

'"The Axis powers welcome you as our ally. The fight against the treacherous British and these deceptive Jews is not easy, and will prove lengthy. As for your request for financial support, I regret to inform you that our coffers are completely dry due to the ongoing war. We can, however, train your soldiers in modern artillery and the latest techniques of war. I am sure this shall provide momentum to your Jihad against the evil forces. Keep in touch."'

There was an aura of doom as the core committee absorbed the bad news. Their flames of hope had just been doused.

'No need to despair, friends!' Ghassan put the letter away. 'Remember the printing press? If we could come this far, we will find our way ahead too. Let's reflect on this and discuss it in the next meeting.'

He walked out with Mokhtar closely following him.

∽

Ghassan was in his office, going through some important papers before leaving for home. Mokhtar stood next to his table. It was late and the other boys in charge of his security had been released.

'What will we do now, Master?' Mokhtar was concerned. The Germans had been their last quarter of hope.

'Close that door and come here.' Ghassan looked at him with a smile. 'We have at hand your most important assignment to date. That letter I read out at the meeting? It was fake! Here's the original one.' He pulled out a letter from his drawer. 'Let me read its latter portion to you.

"'It shall be our pleasure to support your group in our war against these lesser humans. The ethnic cleansing must happen, not merely here in Germany, but everywhere around the world. We can offer financial support by organizing for a valuable cargo, a haul of gold, to be dropped at a port off the coast of Siracusa in Italy. We would have delivered it all the way to Cairo, but these are troubled times and we can only transport it so far across our allied countries to this seaport. Beyond that, the onus to take it safely past the Mediterranean Sea and through the British coast guard is on you. We shall wait for your response to make the necessary arrangements. This transaction should remain highly classified. Please ensure it remains under tight wraps. The more ears you confide in, the more it shall be jeopardized."'

'A haul of gold?' Mokhtar stared at Ghassan in disbelief. 'I don't know what its value would be, but I feel it may just be sufficient to fund our current plans and many future ones.'

'Definitely!' Ghassan grinned. 'I am sure it should amount to a sizeable sum.'

There was silence as Mokhtar tried to absorb the nuances of the offer. Taking up this generous offer seemed too perilous all of a sudden. Bringing the haul across the rough Mediterranean winter seas, and then sneaking it past the coast guards? It was a near impossible job. 'Wouldn't it be too big a risk? Maybe it should be brought in parts.'

'No!' Ghassan stopped him. 'We must pull it off in one stroke. Put in everything you have. This is our doorway to the caliphate.'

Mokhtar nodded, not sure how he would do it. But he was sure as hell that this was their chance to empower the society and make the Islamic dream a reality.

'Why Siracusa, Master, any idea?'

'Probably because it's an idling port near us.'

'And why didn't you read the original letter in front of the board?'

'The sums being implied are too large. As he has rightly pointed out, the fewer the number privy to the affair, the better. Make sure no one else gets to know about this. Not even the fighters who shall accompany you on this mission. I know it's easier said than done, but you have proven yourself to be my nostrum time and again…a rare jewel.'

'I shall give it my best, Master. I would need a few days at the port and its nearby cities, however, before we load the shipment.'

'Don't worry. I will ask them for a month's time. Let me know what you would need. List everything—from ammunition to the kind of ship.'

'Yes, Master. Anything else?' Mokhtar said, although he was still perplexed. *How could that kind of haul be shipped without people on board noticing anything?*

'Yes. Remember that we can do with delay, but not with failure. I don't need this money right away as I don't intend to spend it on simply buying arms.'

'Then what are we going to do with it?'

'Something much more important. I will enlighten you when the time is right.'

21

Olaf: the X-man

Kabir, Olaf and Vladimir sat on a stone bench in the prison cell. They leaned against the rear wall; their heads hanging down as they talked in low voices. The cells were located in an underground tunnel. Meant primarily as shelter from bombing, it was also an ideal location for hiding captives. Theirs was a ten-by-ten-foot room with stone walls on three sides and iron bars in front. Four armed men stood guard outside the cell. They had discussed several escape plans, but nothing seemed viable. Fortunately, they had not been searched that intensively at the entrance as they were already within the camp. They had some knives and small pistols hidden on them, but there was no way that their puny weapons would be of any use against the guards' machine guns.

'Alsamat!' one of the guards shouted, walking up to the bars.

'What happened?' Olaf said, raising his hands. The guard gestured for him to zip his lips, and then returned to his alert position, staring at them angrily. Vladimir put one hand on his stomach and with the other, he brought an imaginary morsel to his mouth, his miserable eyes betraying his hunger.

The guard walked up to the bars, a sympathetic look on his face. He dug into his pocket, took out a peanut and tossed it towards Vladimir. He turned back to face his friends and they broke into hysterical laughter. He then walked up to them, jumping and swaying like a gorilla, massaging his belly, scratching his sides in an attempt to imitate the oversized Siberian. Vladimir charged at him. He hit the bars, his huge body pressing against them and hand sticking out, about half a foot from the guard's throat. The guard aimed his AK-47 at Vladimir's forehead. The other guards took on an alert stance. Kabir and Olaf pulled Vladimir back. The guard retracted, spewing expletives at them. Silence prevailed as the agents sat there staring at the craggy ceiling. The guards relaxed and chatted away, sitting in a circle.

Noticing them absorbed in an animated discussion, Vladimir pulled out a large Lindor bar he had kept hidden under his T-shirt. He secretively tore open the printed cover and golden foil below it. He nibbled at the half-melted chocolate, soiling his mouth and fingers. He offered it to Kabir who broke two clean rows for himself and Olaf.

One of the guards noticed the orgy happening in the cellar. He jumped to his feet and reaching closer, saw the Swiss chocolate wrapper better in the dim light. The calligraphic 'L' in golden on the red base brought back a distant tingling sensation to his taste buds.

'Stop!' he commanded, aiming the gun. He gestured to Vladimir to surrender his booty. Vladimir quickly snapped another row from the bar and mouthed it. He grudgingly walked to the bars and thrust his hand out, holding almost a half of the chocolate out. Kabir and Olaf got up, expecting imminent action. They saw the guard snatch the chocolate from Vladimir's hand, maintaining sufficient distance from his burly fingers. Nothing happened! No pulling the guard, snatching his gun, holding it to his head and asking the other guards to open the door if they wanted to save their friend. None of that happened!

'Scoundrels,' Olaf said, looking at Vladimir as they sat on the bench watching the guards enjoy the treat. 'But we seriously thought you were up to some action!'

'Action? All four of them have AK-47s. Our pistols wouldn't count,' he replied. 'Keep watching.'

Within a few seconds, the guards fell to the floor, holding on to their throats, writhing in pain. They squirmed for a few seconds and then become motionless.

'Genius! So you snapped the last row before handing over the chocolate to make sure the entire leftover portion was poisoned,' said Kabir. 'Doesn't help much though. They are still a good ten feet away and I don't think they even have the keys. The guards who came to lock us here must have taken the key away!'

'14 mm, easily manageable!' Vladimir grinned.

'Millimetres? Hell no! Its ten feet, what's wrong with you man! They are atleast ten feet away,' Olaf groaned.

'I'm talking about the thickness of the iron bars. I checked it out when I charged at the guard who threw the peanut at me,' Vladimir beamed.

He confidently walked up to the bars and stood in front of them. He jerked his arms and legs, relaxing his muscles. Holding two adjacent bars, he started pulling them in opposite directions, putting every shoulder, chest and arm muscle to work. And lo and behold, the bars warped like they had just been heated. Kabir and Olaf looked at each other and smiled. The Siberian had really meant it when he had used the 'me' in place of 'us' during their first meeting!

∽

Keira had tried every possible way to squirm forward. There was no way she could move further! She felt around and figured that she had reached the end of this uphill rafter and it was connected to another perpendicular rafter, a matching square shape. She realized that the whole array of rafters on the four sides of the tent had to be connected to this central rectangular truss. The roof had a small flat plateau atop the four slanting sides. But it was impossible to manoeuvre a human body within the limited space, especially if it belonged to a well-endowed woman.

Oh, bloody hell! Holding on to the bars with her hands and toes, she backed down slightly so her body wouldn't rest on the cloth below. And then, she gazed at her body with a heavy sigh. *It's the only way if you don't want to be caught. Gotta do it. Now!*

She despised the transition every time she had to do it! It reminded her how tough the decision to get operated on had been. But she had made her choice! A transformation that had given her exceptional manoeuvrability and an edge in her profession.

Precariously balancing herself against two bars, she pulled out a plastic bag from a hidden inside pocket of her jeans and held it between her teeth. Her palm then crept up to her forehead and she dug her fingers deep into her roots, pulling her hair back. Off came the auburn wig, revealing a scalp of pointy brown hair. She placed the wig inside the bag. She slipped underneath her shirt and disengaged the nipple-shaped plugs over the pair of skin-coloured pneumatic breasts. The polymer sagged down to a barely discernible layer. Arranging the plugs inside the bag, she zipped it up and slid the packet back into the hidden pocket.

The man was climbing up again, all the while waiting for the torchlight to arrive, with which he would scour the surroundings outside the tent from the vantage point.

Wasting not a second more, she flexed herself as far as she could and finally managed to squeeze her way through the grid. She climbed back down the adjacent rafter truss when she found a joint wide enough to allow her sufficient wiggle room to pass through to the other side. She paused as a thought struck her. All the rafter trusses would have the same symmetry! If she moved horizontally across the parallel rafters at this point, she could reach the other end through these wide joints. The only problem was that the rafters were about ten feet apart, held with only one supporting pipe in between.

She resumed her slow journey towards the other end of the tent, using sheer muscle strength to keep hanging on. She tried to stay parallel to the canvas roof throughout, lest the bump give away her position to someone down below.

Thankfully, the darkness hadn't allowed the guard to spot her yet. In fact, it was so dark and dusty that breathing was becoming a challenge, pushing her endurance to its limits. Out of the blue, she sensed a heavy insect climbing up her bare neck. Unusually heavy! It crossed her chin and parked itself over her lips and nose. She'd never seen a spider so up close. It was a five-inch-long camel spider, the infamous carnivore of the deserts. The predator rubbed its hairy legs on her nose, preparing to pulp it with its jaws and digestive fluids. *Ugh! Get off!* Keira felt a shiver run down her spine.

'*Yasharmouta!*'

An abrupt holler rattled her, her fingers tightening around the pipes just in time so she wouldn't fall.

The man had evidently got hold of a torch now, keen to finish his inspection due to the storm outside. A click later, the beam of yellow light pierced the darkness. It started spanning the space from one side, moving towards her. She flung the spider aside and wriggling out of the rafter, she crawled ahead in desperation. She slid through the two last rafter joints before flexing her body in a right angle to crossover to the adjacent side of the trapezium-shaped roof. The reflection of light from the torch hit her face, but she was lying in a blind spot, tucked into the bottom of the slope on the other side.

'The bitch is not here,' he said as he climbed down, shouting out to his mates. 'Must have clambered out of the roof and escaped.'

'A fricking narrow escape!' She exhaled.

She had survived this one but she couldn't stay here much longer––her outline would be a dead giveaway.

Falling flat on her stomach, she cut a fresh slit in the fabric below. She heaved a sigh of relief. It was a separate enclosure, similar to the room she'd been in, but vacant. A peep through another slit made in the roof revealed guards running away from the tent in all directions—probably in search of her, their chief's latest fancy.

Field clear! Keira jumped down into the empty room.

Retrieving the bag tucked inside the hidden pocket, she plucked the wig and adjusted it back on in less than a few seconds. *Perfect.* She knew how to do this from years of practice. Fishing out the two plugs, she inflated the polymer breasts fixed to her chest, and gave herself a once-over.

Back to normal!

She slid the bag into her pocket and grabbed a large spare keffiyeh neck scarf lying on a table. Wrapping it around her head and face, she dashed out of the main tent. Soon, she was in a blind spot behind a second smaller tent in the distance, trying to recall the name Tareq had called the chief by.

∽

Armed with AK-47s and dressed in the dead guards' costumes, it wasn't too difficult for the trio to make their way out of the underground prison cells. The unsuspecting guards posted outside had not the slightest chance. Only their leader was spared and held captive to show them the way. Hiding the dead bodies in the farthest cell, they seized the militants' truck parked outside.

Concerned for Keira's safety, their first destination was the chief's tent, but it was deserted. The captive militant then guided them towards the tent where Tareq and his men had been detained.

Eight. Olaf counted the number of guards at the tent entrance from the roof of the moving truck he was lying flat on.

In eight successive shots, he took them down, only seconds apart—the constant clatter of machine guns and other artillery from the training grounds drowning out possible noise of his pistol. With the camp inmates none the wiser, Olaf reserved his final shot for the guard they'd taken captive before jumping off the truck roof.

'Wow!' Kabir exclaimed as Olaf struggled awkwardly to pull out food lodged in his molars. 'Bulls eye! All eight, all on the forehead, and from a moving truck! You should be winning Olympics gold medals for your country.'

'I do,' he replied casually, relieved at having excavated the rogue particle that had been bothering him. He cleaned his hand against the bark of a tree and continued, 'That's what I do. Google "Olaf Adler" when you go back. Two gold medals in Tokyo in 2021, but that happens just once in four years. And the rest of the time—I practice!' He pointed at the bodies.

'Earth shattering!' Kabir mumbled. The Germans were a notch above the rest of the world in human resource management.

'But what did you just do?' Kabir walked up to the tree where Olaf had been rubbing his hand and pulled out a small granule; it was the size of a mustard grain. He held it up between his thumb and index finger at eye level, inspecting it closely. 'What's this?'

'A self-adhering wireless Nano-camera.' Olaf winked. 'Never hurts to be prepared. We will know as soon as they get here!'

'Are you kidding me?' Kabir inspected it closely with a fresh wave of intrigue. 'And where's the display device? Where do you see the output?'

'An eight-channel eyelid-controlled nano-film. It's embedded in my left eye.' Olaf grinned.

'Go on... I'm listening.'

'My eyeball acts like the mouse, and flapping my eyelid twice selects the menu option. I have seven such nano-cameras securely lodged in my molars. And they have a powerful GPS tracker too, which I can access on zitis.com/olaf220641...'

Kabir stood still in disbelief. The Protettori had really roped in technical X-men!

'You better use these assets prudently,' he murmured, still trying to absorb what he'd just heard, 'and save a couple for me.' He had something playing in his mind already.

In no time, Tareq and the rest of his men were hustled out of the guest tent. The entire group were now dressed in militant combats. Olaf and Vladimir—the two white men—sat in the back seat with their faces concealed, while Tareq took the wheel. In an encampment of thousands, where many inmates dressed in combats and most were strangers to one another, the taskforce raised not a single suspicious brow as they drove on.

Spotting a group of men pass by, Tareq slowed the vehicle down for a chat to learn about the ongoing symposium at the aviation centre and of the Murshid's arrival. The man looked at his watch. 'The Murshid's talk has just started. It should last about forty to forty-five minutes.'

'Thank you.'

They drove up to the centre, a white sophisticated structure standing tall amid the rustic camp. Having parked the truck a hundred yards away, they decided to approach the building on foot, with Tareq taking the lead. The enclosure was heavily guarded with ten-foot-high electrified barbed wire fencing, with guards stationed every twenty yards. Their plan was to slip in somehow and take the Murshid at gunpoint, thus getting an easy exit too.

Kabir assessed their means of entry. Members were trickling into the building; each one flashing an ID-card before he was let in. 'Photo-bio IDs!' he exclaimed in distress.

'There's no way that we're getting in through the main entry or through the fence!' hissed Olaf. 'And the talk has already started.'

Moreover, someone was bound to spot the dead guards and raise an alarm very soon.

'We have about fifteen minutes at most!' Olaf looked towards Kabir, expecting some quick briefing, but his eyes were equally blank.

22

Trouble In the Mediterranean

Mokhtar reached Siracusa to commence Operation Trident on board a private oil ship, carrying crude black oil, accompanied by thirty-five of his best men. The oil had been billed by an Egyptian refinery to an Italian mill, which rejected it upon inspection. The refinery challenged the judgement of the buyers' inspectors and hence the samples were sent for third-party verification to a private lab. The report would take several weeks to come. So the ship remained docked.

This time was to be utilized in planting the treasure, securely locked in four dozen leather-bound trunks that would sink to the bottom of the oil tanks containing the black viscous oil, making them completely untraceable. And so, a trunk was brought in each night and lowered into one of the tanks. This was to be done discreetly while everyone on board was asleep.

Mokhtar took advantage of the hiatus to go around Siracusa, a centre of rich early European civilization and history. After a few days, he moved inland and travelled north—visiting Sicily, Naples, Rome and Florence. He was awestruck by the beauty and elegance of Italy's history and monuments.

He also had an opportunity to cross borders into Switzerland. The climate and landscapes were like nothing they had ever seen before. The Nazi administration had issued him a letter of authority making his movement easy through Italy, which was a part of the Axis powers. They even arranged for an armoured truck to make his travel smooth and safe. The Swiss, too, though neutral in the war, couldn't disregard the Nazis.

He returned to base as soon as the rejection report from the independent lab arrived. The samples had officially "failed" the verification tests—a fabricated failure—and now the consignment would have to be taken back to Alexandria. It was another thing that the consignment was worth thousands of times more now than its face value. On the last day, one of the leather trunks was brought on board during daylight. The crew was told it was a gift from European Muslim supporters of the society.

Mokhtar's fighters, disguised as refinery officers, were on high alert to protect the treasure round the clock. To avoid rough seas, they took a rather long route, encircling the Ionian Sea, staying within a few kilometres from the shores. They sailed from Siracusa to Malta, southwards to Tripoli and then, east towards Benghazi. Mokhtar had three of the best celestial navigation scientists on board, tracing the exact position of the ship on the map.

The weather had been unusually calm under the partially-lit skies when they had sailed a few hundred nautical miles east of Benghazi. It was well past midnight. They would reach Alexandria by the next afternoon. Mokhtar was sitting in the captain's cabin, sipping on a cup of coffee when he sensed some unusual movement.

He glanced in the telescope and shook his head in disbelief. Three ships were moving towards them, in a wedge formation. A British man-of-war was in the lead, followed by two frigates on either side. These ships were old—replete with masts, mizzen and gun ports. They were no longer used in commercial or defence navigation! Then, he saw the black flags fluttering atop the main mast and it left little doubt in his mind.

'Bastards!' he swore under his breath and turned to the captain. 'Take a look at this… impossible!'

The captain glared at the approaching ships for a while

before finally announcing, 'Sea pirates! Almost extinct in the Mediterranean—thanks to the strong navies of France, Spain and Italy. But remember, we are in Libyan waters. What happens here, stays here. Our ship will disappear and no one will know what happened to us. For all I know, they could be the Libyan private army, the Italian mafia, Turkish vagabonds, or true sea pirates. It could be anyone.' He panicked. 'Anyone who's gotten scent of what we have on board.'

'Can we turn around and out speed them?'

'And flee where? With a trunk full of gold on board?' the captain kneaded his temple. 'Our only safe shores are those of our own country, that too the unguarded ones.'

They thought for a moment.

'They won't risk cannonade.' Mokhtar was confident of his advantage on that front. 'This ship is a powder keg! They wouldn't want the gold melting to irrecoverable splatters.'

'But pirates are masters of siege. They will try to take control through one-to-one combat.'

'How much time do we have?'

'Approximately twenty minutes.'

Mokhtar rushed inside. In one room, the astro-navigators were busy measuring angles and plotting the ship's position to precise quarters. He studied the map. The dotted line seemed well placed. A table to its right contained coordinates for each minute.

'Tuck away the map in one of these thick books, and within the next ten minutes be off to your sleeping stations,' he instructed their leader, a bearded scientist, before dashing off towards the engineering station.

In the room, Mokhtar pushed a corner of the wall. Unlocking a hidden panel that displayed forty red buttons, he pressed them in quick succession, activating the ejectors. Swiftly, the trapdoors dropped the trunks into a hidden inclined channel that led to an ejector door. The tanks had been specially designed to minimize oil leakage. Once the trunks were expelled, no one would know where the treasure lay in the infinite expanse of the ocean bed.

Back in the captain's cabin, he pressed the alarm button. The lights were switched off and the fighters geared up, taking their positions, ready for a gory fight. Mokhtar looked into the telescope. The ships were very close. '*Bloody Italians!*' Their secret must have been compromised at some stage, most probably at the docks. Everything had progressed as per plan until now, but he would need to make it out of the impending clash alive, for the treasure to be retrievable.

'One-on-one combat it shall be…let's show them hell!'

His fighters broke fire. The pirate ships were less than a kilometre away and well within the range of their German Karabiner 98K rifles. The telescopic sights on their guns afforded them a blurry view of the activities on the enemy ships. Strangely, there was none, and no counter-fire occurred either.

The pirates obviously intended to get as close as possible first. They wanted to take over, not take down!

The pirates in this part of the ocean, if any, generally used much smaller ships than the man-of-war or the frigate, making them vulnerable to fusillade from the high decks of the cargo ships. Their modus operandi was to close in discreetly, climb their way up the hull and seize control. Mokhtar's team was well equipped to counter such attacks. But their current situation was unexpected. They were facing three large ships simultaneously. He wished he had cannons or bomber helicopters, but this was a cargo ship and the society didn't have access to such weaponry, not yet.

'Go on,' he said to his deputy. He had to try the last resort. 'Not one of them should make it on board alive… wait… wait… what is that?' He spotted a big round boulder heading towards the captain's cabin.

'Move!' he yelled.

The men barely had a second to jump out of its trajectory

as it came smashing in through the glass, shattering the wooden deckhouse.

The volley of boulders that followed sent the entire crew scurrying in panic, rushing to the lower decks and taking refuge behind the steel structures. The barrage of rocks left huge dents in the deck and the superstructure, immediately killing the few who could not flee in time.

Mokhtar stood at the subsurface deck, thinking long and hard. He had had his counter-attack planned, but the salvo of rocks had barely given him any scope to react. He sighed and hoped his next move would be injurious enough to shatter the enemy's morale.

∽

Adel was lost deep in thought, wondering how time changed people. His meek companion from childhood had turned into a *monster*. So much so that after Adel's promotion to the intelligence wing of the Royal Army, he had been assigned with the sole task of making sure his ex-playmate couldn't continue with his vicious activities. The game of hide-and-seek they used to play had become a bizarre reality.

He clearly remembered a childhood incident that had happened in the park where they used to stroll about in the evenings. It was a beautiful flower garden and the two boys loved the blend of fragrances as well as the bright colours. The children from a building opposite the park used to gather in their balcony to see Mokhtar's crooked walk. As he walked beside Adel on the flower-lined path, he would dog-leg, stumble or miss a step, making his clumsy walk the subject of ridicule amongst the kids. They would jeer at him and shout out teasing remarks. But he would persist with his ways. One day, they decided to escalate their fun and stopped him in his path, standing in a row.

'We love the way you walk,' the burliest of the lot mocked. 'Where did you learn it?' The group broke into laughter.

Mokhtar was not bothered, and continued to stare down as he walked.

The boys took a few steps back so that they could follow his teetering gait, cackling as they did so. This went on till one of them reached out and tripped Mokhtar, making him fall face down. Adel stepped forward and caught the burly boy by his collar.

'Why does your friend walk like that?' the boy guffawed, unruffled. 'Such a jerk!'

Mokhtar sprang to his feet and separated the two. 'I'll show you why!' he said.

He bent down and placed one of his hands tenderly on the mud below, palm down.

'What's your friend trying to do?' The fat boy groaned impatiently after almost a minute had passed.

Just then Mokhtar got up and brought his hand up close, right between their faces. 'Look at these little things! I can't just go squishing them.'

The boys gaped in amazement at the little red ants trailing across the mound of his downturned hand. On the ground, hundreds of ants meandered in the dust, barely visible to an uncaring eye.

'So much for the once-sensitive Mokhtar!' Adel mused, smirking, as he came back from his thoughts. Here was his friend now, killing relatives and strangers alike in cold blood.

'I will stand in your way, Mokhtar!' Adel swore as he tucked his service pistol into his belt. From afar, he had observed the suspicious movement of three ships edging abnormally close to an oil freight. 'Sir,' he radioed the admiral's office, 'we'll need reinforcement—ships full of it!'

∽

The thumping of hundreds of footsteps above told Mokhtar the pirates had landed on the deck. In a few minutes they would find the manholes leading to the sub-decks.

'Stay alert and wait for my signal,' he whispered, commanding his snipers before rushing to grab the public address system.

'Welcome on board!' his announcement rang aloud. 'You shall not rob this ship and get away alive. Our death may be certain, but we will take you down with us. One misfire and the oil will blow up like a bomb.'

He paused, listening for movement.

'I want to talk to your leader,' he added.

He then hastened up the winding staircase that led to a hidden viewing deck. *Around a hundred of them.*

The pirates had stopped fifty metres away from the superstructure. Slowly, a tall man tore through the crowd and stepped forward. Mokhtar then walked out of the hidden deck and confronted him. 'What is it that you want?' he asked.

'All that you have.' The man's scarred face contorted into a wicked smile.

'As I said, I have nothing except the oil. What is this crude oil worth to you?' Mokhtar frowned. 'Why sacrifice your lives for nothing? We are fidayeens. We do it for Allah, and will happily sacrifice our lives on that path. You can rob many more ships if you stay alive. Go back!'

The corsair knew his opponent was playing mind games. 'There are another three hundred men on our ships. Even if you drown this ship, the rest of my men will go after the gold and retrieve it. Give us those black trunks and we will return.'

'Gold? There are no black trunks. There never were!'

'I don't think he gets it. Let's take over!' the leader said, casting a wry glance back at his pirates.

Booooom!

A loud explosion suddenly rocked the seas behind them. The man-of-war had split in two—right through its centre, both pieces sinking. The shock waves jolted their oil ship, causing everyone on board to stagger. Before they could recover, two more explosions followed.

Boooooom!

Boooooom!

The frigates were sinking too—bow, mast and stern. There had been no visible impingement. It was as if the ships had simply imploded from within, leaving the pirates dumbstruck.

They had no idea as to what had just hit them.

'Now, put your guns down, will you?' Mokhtar said. 'Your back-up is gone.'

The pirates complied, in unexpected awe of their adversary.

Mokhtar closed in on their captain. 'I warned you, didn't I?'

'What did you do to our ships?' The bandit was trembling. 'I haven't seen anything like this in all my years!'

'I bet you haven't. We didn't just load the gold from Siracusa, but also these latest incendiaries being used by the Italians in the world war—the human torpedoes. We used three units of the Italian Maiale, deadly human torpedoes, each propelled by two of our fighters. Something like a submarine scooter carrying a missile! They steered the torpedo at slow speed to your ships, used the detachable warhead as a limpet mine and then rode away. Zero casualties on our side. And zero survivors on yours!' Mokhtar's smile chilled the air.

Without warning, his fighters opened fire from atop the roof deck, taking their cue.

The killing machine that he had trained himself to become, Mokhtar unleashed himself upon the pirates.

From the corner of his eye, far in the distance, he could see some steamers heading towards them.

Coast guards from Mersa Matruh port!

'Search the ship, every corner of it!' Adel commanded his men. There were around twelve of them. They had intercepted the oil ship with their steamer. Mokhtar's men began to move, but he signalled for them to stay put.

'Where's the gold?' Adel had his gun aimed between Mokhtar's brows in a face-off between the two. The sight of corpses strewn across the deck was nauseating. How could one man cause so much devastation?

'What gold?' Mokhtar shrugged impassively.

'The gold for which you killed these people and sunk their ships. I have concrete information.' Adel glanced around. 'This is the real face of your society. Terror-mongers!'

'These men were no saints. They were hijackers. Looting and kidnapping is their business. They came after the oil and the crew. Fortunately, we had our own small private army on board,' Mokhtar said. He had to handle this gently. The oil ship belonged to a private company that supported the society. Direct confrontation with the government had been proscribed by Ghassan.

'Didn't I tell you I would come to get you?' Adel hissed. 'A bunch of smugglers, that's all you are! You can't go around throwing dust in everyone's eyes.'

'It's nothing but your imagination.'

Adel's men were coming out, one after the other, each empty-handed. The searches had repeatedly run into dead ends. Vexed, Adel turned around and finally decided to go in himself.

There has to be a mistake! Maybe the oil tanks were too large to be searched properly. He would seize the ship and hand it over to the Royal Navy for a proper scan, if it came to it. However, there was definitely something about Mokhtar's belligerence that didn't sit right with him. He couldn't be so laid-back, not with all that gold on board. *We're missing something here! But how the hell do I figure it out?* He was tying himself in knots till he remembered an ever-so-useful tool from his police training days. *The weak link!*

'Line up the crew,' Adel ordered. 'If no one talks, my gun speaks!'

He strutted from man to man, closely observing their body language and reading their faces. Until he decided to stop by an older man with a long beard. The crew member seemed nervous, his eyes and lips twitching.

'What is it?' he pressed his gun to the man's temple.

∽

Soon enough, Adel and his men were raking the astro-navigator's cabin, slowly taking it apart. They found the map tucked away in a thick old manuscript, with rather large-sized parched pages.

Mokhtar held his breath as Adel flipped through the tattered pages till he discovered the large folded papyrus kept inside it.

Strange place to hide such an important document! Adel cast the parchment aside and studied the map curiously.

The dotted line had been painstakingly plotted, all the way from Siracusa to somewhere near their current position. Why would Mokhtar need such a map?

Unless. His eyes glossed over it. *Unless he plans to return along the same route ...why would he want to do that ... unless...?*

He could feel it—he was getting close!

'Where is his room?' Adel asked his deputy, pointing towards Mokhtar.

The search did not yield any results beyond clothes, armaments, pictures, nuts and a scrapbook containing several familiar drawings. He flipped through some of the pages and shut it. A strange feeling, something like pain, passed through Adel. The pyramid robbers, the murder at the mangrove, and so many more. Mokhtar had given curious titles to his drawings. These sketches had been the only vent to his emotions. And they probably were, to this day. Struck by a pang of painful nostalgia, Adel set the book aside. Apparently, he still cared for Mokhtar, somewhere deep within his heart.

Doesn't matter... He walked out of the room in a daze. He wasn't going to let that stop him from killing the monster.

A few steps and something suddenly dawned upon him. Rushing back in, he picked up the scrapbook and started turning the pages frantically until his fingers stopped at one of the drawings. It was titled 'The Trident Manoeuvre'.

In the centre was a man shaking hands with a military officer. There were trunks full of treasure lined up behind the officer. They were standing at a seashore, a ship docked behind them. To their right, a few men carried this treasure to the ship while a smaller group were towing missiles with scooter handles attached to their front. *The Italian Maiale!* Adel recognized the weapons instantly. These deadly human torpedoes had caused much damage to British ships recently. *Oh, so that's what hit the pirate ships!*

The symbolism was clear, but where was the treasure then? *What am I not seeing? Come on... come on...* He inspected the sketch again, and then he noticed a slight gap in the stern. It might have easily gone unnoticed as a missed pencil stroke, but for the small compartment drawn behind it. It was an inane possibility, but the only one he could figure out. The clues flooded in quick succession from that point on. One of his men reported having spotted oil floating a few nautical miles to their west. Another returned with news about the trap doors beneath the tanks opening into an ejection channel. The ingenuity of Mokhtar's plan was now sinking in. The papyrus in his hand was a treasure map—a treasure that lay deep in the ocean near the point the navigator had stopped plotting. How deep was the ocean at that point? How much of its area would have to be raked? These were things that would take considerable time and resources to unravel. But the key was presently in his hands.

The truth shone clear on his face! Why Mokhtar had named this Operation Trident was also clear now. Mokhtar had made three dents, starting with hiding the gold at the bottom of the oil tanks, then intentionally sabotaging the treasure at a convenient location and finally, the torpedoes, his infallible defence. *Brilliant!*

∽

Mokhtar pursed his lips anxiously as Adel and his team unfolded his plan, layer by layer. Their reinforcement had arrived, the ships were closing in. Adel walked up to Mokhtar, unsure of what he would do with him.

'Let's play a game.' He gestured to his pocket. 'Do you have a coin?'

Mokhtar just stood there, stock-still.

Adel dipped a hand into the young man's pocket and dug out a coin. It had an eagle embossed on one side and an angel on the other.

'Hmm... carrying gold coins in your pockets like the rest of us carry nickels! No less a pirate! Well, then. Eagle, you win, and angel, I do.'

He tossed the coin. It hit the iron surface, tinkling and chiming in the pin-drop silence till it lay dead.

The eagle!

'You are lucky! I'll let you go after you provide some statements at the customs' office,' Adel dropped the coin back into Mokhtar's pocket. 'But remember, this is your last chance to make a fresh start. The treasure is state property now. Dare venture near it and we'll prosecute you. You'll get life imprisonment, or even death!'

And now, Adel Kamaal was going to ensure the entire operation remained classified. The bodies would have to be gotten rid of, and every shred of evidence of the massacre destroyed. But he would do what he had to. He didn't want court cases. He didn't want the public accolades. If the treasure became public knowledge, it would never reach its rightful owner—the state.

'And Mokhtar,' he concluded, 'it will be in your best interest to remain silent.'

Mokhtar's head hung low. He just nodded in acquiescence.

23

Murshid: the Conjurer

The agents could see the imposing structure in the distance—the aviation centre. The Murshid was inside it, hosting an interactive session with the volunteers. He would be leaving shortly. Since nothing convincing had come from their brainstorming session, Kabir decided to take the plunge. He told them to park the truck around a hundred yards away and decided to walk to the aviation centre with Tareq.

Just opposite the aviation centre and to their left, they noticed a tent with an unusual bustle. People were moving in and out of it. A canteen! There were several thousand inmates at the camp and few recognized each other because of the constant flux. And then there were visitors and new admissions. That's how the agents and their troop had made it so far. Desperate to stumble across some method to get inside the aviation centre, they took a table for two in the canteen. A waiter brought them tea and cookies without them having to ask for it.

'Free food, comfortable amenities, some pocket money and a sense of purpose, that's what attracts unemployed youth towards these camps,' Tareq explained.

Kabir tried to look around, hoping something useful would stand out. Each minute the tension was mounting. *Focus! Can't give up now. There has to be a way.* He turned on his aural faculty, processing the mixed cacophony of boisterous voices, all Arabic gibberish. He was separating each strand in search of that useful bit.

Suddenly, he became very still. He had registered a string of perturbed voices, some distance behind his back, and his attention was now glued to there. A rather heated conversation was happening to his southwest. He gestured Tareq to pay attention. Tareq caught on and told him that apparently a senior jihadi officer was seated with a young Chinese man.

The young man spoke with a heavy Cantonese accent, 'What can I do? I tly the entile system just an howal befole and it wolk pelfectly. I have hundleds of hacked ploglams wolking to run the simulation. That's a lot you get for the peanuts you pay me, Mr Saidy.' The first few words were unintelligible, but Kabir soon figured out the Chinese lallation speech defect.

'Goddamn it, Cheng!' The officer banged his hand upon the table. 'I can't believe it. Today of all days! Your software had to crash *today!*'

'I'm sollee. Evely cog in the wheel is impoltent,' Cheng said patiently, 'Maybe one of the tiny codes expiled and needs updating. I just need ten minutes. I'll tlace the bug, hack into the host site and get the updated velsion. The show will go on, don't wallee.'

There was a loud clap and the Chinese man groaned. The officer had slapped him. Hard.

'Don't wallee...Yusuf will only cut your head off!' he mocked. 'This is not that video game that you keep playing all the time, damn it. There's no second and third life here. So get your ass moving son, or we will both be dead.' He looked at his watch. 'The Murshid's talk has already started and will last around thirty more minutes. After that, they will move to the simulator to check on the trainees. If something goes wrong in front of him, we both go to the gallows. Right at the centre of the camp.'

Kabir watched them rush out in a huff, get into a jeep and drive straight through the aviation centre entrance. He saw the officer's hand come out and flash an I-card.

'Let's go!' Kabir tried not to let the urgency show in his

movement lest it attract unwanted attention.

'What is it?' Olaf said as he saw the grin on Kabir's face.

Kabir quickly explained his strategy to Tareq and Olaf. Olaf changed back into his t-shirt. The locals from Tareq's team were told to abandon the stolen truck and drive back out of the camp in the same school bus they had arrived in. Since there was regular movement of inmates in and out of the camp, they would not be questioned. *Militants from another smaller group returning after selling their hostages!* They were to reach a specific location, a few kilometres past the main gate in the desert, and wait for the agents there.

'Bruce was right! Who gave you the authority to decide this?' Vladimir objected. 'I will not go back!'

'The clock is ticking...we need you outside, Vladimir,' Kabir said, placing a hand on his shoulder and looking him in the eye. 'Trust me! You won't regret this.' Kabir extended his open palm towards Olaf. Olaf placed a barely visible small crystal on it—the nano camera. Kabir placed the self-adhering grain on the front of Vladimir's flat cap and smiled. 'Keep the cap on at all times, Comrade.'

They jogged towards the entrance, Tareq and Kabir literally pushing an uncomfortable Olaf at gunpoint. When they were a few yards from the main entrance, within earshot of the guards there, Olaf suddenly turned around and pushed Tareq back. 'Why are you prodding me with that gun. What can I do? I tried the entire system just an hour back. It was working perfectly. I have hundreds of hacked software working in unison to run the simulation. That's a lot I give you for the peanuts you pay me.'

'Goddamn it, Olaf!' Tareq kicked the dust. 'I can't believe it. Today of all days! Your software had to crash today!' He said the last part in Arabic to make sure the guards understood.

'Every cog in the wheel is important,' Olaf said. 'Maybe one of those tiny codes expired and needs an updated version. I'll just need ten minutes. I'll trace the bug, hack into the host site and get the updated version. The show will go on, don't worry.'

Tareq walked up to him and slapped him across the face. Olaf glared at him. This had not been decided. He saw the remorse in Tareq's eyes, but it was not sufficient to stop him from losing control. Kabir tried to stop him, but he punched Tareq in the nose. Blood trickled down immediately. Tareq held his nose in pain as two guards posted at the gate rushed to his aid. They pointed their guns at Olaf's head, waiting for their colleague's command. Kabir too stood there, pointing the gun at Olaf. He could see his plan falling apart. Why did Tareq have to overact? Slapping an agent! He had only told him to be meticulous while repeating the canteen scene.

Tareq pushed the militants back, improvising.

'We can't, he is too important,' he said in Arabic. He signalled for the guards to go back to their post.

He moved towards Olaf and holding up his gun again said, 'Get your ass moving, man, or Yusuf will kill us both.' Turning to Kabir he said in Arabic, 'Mr Saidy has already reached the site with the Chinese boy and he must be waiting for us!' He looked at his watch. 'The Murshid's talk started thirty minutes back and will last twenty more minutes. If something goes wrong in front of him, all three of us go to the gallows. Right at the centre of the camp.'

'Okay, stop nudging me with that gun of yours!' Olaf shook the muzzle off, acting like an eccentric hacker. Kabir kept mumbling some chants in Arabic he had memorized earlier, trying to appear tense.

They moved towards the entrance.

'We need to get to the server room, it's very urgent. This is Olaf, our backup hacking expert,' Tareq told a senior guard in Arabic. 'Mr Saidy told me to fetch him. SOS.'

'I-card please!' The guard demanded. He seemed to have some air of what was happening, but didn't completely understand the conversation they had just had. *Unfortunate!* The language barrier had dampened the impact of their perfectly enacted skit.

'We were having dinner when we got the message, there was no time. We found this guy high on marijuana, dozing off inside the ambulance,' Tareq added.

'Sorry!' the guard replied, indifferent.

'Don't you understand, every second you make us wait here, you put the whole project in jeopardy. I'll make sure you come to the derrick with us,' Tareq snorted, putting up a brave front.

'Let me talk to Mr Saidy.' The guard brought out his walkie-talkie.

Their game was over. Kabir looked around quickly. Around ten guards stood alert following the heated discussion. Their chances of being taken to the gibbet had just escalated. If only somebody had known English around here, their plan wouldn't have failed.

'Let them go!' An officer walked up to them. 'It seems the software is down and we don't want any hold-ups.'

'You Indian?' He held out his hand to Kabir.

'No Pakistani. I'm Farhan.' Kabir shook his hand.

'Wow! Me too, Akram…' He smiled and patted him on the back. 'Now rush.' He sent one of his boys with them.

'Nice,' Olaf muttered as they walked through the entrance of the main building, their RPK light machine guns deposited. 'But how will we ever make it to the Murshid. Yusuf will recognize us as soon as he sees our faces.' The guard's impassive face attested to the fact that he didn't understand a word of English. He accepted their chatter. Some makeup conversation was apt after the scuffle.

'He will definitely recognize me,' Tareq said. 'But I am not sure about you and Kabir. He only saw you once.'

They had walked maybe a hundred-odd yards straight from the entrance, when they reached the auditorium complex gates, flanked by armed security, both from the Al Sharia as well as the Murshid's private security, dressed in navy blue uniforms.

'Where are you taking us?' Tareq asked the guard in Arabic. 'We need to go to the server room.'

'The servers are located inside the main auditorium just behind the stage,' the guard replied.

'So? There must be a back door? A side alley or something leading to it? Or do we just walk through the auditorium, disrupting their proceedings?' Tareq hissed.

'See anything on the cams yet?' Kabir looked at Olaf. Olaf shook his head in the negative.

He was thinking hard. The moment they entered the auditorium, their position would be very vulnerable. It seemed improbable that Yusuf would not recognize the faces of his prized hostages, even though he had had only a fleeting look at them this afternoon.

'I will stay outside. Yusuf will not appreciate too many people,' Tareq told the guard.

As the guard opened the heavy soundproof door of the auditorium, they saw the Murshid standing at a podium, addressing the fidayeens. Kabir realized how much more imposing he looked compared to the image Victor had shown them. Yusuf was at the back, sitting behind a table kept on the stage. The door opened right onto the wide central alley sloping down to the stage. The hall was well lit with a large chandelier in the centre and numerous small ones placed symmetrically along the roof. A green carpet ran wall to wall and the fidayeens, the hundred selected ones, sat on velvet chairs placed in the usual stepped formation on either side of the central alley.

'The laurels of martyrdom, my friends,' the Murshid was saying in Arabic, 'are bestowed on the ones who slay or are slain in the path of Allah. Each one of you, inshallah, shall slay a thousand kafirs, turning their own weapons against them. Their drones kill our innocent women and children, and now, the time has come for them to pay the price!' Kabir couldn't understand a word, but the fidayeens seemed to be glued in attention. Dressed in white thwabs, they nodded their heads in agreement as he spoke. It struck Kabir that unlike the usual fiery orators, there was no aggression in the Murshid's voice. His soothing tone caused the magical effect Victor had talked about.

The guard escorted them down the central alley and then turned right, opposite to the direction in which the podium was placed. The steps next to the stage led to the server room, located just behind it.

Kabir could feel the weight of Yusuf's gaze on them as they headed towards the server room, his guts twisting in anticipation. He noticed a security guard rushing towards the stage. He was stopped by the Murshid's security and was trying to fervently explain something to them. Kabir could feel the heat building. They would have to act. Fast.

'Stop!' a voice suddenly thundered at them.

He looked up to see Yusuf standing up on the stage. He took steady steps, rushing towards them. 'Aren't you two the Red Cross volunteers Tareq brought to me a while ago? How did you get in here?' Yusuf was hollering in Arabic.

Abu Bakr paused his speech, staring in their direction.

Think of something... think of something... Kabir's thoughts were whirling, until they abruptly landed on a safety net.

'How's your red Jaguar, Uncle Neel?' Kabir moved out of Yusuf's path.

Olaf took the cue and intercepted the old cleric. And to buy time, began offering explanations to Yusuf in a language he didn't understand.

The security personnel restrained Kabir midway. However, Abu Bakr signalled to them to release him. No one knew about his Jaguar. And no one knew his pseudonym—'Neel'. Not even his security. None except those who had personally served him at his house in Cairo. So who was this young man? And how did this man know these private details? 'Go on...'

'Farhan...your driver, Jamil's son?' Kabir announced as he moved closer to the man, his eyes rife with emotion, right hand placed delicately over his heart as a sign of respect.

'Jamil's son...?'

Kabir had needed an excuse to flummox Abu Bakr for a second, and it had worked. Yusuf was still yelling when he immediately pulled out the padded mini pistol that had been securely assembled and tucked around his hips. In a flash, he swung his body behind Abu, his left arm strangling his neck and right hand holding the pistol right to his temple.

The Murshid felt the pressure building at the back of his head. 'Whoever you are, you have no idea what you're doing!'

'Freeze. Everyone!' Kabir brandished his pistol, warning Abu's bodyguards to move back. One of them tried to edge in, but he pressed the pistol so hard against Abu's temple that it made Abu cringe in pain. The security had to back off briefly.

Kabir looked at Olaf. And winked. That was the signal!

Olaf instantly flapped his eyelids, navigating through the nano-camera channels until he had a clear view of the scenes outside the hall. *Nothing.* He shook his head in the negative. Everything seemed to be normal. *No movement whatsoever! Wait a sec... wh... what is that?* He gawked at his camera all of a sudden, unable to believe the events unfolding outside.

Kabir got his cue from the surprise that'd descended on Olaf's face.

'This is a NATO attack,' he leaned over and announced on the mic. 'Our tanks have arrived and the air strikes will follow. The Murshid will not get out of here alive. Nor will you... unless you vacate the aviation centre immediately.'

Olaf's head was still reeling from disbelief, when the sound of deafening explosions outside validated Kabir's announcement. Agent Rathore had proven himself a worthy captain so far, his uncanny ability to come up with instantaneous plans had gotten them here after all.

And soon enough, the detonations sounded in rapid succession, apparently heading their way. 'Damn, man… this is impressive… perfect timing!' he acknowledged the taskforce captain with a nod.

Meanwhile, all hell broke loose in the auditorium as the fidayeens, militants and staff from the Al Sharia scrambled to vacate the aviation centre. Yusuf too was nowhere in sight. Four men from the Murshid's personal security were the only ones who held their ground. Stripping them of their arms, Olaf aimed an AK-47 at Abu Bakr, securing Kabir's position.

'One billion US dollars cash!' the Murshid shouted out loud. 'If you get me out of here alive, this amount will be transferred to your account, no questions asked.'

'What do you say?' Kabir asked Olaf. However, Olaf was far too busy following the spectacle unfolding outdoors. The output from the nano-camera on Vladimir's cap showed the muzzle of a tank spewing fire at the training tents and enclosures. The news about the NATO attack had travelled across the camp. Militants who did not succumb to the detonations fled instead of resisting the attack. They knew there would be no escape from the air strikes which would soon follow.

'One million? Before I answer that, Kabir, will you tell me what's going on here?'

'It's Bruce,' Kabir chipped in, 'driving the Wiesel. Vladimir is covering him from a transparent bulletproof cubicle with a bazooka and a machine gun.'

'Oh!' The German agent arched his brows. 'So you lied to me?'

'No.' Kabir winked. 'I did tell you he was meant for bigger and better stuff.'

Olaf smiled, working out the rest in no time. When Kabir had taken Bruce aside after the funeral, they had evidently resolved their differences. That was when he had sent Bruce to fetch the arsenal and told him to prepare for the imminent rampage at the camp. He would just have to wait for the cue, which was Vladimir's arrival outside the camps.

The very next instant, Olaf bellowed at Abu Bakr, 'Offer declined!'

And then, he shot down the four security guards. 'Let's get the hell out of here. I can see the aviation centre from Vladimir's output. The Wiesel has arrived. All clear outside.'

'You bring the Murshid out. Be very careful,' said Kabir. 'Let me check on Keira. If she was hiding, she may have come out and followed the Wiesel. I hope she's not in trouble or hurt.'

∽

Unable to figure how to locate her, Kabir sprinted towards the tank parked a few yards away. He smiled at Bruce and Vladimir, giving them a thumbs up. 'There's good news and bad, guys! We've got the Murshid. There's space for three in here. Take him in. Me and Olaf will lead in that,' he said, pointing to a solitary Land Rover parked a few yards away that had surprisingly survived the shelling. 'You give us cover. We may have to take a detour as we are missing Keira.'

'Roger that!' Bruce replied, his hatch up. He was looking towards the aviation centre exit. 'Shit!' he suddenly exclaimed, his eyes widening in horror, causing Kabir to wheel.

Olaf was scurrying out of the exit—alone—holding his left arm with his right hand, his T-shirt soaked in blood.

'Fuck! What happened?' Kabir sprinted in his direction, his face blanched. 'How did you lose him, Olaf?'

'There were more of them…his security. I tried, but he got away.' Hearing this, Vladimir jumped off the tank and was bolting towards the camp, holding machine guns in both his hands. 'They came from the back entrance. There were around eight to ten of them. I got three of them down, but then…' His face contorted in pain. He was losing blood.

'Don't!' Olaf lifted his other arm and shouted out to Vladimir.

'Stop Agent Vladimir,' Kabir turned back and commanded the fuming Siberian. He felt exhausted and defeated. He had tasted victory after a long-drawn battle and now had been robbed of it in a single harsh blow.

'They couldn't have gone far. Should I shell the aviation centre down?' asked Bruce.

'No! Can't take that risk. We need him alive, remember,' Kabir said, still thinking what to do next. 'You get Olaf in. Give him a tight wrap.'

He couldn't come to terms with it. For an instant the thought of Olaf having accepted the Murshid's offer struck Kabir. He looked at Olaf. Nothing! No point even trying! He was a hardened agent.

He should never have come out without the Murshid. The mission was falling apart. They had lost Abu Bakr and an agent was missing. The one who had saved his life! He considered all scenarios. Dismal! Whether she was alive and captive or had run away alone to safe grounds, her chances of making it were marginal.

He jumped into the Land Rover and drove to the rear of the aviation centre, the Wiesel in tow. A tiny black dot moved along the road leading away from the camp, casting a cloudy trail of desert sand behind it. The Murshid was getting away in his black armoured vehicle, a good ten to twelve miles ahead of them.

Kabir was in a dilemma—if he pursued the Murshid, Keira would be left behind in the hostile, militant infested desert. But he didn't have a choice, he figured. The mission was paramount.

'Get the chopper in,' he commanded.

24

The Palimpsest, Double Eagle and LSD

'I still can't believe you failed our most vital mission!' muttered Ghassan.

Mokhtar stood in front of him at the society headquarters. The pain and disappointment on Ghassan's face was evident, but his voice was gentle. He had given Mokhtar every resource and support he needed for this operation, but it had all been in vain.

'I didn't!' The haze from Mokhtar's eyes lifted, making them come alive with a sparkle. 'How could I fail your trust?'

'What?' Ghassan sounded piqued. 'Have you lost it? You are unable to keep the mission discreet, get into a tussle with pirates, drown the treasures and finally get arrested by the police. And now you stand here boldly before me claiming success!'

'No, Master! The treasure is inside our headquarters already. Do you remember I named this Operation Trident? When you told me about the large haul of gold, I was taken aback. That kind of quantity would be almost impossible to keep hidden from the common eye, let aside the crew. So I thought of converting it to something costlier. Diamonds were the first thing that came to my mind. But diamonds would only be about ten times more valuable. I still had a month to execute the plan. So I began my research. And I finally decided to convert the gold into three very expensive—almost priceless—objects. Hence the name of the operation.' Mokhtar smiled, letting the gravity of his words settle.

'During my research, I learnt that Siracusa or Syracuse is

famous for being the birthplace of Archimedes, the greatest mathematician of antiquity who lived around 250 BC. Although very little is known about his early life, it is said that he came to Alexandria for education, where he worked with Euclid. Later, when he returned to Syracuse, he endeared himself to King Heiro II, discovering solutions to problems that vexed the king. He invented the screw to empty rainwater from his ship's hulls…and while solving the puzzle of the king's crown, he is said to have run down the streets of Syracuse naked, shouting "Eureka! Eureka!"'

Mokhtar paused, he could sense the agitation in Ghassan's eyes. But he couldn't skip the backdrop.

'When the Roman general Marecellus laid siege on Syracuse, it was his machinations alone that could defend the city for two long years—iron claws seizing ships straight by the prow and plunging them into the water, specially designed mirrors that could burn down ships by focusing sunlight on their masts. He was a genius, way ahead of his times. It is said that he was accidentally killed by a Roman soldier during a siege, who thought that the mathematical instruments he was carrying were some kind of valuables.'

'But why are you telling me all this?' Ghassan finally spoke.

'I am getting to it. My point here is that his life story is one of the most intriguing ones till date. His works were compiled and quoted by mathematicians in Alexandria and Byzantine Constantinople through the ages. I came to know that a local in Syracuse had recently discovered a palimpsest in his basement.'

Ghassan was sorely confused. 'What is a palimpsest?'

'It's a manuscript on which something has been overwritten, but which still bears visible traces of the earlier writing. This one contains the biography of Archimedes written by his friend, Heracleids. The original work had been lost, leaving the details of Archimedes' life obscure. Therefore, this rediscovery makes this palimpsest almost priceless to a collector with scientific or historical interests. It not only has details about Archimedes, but it also brings to light the life and culture thousands of years ago. The local was unable to find a buyer willing to pay him unaccounted hard cash for an antique as valuable as this one. If word got out, the book would have been confiscated by the government. I exchanged it for one-fourth of the treasure.'

Mokhtar remembered how roughly Adel had handled the palimpsest when looking for the astrological map, flipping it around like scrap, making the heart skip a beat. 'It's there,' he said, pointing to a frayed three-inch-thick book. It was stacked between the religious texts on top of the cupboard behind Ghassan.

The tension on Ghassan's face eased. 'Oh!'

'We then moved to Naples to meet a collector. You are aware of how passionate our King Faoud is about his coin collection. Now, this man in Naples had in his possession a St Gauden's double eagle of 1933, a gold coin that never made it to circulation as President Roosevelt forbade the minting of gold coins that year. All the double eagles were thus melted again, with the exception of two that were stolen from the treasury soon after the minting. King Faoud already owns one of those two. I believe he would offer any price to complete the set. So I exchanged this for another one-fourth of the treasure.' It was the same coin that Adel had flipped in front of his eyes. The coin had turned out to be really lucky for Mokhtar as it had saved his life before making it back into his pocket.

Fishing out the coin, he placed it on the table. Ghassan flipped it between his fingers. The design was indeed one of the finest he had ever seen.

'Beautiful...'

'Now the last and final barter—the third prong of the trident. Do you remember that I requested for a truck? We used it to cross over, into Switzerland.' Mokhtar paused, his mouth twisting into a half-smile. 'I had been in touch with a man, a research assistant to the great scientist Albert Hoffman. Two years back, this scientist synthesized a chemical which his assistant accidentally ingested during one of his late-night shifts in the lab. The effect was like something he had never experienced before—recreational, spiritual and ecstatic. This assistant had snorted heroin occasionally, but this chemical was a trip to another realm entirely. Realizing its potential in the narcotics market, he decided not to share this finding with Albert. He started clandestinely synthesizing small quantities of it during his night shifts. When I met him, he had processed nearly seventy whole pounds of it. I exchanged the remaining half of the treasure for sixty pounds of this wonder drug. Two hundred and fifty micrograms of this drug would cost about half a dollar, making it forty thousand times more expensive than gold.'

'Ohhh... that's freakish. Does this drug have a name?'

'They haven't named it yet, but he did give me an acronym. LSD, I think.'

'Where is it now?'

'Lying in a gunny sack in our store along with the salt that came in from the ship's kitchen.' He held his head up with pride.

'Unbelievable!' Ghassan shook his head.

'Why then did we need all that confrontation and bloodshed? You could have easily travelled on a passenger ship with these goods.'

'That's easier said than done, Master! The customs officers at Siracusa or Alexandria would scan individuals thoroughly. A man with a sack of white powder, an old scripture and a gold coin on a passenger ship is much more vulnerable than one travelling as the crew member of a cargo ship with his best men. I managed to smuggle the goods out from right under the noses of steamers full of customs officers because their focus was elsewhere! The point at which we dropped those empty black trunks is almost two thousand feet deep,' added Mokhtar, 'which would make it impossible for them to get to it immediately. They will live under the delusion of a false victory for years.'

Ghassan smiled.

'You have proven yourself worthy of much bigger responsibilities, Mokhtar! Not that I had any doubt earlier, but now I know for sure that you have a rare gift.' Ghassan stood up and held the man's shoulders. 'Remember, I told you that I have a bigger purpose for this gold, which is why I hid the details from the board. I will now tell you exactly why.'

25

The Mission Falls Apart

The Murshid's armoured van was no less than a bunker. It contained the latest assault weapons and had comfortable interiors, a miniature version of the Cove. It had no windows, except for the driver's windshield, made of bulletproof glass. He knew the NATO commandos would tail him, so he had his insurance in place. An infallible trump card! The hovering chopper did not worry him.

He watched the antics of the commandos with amusement. They obviously didn't want him dead. For a few moments, when one of them had had him strangled in the auditorium, he had felt he had reached the end. As soon as this man had left, he had played his cards…and it had worked. Like always! And now that he was in his little fortress, he was smug. That same commando was now making his way down a rope ladder. The night-vision cameras embedded on the roof of the van provided the Murshid with a 360-degree view of the surroundings. The commando hung precariously from the rope, like a circus gymnast. The robotic guns embedded in the body of the van could kill him any moment he wanted, but he did not want to make a hasty decision.

Back in the copter, Olaf's bleeding arm had been tinctured and bandaged. He was keenly fishing around in his trunk for something. He was no longer sure whether the one billion dollars would make their way home. The Murshid was getting away, and had ample chance to change his mind. After all, it was a huge amount, the size of a small economy. The Ikhwan could afford it, but he intended to make sure.

Bruce sat buckled to a front seat in the chopper, looking out of the window. 'What about the communication systems in the van? I think we should disable them right away,' he said, looking at Tareq seated in the cockpit, his back towards Bruce. 'Do we have a jammer on board?'

Tareq did not reply. He had narrowed his eyes at the windscreen, trying to focus on a strange dark object visible in the distance. A moving figure that did not quite look like a bird or an aircraft. It swerved and flew left, out of his vision. '*Queer!*'

'Don't worry about it! It won't be needed,' Olaf commented, looking up at Bruce. A few moments from now, the Murshid will be inaccessible to any help.

'Why? What are you guys up to? You have already lost him once, why don't we get it over and done with?' Bruce said, sniggering.

'Oh yeah! Over and done with as in? Bomb the van? We want him alive. If he dies, everything is finished,' Olaf shot back. 'Do you understand?'

The Murshid's gaze was fixed on his monitor, watching the agent fidgeting with his backpack. He wondered what this man hanging above his roof was trying to do. *Maybe I should end this now. No games! This is not the time! Maybe I shouldn't have ventured out at all.* As he pondered over which nifty gadget to use, still staring at the monitor, the blocks on it started blacking out, one by one. Kabir was spraying black aerosol on the cameras. What he did not see was a tiny robotic spider making its way down the rope ladder.

'Fire the guns,' he commanded. 'Position the guide-grid over the roof of the van.'

The guns rattled. But they did not hit flesh. The chopper had banked sharply and risen, taking Kabir with it. However, the spider was at its job, hanging from a spool of high tensile steel cord from the copter. It scurried around the body of the van, around the bottom, looking for an inlet to inject the nano-camera it was carrying. It took several rounds, but did not find one. Olaf was busy controlling its movement through a joystick remote above. The spool was almost at its end, its last segment of a much thicker multi-filament steel rope now connecting it with the spider. The spider ran to the centre of the roof and spread-eagled itself there. Mission aborted!

Inside the van, the Murshid was going berserk. 'Bring on the infra-red homing missile. I want the chopper down. Now!'

A hydraulic arm, fitted with a wide-angle dome camera, projected itself out of the van. It showed the CH-53 flying high above to the left. The red crosshairs were positioned over the helicopter and the 'set target' button pressed. The target's heat signature had been mapped, which would now guide the missile to it. The Murshid's finger hovered over the red button—positioned to fire—evaluating the final pros and cons. He stopped and picked up the satellite phone. *The Cove should know my coordinates!*

'All clear?' Olaf asked Vladimir, who was leaning against a window, carelessly munching pretzels. He gave one final look out the window and shook his head in the affirmative.

'Good to go!'

Olaf pressed the rewind button on the joystick.

The sudden jerk caused the phone to fall out of the Murshid's hand. The van had been lifted off the ground! It was see-sawing back and forth, throwing the men inside out of balance. Before they could understand what was happening, the van was a good hundred metres in the air. The Murshid realized his blunder. He should have pressed the button while there was still time. Now if the copter crashed, the van would go down with it and be blown apart.

The robotic spider had looped several rounds of steel cord around the van and finally clutched them together, its body forming a central hook that connected the thicker steel cord from the copter to the web of fine cords wound around the van.

Vladimir walked up to Olaf and high-fived him. He turned around to see Kabir looking at him with an amused expression.

'What?' Vladimir became conscious.

'Nothing!' Kabir said, 'College students, right! Weren't you saying something like that this afternoon?' He burst out laughing, unable to control himself.

Everybody on board was jubilant. They finally had Abu Bakr in their grip, like a rat in a cage. In less than four hours, they would be on the Protettori's cargo ship. Kabir, however, stood at the rear, looking out of one of the back windows towards the vast stretch of moonlit desert sand. He was in a melancholic mood. The memories of Keira—her first sight as she had popped up the manhole cover, how pretty she had looked in the blue gown the day before, her sudden fainting in the van today—it kept playing over in his mind. He felt a pang of regret at having failed her.

His thoughts were interrupted by a strange sight. Something just whizzed past his line of vision It was a man, standing erect on a hoverboard jet. Olaf had definitely been presumptuous in thinking help couldn't reach the Murshid once the van was suspended.

He ran to a side window on his left, the direction in which the man had swooped. The rider was flying past the copter at window level, his middle finger raised up from his clenched fist in a gesture of disdain. Kabir recognized him instantly, even though his face was covered with a helmet. The frail figure! It was the killer. Khabib! Abu Bakr's man-at-arms! The twin flames from the jet-pack below his feet enhanced the visibility around him. He was riding a Zapata Flyboard IV, the most advanced stand-over jet-pack.

He wondered what chances this man stood, fighting alone against four of the world's best commandos. And then, he remembered those deep-set cold hazel eyes. Underestimating him would be foolish!

By now, everyone on board had noticed the man on the hoverboard cruising along with them. It was an unusual sight.

Not only did air traffic rules prohibit riding at this elevation, it was suicidal!

'What the fuck!' Bruce cursed. 'Now who's this? Let's get him down!'

He unbuckled himself from his seat, got up and pulled out a sniper hanging from a wall nearby. He had been right about the jamming device. They should have used it. The Murshid had probably used satellite communication to call this joker for help.

'Wait! Don't go by his puny figure. This man is evil personified—the same heinous terrorist Victor introduced us to—Abu Bakr's right hand!' Kabir said quickly. 'He is the one Keira had been chasing before coming on this mission. And for some frickin' reason, he desperately wants me dead. He attacked me while I was in a hospital in Kuala Lumpur.'

'Don't tell me! So this guy tracks us all the way down to the deserts of Libya,' Olaf cackled, 'and chooses to confront us in a military helicopter, riding a hoverboard. Some balls he has!'

'I'm sure the Murshid had him stationed nearby for backup. He's his last resort, his trump card of sorts,' said Vladimir. 'I agree with Bruce, we should have shot him on sight.'

Vladimir and Bruce were probably right, but it was too late now. Khabib had completed his reconnaissance and was rapidly descending below the helicopter. He landed on the roof of the van, the safest spot for him. Kabir was hastily evaluating the possibilities. They couldn't shoot at Khabib now, they would not want the web holding the van to fall apart. They wanted the Murshid alive. And so did Khabib! For that reason alone, he hadn't blown up the helicopter. Nor attempted to cut the rope holding the van—if he had, the fall would have been fatal for its occupants. Kabir asked everyone to be alert, waiting for Khabib's next move.

He watched as Khabib began to talk on his satellite phone.

What happened next was something none of the agents had expected. Suddenly the back door of the van opened and bodies enveloped in jumpsuits started falling out in quick succession, barely discernible from each other in the moonlight.

'Don't shoot!' Kabir held up his hand towards Olaf and Bruce, who had their guns aimed at the copter. 'Get the Chinook down, and keep as close to them as possible.'

The falling bodies were rapidly diminishing to specks. Khabib's jet spurted fire again as he flashed before the open van door. Holding the sixth and last occupant of the van, he succumbed to the gravitational pull. The specks had now mushroomed to remarkable sizes, their parachutes open. As the helicopter banked sharply, trying to imitate the fall, Kabir was the first to jump off.

He dived head down, like a spear cutting through the atmospheric resistance, trying to catch up with the fleeing captives and Khabib. The person in Khabib's grip had to be the Murshid. He steered himself in their direction, taking a parallel accelerated line of fall to the van's occupants, which was slowed down by their open parachutes. He pulled out his gun, just in case… Khabib had no reason to spare him, except saving the Murshid.

As he approached closer, he stared wide-eyed, trying to make sure that what he was seeing was true. He pressed the button to unfurl his parachute. It was not the Murshid standing over the hoverboard with Khabib.

It was Keira!

She wore a jacket sequined with explosives. The hoverboard supported both their lean frames well. The killer gestured Kabir to back off. He probably wanted to avoid any kind of crossfire that could pose a risk to the falling Murshid's life. Besides, he knew they would be outnumbered, him and the Murshid's guards. There were about a dozen of Kabir's men who had jumped off the helicopter and were quickly catching up. He chose to go with the Murshid's insurance card instead. With Keira as his hostage, he had a good chance to fend them off. He looked up to see Bruce descending with his gun aimed at Khabib.

Kabir looked into Keira's eyes. They were moist. He did not know whether it was due to the air gushing into her bare eyes or an overflow of emotions. There were so many questions he needed to ask her. But most of all he wanted to save her first, free her from the clutches of this monster. She had bravely taken the decision to split from the team in the first place, and then managed to escape from Yusuf's den unassisted. Even now, with the explosive jacket around her, there was not an ounce of fear in those evocative eyes. He felt a flutter in his chest. She had saved him from this brute when he had cornered him, putting her life at stake. Now it was his turn.

The gunshots brought Kabir back from his thoughts. His gaze had been fixed on Keira's face and Khabib's hand holding her around the waist. He could drop Keira off at any moment and press the remote button. Kabir glanced upwards in the direction in which Khabib's other hand was extended. He saw three of Tareq's men come tumbling down, hit by his bullets. They had probably been holding hands in their sky-dive, trying to catch up with the fugitives and planning to open their parachutes once they were nearer to the ground. But their bodies were now rolling down awkwardly, unable to hold posture. It boggled Kabir how this man could shoot men in free fall. Khabib had already started raking up casualties. It was also a signal for the agents to back off. They were about to hit the ground, and he wanted to focus on rescuing the Murshid. Holding Keira as his shield, he already had them handicapped. He had turned his body, taking cover behind Keira so that Bruce or Kabir could not aim at him. He also had the option of jetting away, but he had to stay close to the Murshid's line of fall.

Kabir instinctively knew what he would have to do, but his heart and mind would not come to terms with it. *Sacrifice Keira!* How could he render such a horrible death to a brave and selfless agent! She would be blown to shreds.

They were less than a hundred feet in the air, about to hit the ground. The terrain below was full of tall sand dunes. The figures in jumpsuits had landed, shed the parachutes and were scurrying away from the landing site towards a colony of tents some distance away. It was some kind of settlement. Camels and horses were parked along its wooden palisade. Kabir got ready for the act, extending his hand to fire the gun right through Keira's jacket. Once Khabib was out of their way, they would get the Murshid easily. His guards would be no match for the four agents. His hands shivered as he looked into Keira's fearless eyes, urging him on.

And then something unexpected happened. Khabib ducked low behind Keira, making himself inaccessible to Bruce's fire. He swept his hand upwards, firing three shots in swift succession. Kabir flipped on impulse, the first bullet missing him by an inch. The second bullet missed its target too, puncturing a hole in Bruce's parachute. But the third bullet hit its mark. Kabir and Bruce let out terrified screams as Olaf slumped in his harness, the parachute bringing down his lifeless body.

The killer then straightened his other arm, releasing Keira. Kabir and Bruce watched in horror as Keira plummeted in free fall, tumbling towards the sand below.

∽

The fusillade from Bruce's gun was futile as the landing trammelled his aim. Khabib darted off on a zigzag path upwards in the Murshid's direction on the hover-jet, firing back at the agents.

Kabir told Vladimir and two of Tareq's men to go after the Murshid and another two towards the north where Keira would have hit the ground. There was little chance of her survival after the 100-foot fall and the explosion from the jacket. They hadn't heard anything but the incessant crossfire. The distance and the burying of an accelerated body in the sand could have easily dampened the sound. The rest of them attended the three black men who had been shot down by Khabib. Tareq was trying to land the helicopter some distance away on relatively flat ground. Bruce and Kabir rushed towards Olaf, who seemed to be in bad shape. He was bleeding profusely from the bowels. Khabib's bullet had passed right through them.

'Hang on, partner!' Kabir said, looking Olaf in the eye. He wrapped his jacket tightly around his wound, trying to arrest the flow of blood. 'We'll get first aid as soon as the helicopter is grounded, and we will transport you to the nearest hospital.' Bruce held Olaf's hand, praying hard for him.

'Won't be necessary,' Olaf moaned. 'I have to confess something before I go.'

'Don't say that! You're not going anywhere,' Kabir pleaded, taking Olaf's head in his lap to elevate his upper body.

'I noticed the suspicion in your eyes when you looked at the close range shot on my arm. You were right. I traded Abu's safe passage for one billion dollars!'

'What! Fuck...no! I don't believe you,' Bruce erupted. 'Why would you do that, man?'

'There were around eight of them with machine guns. I was surrounded... I didn't stand a chance. So I took the offer.'

'What...you took the offer? Just like that?' Kabir felt stabbed.

'But why did he make you the offer then, if you were surrounded?' Bruce asked, shaking with indignation.

'Because he didn't know that I wouldn't shoot him. That we want him alive! So I thought—why not eat the pie and keep it too... It didn't feel wrong to shave some money off the bastard. He saved my account number on his mobile and promised to transfer the money to my account the moment he was safely inside his van... The chit with my account details is still...in my right pocket.' Olaf was finding it difficult to breathe, choking from the upsurge of blood into his wind pipe.

'You probably did the logical thing. But what about pride and honour, man? I would have at least tried,' Bruce said. 'What good is this dirty money now?'

Olaf shook his head. 'Don't judge me. I'm a single father...of a spastic son.' It was taking him huge effort to utter each word. 'I wanted to donate it...to the Spastic Society...that takes care of him. There are...hundreds of children there...the society is always struggling... to make both ends meet. They could do... with a... corpus fund. Please make sure...' Olaf breathed his last, before conveying his last wish.

Kabir ran his hand over Olaf's eyelids. He looked at Bruce, both of them guilty of having momentarily mistaken his intentions. They had lost the techie of their team. Without his help, they would never have reached this far. The spider trap, the nano-cameras... his impeccable aim! Khabib had made a massive dent in the team's count and confidence. Two out of five down already! His appearance on the scene, like always, had been horrifying. And he had left behind a ghastly trail of dead bodies.

'No survivors amongst my three men.' Tareq rushed to the spot, carrying first aid. 'Gosh! Olaf too!' He held his forehead in despair.

'Arrange their burial,' Kabir said, taking out the paper with the account details from Olaf's trouser pocket. 'Bruce and I will check on Keira.' He wanted to look at her face one last time before bidding her goodbye.

༶

Keira was rolling down a high sand dune, the soft sand at the peak having cushioned the impact of her fall. She had hit the dune feet first, immediately crumpling her body like an accordion, bending it to roll down the slope. In the academy, she had been trained to sustain jumps as high as thirty feet. This, of course, had been a far steeper fall—but the soft terrain had saved her. Magically, the jacket had not blown up.

But she could already tell from the awful spasms in her right foot that her ankle had sustained either a fracture or a severe sprain. Adjusting and clipping her wig securely, she gathered every fibre of strength to pick herself up, before dragging her leg through the dunes, moving southwards.

Bruce and Kabir had barely walked a few hundred yards when they saw a movement on a dune to their south. A closer look revealed the outline of a woman limping towards them. 'Oh my god... I can't believe it!' Kabir laughed in relief, as he shook his head. *Finally!* A welcome stroke of luck after the string of disasters they'd just gone through, giving his spirits several reasons to rejoice. The positive tidings would uplift the team's nosediving morale and assuage him of the crippling guilt at having failed her. More importantly, he was just happy she was alive.

'She's taken a different route around the dunes...' Bruce said. 'No wonder the rescue team missed her.'

'Yes. And look there,' Kabir said, pointing to an object in the distance. It was the explosive jacket that lay in the sand, intact. 'Sham jacket. Smart move!' It would've allowed Khabib to use her as a shield, without putting his own life at risk.

As the men reached her and examined her foot, it became increasingly obvious that the swelling was more than a simple sprain. Still, both the sand and her own vaulting skills had broken the overall impact of the fall, protecting her spine and neck from fatal injury.

Kabir pulled out a crepe bandage from the first aid kit. She grimaced in pain as he propped her leg on his thigh to tie the bandaging around her foot. 'It'll be okay.' He nodded in reassurance and paused for her to recoup. And then, in a flash, holding her foot and shin, he tugged them apart and twisted her ankle.

'Ahhh!' She bit her lip to smother the pain from the snapping sound.

'Thanks!' She smiled at him a few moments later, knowing her ankle had been fixed.

As Kabir tied a crepe bandage over her ankle, his gaze was fixed on her face. Her hair was scruffy, and her features had taken a battering—her appearance a striking contrast from the attractive woman who had chatted him up over wine. But the lure of those emerald eyes was just as profound. And under the mellow light from the moon above, her expression exuded a warmth that sent his heart racing, much like it had done the previous day. He decided against putting her through any further emotional turmoil for the moment, holding off the many questions in his head for later.

26

The Sheepdogs and the Eliminators

Mokhtar was driving up the winding mountain road, watching the ice-clad trees in the dim moonlight. The chilly wind pierced his thick overcoat and went right to his bones. A solitary house on the hilltop stood out like a beacon, the yellow light from its lamps in stark contrast to the shrouding darkness. This was his destination tonight.

He lapsed into thoughts of how it had all started—this role he had taken of a phantom trotting the globe, punishing evil. He had lost count of how many people he had brought to justice in these few years.

∽

'Hanif, meet Mokhtar, the man who made it possible!' Ghassan gestured as he walked into an isolated room on the second floor of the headquarters building a few days after the Trident mission.

'And Mokhtar, this is Hanif, one of my brightest disciples, a brilliant planner and administrator! He has been working as our lead strategist in Tunisia.'

Mokhtar threw a curt glance at Hanif—a sober, fair young man of medium height, about the same age as himself. He was trim, dressed in a suit, exuding confidence and positivity. He smiled at Mokhtar.

'We meet here in secret today as I wish to entrust you both with a great responsibility, the biggest project of my life. A project which will surpass my lifespan, and maybe yours too. Your sacrifices on this path may never be applauded, as you will have no identity from this moment onwards. Are you both ready?'

They nodded in unison, curious to find out what the project was.

'Good! As I have always said, Islam is the solution. The only way to apply God's rule over the world. The time has come for us to start working on it. While our struggle for independence continues in Egypt and other parts of the Arab world, we need to start spreading out. Not only into the countries of our colonizers, but to every corner of the world. That's where you both come in.'

Ghassan paused to make sure the boys were following. 'Roots need nourishment, else the plant dies. You have to be that underground nourishment, invisible but indispensable. The saplings that you shall plant all over the world will grow into trees one day. Massive branching trees! And when this forest is dense enough, it will provide a canopy for the world to flourish. The canopy of Islam! Our worldwide caliphate!'

'Got it!' Hanif nodded, 'means our job is to recruit loads of people and facilitate their migration, right? To help them develop communities which are self-sustaining and will proliferate.'

'No! All that the society shall take care of. Migrations, building mosques, charitable work and all of that stuff! Your job is much more subtle, yet vital.'

'You shall develop assets. During the first few decades, these assets will make sure that our communities don't get lost in the blitz and remain loyal to Islam. The assets should never ever bring up the caliphate. Better still, they shouldn't even be made aware of that angle to avoid drawing untoward attention from non-believers. The assets should win the trust of the locals, blend with them and rise to higher positions there. Your narrative to the assets should always be towards spreading Islam, and their responsibility towards everyone else will be to help Muslims follow their religion peacefully.'

'How many people can one asset really control?' Hanif asked, wondering if the silent Mokhtar had similar questions running in his mind. 'Won't the numbers get out of hand?'

Ghassan smiled. 'Think of the sheepdog. It moves around large flocks of sheep, herds them together and keeps them moving in the right direction! We won't need a large number—just enough to keep the populace moving in the right direction.'

'And what if a sheepdog himself goes rogue?'

'That's where our eliminators come in,' said Ghassan, turning to Mokhtar.

'But I can't leave your side, Master!' Mokhtar finally spoke up to voice his objection.

'It's the Islamic dream that needs protection at this point, more than I do! That's what we're all working for, isn't it?'

'But, Master...'

'It's an order!'

A brief silence followed until Hanif resumed the conversation. 'So when do we begin?'

'Right away! I'll see you in three days. Be ready with a blueprint.'

'Th...three days?' Hanif muttered. 'Is this where we work from? Our new office?'

'No, there shall be no office. It's best to keep changing locations so that no one can trace you. Right now, you work from your hostel rooms.'

'With what name should we refer to our new organization?'

'No names! Anything that has a name exists. Any further questions?'

Both of them shook their heads.

Mokhtar didn't quite understand what sort of defence an underground organization would need in its formative years. He was already preparing himself for the boring new role that had been thrust upon him.

He couldn't have been more wrong.

∽

Returning from the flashback, he switched off the headlight. He was one turn short of the hilltop. Parking his car, he stepped out and pulled the monkey cap over his face. The lights from the torches and the fireplace inside the house had waned. It was 2 a.m. His target was probably in deep sleep. Mokhtar hadn't expected that the need for eliminations would arise so soon. This particular asset had turned out to be a spy, reportedly trying to collect inside information about the society for the French.

He checked the main door. *Bolted from inside.* A quick stroll around the house gave him the access he needed—a glass window protected with an iron grille behind it. He cut through the glass neatly with a diamond cutter and undid the screws holding the grille in place. Half an hour later, he was inside the kitchen. Treading lightly over the wooden floor to minimize the creaking noises, Mokhtar opened the door of the room to his right and peeped in, his eyes used to the darkness by now. The man on the bed slept straight on his back. He could see his face. He was handsome, almost like royalty. Like the British officers who carted around their streets back home in all arrogance! His assignment was to finish off the husband and wife as quietly as possible, ransack the furniture and belongings to make it appear like a robbery, and leave.

He took out the poisoned dart shooter, his staple weapon—lethal, light and lissome, easier than a gun to smuggle across borders any day. He put the pipe to his lips, ready to blow the dart, when the squeak of door hinges forced him to spin around.

The shadow of a little boy emerged in front of him.

'Who are you?' the boy shrieked, startling his parents awake.

In a flash, Mokhtar brought the tiny dart shooter to his lips and blew his first dart at the man. But it missed its target. The man had rolled out of bed and hurled himself in Mokhtar's direction. He punched Mokhtar hard in the face, rupturing his lips.

Mokhtar stood there paralysed, unable to respond. His gaze was fixed on the woman, sitting up on the bed, glaring at the masked intruder. *Nouran!*

The European landed another solid punch in Mokhtar's stomach, making him stumble backwards, as he rushed to the closet. He pulled out a double barrel and aimed it at Mokhtar.

'Close your eyes, boy,' the man hollered at his son—who did as he was told—before pointing the muzzle at the intruder. 'Who are you, bastard? Remove your cap!'

Mokhtar complied. After all, the man could easily press the trigger and then unmask him.

'It's you! Ya Allah,' Nouran cried in disbelief on recognizing the silhouette of his familiar features in the dimness, her cry making her husband's attention falter.

Mokhtar seized the opportunity and launched himself at the husband like a bolt. Drawing the karambit from his socks, he sliced the man's gun-wielding arm. The white man stumbled backwards and landed on the bed. Mokhtar snatched the gun and aimed it at him, the bloodstained karambit lying on the bed behind the man.

Mokhtar felt little fists jabbing at his back. 'Let go of my father, you thief!' The little boy was yelling in frenzy. It pained Mokhtar that he would have to kill him too.

Realizing that his attack had had little impact on the intruder, the little boy scurried to the security of his mother's arms and covered his face in terror.

All three targets were in clear sight now. Mokhtar was about to press the trigger, when Nouran suddenly picked up the karambit lying in front of her and brought it to the child's throat. 'Stop, she cried! Or I will have to kill him.' The little boy peeked up at his mother in shock, unable to understand what was going on.

'What?' Mokhtar scoffed with spite. 'Go ahead!'

'He's your son!' she yelled back.

Mokhtar's head reeled, as he tried to observe the boy in the darkness. The child was around five years old. He had deserted Nouran six years back. Why should it matter to him? How was he supposed to feel anything for a son he had never known? Strangely, he did. 'When I suggested you marry a pious Muslim and settle down, did you decide to marry a French spy trying to intrude into our society! Simply to get back at me?' he scoffed, struggling to maintain a spiteful look on his face. 'Didn't you consider that one day it would come to this?'

'Wait, what? Jameel works at the foreign affairs ministry, he is no spy! It's a misunderstanding… I would never dare to come in your way!' She begged with folded hands.

Taking advantage of Mokhtar's lapse of attention, the white man jumped at him. Mokhtar pressed the trigger on impulse. The impact of the lead from the double barrel sent him flying back as he hit Nouran, making the karambit fall aside.

Watching his father's body sprawled on the bed the little boy squalled in horror and glued his tiny hands on his eyes.

The next second, Nouran fell motionless on the bed, blood oozing out from her throat. A shrapnel had cut through her carotid artery. She probably had a minute before she would breathe her last.

'I didn't want to kill you!' Mokhtar found himself confessing to her on impulse, as he kneeled on the floor beside her.

'Stay away from my son,' Nouran managed to croak before her eyes turned blank.

Mokhtar sat on the floor, holding his head in his hands. For the first time in years, he heard himself sobbing.

He looked at the little boy huddled in a corner, shivering and weeping. *Would I ever be able to raise him to forgive his parents' murderer?*

He felt a strange shudder as he aimed the gun at the boy. *No one, absolutely no one should ever get scent of our mission!*

27

Village of the Gypsy Women

In the dim moonlight, hidden behind a low mound, Vladimir and the two men from Tareq's team could spot the Murshid, his security guards and Khabib, all making a beeline for the tents. 'Khabib could not have carried the two of them on the hover-jet,' Vladimir reckoned. He wouldn't risk the extra weight. Or maybe, he had run out of the special jet fuel required for propulsion. Anyway, the flyboard was nowhere in sight…probably discarded.

The plains around the settlement, surrounded by dunes, provided him with a clear view of the silhouettes as they edged closer to the tents. They would steal a few horses or camels and try to make it to the nearest city. He took out a laminated pocket map the Protettori had provided each agent with. They had been travelling north of the Al Sharia's Kufra camps and would be close to Al Wahat district, which had several airports. The Murshid's men were well armed in case of a confrontation with the tents' occupants, who in all probability would be primitively armed nomads.

He had to rapidly figure out what to do. He couldn't let them get away. His only option was to directly confront and stop them till the rest of the team arrived. The Chinook would then witness another successful mission, transporting the world's most wanted man to justice. He was quickly ruminating over a feasible strategy for minimum damage. He was around two hundred metres away. Murshid and his men did not know his location. Only once he fired, would they know and fire back. The camp's inhabitants would wake up and rush out in a frenzy, the ensuing mayhem would provide the targets with better opportunities to escape. Not good! But what if he could get closer to his targets and buy some time? This seemed more appropriate.

'Cover me!' he told the two men accompanying him. They moved immediately at his command, keeping low. 'The Murshid shouldn't be hit under any circumstances. Open fire at his guards and at the assassin, Khabib, only when you hear my command. My voice should travel easily across this open stretch.'

They gestured to say yes.

The outlines of the tents grew clearer as they approached the settlement. Vladimir sprinted his way around the dunes to the west, still out of sight of Murshid and his men. When they reached a mound that was barely fifty metres from the stables, they paused to study their targets. Khabib was keeping watch. The remaining security team were busy feeding the horses to keep them quiet, untying the animals while they did so. *Shit! No sign of the taskforce yet!* Khabib had definitely kept them busy with the casualties earlier, hadn't he? *Swine!*

Vladimir walked out from behind the mound, holding his hands behind his head in surrender.

'Peace!' he shouted.

Murshid spun around, startled. Khabib had to fight his instincts to shoot down the giant at once. What purpose could the commando have in giving himself up now? Was there a catch, a trap?

The assassin surveyed the man hardly twenty metres away, still ambling towards them. No sign of weapons or arms. So why was the man throwing his life away by walking towards sure death, unarmed? Was it a desperate move? An outburst caused by their failed mission? An attempt to die in honour?

Should I kill him? Without wasting any more time, Khabib grabbed hold of his gun and decided to stick to the middle path for a bit.

Bang!
Bang!
Bang!

Two of his bullets had taken down the two men hiding behind the mound, followed by a third that went right through the commando's thigh, forcing him to his knees.

'Stay where you are,' he growled at Vladimir, 'or the next bullet goes through your head.'

Shit! Vladimir winced as he turned and saw the heads of his accomplices hit sand. His only backup was dead. It boggled him how this assassin could've spotted and shot the hidden men in such darkness. But he didn't allow any sign of shock to show on his face. Instead, he ploughed along, casting a bloody trail on the golden sand, his hands still glued behind his head.

'There is something amiss! Maybe I should have shot him in the head in the first place,' Khabib mused.

Dawn was now making its presence the first rays from the sun beginning to illuminate the horizon. The gunshot had woken up the nomads. A few women dressed in hooded kaftans began to gather around them.

And with the gap between them closing, Khabib spotted something he hadn't until a few minutes ago. Instantly, the whole ploy became clear like the light coming up in the sky. '*Ya Allah!*' He sighed, glad he hadn't acted on an impulse. There were little rings around the fingers of the giant's half-stretched hands, thin white threads running down from them into his backpack. Had Khabib shot him, the pins would've automatically been pulled out as his hands would have fallen apart. And with barely twenty metres between them, the powerful detonation of the grenade-bank would've taken all of them along with him. Stepping close, he mumbled caution into the Murshid's ear.

'What do you want, Siberian?' the Murshid asked, stepping forward. 'I have nothing against you. I just need to get back somewhere. I have an urgent appointment to keep. I'm willing to pay a ransom. Whatever price you ask!' There wasn't an ounce of tremor in his voice.

Vladimir stayed silent. He was waiting for the others to show up. The local gypsy women in hooded kaftans were flocking around them now, enjoying the spectacle, unaware of the impending danger. He would have to find a way to warn them, drive them away from the scene.

Khabib leered at the gigantic agent and realized how the tables had turned. The wholesale buyers of fidayeens were now hostage to a Russian one. There did not seem to be an immediate way out, except for the negotiations the Murshid had embarked upon.

Or was there one? He recalled something else—an infallible device that had served him well during numerous confrontations.

Vladimir noticed the assassin's right hand stealthily creeping towards the pocket of his cargo trousers, through which was visible the distinctive outline of a tube. 'Stop that!' he yelled instantly. 'I will pull the strings before you bring that windpipe to your lips.'

Khabib's hand froze. How had the agent known? The deadly venom from his blowdart would have killed him before he could twitch his biceps, turning every muscle to stone the moment it pierced his skin.

What the assassin didn't know was that venom darts were a regular in Russian espionage.

'I am waiting for your answer, Siberian,' Murshid pressed on.

Vladimir noticed that there was still no sign of his team. He would have to keep them engaged. 'A life for a life!' he said firmly.

Abu raised an eyebrow. 'Care to elaborate?'

'Your man just killed half a dozen of our men. I want his life in return. Shoot him now… and I will let you walk away.'

Khabib was taken aback by this unexpected demand. Dousing the little surge of anxiety within, he darted Murshid a look that conveyed his consent in case this was needed. Nothing was more important than the Ikhwan's mission at hand.

'I can't do that,' smirked Murshid. 'Besides, how can I be sure you will not pull the strings even if I follow through with your demand? I'll pay you in dollars, just as I paid your friend—one billion to his account. Here's the proof.' He held up his mobile screen. It displayed a confirmation of the transaction.

Vladimir was shocked by this sudden revelation.

But he had to go on. 'I have no interest in money. I have tons of it already. Consider this: for each bullet that you put through him, I will release one of my fingers, disengaging a grenade. Ten shots. Start from the legs. I'll tell you where to shoot. The last bullet goes through his head, before which I will hand over my backpack to you. Hurry, we may not have that much time. My friends will arrive any moment. And yes, ask the locals to return to their tents.'

Abu saw the burning vengeance in Vladimir's eyes. He was speaking the truth. If he sacrificed Khabib, he could probably save the mission.

He then cast a glance at his unfamiliar audience. There were around forty locals who had gathered in a circle around them. The Moroccan gypsies rarely got to see such dramatic confrontations in the desert. Their eyes feasted upon this early morning treat. *Odd!* The crowd was comprised entirely women. *Where were the male members of the pack?* In any case, he had decided.

'Okay, step back!' He waved at the onlookers, bringing out his thirty-round Kel-Tec PMR-30 pistol. He aimed it at Khabib's left calf, waiting for the Siberian's call.

The sound of the first shot, however, came from another direction, much before the call. A tall woman tore through the crowd, holding up an assault F-2000. Wearing a hooded kaftan like the rest of the throng, she had fired a round in the air to grab their attention.

'Who the hell…?' Abu was perplexed. He had assumed

the gypsies would come out with spears and swords, spouting aboriginal gibberish. *But, an assault F-2000?*

'What's going on here?' She spoke authoritatively, in clear English. 'All guns down. No one wages their private wars on my land.'

'Your land?' Abu swallowed as he noticed the other gypsies drawing out light machine guns from their kaftans, securing their leader's position. There was another rustle as Kabir, Bruce and Keira tore through the crowd from behind, to reach their bleeding friend.

Before they could ascertain the situation, everyone was forced to raise their hands above their shoulders in surrender.

The commanding woman spoke. 'Strip them of their weapons and bring them to my barrack,' she instructed her group in a gruff voice. 'And see what we can do with the injured giant.'

∽

Nusrat, the leader of this strange all-women tribe, listened patiently to Keira's narration of the whole episode. She sat regally on a sofa, while the three agents and Abu, all seemingly compliant, stood on either side of her. It was an arrangement that resembled a courtroom. Khabib was restrained at the rear of the tent, near the entrance, flanked by Nusrat's fighters.

The agents had assessed that this group was a female wing of the Libyan shield—the combined force of private militias that defended oil-rich Libya from external threats. In a politically unstable country such as this one, the military alone was not powerful enough to protect all borders. The gaps were filled by numerous militias that had empowered themselves with the passage of time, developing territorial strongholds. So the only option in front of the agents was to appeal to the nobler senses of this lady warlord.

Keira had taken the lead. She explained how the Brotherhood was planning to take over the world with the orchestrated terror attacks masterminded by Abu Bakr—the man in Nusrat's custody.

'The lady here has spoken as a representative of the West. You,' Nusrat turned to Abu, ready to listen to his version, 'the proponent of Islam. Speak up.'

Abu began in a sombre tone. 'What this lady has told you is a distorted and hypocritical view, that of the Western world... as a Muslim, I am sure you are aware of how they have oppressed us for centuries. This plan was a reprisal, and it was not made today. It took birth in the mind of a devout Muslim, around a hundred years ago. It was sown as a seed in his son's mind—a random idea over a meal. But the son took it very seriously. He witnessed the fall of the Ottoman empire at the hand of the Europeans after the First World War—an empire which had been the social and political representation of Islamic pride and culture for fourteen centuries! It further anguished him to see his own country enslaved and dominated by the colonial powers. As fate would have it, he turned out to be a powerful leader, a genius, a man with the intellect and means to set the ball rolling towards this Islamic dream. We are just hours away from the consummation of a hundred years of toil and sacrifices by Muslims...made over generations. The clock is ticking. I beseech you to let me go...for the sake of Islam.'

Nusrat gave him a skewed smile. 'Easy, commander! This parley just got more interesting. I will not be coaxed into making a hasty decision. Besides, I have plenty to say too. Now...,' she cracked her fingers 'you must be wondering about us.' She looked them over.

'Look at us. A group of armed women wandering the desert in an Islamic theocracy. Well, we are a group of Berber women, the original inhabitants of North Africa, as opposed to the Arabs who migrated from the Middle East. These hooded kaftans that our fighters are wearing is our ethnic dress, a symbol of our strength, our Amazigh culture. Our name signifies "free people". We are Sunni Muslims too. And we fight to protect Islam. But...,' she then addressed Abu in particular, 'the intentional misinterpretation of the Hadiths by the ulama and their sponsors for their personal gains has demonized Islam. The Shia-Sunni conflict is a source of power and money for many. The ego clash of the two most affluent Islamic countries, Saudi Arab and Iran, backed respectively by the US and Russia, has led to relentless war, pain and misery all over.'

'Exactly!' Abu nodded. 'The US and Europe have been waging proxy wars on our lands, using ignorant militant organizations as puppets that are much too eager to spread Islam. Our organization is on the apogean path to eternal peace! There cannot be peace while there are so many power centres. It's impossible to strike a balance between them. The only way to contain this violence is through Islam. It is a complete way of life that does not separate politics from religion. Once the caliphate is established, this bloodbath will end.'

'And what about the holocaust you shall cause?' Keira said, out of turn.

'Please do not preach about saving lives!' Abu shot back. 'The US and Russia have eight thousand nuclear weapons each. Britain, France and Italy around five hundred each. And Pakistan, the only Muslim nation that has nuclear weapons, has barely eighty. You bully and corner nations with your sanctions! Muslims don't have the power to threaten the West—not even to impose sanctions! So who are you trying to protect? Every day your jets and drones kill hundreds of our women and children. No Muslim country does that.'

'Much less than those you kill yourselves!' Keira countered. She noticed Nusrat and her aides nodding in agreement as the Murshid hypnotized yet another audience. Kabir and Bruce waited for Keira to make her final, game-changing pitch.

'We will continue our fight against terrorism,' she continued, unfazed by Nusrat's accomplices twitching their lips in anger. 'Without fear there is no discipline. Without a leader there is no order. The US is a morally upright country. We believe in equality and liberty, values that are not exactly the Sharia's favourites. We have taken on the onus to fight for what is right, even at the cost of earning the ill will of many countries. We have lost so many lives in wars which were fought for world welfare, rather than our own. It's a thankless job!'

'It is no secret that you have twenty-eight Muslim organizations with hundreds of chapters operating in America, to spread Islam and infiltrate our system,' she continued. 'There is nothing hidden about how much you hate America because it stands in the way of your religious dominance plan. Let me tell you how you work! You stand for a totalitarian theocracy that introduces itself in naive societies as a religious group. Then you grow using high birth rates, polygamy, by proselytising and attracting people from discriminated sections of society. And finally, when you have enough members, you launch political efforts to implement the Sharia, bit by bit, till the land is controlled by the law of Muslims. You use terror as a weapon in the process, to intimidate people and snatch resources. That's what your current plan does, right? On a much bigger scale! Much more insidiously, isn't it?'

Kabir and Bruce exchanged a tense frown. They had chosen not to interrupt the debate so far, but with Keira's inflammatory tone, they were beginning to seriously doubt their choice. What was Keira trying to do?

'Enough, lady!' Nusrat snarled. 'How dare you! Is it not true that developed countries like yours make huge profits from the sale of arms, propagating fear and warmongering secretly? America has seventy per cent of the top arms producing companies in the world, and sixty per cent of your population has private guns. You have militarized the world by setting up military bases in over four hundred locations across the globe. You project yourselves as saviours, but you dominate the world by controlling oil and selling arms.'

'I apologize, Madam Nusrat,' Kabir intervened, attempting at swift damage control. He had an inkling that Nusrat was not just another radical fanatic. 'Our agent was carried away, and I'm sure

Village of the Gypsy Women • 219

she meant no disrespect to your religion. But I do believe that despite your fight for Islam, you wouldn't do so at the cost of innumerable innocent lives. That, too, based on a crazy plan that involves taking over the world.'

'Crazy plan! You don't even know our true plan,' Abu snapped back. 'The 9/11-style crashes are just a part of the whole scheme. Parallelly, we will do something that will cripple the essential support systems of your world and subjugate the people in power in one go. Something our scientists have been working on in your own advanced laboratories, seeds that our engineers have been planting at every critical location in your countries. Come on, Nusrat! How can they land up in our territory, amongst our people and try to stop us? It's time they had a taste of their own medicine. Let their people feel the helplessness and horror that their bombings bring.'

'Oh shut up, will you?' Nusrat suddenly shouted out. She glared at Abu.

'I told you, I fight for Islam. That doesn't mean I do that by killing innocent people. My Jihad is directed inwards, towards our flaws within. Every time an innocent Muslim is referred to as a terrorist due to the actions of our extremists, my head hangs in shame. My family was ostracized from a French colony in Morocco after an explosion in our locality. We had lived with them for ages. I was devastated, but I could not blame them. They merely wanted their families to be safe. I realized that my own people were wrong. But sadly, no one had the guts to challenge them. If Islam has to be sanitized, it must happen from within. It's rare to find Muslims who would dare to recognize the flaws in their system, or demand evolution from the medieval way of life, where women are considered the inferior sex, an object to derive pleasure from. My sisters and I took up arms thereafter and our movement has only grown stronger every day.'

This came as an unexpected turn. Keira, Kabir and Bruce exchanged relieved looks.

'We need to take this man in our custody for interrogation and to stall the cataclysm,' Bruce requested Nusrat. 'We have a CH-53 waiting outside. Time is short and we need your permission.'

Nusrat seemed to consider this when suddenly, Abu spoke up. His chilly voice rented the air.

'Before you do anything as silly as that, would you not like to know whom you are working for?' Abu looked at Bruce and Kabir. 'You are brave men, but it's a pity that all of you have been taken for a ride. By this woman, right here.'

He raised a hand and pointed it towards Keira.

'She is not a US secret service agent,' Abu continued casually. 'What I am about to tell you will blow your mind. Listen carefully.'

Kabir stood still for a second, glaring into the emptiness. And then, he finally turned to Keira, to gauge her reaction. But there was none. That same placid face—no fear, no aggression. He looked back at Abu, who continued, addressing him directly.

'You were eager to learn what happened to your friend, were you not, Agent Kabir? Wasn't that one of the incentives they promised you when you joined the mission? Then, let me tell you a little secret that your Protettori conveniently forgot to mention! MH-370 was not hijacked by any person on board, but by the people working in the technology centre of Air-Bee that fateful night.'

He paused to bask in the pleasure of how his revelations were evidently affecting the dynamics of the taskforce.

'On that fateful night, Air-Bee switched off the transponder and took the aircraft's navigation into its control. The real reason was simply this: twenty Chinese and Malaysian employees of Treescale Semi-Conductors, a US-based multinational, were on board. Treescale has to its credit several of the earliest inventions in the field, did you know? Like the transponder used to put man on the moon in the 1960s. Earlier, one of Treescale's engineers, a Chinese spy, had broken into the company's servers and stolen some cutting-edge technology that powers Air-Bee's ground control—the latest in satellite-based monitoring.'

Kabir waited for him to continue.

Abu smiled as the words sank in. 'If the flight would have reached Beijing, both the spy and the technology would've slipped out of American hands. When the Americans learnt of this, they took over the flight, using the very technology developed by these scientists. Using another latest technology—a radiation envelope—to hide the aircraft from radars, they landed it in Deigo Garcia, their military base in the Indian Ocean. All this while allowing the rest of the world to believe that the aircraft had crashed.'

Kabir's features turned graver as he continued to watch Abu Bakr. He could not deny that the terrorist's explanation had filled in all the blank spaces perfectly. No debris in the ocean bed at the suspected crash site, his calculations pointing to an entirely different location to the northwest, and now, the mention of Diego Garcia. It was spot on!

'You may probably be aware that Air-Bee doesn't manufacture aircraft alone.' Abu Bakr continued, 'It is also the largest arms supplier in the world, after Lockseed Perkin. And your friend here works for that very division.' He tilted his head upwards, as if trying to cite facts from memory. 'Of what I recall from the encrypted messages that my team cracked, her assignment was to spy on you for information, then mislead you from discovering the truth. Basically, to do anything to ensure Air-Bee's secret remained a secret. And I take it that is why she intercepted your path in Malaysia.' He darted her a quizzical look. 'Am I right?'

Kabir was shell-shocked. Had his intuition at the dinner table that day been correct? That day! The last few days had been the most tempestuous of his life. So much had happened that he had kind of lost sense of time.

'She put her life at stake to save mine,' he hissed, trying to resist the man's ploys. 'She could have easily let your assassin put me out of her way forever!'

Abu smirked. 'Mr Kabir, do you remember that little amulet you used to wear around your arm? If it would have fallen into our hands, it would have meant certain exposure. It was too big a risk for Air-Bee. That was the only solid evidence proving that they had hijacked the MH470. And then, they got scent of me and thought what better option than to put you on this mission. Their business would be finished if the Ikhwan came to power. So their first priority switched to stopping us…and with the kind of chemistry I see building between the two of you, I'm sure she would have acquired the amulet anywhere along the way later.'

Kabir understood in a flash. While Abu Bakr's intentions at dredging up the truth at this point were a malicious attempt to weaken their taskforce, his facts were impossible to rebut. It also explained why Khabib had been hot on his trail—not just to finish him, but to attain the amulet. He felt his repressed rage as he turned to Keira. Her silence spoke far more than Abu's lengthy monologue.

'You are juggling with facts. Why would the Protettori take her on board this mission then, if she's just an Air-Bee spy?' Kabir tried his last counter.

'Exactly! So this brings us to the most important bit. The consortium for world safety, the Protettori…or whatever they call themselves,' Abu scoffed, 'is nothing but an arms syndicate, a group of top liaisons from arms producing companies working in coordination with their country's governments. The directors on their board hail from countries that are the largest producers of weapons—think about it!'

'They have nothing to do with world welfare. Peace.' Abu stopped to guffaw. 'Their only objective is to secretly propagate unrest in the world so that their stock keeps moving. They do it by lobbying with government, press and media to spread a strong anti-Muslim feeling, making people feel insecure. Oh, and also by fuelling the Shia-Sunni discord to make sure Muslims keep killing each other with their own lands while they sit safely in the lap of luxury.'

The Murshid suddenly turned to the warlord, aware of the discord he had caused. 'Choose wisely, Nusrat! Would you side with a private syndicate that works for profit? Or with a pious group that believes in a new world order, one where all humans would be equal, countries wouldn't push each other around and there would be complete nuclear disarmament,' Abu played his final card.

The momentary lull was broken by a loud sound. Everyone turned towards Kabir and Keira. Kabir had slapped her.

'You ... you were using me all along! It was all a big mistake, I should have trusted my instinct,' he burst out. 'When I saw you missing from the camp yesterday, I was heartbroken. We agents don't succumb to our feelings so easily. But I had genuinely begun to care for you. Begun to sense possibilities. And look where you've got me. On one side, I have this zealot to deal with and on the other, people like you, people who sell death.'

No remorse! Keira was standing with her head held high, looking straight into his eyes.

She finally spoke. 'Kabir, I did what a good agent is supposed to do, acting in the best interest of my country and my company.'

Kabir thought he sensed an ever so slight moistness in those stubborn eyes. Or, was it just wishful thinking?

The pair had now become the centre of everyone's attention.

Nusrat and her militia stared. Bruce was livid. Had Abu Bakr not spilled the truth, they would never have come to know the real face of the Protettori. Olaf and five of Tareq's men had sacrificed their lives. Vladimir lay bleeding outside. For what? To assist weapon sellers?

'It is true that I work for Air-Bee,' Keira said. 'It is also true that my mission was to distract you. And I am sure you would have done the same to me, given such an assignment. But beyond that...,' she shook her head, 'Abu Bakr's revelation about the Protettori is as much of a shock to me as it is to you. I was sent here on a sudden deputation by Air-Bee and I complied. It was my first introduction to this organization and I still find it hard to believe that they could be an arms syndicate.'

Unable to rein his temper in any longer, Bruce opened his mouth as if to argue.

Boom!

There was a deafening explosion just outside the tent. A few splinters flew in wounding the guards at the entrance, whose attention had been glued to the argument in front of them.

By the time they had realized their mistake it was too late.

Khabib had slipped out of the tent, taking advantage of the distraction. Had they known the monstrosity of the skinny man they were guarding, they would never have let their attention wander.

Outside, dressed in a hoodie, Khabib mingled with the fighters running amok. He slid another grenade stealthily behind the tent, making sure it was flung at a calculated distance away from the Murshid. The explosion sent Nusrat's chair flying forward. Fortunately, she wasn't on it—having already rushed towards the exit upon hearing the first explosion.

Bruce pulled Kabir down—just in time—to avoid the shrapnels coming at them. The tinnitus in their ears and the dense smoke immobilized them for a while. As the smog cleared, all they could see around them were smouldering bits of fabric and injured bodies.

The scene outside was no different.

There were explosions all around the area, each sending up thick clouds of smoke and dust. Khabib must have slipped out and freed Abu's guards. Dressed in hoodies from the fighters guarding them, it would have been easy for Abu's guards to go along with the crowd, letting the grenades slip underneath their kaftans and stepping on them to bury them in the sand. The time-delay grenades would have provided them ample time to move ahead, leaving behind a carnage of unsuspecting fighters, while providing cover for Abu and Khabib to flee.

Flee where? Kabir thought. They wouldn't reach far in this desolate desert without a vehicle. The camels and horses wouldn't carry them far out of reach. Rising to his feet, he extended his hand to pull up Bruce. There was a splinter sticking out from his thigh, making him bleed profusely. The crowd seemed to be drifting to the east. Kabir supported Bruce as they plodded in that direction. It was a gory sight all around. Disembodied limbs and bleeding corpses scattered everywhere. Beautiful Berber women who had been fighting for peace! The cult they were trying to stop truly was evil.

And all of this brought on by the machinations of one man. The Ghost! He had swept in from thin air, rescued the Murshid, and vanished—his appearance on the scene infernal as always, leaving behind a ghastly pile of corpses.

'Hang in there!' he yelled to Bruce after sitting him down in a safe corner, trying to keep his morale high. 'I'll come for you in a while—both, you and Vladimir. I am going to get Tareq and the CH-53.'

He sprinted south towards the mounds. He would run around them to the east where Tareq would be waiting with the helicopter. He was barely half a mile from the flatlands when he stopped dead in his tracks.

'No... no... this can't be happening! Fricking hell, no...'

Kabir fought back the daze—his worst fears coming true. Mustering all his power, he bolted in the direction of the rattle of the rotor blades.

The CH-53 was taking off, flying away further east.

As he drew closer, he saw a group of Berbers standing there, amidst strewn bodies and belongings, right at the place where the CH-53 had been parked. The women were glaring at the copter angrily, some of them firing at it with their Light Machine Guns—but it was well out of reach now.

'He escaped!' Nusrat announced dejectedly.

Kabir looked around at the dead bodies on the flat patch. Three of Abu Bakr's guards, two Berbers, two of Tareq's men, and Tareq himself!

'Tareq? Oh god…I'm sorry, man! So sorry…' Kabir saluted the black man, remembering his misleading grin. Without Tareq, they wouldn't have gotten anywhere close to Abu. But now what? Abu and Khabib would be on a rampage after this, and it would be impossible to stop them. He had no clue where they were headed.

'They got away unscathed! After massacring our people?' he growled from frustration.

'We shot the bastard in the waist.' Nusrat spat. 'May he die and burn in hell.'

'How many men got away?'

'Him and three others.'

'Where's Keira? Have you seen her?'

'She's their hostage,' Nusrat replied calmly. 'She fought back, but Abu's bodyguard—he's too strong…like a predator, he dragged her away…'

'Oh god, not again!'

Kabir stumbled, then sat down in the sand for a while. Olaf and Tareq were dead. Vladimir and Bruce were gravely injured. Had the taskforce failed in its mission? Were millions doomed to die? He opened his throbbing palms, staring into them. He had been clenching his fists so hard, his nails had left indents. 'And Keira…'

Her indignant face materialized before his eyes, while her words rang inside his head. *And I am sure you would have done the same to me, given such an assignment…!*

He had despised the words she had thrown at him. Had she never, not once, felt remorse when deceiving him? Surely, she must have felt something, he had seen it in her eyes. She was a strong woman and had faced the Murshid, Nusrat and Kabir's belligerent teammates bravely, holding her ground. Had she expected Kabir to stand for her when she was cornered? Obviously, she had let none of that show!

Damn it! He wished he could vent his anger out. She was the one who had betrayed him. But here he was, feeling guilty that he had failed to protect her?

And yet, there was a positive side to Murshid's revelations too. If the man was right, it meant that Jayant could still be alive... living in a prison cell somewhere. On the island of Diego Garcia where the MH470 was allegedly landed! Or, in any of the three hundred-odd US military bases. Or in a private detainment camp secretly set up by Air-Bee in some desolate out-of-reach location. There was no way of knowing exactly where! Only Keira could have taken him there!

'But...'

He looked up, staring at the pile of bodies. And there was her backpack, lying in the midst of the carnage.

28

Hanif, the Saviour

The interiors of the fort were austere. The yellow limestone walls of the central hall had rugged surfaces with oil torches fixed high up along the entire span. The floor was covered entirely with thick green handmade carpets, comfortable mattresses spread along its periphery for the participants to rest and mingle.

There were no logos, no symbolism in this decor. If one walked into the evacuated hall after the ceremony, there would have been absolutely no clue about the men who had been there. The assets, or the sheepdogs as Ghassan had called them, were gathered here for the annual re-avouchment ceremony. Hanif had contrived the structure and functioning codes with great ingenuity. The programme was designed to strengthen the cult through various ceremonies that were conducted through a full-day conclave. Each of the fifty-five assets wore a mask, and so did the two dozen organizers. Their identification codes and countries of origin were embroidered in gold on the black robes that they wore.

Hanif went by the title 'Murshid'. No one knew him by his real name or face.

'*Lā'ilāha'illāllāh muhammadunrasūlullāh.*' The hall echoed with the universal chant that bound these brothers together. The prayers were followed by a communal lunch. Eight volunteers rolled out a massive brass wheel, fifteen feet across, towards the centre of the hall, where it was laid flat carefully and wiped down with a linen cloth. It was a giant food plate. A hand cart was driven in and the volunteers emptied buckets full of saffron-flavoured rice with meatballs along its circumference. The assets took their seats around the plate and rolled up their sleeves.

Mokhtar stood on one of the high steps of the staircase. It offered him a clear view of the entire gathering. His men were on their toes, prepared for the worst. They had sufficient munitions to ward off a small army assault, the high bastions of the fort providing them with a position of advantage.

Mokhtar spared Hanif a glance. He wore a French cut that accentuated his soft features and gave him a much more authoritative look, compared to their first acquaintance. The man was serving the assets glasses of water, working as if he were simply a volunteer. Mokhtar knew that this gave him an opportunity to bond with the assets. He wasn't just exchanging pleasantries; he knew each of them by name. While he talked business he also read their eyes. Three of his deputies sat at a table, perusing the annual reports submitted by the assets.

When Ghassan had introduced Hanif to Mokhtar the very first day, his first impulse had been that of jealousy. In fact, he had felt cheated. After all, he had been fiercely loyal, brought in the seed fund, and had the required brains and muscle power to run the new organization. Yet, someone else would be his master, someone he hardly even knew! But as of today, it had all changed.

He had begun to admire this man's organizational genius. And he was glad that Hanif had proven himself worthy of Ghassan's choice by working day and night for the mission since.

But what had truly changed it all was an incident that transpired two years ago, on the fateful day when a haggard Mokhtar had returned with a sedated little boy in his arms.

'I couldn't kill him!' Mokhtar had said, his shoulders slumped, weary after three long days of a gruelling journey with a child on his back, all the while battling to stay hidden from the police.

'You did the right thing,' Hanif said kindly, staring at the fair boy. 'Who is the boy?'

'My son!'

'Your son?' Hanif raised a brow.

Mokhtar then went on to narrate the entire story. 'Yes, I should have done it,' he said, 'but I just couldn't bring myself to kill him. I drugged him and carried him here. But what will he do when he wakes up? He will hate me. He will want to kill me someday. He will hate all of us... our religion... our people!'

'You underestimate the power of our great religion!' Hanif came forward and sat down beside him on the ground. 'He will grow up to cherish you and Islam. He will be a devout Muslim, just like the rest of us.'

Mokhtar shook his head in despair. 'That is never going to happen.'

'I will make sure it happens. But for that, you must trust my decisions. Stay away from him for a while. We will have him admitted into the society's boarding school. He will be told that a good Samaritan rescued him from his kidnapper and left him there. He is still below six years of age. Do you know children start forming explicit memories around the age of seven? From what you've told me, he isn't aware of your name... nor has he seen your face clearly. His memories will fade with time... memories of the murder scene... and everything else. He is too young to have comprehended Nouran's words. All he will remember is that his mother placed a knife to his throat. An implicit, fuzzy and discomforting memory that may or may not ever seem real. And even if it does, that might eventually work to our advantage.'

Yes! This is so simple! Really. Why didn't any of it strike me? Mokhtar shuddered with tear-stung eyes. He hadn't been thinking straight, probably because he had been emotionally wrecked for the first time in years. But Hanif had redeemed him. And now, his son would live.

'I can watch him grow from a distance. Watch him turn into a young man!' Mokhtar hugged Hanif, who gently patted his back and comforted him. His concern was genuine, like that of a brother.

29

Brotherhood and Air-Bee: the Baffling Connection

Temperatures soared high. The sun scorched the narrow lanes that were scattered with rows of dilapidated shanties on either side. Hardly was there a spot of green or a body of water in the arid outskirts of this little Libyan town. Nothing to counter the heat. But Kabir was far too preoccupied by the numerous stressors wreaking havoc to note the sweltering weather.

Seated at a table in the dingy corrugated basement one floor beneath a dairy shop, he waited, restlessly tapping his feet on the floor. Close to the low ceiling were small windows covered with mould and dirt, hardly letting sunlight enter. The only source of light in the basement was a single bulb, dangling askew from the ceiling.

Across the table sat a hippy Arabic hacker, relentlessly puffing out wisps of cigarette smoke as he worked away on a laptop. The laptop that belonged to Keira Brooks. Kabir had managed to get her backpack. It had been lying in the sand after the helicopter had taken off. *She must have tried to get her backpack from the copter but Zain and Murshid got to her before that!* Nusrat had told him that Khabib had forcefully pulled her into the copter before taking off. *So she cleverly discarded this highly secure laptop in the desert sand amidst the scuffle, knowing very well it would do no harm there. Air-Bee employees wouldn't have to worry about their data backup anyway.*

When he hadn't been able to make it through the security locks, he decided he needed a hacker's help. And after several local inquiries, he had come to this dingy basement. For nearly two hours now, the chap had buried his face into the screen, but showed no sign of cracking its security web.

Kabir felt agonizing spasms around his rotator cuff as he sat back. The effect of the morphine was wearing off. A soft beep from his wrist drew his glance to the dial on his Tissot. *Shit!* He swore, swatting a pesky fly off. *1400 hours.* One more hour lost. That left them with a nerve-wracking eleven hours to stop the attacks. He had allowed himself not more than a few hours to follow this lead. If it led to a dead end he would have to move on, and shift track.

Governments of the concerned countries were now coming together, pooling in all of their intel and resources and toiling round the clock to track down and stop the Ikhwan before it was too late. The rest of the taskforce had picked up the few remaining fragments following the splintered mission and were working themselves to exhaustion to get back on track. And while the world was in a feverish race to stop the air strikes, Kabir Rathore was here, alone in this fly-infested basement, trying to hack this laptop. *God!* He kneaded his forehead, questioning his choices briefly. *What am I doing?*

But the sceptic in him could not stop those gnawing hunches of an intelligence officer. There were a couple of links missing in the whole puzzle. Links crucial to stopping the air strikes. After all, it was evident that Ikhwan had been trailing Air-Bee closely, which was why Murshid could spew so much information about an air crash that had taken place a decade ago.

But why have the Brotherhood been trailing Air-Bee? He had approached this very query in a few different ways. And each one pointed to one clue—the remote navigation technology! It was what had been allegedly used to hijack the MH470. Could this be what the Ikhwan were planning to use for the terror strikes slated to take place in eleven hours?

And the Air-Bee files in this laptop could actually contain those missing links of information. Information on the details of MH470 disappearance. The technology that had been used to hijack it. The engineers who had developed it. Those involved in the hijacking. These were the missing links, which if pieced together could help avoid the attacks.

But if the technology is so critical that it warrants even hijacking planes to keep it a secret, how could the Ikhwan have gotten hold of it? He rested his elbows on the table, his fingers steepled as his mind delved deeper into the conspiracy. *Maybe I am overthinking it. But there is something... something about what Murshid had said in Nusrat's tent... to us and to...her!*

His thoughts wandered back to the episode. And to Keira. Kabir still couldn't believe he had been hoodwinked by her charms. His years in the dark world of espionage had taught him to never get too attached. While his suave looks and manner gave him an advantage in the field, he had often been playfully accused of turning down attention from attractive girls he wouldn't trust. But here, the tables had turned. A mere two days with Keira and he had somehow been acting like a different man, letting his guard down.

The shock had still not worn off entirely. Had he not passed on the amulet to Sarah in time, and had it reached Air-Bee—the damage would have been irreversible. They would wipe out any remaining traces of evidence. The episode had come at a cost, but it was a lesson well learnt. And now, this very Air-Bee employee, one who had double-crossed him, was going to help him crack the case, as soon as he broke into this murky secret triad of the Air-Bee technology-MH470-Ikhwan strikes!

1435 hours... Oh, come on! He stood up and paced about. Time was ticking away, and this lackadaisical hacker showed little sign of progress. 'Should've just flown up to Turkey.' Kabir whispered under his breath, just loud enough to be heard by the hacker. 'The world's best hackers are there anyway.'

'Hey!' The hacker appeared miffed as he paused to take a cigarette break. 'Too many firewalls and security blocks. It'll take me...'

Kabir cut him short by pulling out a bundle of notes with one hand. 'Stop with the cigarette breaks. Finish it within the next half an hour, and you get all of it. The alternative might not be so pleasant,' he said while adjusting his jacket slightly, flaunting the butt end of his Glock. 'Get to work!'

The chap's stares turned glassy from fear.

'Get working!' Kabir slammed a fist on the table to snap the man out of his daze.

'Y... yes...' The hacker instantly doused the fresh cigarette, his fingers and mind beginning to move faster than ever.

Back in his hotel room, Kabir's eyes were glued to the laptop screen. He downed a glass of ice-cold water, his pulse racing. A plate of crusty sandwiches lay untouched on the table nearby. In the couple of hours he had till the taskforce was meant to reassemble, he had scoured through the drives. Hundreds and hundreds of documents: protected files in hidden folders, each stored under various cryptic names. All of them classified. Most of them related to Air-Bee and its affiliate companies. And many of them, as expected, were quite incriminating.

Just as he was arriving at the highly frustrating conclusion that it probably had none of the missing links he was looking for, Kabir stumbled upon something. A particular reference to a location. An American address in Idaho. Had it not been highlighted, he might have missed its significance; it sat in a remote corner of a lengthy 200-page document on the MH470 crash, dated a month after the accident.

A quick glance on the navigator told him it was a remote location. Miles away from civilisation, a tiny speck in a vast expanse of uninhabited forest land. One that was most certainly not easy to access for large vehicles. Which meant that it could neither be a dwelling nor a warehouse of any sort. So what was it about the place that made Keira highlight the address?

He pulled up the coordinates on satellite images. And moved the screen around. The photos showed up as thickets, twigs and trees everywhere. Not even a shed in sight!

Until he spotted a peculiarity. A rusty fleck on the ground.

He zoomed the image as far as he could. Nearly buried under piles of twigs and leaves was a circular metallic lid that appeared like it had been recently opened. It resembled a rusty old manhole cover. *A manhole lid in the middle of a forest? Highly unlikely!* He zoomed the image further to its maximum resolution until it became clear that it wasn't a manhole lid—the protruding heavy-duty hinges were a dead giveaway. And as an officer who had served in many warzones, he instantly recognized it for what it really was! *A bunker!* What place did an obsolete war bunker have in a classified Air-Bee document?

Kabir stared at the image of the hatch...the date the file was created...the address—Idaho, the north western US state known for mountainous landscapes, vast swaths of protected wilderness... the secrecy surrounding it. All of this could only imply one thing.

It's a safe-house! He set his phone down numbed. *For hiding something from the public eye. Or, worse, hiding 'someone' from the public eye!*

What if this bunker was where Air-Bee had been keeping its most guarded secret: its prisoners? Then, this was where the engineers would be—if they were still alive. If that was the case, then at least part of the answer to stopping the airstrikes lay inside that bunker. For these were the engineers who had developed the technology in the first place. Even if the Ikhwan had decided to modify the technology over the years, they would have a better chance at stopping them with these engineers on their side.

After contemplating his next course of action, Kabir decided to send an end-to-end encrypted message on a private line to his boss, Mr Menon. Having burnt his fingers with Colonel Bakshi and the Protettori already, he decided to keep it short and effective. He typed: 'Important developments. Top secret address. Need more details.' He sent across the bunker's coordinates.

If his hunch was right, Air-Bee was wilfully refusing to bring this information out in the open, even in crisis. It was more concerned about saving billions of dollars than it was about saving millions of lives. This meant that it wouldn't welcome any form of open inquiry. He would have to resort to back-door channels to hasten the process. When he had last spoken to him, he had told Mr Menon about his friend in Sri Lanka whom he had intended to visit shortly. Based on the data in his amulet shaped pen drive and certain specialized interface his friend had developed, they would have been able to locate the exact coordinates of the MH 370's landing. But after the Murshid's revelation ... that exercise had become redundant. And now if the Idaho thing turned out to be true, the whole MH470 mystery could be laid bare before the world in one straight shot.

Mr Menon's response was with him before long. The crisis had evidently rendered the man more alert than ever. 'No traceable records of the address,' he wrote.

Kabir replied: 'Urgently need backup. A private company that specializes in ground penetration radar tech needed at site in three hours. And clearance to land on American soil.'

While awaiting a response from higher command, he sent Bruce a coded message on the same secure connection.

'What news on the location of the nano-camera?'

Olaf continued to be a part of this mission even after he was gone, thanks to his tiny nano-crystals that Kabir had borrowed. While one had come in handy to get them out of the Kufra camp, the other was now being used to track Abu Bakr. During the scuffle at the aviation centre, when he had had his hand around the Murshid's neck—on a hunch—Kabir had stealthily fastened the second nano-camera to the back of his captive's head. Of course, he hadn't known then how effective the GPS on the nano-camera would be. But it was proving to be a powerful tracker so far.

Bruce was prompt with his reply. 'Tracker reveals movement in the outskirts of Libya. All eyes on him.'

Good. But why are they still lingering in Libya... A faint grin curled his lips even before he had finished the sentence. *Abu Bakr must've been forced to stop for medical help. Nusrat's bullet had drastically slowed him down.*

Within a few minutes, he was alerted to a second message from Mr Menon.

'Had to loop in the PM... clearance granted. Backup arranged. You may be onto something. Proceed with caution.'

Kabir immediately peeked into his watch. Nine hours left! There was only one way to do this. Without further delay, he responded to Bruce's text with an encrypted message that hinted at a dangerous game plan—in line with their strategy to play along with the Protettori till they could

'Urgently need the Xssault to fly us to America to intercept their supreme leader. Tell the Protettori every single minute is vital!'

He swiftly added: 'Details later.'

30

The King's Secret Army

The occasional whizzing of shots echoed around the training ground. Boys and men were busy trying to master the use of weapons. Mokhtar walked amongst them, supervising the training, but his eyes mostly hovered over one trainee. A boy. A wave of affection and pride washed over his features as he watched him swinging a scimitar masterfully.

There was a sudden bustle in the camp ground. Mokhtar spotted Hanif approaching him with a box of basbousa.

'Allah has blessed me with a son, brother.' Hanif beamed. 'We have named him Zahur.'

Mokhtar had never seen him so joyous. 'Congratulations!' He embraced the new father. 'May the Lord bestow him with a long and happy life.' The two men sat down under a tree in the secluded camp grounds.

The friends were happy with how their lives had been taking shape lately—both within the Ikhwan movement that was fast gaining pace and outside of it.

'It's a special feeling to see your child grow.' Mokhtar took a bite of the sweet. 'Reminds me of my own childhood... helps to make up for what we might have missed.'

The men looked up at the boy who was on his way to becoming a master warrior, just like his father. At thirteen, he had reached the final stages of his training and would soon be indoctrinated and brought into their fold. 'Bilal.' Mokhtar smiled. On these very grounds, he had arrived years ago, lost and apprehensive. The initial journey had been gruelling—isolating and frightening! Yet by the sheer strength of his determination he had forged ahead into becoming a fearsome soldier. And Bilal was turning out to be quite the same.

Mokhtar added, 'I had no one with me in my early days of training, no one whom I could call my own. But Bilal has me on this journey now, and for that I am thankful to you, brother.' He meant it sincerely. He embraced Hanif once more, caught up in his gratitude, before Hanif left to meet others in the camp.

It was nearing noon and there was something important he had to do. Important for the boy and for him.

'Bilal!' he yelled out. 'Remember what I told you yesterday. It is time now. You must wrap up your practice and join me.'

The boy's eyes brightened with joy. He put the scimitar down, rubbed his sweaty palm on his trousers and ran his fingers through his wavy hair.

Replacing the weapon from where he had taken it, he gulped down a glass of water from a pot under the tent and then splashed some on his face too. He looked fresh now—more so because he was ecstatic.

A warrior, one all the boys looked up to, had chosen to adopt him. A man who had earnestly cared for him throughout, was now going to make him his son. He was going to have a real home, finally! What else could an orphan wish for? Try hard as he would, he had no recollection of his early childhood. A few fuzzy images of a woman holding a blade to his neck, probably his mother, would come around at times, arousing an implicit discomfort. A feeling of betrayal!

In fact, he had grown to regard all women as untrustworthy, and a hindrance in men's path to glory. It had to be why Mokhtar had never had a woman in his life. Following his mentor's footsteps, he too had taken an oath to stay away from them forever.

Regardless, today was a new day. He was going to have a new identity. A new surname. And someone he could call 'Baba'. The boy straightened his dress and rushed towards the camp ground where his new father was waiting for him.

Mokhtar held Bilal's shoulders with both his hands. 'Shall we leave now?'

'I am ready.' The boy beamed, watching his foster father take his fingers within his palm as he led him out.

Mokhtar was still holding his son's hands as he climbed the steps that led to the bustling office building. It was a crowded place. It thronged with an assortment of people, but Bilal was oblivious to everything around him. He looked up at the man whose strong hands held his, eagerly anticipating the new identity he was about to be given.

They turned right and were greeted by two men. They offered their congratulations and said, 'The papers are ready, brother Mokhtar. We were waiting for your arrival.'

Mokhtar nodded genially. He wished Hanif could have been present as a witness at the registration office today. But it would be unfair to deny the man the company of his new born son on this special day. So he had called for two others from the society instead.

They approached the table where the officer-in-charge handed him the papers.

Mokhtar signed the documents. He was now a very pleased man. He had been looking forward to this day for quite some time. The world would know Bilal as his son now.

'Congratulations, brother!' The voices of his mates shook him from his thoughts.

'Thank you.'

He turned to Bilal. 'Are you happy?'

The boy nodded with enthusiasm. 'Indeed,' he said. 'Baba!'

Baba. The word brought back to Mokhtar memories of his own childhood. Memories of his father. He had not seen him for years now. How could he? The rumours lingering over the mysterious death of his wife must have reached him too. Besides, his father was a weak man and he wouldn't allow any such influence over his son.

Pushing those memories aside, Mokhtar left the office and climbed down the stairs.

Suddenly, the streets that should have been bustling with the humdrum of routine sights and sounds had turned chaotic. People wore expressions of tension. Traffic had come to a standstill. Hawkers were shutting down their businesses, scurrying about in panic. There was pandemonium—hollers and cries, voices overlapping one another.

The repeated mention of a name caught Mokhtar's attention. *'Ghassan?'*

He stopped to listen clearly.

'Ghassan has been assassinated,' cried an old man.

An ominous expression came over Mokhtar's face. *No! It could not be true.* He held a passer-by by the shoulders and hurriedly questioned him. 'What's happened?'

'Ghassan! He has been murdered! May his soul rest in peace,' confirmed the passer-by.

'How? Where?'

'Near the district administration office. Two unidentified men shot him point blank and got away.'

Letting go of his arm, Mokhtar sank down onto the footpath.

'Baba!' Bilal tried to support him. His fellowmen were equally aghast.

'Ghassan is no more? Murdered?' Mokhtar found it impossible to believe. He was in shock. Ever since he had taken on the role in the secret society, he had not been in charge of Ghassan's personal security. And they didn't meet as often as they used to. But he always considered the man his godfather—the one who had given his lost soul a new direction and purpose. And now, his mentor had been killed! Just as he was rejoicing at having gained a son, he had lost a father.

'Ya Allah!' Mokhtar stood up and rushed to his vehicle. He had to know the details. As he accelerated his car, his mind raced faster. *Who could it be? Who could have committed such a dastardly act? Where had Ghassan's security been? Was it the King's Royal Army avenging the death of their minister, allegedly killed by Brotherhood affiliates a few weeks ago? Or was it someone with a personal grudge? I should never have left his side!*

The aura in the car was sombre and silent. Bilal kept his thoughts to himself. He had never seen Mokhtar so worried or lost before.

And Bilal was right. The bitterness that had enveloped Mokhtar years ago came back with a vengeance. All of a sudden, he applied the brakes, bringing the vehicle to a screeching halt as a thought struck him.

Isn't Adel the head of the King's secret army? Could Adel be behind this? Was this a bait to bring him out in the open after Adel's repeated failures at unearthing their secret society?

Mokhtar's pulse raced. He fought the temptation to turn his car around, crash through the gates of the Royal Palace and open wild fire till he reached King Faoud. Then he would have his revenge.

Bilal placed a hand over his. 'I know what you are going through, Baba. But you must be patient. We will get our revenge, a much bigger prize.'

Mokhtar paused on realizing his son was right. Ghassan had probably separated him from the Society for this day. Only a great leader like Ghassan could foresee and plan the future of the movement after his death. He had planted a seed fund for Mokhtar and Hanif's organization that would keep proliferating to keep the secret mission going as long as it took.

Mokhtar would make no stupid moves!

31

Off To Nowhere

The British agent was busy on his phone. He was updating his senior intelligence officer on the plans as he walked down the corridors of the mechanical room and into the runway. A five o'clock stubble made him seem unkempt, and his blonde hair hadn't even been brushed.

Kabir, who had been waiting at the bottom of the air stairs by the Xssault, greeted him as soon as he cut the call.

'Agent Wilson.'

'Aye aye, Captain!' He saluted the man. The banter had become quite typical of them now. He wore an amused frown as he looked at Kabir's face. 'You look like shit!'

'Speak for yourself.'

With a chuckle, Bruce shifted his attention to the supersonic jet parked beside them. 'Sweet ride!' He whistled, studying the jet—a humbling reminder of how potent technology could be. In the right hands, it created marvels. And in the wrong hands, it literally brought worlds down. 'Poor Vladimir. He's missing out on all the fun.'

'Speaking of which, how is our friend holding up?'

'Oh, you know him,' Bruce began ascending the stairs of the jet, 'holding up like the seven-foot-tall Siberian that he is!'

'Good.' Kabir sighed in relief.

'By the way, nice work on the nano-cameras. The technical team have their eyes on him each fricking millisecond!'

'We have Olaf to thank for that,' added Kabir as he joined his teammate in the canopy of the cockpit.

The pilot was already seated. He quickly gave them the safety drill.

'The Protettori were quite swift in sending this cool carrier for our upcoming mission.' Bruce patted the cushy armrest of his seats.

'After everything they put us through, they ought to be!' Kabir strapped himself in. 'Besides, if they need people to buy their arms, they better help save the world first.'

The two men exchanged a bitter laugh.

Kabir was now sure that the news of their visit to Idaho had not reached Air-Bee, not yet. Or else, they would have used their influence in the Protettori to stop them. Which could mean two things—first that Keira was still a hostage with the Murshid or second, there was nothing worth hiding in the bunker at Idaho. Or both! It had been a big gamble to call for the Black Moth, but the ticking clock had left him with no other option.

'So,' Bruce looked up the time on his mobile screen. 'A few hours to Idaho? Impossible to believe!'

'Wait and watch.' Kabir looked at the front as the wings were about to launch into a vertical take-off. 'A few hours, and we'll be in the US.'

A few hours. The same thoughts coursed through both their minds. The ongoing countdown. About eight hours was all they had—and every passing hour grew increasingly priceless.

Kabir watched as Bruce buckled his seatbelt. The image somehow brought back a memory from the last time he had been in the craft, with Keira, while she nervously sat with eyes shut, mistakenly holding onto his seatbelt retractor.

Bruce saw the shades of grimness emerging on his teammate's features. 'So,' he exhaled, 'any news of Keira?'

'No,' Kabir was quick to reply.

Bruce got the hint, and then decided to change the subject

straightaway. 'Anyway, care to elaborate on the "details"? The Murshid is still in Libya. He doesn't have a Black Moth to bring him to America all that quickly. With just eight hours left, why then are we headed in the opposite direction?'

32

The Caliphate Dream

Mokhtar entered the ground floor of the swanky Cairene mansion that belonged to a wealthy businessman from Aswan. It was tucked in a leafy corner of Ma'adi. After walking through a series of narrow stone portals, he entered the private receiving room at the rear. It boasted of tall ceilings and exquisite gold panelling. On the wall, adjacent to the garden, projected a pair of the traditional mashrabiyyas—overhanging wooden balconies that had been screened off by thick curtains.

He greeted the masked men seated on the settees before smiling at Bilal. The boy was standing behind Hanif. Then, he took his spot in a corner of the room, taking note of the large group assembled. Some were dressed in thwabs, and others in three-piece suits. Some were from Egypt, and others from countries far beyond. But they were all influential men in their own right, and willing patrons of the secret society.

It was a good sign. A lucid step towards their global expansion. Amassing these patrons had taken years of networking and strategic planning. But now that they were finally assembled, he could see the society's long-standing goals for international growth finally taking shape.

After Ghassan's death almost a decade back, a lot of leadership changes had happened in their parent organization, the Brotherhood's structure, but the governing council had borne the brunt of the turmoil well, managing to stay cohesive. Despite the fact that the military had betrayed them and seized power after ousting the British from Egypt, the Brotherhood was only growing stronger with increasing public support. In fact, they wielded enough power to topple governments in several nations, change ideologies and to bring partisan Islamic groups together. Ghassan's dream was taking shape well in the Arabic region. But all this did not bring them anywhere near the caliphate—a much bigger dream. For that, Ghassan had entrusted Hanif and Mokhtar with the game plan, making them an independent entity.

'Saudi Arabia,' suggested one of the younger members in the gathering.

A lengthy debate on the countries that could make another ideal base for the secret society had been ongoing, and the suggestion was instantly met with consensual nods and murmurs.

'And from there,' continued the young man, 'to the West... maybe even the United States of America!'

'What? Branching out to the US? That is far-fetched!' argued an older man dressed in a jalabiya. The gathering soon broke out into a string of inaudible whispers, most in agreement with the old man. America had emerged as the true world power after dropping the bomb on Hiroshima, concluding the world war and forming the United Nations.

'Trespassing their territory could be suicidal,' the man added.

Hanif listened to these mixed responses quietly. Despite their apprehensions, he did not think that the young man's proposal of establishing their roots in the West was wrong at all. If anything, it was an idea that had been lingering in his mind for a while too. Once the whispers subsided, he spoke up.

'Oil!' he said. 'Black gold that drives economies. Those who know how to wield it shall be the puppeteers. And those who don't, shall remain the puppets!' He spread his arms.

'What has *oil* got to do with our new base?' the old man asked.

'Why, look at ourselves. Until a decade or two ago, America was the world's biggest oil supplier. Today, our Arabian region has more oil than all of them put together. So they've improvised. They have come up with sanctions and new foreign policies, befriending those of us who were happy to shake hands with them. Governments that didn't follow their endgame were overthrown with the covert help of their intelligence agencies. And thus, with all the oil in the world, we still remain their puppets, while they continue to grow as a superpower.'

The men nodded.

Hanif continued. 'The Ikhwan would benefit from landing on their shores and establishing a subtle presence there. Spreading our principles of Islam amongst those we can, while we learn a trick or two from them. Infiltrate their system surreptitiously, till we are ready to deal the final blow!'

The gathering fell quiet. It was an ambitious goal. But with Hanif having put it across, they knew he would have a plan to make it real.

'Besides,' he added, 'do you think we could ever establish the caliphate without subduing them?'

'Yes, I agree, brother Hanif.'

'I do too.'

They chipped in, one by one.

'We have to make an early start!'

Mokhtar's attention shifted from the discussions when he caught sight of the gaunt servant boy edging nervously into the room. The boy stopped walking when he was next to Hanif and whispered something into his ears.

A second later, Hanif's eyes sought Mokhtar out in the crowd, and gestured with a brief nod towards the corridors.

'Phone call,' he pantomimed.

Mokhtar understood. His friend did not wish to interrupt the crucial discussion midway and wanted him to attend to it instead.

Returning to the corridors, Mokhtar picked up the receiver.

When he heard the message from the other end, his lips parted in shock. It was a tip off from an informer. The location of the safe house had been compromised. The hideout where Hanif's family were staying had been discovered by the army.

Hanif was a wanted man. He had always been.

Though Hanif and Mokhtar had done everything to remain underground, Adel had slowly spun his web around them. He had gathered scattered evidence that the duo were the masterminds of this ignoble secret society. Custodial interrogation was what he needed to solve the case. He and his deputies had been doing everything in their power to bring Hanif in, and to have him tried for insurgency, but Mokhtar had outsmarted him every time.

But now, if the army got hold of Hanif's family, it would be easy for them to manipulate their leader into surrender. As he cut the call, Mokhtar glanced over his shoulder and noticed that Bilal had followed him into the corridors.

'What is it, Baba?'

'Unsettling news. I have to leave, my son,' he paused, 'take care of yourself.'

'I'll accompany you, Baba.'

Mokhtar studied the frown on his son's face. He could sense a hard lump forming in his throat. He hugged Bilal, who was now a strapping man, much taller than him. It was strange, but his emotions were rising and he could not understand why. He had felt this way only on two occasions—the day he had made love to Bilal's mother, and the day he had adopted his son.

'No. Stay. Look out for Hanif. Keep him safe from harm.'

33

The Lost World

'Hello, Agent Rathore here.'
    'I'm Agent Wilson.'
'Pleased to meet you.'

Kabir and Bruce shook hands with the Japanese man who had introduced himself as the chief engineer. And then they shook hands with the captain of their backup security team. Mr Menon had been highly effective as usual. Air-Bee—or the Protettori—probably had no idea that the taskforce was on to their little secret. The Black Moth pilot's communication channels had been cut off, both on and off board. They had landed in a warehouse, the automated roof now closing into position. The agents had made the best use of their time by sliding into a short meditative sleep.

'How far to the bunker?' asked Bruce.

'Roughly thirty minutes,' replied the Japanese.

'Why the hell. We don't have that much time.' Bruce hung his head, exasperated.

'Because we go out on those,' the Japanese said calmly, pointing out towards half a dozen kayaks, four of them already occupied by armed marines.

The agents gasped. They finally noticed their surroundings. It was a marshland as far as the eye could see. Tall grass covering every surface, interspersed with dense trees, which they would have to meander around.

'But the coordinates I checked stated that this was plain

land,' Kabir shot back, looking at the Protettori-appointed officers suspiciously. 'Besides, you can't have a bunker in the middle of a swamp, right?'

'Right!' countered the Japanese. 'We have conducted a drill already. There is a hammock, a few hundred metres square, right in the middle of this quagmire. That's where we are headed.'

Bruce and Kabir processed the facts being laid out as they slipped into specially designed bodysuits. This was as ingenious and resourceful as a corporation could get. Buying a large piece of valueless swampland from the government and having a hideout in the middle of nowhere. Who would come to check on them here?

As the group waded through the chest-deep muddy waters on the kayaks, they were met by nature's rarest painting of vivid contrasts. All around them were miles and miles of trees, protruding from the waters, splattered with green and brown shrubbery, with a few streaks of pink sunset shining in through the gaps. All of this beauty would amount to nothing if they couldn't stop the attacks in time.

A soft beep went off on Kabir's watch. Five hours! 'We'd better be quick.'

'We'll be there in five minutes. Care to brief us about the plan? We do know something major is unfolding here, Agent. We've seen the news.' The Japanese replied. 'That said, our geotechnical GPR system is generally hired to solve cold case mysteries and for rescue operations—for instance, when people are trapped under rubble.'

Bruce exchanged a quick frown with Kabir. 'Perfect. You are just the men for our job then!'

Kabir added, 'Let's just say that both your timely efforts and your discreetness in this delicate matter will be much appreciated. No interactions with the press, please!'

The Japanese gave an all too willing nod. These were exactly the directions his patrons would have given him.

The hammock was fully covered with vegetation and visibility was low. They moored the kayaks, unloaded their weapons and equipment and started treading towards the bunker hatch co-ordinates in tow. The hammock was so small it was barely a few metres before they could see the protruding lid.

'Let's not get too close.' Kabir held up his hand and signalled for the team to spread out.

The engineers set up the survivor search system by affixing it to a robotic vehicle that was then manoeuvred by a controller. 'So what do the readings say?' Kabir peered into the small monitor registering the readings.

'Not certain how many but there are definitely people down there,' the engineer said as he steered the vehicle to the left of the bunker hatch. 'It has picked up a range of vitals so far.'

'Maybe it's just a group of hippies living in there,' offered one of the marines. 'So that they don't have to pay taxes.'

'Highly unlikely!' the chief engineer spoke up, pointing to the monitor. 'The constant interference in the readings… that's from radiofrequency waves. There's some pretty sophisticated technology down there too.'

'Something's off,' Bruce whispered over Kabir's shoulder. 'If there's an entire murky world down there, as you were suspecting—why is there no security around?'

Kabir gave their surroundings another glance, his colleague having echoed his own doubts. *What if we are being watched?*

Bang!

'Duck!' Bruce shouted as a bullet suddenly went whizzing past his ear.

Bang! Bang!

'He's hit!' rang a cry, forcing everyone to instantly plunge down to the floor.

The team frantically crawled towards the trees to take cover.

'There!' the captain pointed at the rounds that were being fired from strategically drilled holes in the ceiling of the bunker.

Holes equipped with sensors and recording devices that had been camouflaged by the forest floor. From how comprehensive the entire set up was, it was clear they were being watched on the screens of a well-staffed subterranean surveillance room of some sort!

'Sedative shots,' shouted out a marine tending to the hit soldier. 'They don't shoot to kill.'

'Equally damaging! We have to move in. Fast!' Kabir shouted back to his team. 'They have the position of advantage right now.'

Another sign that the bunker is owned by a corporation.

'Yes,' said the captain, 'the radar hasn't picked up any explosives either. Agent Rathore, Agent Wilson, you storm open the hatch. We'll give you cover.'

Shoving over two tactical ballistic shields towards the duo, he then turned to his men, who instantly knew what had to be done.

The men jerkily brought out four capsules and rolled them towards the centre.

Soon, the forest floor, which formed the ceiling of the bunker, was covered by a blanket of thick fog from four smoke bombs. It left the men in the surveillance room below with zero visuals of what was going on above.

'Let's go!'

Racing towards the hatch, the two commandos used an explosive to quickly crack it open. 'Yes,' Kabir gasped as the door swung open with a groan. As planned, the blast had taken down two guards who'd been standing there.

Stalling for a second till the smoke and dust cleared, Kabir and Bruce stealthily descended into the bunker, unaware of what to expect in this forgotten world.

34

The Face-off

Visibility was steadily reducing along with the twilight sun, draping the woodlands in a thick shroud of grey mist. More overpowering than the smell of moss was that of petrol from the many engines that had just been switched off. Treading light to avoid the sound of their footsteps, Mokhtar and his men crept through low-hanging branches, inching closer towards the safe house.

In a small clearing, amidst miles of crevices and cliffs, sat the lone hideaway, unaware of the eerie dangers looming over it. It was tough to imagine how such a desolate location had been compromised. But the intelligence officer in question was Adel Kamaal—a man just as tenacious as him!

Mokhtar surveyed the area. *It seems like they have not yet infiltrated the safe house!*

Using his binoculars, Mokhtar tried to gauge the strength of his enemy. Beams from half a dozen torch lights came piercing through the endless silhouettes of tall trees. *Seven cars. Thirty-two officers.* He took note. The unit had strength in numbers. And they had seven vehicles to take cover too—making it very difficult to get a clean shot, especially in such poor light. His own group comprised just ten men, apart from the two servants and two bodyguards stationed within the house.

Currently, the only thing Mokhtar and his men had going for them was the advantage of a stealth attack. He would have to get very clever to rescue Hanif's family out of this alive.

After brief reflection, he split his ten-member group into three batches. Since the valleys were an echo trap—even the quietest sounds carried farther than he would like—he instructed the first team using signs and gestures. 'You four, creep around to the north, towards that range of rockery overlooking the back of the house… try and get the unit's attention drawn to that side.' He turned to the second team. 'You five… give me cover as I try to make my way to the house.' The general guideline was to take down as many soldiers as they could, without compromising their own positions.

Go! The first batch was given the signal and they began immediately, sneaking around the cliff face towards the north end. They were about fifty metres away from their intended hideouts when the rustle of their movement caught the attention of the army.

'There's someone's out there!' the soldiers roared.

'Behind the rockery!'

Within the next second, bullets were fired back and forth, causing an uproar in the zone behind the house. Mokhtar had to take advantage of the diversion at once or he would never be able to make it. The last streaks of light in the sky had dissolved. It was the time for Salat al-Isha, the final prayer of the day. He glanced up at the heavens and noticed a raven perched at the top branch of a tree, carrying the torn flesh of a dead mouse. It was an omen.

Muttering a quick prayer, he gave the second batch the go-ahead. The unit had begun shooting directly at the windows of the house now! Using the enemy's spotlights, he leapt across, zigzagging towards the safehouse, when he heard a fresh surge of alarms from the officers.

'Here!'

'There are more!'

'On this side too.'

His second team attempted to cover for him, but without sniper rifles and in such poor visibility, all they could do was fend the soldiers off with a few bullets. Just as Mokhtar was about to cut across to the entrance of the hideout, he ducked from the shots coming his way and pulled out two hand grenades from his back pocket. Simultaneously flicking out both pins while bolting past, he hurled them under the army trucks behind which most of the soldiers were taking cover.

'Grenades!' one shouted.

'Run!'

'Move!'

'Mokhtar?'

A familiar gasp echoed from behind him. From the corner of his eye he spotted Adel standing by the edge of the building.

Instantaneously, two deafening blasts went off, one after the other, their salvos swallowing nearly half the unit. Adel's body flew through the air.

It was the perfect opportunity for Mokhtar to break down the front door and dash into the house.

However, for whatever reason, his feet slowed down for a second. And he glanced behind his shoulder, curious to know if he had avenged his mentor's death. The body of the intelligence officer lay still somewhere amidst the carnage. He searched his jacket frantically. No more grenades!

Just go! His own panic jerked him out of the trance, and he leapt to the porch.

Announcing himself so the bodyguards within would know he was one of them, Mokhtar kicked open the door, darted inside and locked it behind him. The small empty living room was dark, its lights blown by stray bullets. The windowpanes had been shattered to bits. Wind was howling in through the wooden frames, flapping the curtains wildly. And fragmented pieces of furniture lay strewn around, their shards crunching under his boots as he tried keeping low.

'Zahur, sister? It's me... Mokhtar,' he whispered. The reverberations of bullets and the shrieks of injured army officers were still raging in the background. The second group was at their job, holding the remaining soldiers from coming closer. 'I'm here to get you all out to safety... are you there?'

There was no response!

Crawling from the living room, he moved into the narrow corridors. And from there, into the kitchen.

Zing! A bullet rushed through an open window and shot right over his head, forcing him to fall flat on the glass shards.

'Zahur... sister,' he whispered again, 'it's me... Mokhtar.'

Still no response! At least there was no blood splattered on the walls. Had the bodyguards been forewarned of the attack and taken them away to safety? Plucking out a piece of glass from his hand, he yanked down a couple of kitchen towels from the door and wrapped them around his fist to cushion his skin from the debris as he slithered to the last room, reaching the back of the house.

If this room was empty too, it meant the family had fled, and he could breathe a sigh of relief.

'Zahur... sister... it's me Mokhtar!' he said again, his voice trembling.

He slowly nudged the bedroom door with his gun. The door creaked open. And as the light from the spotlights flitted in through the bullet holes in the wall, his jaw dropped in horror.

All four walls were dripping with fresh spatters of blood. Four bodies lay sprawled on the floor, shot several times over. Two men and two women lay dead, glass and wood fragments sticking out of their still faces and hands.

Mokhtar cupped his mouth in shock, wondering how he might convey the tragedy to Hanif, when something suddenly struck him. *Wait...* a tint of colour returned to his pale face. There was no body of a child amongst the dead. *Where is Zahur? Hiding somewhere?* As he put his ear to the ground, he could hear a whimper. The boy was alive. Hiding somewhere!

He removed a penlight from his pocket and flashed it at the

faces of the dead when the source of the whimper swiftly became clearer. Hiding flat, underneath the bodies of the dead, were Zahur and his mother. They had both managed to stay alive thus far from the shower of bullets. He quickly and quietly dragged them out.

The boy's mother had ended up with bullet wounds in her arm and shoulder, but Zahur was slimmer, and had managed to escape unscathed.

Mokhtar ran a quick look over her injuries, as she lay still, paralysed by fear. *'Flesh wounds.'* She would survive.

The sounds of gunfire were beginning to fade away. Mokhtar wondered whether all his men had perished or the entire army unit had been taken down. A swift peek through a hole in the wall unfortunately revealed the former to be true. There were heavy casualties amongst the officers, but his whole crew was now dead. He was alone, and he had two injured to save!

'Quick! You have to snap out of it, sister.' Giving her a towel to stem the bleeding, he tied Zahur's eyes with the second one. *He should not have to watch this!*

Breathing in a chest full of air, he pushed the bed to a corner. The sounds of moving furniture would draw the attention of the soldiers outside, but he had to. He had no time to waste! He pulled out a faded dusty rug from below the bed. Underneath it lay a trapdoor.

'Ya Allah.' Hanif's wife shuddered. She had been here a month and had had no idea about such a door.

Opening its hatch, he helped the duo descend its steps after handing them a bag of supplies. 'The tunnel is long, but it will eventually take you to the other side of the valley. From there, you'll have to walk a mile or two to reach the nearest town.' He dropped close to the boy. 'Zahur, if you're brave and clever, you'll both be able to make it out alive!'

'Yes,' stuttered the boy, with his blindfold still on.

'Now, quick. Yallayall…'

Zing!

Zing!

A bullet had come through. And another. Mokhtar briefly froze by the trapdoor. He could feel a wet patch forming on the back of his shirt.

'What happened? Are you hit, Mokhtar?' She exclaimed, her eyes widening.

'No. I am fine. I'll hold them off. Now move... yalla...' Handing her both his penlight and his own gun for their safety, he hurriedly shut the trapdoor and replaced the rug.

He could hear the guards approaching the front entrance. They would come barging in any moment now. Grinding his teeth, he hauled the bed back to its spot, battling the agonizing spasms radiating across his back. In the darkness, the soldiers would never know something was amiss.

Exhausted, Mokhtar then plonked to the floor, crouched in his own pool of blood.

When the door to the bedroom opened, Mokhtar had to crinkle his eyes as the light from several torches hit his face.

A string of happy sighs and cheers swept across the room as the officers spotted the notorious man sitting in the corner. The assassin had no gun on him, and he was fatally wounded. They had finally gotten one of the most wanted terrorists on their list!

'We beat you finally. You've taken too many of our lives.' A soldier pointed the muzzle between Mokhtar's eyes.

'Wait!' came a loud order.

The soldier fell back.

'My friend!' Mokhtar laughed slowly, blood trickling down his bluing lips. 'You're alive, Adel Kamaal!' He raised his head, mastering the pain to take a good look at his former friend. His handsome face hadn't been touched by age, nor tufts of grey hair charred today by the force of his blasts.

'Where is Hanif's family?' Adel demanded.

Mokhtar weakly gestured towards the dead bodies on the floor. 'You already... g...' he wheezed, 'got them...'

Adel was not buying it. 'And where is Hanif's son?'

'He must be around here somewhere.' His head was lolling over his shoulders, life draining out of him, bit by bit.

'Don't lie to me!' Adel thundered. 'Who are you working for? What is your plan?'

Mokhtar continued to stare at him defiantly, blood trickling down his lopsided mouth.

'Speak up, Mokhtar! You can't outsmart the Royal Force. I can get you immunity. I stopped you earlier on the oil ship and will again this time around! Confess!'

Mokhtar just grinned, thinking how miserably his friend had failed. Both times.

Asking his subordinates to step out, Adel approached the dying man and knelt by him. 'Mokhtar...' there was a tinge of grief in his voice as he raised the man's face to his. 'What have you done to yourself?'

Mokhtar's glassy stares met the officer's blue eyes. 'Two decades in the police and it hasn't toughened you the slightest, has it?'

Adel grunted, 'Sorry, my friend, but you should have surrendered while you had the chance.'

Mokhtar grinned weakly. 'Sorry, my friend, but you should have killed me while you had the chance. The secret must live!'

In a flash, he whipped out the tiny blowdart that had been hiding beneath his palm. By the time Adel could grab his wrist, the needle had already lodged into his neck.

There were so many questions in his wide glare, quietened as the expressions froze on Adel's face, paralysed by the venom. But Mokhtar had already shut his eyelids—probably unwilling to face any of those questions.

Adel had never stopped caring, right until the point he had been killed.

Mokhtar, the protector, had never stopped killing all of those who had cared for him. His mother. Nouran. And now, Adel Kamaal. His first friend. The irony!

A sordid minute later, the men returned and the valley echoed with relentless tremors as Adel's deputies continued to empty their bullets into Mokhtar's body, long after he was gone.

35

Kabir Strikes Gold

At first glance, the bunker was essentially a long musty corridor. It had several arterial paths, which led off into more hallways. Expecting to find resistance in every nook and corner, the duo snuck through the passage slowly, a yard at a time. And just as they had expected, tucked behind the very first alleyway on the left were two heavily armed guards. The shots came at them in coordinated attacks, every three seconds, giving them no time to retaliate. If not for the ballistic shields fending off the gunfire, they couldn't have survived the onslaught.

A minute into the heavy fusillade, Bruce pulled out a canister and let it quietly roll into the alleyway. As soon as the unwitting guards began to cough their lungs out, the duo took them down with non-fatal shots.

Smothering their noses and mouths, they crossed over the bodies and the plume of smoke to enter the alleyway. It soon became clear that the alleys were a network of dormitories—rows of cells barely enough to house a man. Each cell was segregated from the other by a thin wooden wall.

With Kabir posed to take on the resistance from within, Bruce cautiously kicked the first cell door. The door fell open.

'Jesus!' Bruce crunched his nose. The cell smelled terrible. Within it was a mouldy mattress with a man sprawled across it.

'Dead?' They shared a confused stare.

But a rumble of snores put their doubts to rest.

The second cell presented a similar scenario. So did the third.

As they moved through the corridor, they were met with further resistance in the adjacent alleys. But all the lurking guards were overcome by the two commandos, backed by the special forces with tactical efficiency, one at a time. Once certain there was no further threat, they moved ahead. They kept going until they reached a heavy door at the very end.

With their guard up, the duo gradually nudged the lever, wondering what the heavy door concealed. But when the door unlocked, the sight that greeted them made their jaws drop.

'Oh my god!' Bruce grunted.

It was a spectacle straight out of a science fiction film; definitely not something one would expect in a desolate forgotten bunker under a forest floor. In a brightly lit room of solid walls, several tables ran symmetrically along the centre. While the walls were teeming with screens and wires, the tables were stocked with cutting edge hardware. They could spot several programs simultaneously being developed. It was an advanced software lab of some sort. And apart from the whirring noise of fans, the room held a deathly silence.

And yet, it wasn't empty.

A group of shabbily dressed men were seated behind the tables, working away at the systems indifferently. The blasts. The gunfire. The dead guards. Nothing seemed to matter. It was as if they were all in a world of their own. All of them. And they shared another common trait too: East Asian features. Except one. An old man, who was hunched over the table unlike the rest.

'Oh my god,' gasped Bruce, 'are these the Treescale engineers? One of these then must be the Chinese spy who stole the Air-Bee technology, just as Abu Bakr had mentioned.'

'I'd think so,' Kabir said, still in a daze at the sight, 'and I'll hazard a guess that they've been doped!'

The rest of the team barged in soon thereafter. The engineers barely looked up at the stream of unfamiliar faces who had just charged into their lab. A second later, they returned to their desktops, as if it was just a normal day at work.

The captain of the backup security team gradually approached the old man at the end and tapped his muzzle on the table. Holding up his torchlight, he flashed it on the man's face through his unruly hair, forcing him to sit up.

The old man cringed. 'I've done nothing...'

'Speak up.' Kabir was about to join the captain in the interrogation, when his boots slowed in their tracks. The man who had turned to him with a sorry frown, appeared eerily familiar. 'C... can't be!' He said, nearly dropping his gun. 'M... Jayant... is that you?'

The vagabond nodded slowly, his features brightening. 'That is my name.'

Rushing around the table, Kabir took a good look at the man's face.

In place of the neatly trimmed goatee that his mate used to sport, the man wore a long monkish beard, some of it with streaks of grey. There were puffy bags underneath the eyes that used to sparkle with the smartness typical of an acclaimed intelligence officer. Crow lines had crept up on the sides of his face. All of this lent him the appearance of a sixty-year-old rather than a man in his thirties. But it was him all right. 'What have they done to you?' Kabir sensed a lump curling up in his throat as he approached the chair. 'Jayant... I... I can't tell you how glad I am to have found you. Everyone else had given up hope... but I never stopped looking... never stopped searching for answers...and now... after ten years... finally...'

Kabir was about to grab his friend by the shoulder and give him a hug when the vagabond interrupted him and patted his arm instead. He spoke softly, 'Okay. But who are you?'

36

A Parallel Headquarter

'But I don't want to go, Baba,' the young thirteen-year-old boy said, wiping his drenched cheeks.

The airline announcement rang out. It was time for all passengers boarding the flight bound for New York via Geneva to proceed towards the final security.

'Zahur!' Hanif stared him down sternly. 'You have to be brave. America is a land of opportunity. This will be a learning experience for you. You will see more, discover more about other cultures and other people. Their ways, their lifestyles, their beliefs.' When he observed the unconvinced scowl on his son's face, he stepped closer and whispered. 'You know how dangerous things have gotten around here.'

Hanif paused briefly. Ever since Mokhtar's death, circumstances were no longer the same. True, Hanif was a brave man. He had willingly taken up the secret assignment, aware that his days would be fraught with peril, aware that life could be snatched away any moment. And he was willing to embrace it all for the greater good.

Up until he was gifted with a son!

Now, after the tragedy that'd snatched away the life of his dear friend, the undercurrents had shifted ever so slightly. Hanif hadn't realized how much support and strength he'd derived from the presence of his late friend. But with Mokhtar gone, he could sense that the Ikhwan was turning from the offensive to defensive.

While they needed to continue pursuing their agenda

aggressively, everything needed to be kept under the wraps. They would have to go underground. He had been receiving information of how the deputies of Adel Kamaal had vowed to finish off what Adel couldn't. With the Royal Army hell bent upon unearthing them, they would have to lie low. He had spent many sleepless nights wondering how the safehouse location had been compromised and what would happen if such a situation was to repeat itself. And he definitely did not wish to see his child taken away in front of his eyes. Life had suddenly become precious. So until he had firmly reclaimed his foothold, his son would have to be away.

But Zahur was not willing to leave his family's side. No child his age would! That said, an idea struck him. Zahur was now thirteen years old, a sober and sincere child. Old enough to keep secrets and harbour thoughts that would give his future a worthy direction!

'Zahur,' he lowered his voice, 'you know the Brotherhood, right? Uncle Ghassan's Muslim Brotherhood! They are special, they help people. Thousands of poor people!'

Zahur had stopped sobbing. He was now listening carefully.

'*We* are even more special,' Hanif said, 'Out of lakhs of its members, *our* family was chosen to carry out a secret mission. Ours and Uncle Mokhtar's. A mission that will change the destiny of the world and bring eternal peace and happiness to all. And we are the blessed ones endowed with this divine responsibility. We have to protect this secret at any cost. Our lineage shall live and die for it! Do you understand, son?'

Zahur shook his head innocently.

'I need your support,' Hanif said, 'I envision you taking the reins after me. I envision you nourishing our movement in the West. For that, I need you to be bold, and I need you to proceed with foresight as well. Will you do that for me?' He tapped his son's cheeks, his kind tone working its charm.

'Yes, Baba.' Zahur wiped his face on his sleeve. 'But, will you come visit me?'

'Yes, I will.'

'And will you bring Bilal with you when you come? We are supposed to work on this together, right? To avenge Uncle Mokhtar's murder?'

'Yes, I will.' Hanif heaved a sigh of relief.

He could see the glow in his son's eyes.

37

Green Dots All Over the Map

The metal-panelled fencing that ran around the expansive enclosure was shut and sealed at every intersection. Armed guards were patrolling the grounds. They constantly reported back to a team of personnel, all equipped with the most advanced surveillance system and television monitors. Security had been raised following the spate of unsettling events in oilfields around the world.

This was the last of sixty subterranean caverns carved into rock salt, far beneath the surface, that constituted America's Strategic Petroleum Reserve. Hidden across four secure sites, running along America's gulf coast—from Baton Rouge, Louisiana, to the largest of the four, near the tiny city of Freeport, Texas—these unassuming locations stored 900 million barrels of oil. Unassuming because there wasn't much to see above ground, merely some well bore heads and pipelines.

No nation could be a superpower without such reserves. They were the key to foreign policy. They provided the nation with a shield to guard against oil import cut-offs and a dependence on the Middle East.

Chewing loudly on his stick of gum, a surveillance officer moved towards the monitors, studying the footage on a screen in the top right corner. A member from the ground staff was beaming his light at the entrance of a well head. He stared at the screen for a minute, longer than usual, before relaying his instructions to a few armed guards through his transmitter.

'I think a member of our staff has spotted something at the north-side entrance. He might need backup.'

'Yes sir.'

The rest of the team in the surveillance room edged closer to watch the developments, while the officer zoomed into the images on the monitor for a hawk-eyed view of the north side entrance. The member of the ground staff in question, had paused by the wellhead and fished out a packet of crisps from his jacket.

'Seems like the man wants to catch up on his dinner while waiting for backup!' the surveillance officer remarked, sending his team into a series of chuckles.

However, the next second, instead of eating the contents, the ground staff member began emptying the contents of the packet into the oil well.

'What?'

'Has he gone mad?'

'Why would he do that?'

'Look! A powder...'

'Shit! Fuck!'

An emergency button was pushed. An alarm was instantly raised. Announcements blared across several speakers and transmitters throughout the ground.

'Security breach! Security breach! North-side entrance. A man in overalls has dropped the contents of a packet into the oil well.'

While the shocked surveillance team watched on, waiting for the man to be caught, the intruder gazed up, straight into the cameras. And then, as the last clunks of powder were emptied into the well, he smiled, as if mocking the surveillance team, right through their monitors, to their faces. With his mission accomplished, he then pressed an icon on his mobile. The strategic reserves of Japan, China, Russia, Canada, India had all been contaminated in a similar way by his colleagues. This was the last nail in the coffin! His part complete, he quickly bit the cyanide tip off his index finger ring.

∽

Bleep. Bleep. Bleep.

The signal went off in a receptor in the communications wing of the Cove.

'Yes!' The Murshid shook his fist in victory.

The final oil reserve had been contaminated. All the dots on the world map were now flashing green.

'Sayyid will be very pleased. All hail the leader! Everything has gone as planned, and we are on time!' he celebrated.

He turned around cheerfully, addressing the experts who had assembled in the control room.

'Chevron, ExxonMobil, BP, Shell, IOCL, Sinopec… you have the schedules, and the designated times at which the microcapsules have to be activated to seize control of their respective rigs. Let's get working to ensure a perfectly timed siege.'

38

Bilal Sows His Seed

The 6B graphite tip curved around the edges of the masterful greyscale portrait. Each shade was rendered in hair thin strokes. It depicted a man surrounded by armed soldiers. There were around eight of them, their guns pointed at him...five of them taking a shot, whereas three were falling backwards. Blood flowed freely from the man's wounds. A young boy was hiding behind the killer, his expressions wrathful as he peeped. In his little hands he held a pistol, pointed towards the fourth soldier.

Bilal took a step back to study his artwork resting on an easel that stood in the middle of the room. The encounter at the hideout had become a legend within the society. His father, his now-dead father, had protected his friend's family. He died protecting the society, putting an end to its greatest enemy, the head of the King's Royal Force. The man who had killed Ghassan.

And indirectly saving Bilal, who had insisted on accompanying him that fateful night.

Bilal had proven to be a capable heir, taking on the role of the chief eliminator naturally. He had stood by Hanif, much like his father had, giving him free rein to expand the society's web across the globe. Their assets were growing exponentially. And if there ever arose a threat, Bilal was swift to act.

As a forty-year-old, the first flecks of grey hair had begun to emerge. If one were to look at him, gloating over his sketch, they would feel that Bilal was a happy man. But he was not truly content.

There was one element missing in his life—human connection. And he craved for it. Having vowed to never seek the company of a woman, he had neither been intimate with one, nor wished for it. However, he did crave for the sort of connection he had had with his father. Even if brief, those were the happiest years of his life. He'd hoped to adopt a son. He'd even met a few children from the orphanages of the Brotherhood. However, none of them could ever stir his fatherly emotions. He wanted a son of his own. He wanted to bring into the world his own flesh and blood, his progeny. And while he'd been languishing under the burden of such a dilemma, who else could help him other than Hanif!

He should be here any moment now.

A car pulled into the driveway. Bilal set the pencil down and strolled up to the lobby to welcome the older man. They met with a hug.

Hanif observed his foster son with a smile. Tall, sharp features, dressed in a smart blue suit, Bilal remined him of Mokhtar.

'She's here,' Hanif whispered into Bilal's ear. 'Chaste. Virginal. And from a respectable family. She'll give you what you desire. Your very own son.'

Turning around towards the entrance, he murmured the holy verses.

The driver escorted their awaited guest inside. She was a young woman, clothed in a loose abaya from head to toe. But her face revealed a set of comely features. A maulvi was at their heels.

Following a short bout of introductions and a makeshift nikah ceremony, Hanif left. Without hesitation, Bilal led her inside the house, towards his bedroom.

'Are you nervous?' he asked kindly.

'No. Why should I be?' she answered demurely as she sat down on the bed.

'We are strangers. I know you must have had some compulsions, some pressing needs, otherwise why would you have agreed to this?'

Bilal Sows His Seed • 273

'No. No such thing...' Her voice trailed off. She was clearly not comfortable with this discussion.

'Then what is it? I need to know before we do this.' He held her by the shoulders, his firm grip conveying his resolve.

'It's for Hanif baba!' she finally said. Her gaze was affixed to the ground.

'Hanif baba? How long have you known him? I get it, your family must be under obligation to Hanif baba, right?'

'No, I'm his niece!'

Feeling the firm grip on her shoulders thaw, she looked up to see the teary-eyed handsome man standing there, frozen in shock.

39

The Chinese Engineers

The doctor swung the medical penlight in front of the captive's eyes, turned and then flashed it again, peering into his pupils. The medical team had been baffled when they were brought in to examine the rescued hostages. And quite a while later, continued to be so. There was no precedent for such horrific circumstances.

'He *seems* fine.' She set aside the penlight. 'Of course, we would need to do further tests.'

'Fine? Why, thank you, ma'am,' Jayant smiled. 'I have been saying the same thing. But this young man here, he refuses to believe me.'

'Of course not. What would he know?' The doctor played along.

Kabir shook his head with a faint grin. His friend might have lost his memory, but he had not lost his ability to switch on the charm around an attractive woman, had he?

After having finished her preliminary examination of the lone Indian survivor, she nodded at Kabir, indicating that he step outside. They walked into the makeshift canopy—one of many that had been set up around the perimeters of the bunker.

'Continued oxygen deprivation-triggered memory loss. That is my first suspicion,' she declared, going on to explain her patient's condition in detail, while Kabir continued to observe his mate through the open door. The man he was looking at was Jayant. But somehow, it was not the friend he knew. And staring at such a reality in the face, was tough.

'Agent Rathore,' the doctor's voice pulled him from his thoughts as she pointed to a second canopy wherein a few engineers were being examined, 'as for them, they have been drugged.'

'They are displaying signs of disorientation, because of both, chemical imbalances from the drugs and from having been held in a bunker for over ten years! So I cannot imagine how cooperative they are going to be or whether they have the information you're looking for.'

'Kabir.' Bruce joined the pair. Having just emerged from the bunker, he had an update to share. 'There are a couple of hostages who appear somewhat coherent.' He tilted his head towards the bunker hatch. 'Do you want to have a chat with them?'

Kabir understood. 'I'm coming.'

'Before you leave, Mr Rathore...' the doctor stalled their departure. 'Your shoulder, if you do not rest it, you risk injuring it permanently. I will prescribe a powerful painkiller for now... morphine. It will knock you out for a while. But you'll need some intensive physiotherapy to get it back to working condition.'

'Morphine. Physiotherapy. Gotcha.' He acknowledged with an affable smile, before heading off with Bruce. The shoulder did hurt like hell!

As the duo re-entered the bunker, an unsettling silence kept them brief company.

'Eighteen of them rescued and accounted for, so far.' Bruce broke the lull with a scoff. 'All MH470 passengers. All engineers who used to work for Treescale, apart from your pal, of course. So where are the rest? The families? The women? The children? No one knows yet. And what about the spy—the one who stole the information?'

'My guess is that he was taken out immediately. The remaining passengers would have had to be silenced, since they knew too much about the hijack... I don't know what they chose to do to the rest. But these eighteen scientists could take Air-Bee's remote access to another level. The kind of expertise money couldn't buy, loyalties that couldn't be seduced otherwise. They were too precious to be sent to the sacrificial altar.' Kabir theorized, glancing at the dinghy beds the engineers had been forced to share for the last ten years—as if they were criminals. 'So they kept them alive, imprisoned them here, plugged them on drugs and forced them to work like machines, developing technology that could be used by Air-Bee for a variety of purposes. Of course, we can never be sure until someone actually coughs up the truth.'

'If this is how they treated people who were useful to them,' spat Bruce, 'I shudder to imagine what they might have done to the rest!' He paused. 'And what is the story with your friend?'

'I ... don't know exactly, but I have a hypothesis!' Kabir said, clearing his throat. 'Jayant was carrying an advanced signalling device, which they discovered on him. They came to know that this device was used to transmit the MH470 location at some point close to its final destination during the flight. There are signs of torture on him. They have been subjecting him to bouts of oxygen deprivation and revival as a mode of interrogation.'

'Oxygen deprivation?' gasped Bruce.

'To dig into his memory and still keep him incapacitated. His dorm, like the others, is maintained at just the right oxygen levels to bring about temporary loss of memory. They want to find out where the transmitted signal would have gone. How seriously and in what way it would be handled by his command? And to find out as much as they can about India's military capabilities and secrets.'

'Who, Air-Bee? And for this they have been torturing the poor guy for nine years…'

'Yes Air-Bee…after all, they must be in cahoots with the US defence Other Government Agencies. An Indian spy in undeclared custody is worth millions of dollars in term of information. No human rights, no limitations!' Kabir conjectured sadly.

'Air-Bee is going to be facing some serious shit in the upcoming tribunal.' Bruce turned away and punched a thin wooden cell wall, denting its structure.

'Well, that only time will tell! For instance, this bunker. There are no markers, no evidence against Air-Bee, nothing that would lead back to them specifically. Keira's laptop too had several files, but all unauthenticated! We still don't know for sure whether she is an on-roll employee of Air-Bee, so all the documents on her laptop mean nothing unless we can prove otherwise,' said Kabir.

'Do you think the US government is in this with them?' mused Bruce.

'You know how the lobbying works out there. If not the government itself, someone really high up must be.'

∽

Inside the lab, the doctor who had been tending to a pair of engineers intercepted the two commandos before they could sit the dazed patients down for an interrogation.

'Officers, I advise that you please go gently on them.'

'Yeah, right!' Bruce let out an exhausted laugh. 'Apologies, but we are a little hard-pressed for time.' He flashed his mobile timer. 'Four and a half hours, to be precise!'

'You will not get your results if you rush this or if you push too hard.' The doctor glanced over his shoulder at the engineers who were still staring at their desktop screens with hollow eyes. 'They have lost their sense of reality.'

Bearing the advice in mind, the commandos pulled out two chairs for themselves. They faced the engineers and made introductions.

Kabir studied the man seated opposite him. He was the chief scientist, Mr Huang. A lean man in his early fifties, he resembled an ageing professor, someone who could have been an interesting personality a decade ago.

'Mr Huang, we have been informed that you are the lead

developer.' Against every fibre in his being that was urging him to rush on, he tried to ease into the conversation. 'You were the brains behind the inception of the remote navigation technology. A technology that has been stolen by a terrorist group, who now plan to use it to destroy the world. We need your help to stop them.'

The engineers stared at each other, and then straight ahead again.

Kabir placed his palm on the table, trying to keep his restless fingers still. 'We have technical teams working round the clock to try and stop then. But, if the Ikhwan have modified the codes in such a way that the experts are unable to override it, would you be able to help us?'

The engineers exchanged a blank look. But no response followed. Not even a sound.

Kabir went into a few more details to explain the gravity of the crisis. When that didn't bring the desired result, he attempted to sketch a few pictures. That failed too. Finally, the commandos showed them a few online news snippets in Mandarin, hoping that that might snap them out of the stupor.

Unfortunately, they sat like statues in a park. Stone cold.

Bruce tapped his boots on the floor as he hissed, 'We were told that you men can understand and speak English. Do you need me to bring you a translator?'

When the scientists continued to display no reaction whatsoever, Kabir tugged at his hair. He could feel a headache coming on. 'Oh god! Give me strength.'

'Fuck strength!' Bruce lost it. He thumped his fist on the table so hard that it caused the equipment to jump. The next moment he pulled out his pistol and shot the two engineers.

Blood trickled down the shoulder of one while the other held his face, white pain searing through his temple, his ear half blown. They whined in pain, their first sounds since the interrogation had begun. Pushing his chair back, he leaned across, ranting right into their shocked faces, 'Didn't I tell you we have no time to be pussyfooting around your asses!'

'Yes, yes,' the scientist said. A second later their nervous shudders came through. 'Please don't shoot us, we have been conditioned not to respond.'

'Not to divulge anything.'

'Please help us! Doctor!'

Bruce and Kabir frowned at each other in disbelief before darting an angry glare at the doctor. So much for not rushing this and not pushing too hard. They had wasted a precious half hour because of it.

'Fine then.' Bruce adjusted his sleeves, feeling quite pleased with himself. 'Let's get it all set. I promise you, the wounds are harmless.'

'Let's begin with the most important question,' Kabir looked at the engineers. 'Who is holding you here?'

'We really have no idea!' said one of the engineers.

'Maybe the US government!' said another.

The engineers' expressions told them that they were not lying. Kabir and Bruce exchanged a worried frown. Incriminating Air-Bee was not going to be all that easy.

∽

Within the next few hours, the tiny hammock had gotten more chaotic than a seabed on the brink of a tsunami. The entire locale had been cordoned off by the military to keep media and neighbours out—but news of the bizarre developments in the forests had already spread. Food and supplies had been stockpiled. Medical staff and psychologists were to remain on site 24x7 to support the hostages in case of an emergency. An array of helicopters arrived with dignitaries from several departments, brought in for both damage control and to fast-track clearances.

A separate control room had been set up so the engineers could liaise with the other worldwide anti-terrorist technical teams without interruption. And technical crews were being flown in too.

The two commandos stood by their vehicle, darting one final glance back at the unlikely locale that was gearing up to counter an unprecedented terrorist-attack. And they breathed a brief sigh of relief. It was their first such moment in two whole days. This part of the mission had been a success on many counts. Of course, all of this would be for naught if they could not stop the Ikhwan now.

A beep went off on his watch. But Kabir didn't bother looking at his dial. He knew what it meant, his pulse now attuned to every passing second. *Four hours left!* His eyes continued lingering on the rotary blades of the helicopter that was gaining speed by the moment. A stretcher was about to be hauled into it to airlift a patient to a medical facility nearby for further treatment.

'One sec,' he mumbled a request to his team before treading up to the helicopter, where he came to a standstill beside the gurney.

Kabir couldn't tell if he would return from the mission. He couldn't tell if this was to be a final farewell to his friend. Getting to meet Jayant after ten years, only to let him go once again, was a tough cord to snap clean. For a few moments, he had been concerned for Jayant's safety, leaving him once again in the custody of American medics, but with the details of the bunker now an open secret, it wouldn't be easy for them to act funny.

'Hey buddy.' He smiled.

'Hey stranger.' Jayant smiled back.

'You'll get well soon. I'll be back, and we'll holiday on Goan shores, like I'd promised you on our last assignment together.' Kabir was about to pat his shoulder, but his friend recoiled, evidently not at ease with him.

An awkward second later, Jayant looked at the commando's face and noted his earnest expression. 'Terrorists. Such buggers, eh?' The lines on his temple gently furrowed. 'They say you're going to stop them!'

Kabir shrugged. 'Well, I'm going to try.'

The medics began hauling the stretcher into the helicopter, ready for lift-off. A quick wave later, Kabir began retracing his steps towards the kayaks.

Jayant observed the receding silhouette of the commando. And though he could not recognize the man, he somehow felt a sudden overpowering urge to wish him luck. 'I'm sure you'll hunt those buggers wherever they are,' he yelled over the deafening sounds of the rotor blades, 'hunt them down to the bottom of the ocean, if that's what it takes.'

Halting abruptly, Kabir spun around. 'Jayant?' He stared in the direction of the soaring chopper, a poignant smile washing over his face as his mate's farewell words replayed in his mind. 'You're still in there somewhere, aren't you?'

40

Hanif's Grief

Reclining against the leather seat of the Lincoln Continental, Hanif rubbed his knees, sore after several hours of travel. His gaze travelled. He saw the bustling New Jersey roads on the other side of the car's window. At eighty-seven, his best years were well behind him. He knew he'd led a fruitful life. The seed fund created with the help of the Nazis, three-quarters of a century ago, had grown to unimaginable proportions, making the Ikhwan a self-sustaining and highly resourceful organization. The financial independence was what had facilitated its covert existence too. With thousands of assets across hundreds of countries, the Ikhwan was well on its way to reaching its pinnacle. What Hanif was leaving behind was not a secret society but a canopy engulfing the world, as Ghassan had imagined. And a bigger achievement yet, the society had done all this in obscurity.

A large part of that legacy he owed to his own son. Zahur had helped drive those dreams to fruition from Western shores, just as he had envisioned. Serving as a senior asset for nearly two decades, Zahur had orchestrated a slow, yet steady, influx of the movement towards the West. Today, a permanent footing had been gained in Europe and America, in the form of numerous underground sleeper cells, while the institutions they worked for had not the slightest inkling of it. These sleepers or assets would not plant bombs, but achieve something much more important once the bell was sounded. They would take the power in their hands!

His foster son had proven to be no less of a leader either. Mokhtar's soul would be brimming with delight in the heavens above at how his own flesh-and-blood had served the cause. First his son, Bilal, and now, his grandson, too. Bilal had not for a moment let Hanif feel Mokhtar's absence. He had not only reinforced the security and elimination team of the Ikhwan, but had also been instrumental in keeping the organization hidden from the public and government scanners for four decades. Not surprising then that Allah had granted Bilal his most heartfelt wish—in the form of his surrogate son. Thirty years on, the blessing had been gratified by Bilal, who had made an inimitable soldier of that son. Khabib, or Zain, as he had been titled for his achievements.

Bilal had personally trained Khabib to be better than himself, better than anyone—with training such as the ice-lake immune response, bear fighting and white torture. It probably ran in their genes—each successive generation surpassing the previous in skill and ferocity. And above all, in protective instinct!

Hanif's gaze trailed away from the sights outside the window towards the profile of the slim warrior seated to his right. Most high-profile personas would travel with an entire security detail flanking them. Not Hanif, no. Why would he need any protection at all, when he had Khabib by his side?

'Alhamdulillah!' exhaled the old man, stretching against the backrest. He had no complaints. Not even when doctors had told him a few months earlier that he only had a short while to live. God truly had given him no reason to gripe. Not until a week ago, that is. When an unexpected tragedy had befallen Zahur's family. Which was why, despite his ill health, he'd made this one last trip overseas to meet his grandchildren. And to be a source of strength to his own son during these tough times.

No sooner was the door to the million-dollar Englewood Cliffs mansion opened than he was greeted with the welcoming presence of his son at its tasteful porch. A stark contrast to the austere life he led! As an asset, unlike the core members, Zahur could flaunt a lifestyle without any apparent risk.

While Zahur was furthering the Ikhwan's agenda in the West, Hanif had handled the reins of the Ikhwan single-handedly for three long decades. But then he had begun to feel the effects of age. Hanif needed someone to work in tandem back in Egypt for the overall coordination of the Ikhwan's operations. He needed someone to support him and also take over after his retirement. Both Hanif and Zahur had agreed upon this. The mission was paramount. He had found an able successor in Abu Bakr. Abu had been working in his core team for around a decade. His organizational skills and oratory skills reflected the genius of his mentor, Ghassan. With Abu Bakr in the headquarters and Zahur here, Hanif could retire peacefully.

'Where's Bilal?' Zahur asked fondly. 'Has he no time for his friend, or do you keep him that busy?'

'He's with Abu. There's a lot going on there. But look who I have here!' He pointed to the young man who was entering the living room after completing his recon of the villa.

'Your nephew, Khabib! No less than Bilal, he is helping the Ikhwan multiply its strength.'

'Oh! Welcome, son.' Zahur got up and hugged him. 'You remind me so much of your father. Come, make yourself comfortable.'

'Fatih! Fatima!' Zahur called out to his children.

Twin siblings, brother and sister, came scurrying out to meet their grandfather. Fatima was an effervescent girl of sixteen, pretty features and a pair of keen hazel eyes that seemed ever willing to learn. Fatih tried hard to match his sister's spirits, but with the illness having rendered his form much weaker, he could not keep up.

'He is a bright boy, dreams of life. Wishes to go back to Egypt and lead after you!' Zahur lamented to his father, once the two men had retired indoors to the quiet confines of the study. 'Why did Allah have to riddle his youth with an incurable disease?'

'And his dreams shall come true, my son. Be brave.' Setting his own grief and tears aside, Hanif patted his son's shoulders, holding him close till the man had regained some composure.

After spending a short while catching up, they sat in the dining room to have some tea. Sipping on the hot brew, Hanif watched his grandchildren who were busy bantering in the adjacent reception room. Fatima was poking her brother's shoulder with a finger, in the hope that he would relent and play a game of hockey with her. Fatih was too fatigued to indulge her whims. But he wouldn't say so aloud. Instead, he contorted his face into a scowl. 'What happened? No episodes to catch up on? Stop bugging me, Fatima!'

'Oh come on. I'm not interested in watching serials. Hockey... Will you...?' She ruffled his hair.

It irked him whenever she did it, even when he had had a head full of hair. And now that his hair was thinning, it irked him even more. 'Stop,' he said, swatting her hand away. 'Later... I'm feeling lazy now!'

'Lazy?' She mocked him by miming his voice and expression. 'A glass of water, and you'll be fine!'

'Nope. And anyway,' Fatih chortled, 'your hockey stick has cracked from all the abuse it's suffered at your hands, Fatima!'

Fatima fell silent. He was right. She had forgotten about the cracks on its shaft from a day ago. A second later, she sprang to her feet and approached her father quietly. 'Baba...' She fidgeted with a curl, tucking it behind her ears. 'Can I pop down to the sports store to get myself a hockey stick?'

'No.' Zahur frowned.

'Please, Baba...'

'I got you one two months ago!'

'Baba, please...' She put on a puppy-eyed expression.

'No.' His tone grew grave.

'But I love hockey and can't play in my school team!'

'I don't care. You shouldn't be playing sports in school teams anyway. I've told you to stay at home, learn chores and cooking from your mother, but...'

'One second, Zahur.' Hanif was intrigued by the cause of the entire drama. 'Why can't you play hockey in your school team, my child?'

'Because,' she lowered her eyes and her tone out of respect for the old man, 'despite the fact that I'm the school's best player, I am not allowed to practise or play matches wearing my hijab. So I had to quit.' She shrugged nonchalantly. 'I won't play with girls who tease me for the manner in which I lead my life!'

'Stubborn girl,' scoffed Zahur, worried his father might be offended by her brazenness.

Hanif, however, was not offended in the least. If anything, he was quite impressed with his granddaughters' mettle.

'Now leave, Fatima,' Zahur said, 'and let me and your grandpa be in peace!'

With a groan, Fatima returned to the reception room and plonked herself on the couch, only to face another bout of taunts from Fatih. Until an idea struck her. Running up the stairs, she barged into the old playroom and pulled down a hobbyhorse that had been gathering dust atop a cupboard.

With a hard tug, she managed to pluck the horse-head, along with its supporting pole, right out of its base. 'This will do!' A few seconds later, Fatima was standing in the reception room, tapping the stick on her palm like a seasoned hockey player. 'I have my hockey stick. Now grab yours and come out to the garden, you bag of lazybones!'

Zahur stared in annoyance at the scene on the other side of the patio glass door. His son was clearly straining himself to keep up with Fatima's moves in the game. 'Fatima! Why are you driving him to exhaustion? Fatima!'

When his screams fell on deaf ears, he turned to his old father, exasperated. 'She is in denial. Refuses to acknowledge his illness… my Fatih.'

'Don't worry,' Hanif reached out to hold his son's hand. 'Fatih will live. Fatih will lead the movement.' He ended his assurance with a prophetic smile.

Hanif was right about many observations during that fateful visit. One of it being the fact that it would be his last trip to the US. He breathed his last in Cairo a month later. Ironically, it was not the illness that killed him, but a bullet from the Egyptian forces in a stakeout.

41

Hell Breaks Loose

A firm voice shook him awake.

'Woah.' Kabir sat up with a jolt. After pressing his heavy eyelids, he glanced up at his teammate. A prickle climbed up the nape of his neck as the fog lifted and he noticed the horror in Bruce's eyes. 'What's going on?'

'We've failed!'

'F...' He cleared his groggy throat. 'Failed?' Kabir glared ahead through the hatch visor. The little rectangular patches on the vast expanse of green were getting clearer and closer. They were landing. 'Where are we?'

'W... we had to take a detour.' Bruce sounded nervous, unlike himself.

'Detour? Where?' He spotted the thatched huts and the water pumps at the fringes of the paddy fields—it was all frighteningly familiar! 'Wait, where are we?' Kabir unbuckled his seatbelt.

'Sir, you will have to take a seat. We haven't landed yet!' the pilot's stern warning rang out.

Unbothered, he hurriedly angled forward for a better view. 'New Delhi?' He could hear his pitch rising. 'What are we doing here. Why are we landing in India?'

'Kabir, calm down.' Bruce tried to get the man to return to his seat. 'We just received a message on our communicator, asking that we land here instead.'

'Why?'

Bruce took a forlorn pause, his jawline stiffening. 'We failed, the Ikhwan rescheduled the attacks. We were preparing ourselves for New York, London, Sydney, Paris, Berlin, Tel Aviv...instead, they've hit India, China, Japan and South Korea first.'

'What?' Kabir raised his fists and banged them against the interiors of the Xssault in a frenzy. 'H...how did...I need to get to...'

'Sir, you will need to be seated!' the pilot announced again, 'Stay calm.'

Bruce grabbed his colleague by the shoulder and yanked him back onto his seat. 'Kabir, no point losing your cool. Sit down. Once we touch ground, you'll be able to assess the situation!'

It took no longer than a few minutes thereafter, but it felt like forever had passed before the jet actually landed. As soon as the hatch was opened, Kabir propped himself up and jumped onto the landing mattress that had been laid out by the emergency crew. Rolling off the mattress, he rushed towards the squad of police jeeps that were out there waiting for him.

'Mr Menon? When did this happen?' he said, panting.

'Approximately thirteen ... no, fourteen minutes ago.'

'But why have we landed out here? In the fields? It will take us hours to get to Delhi!'

'Because the expressways and roads have been blocked. The Parliament, the Secretariat and our headquarters are hit too,' he said, huffing as they dashed back into the squad cars.

As the cars raced through the fields to make it to the capital, Kabir realized it looked nothing like the suburb he knew it to be. There was no horizon. It had all been engulfed by plumes of smoke.

Next to him, Mr Menon was screaming hysteric commands over the wireless system, one after another, but he heard none of it. The shrieks and sirens in the background drowned it all. However, the worst aspect of their failure to stop the apocalypse that had descended upon them was yet to unveil itself. And it came a few miles on, as the soot briefly cleared from the distant northern skyline.

'The Taj!' Kabir kneaded his temple. Two of its minarets were missing.

'Callous precision!' Mr Menon shook his head. 'The remote navigation technology has proven to be such a curse!'

'Oh my God!' Kabir said. The colour in his features had been sucked dry. A four-hundred-year-old historical structure, one that defined an entire nation. The building had been ruthlessly devastated. Something that had managed to withstand typhoons, quakes and many other natural calamities had been torn down by man.

'You should see what they've done to the Great Wall of China!' Menon flicked open an image on his mobile to show him the latest newsflash.

'Bloody hell!'

Kabir couldn't tell what had happened. Had the technical team been unable to stall their assault? How? Had the Ikhwan gotten wind of the original engineers being unearthed? Is that why they'd preponed the attacks?

They tore through the roads converging at the Lodhi Gardens, leading to the CGO Complex, where the research and analysis wing headquarters stood. The famous Mughal monuments that lined the roads were now a graveyard of ruins. Scenes of annihilation were rampant, forcing the people to flee for their lives through fragments of carts of fruits, flowers and terracotta. There were more stretches of red on the streets than there were grey. Riots had broken out. Men donning saffron and green were butchering each other. And despite being commandos, they could not pause and get off to stop them.

Instead, they were compelled to turn a blind eye. They raced onwards, hoping more riot police would turn up in time. A few metres ahead, a large crowd was amassing around a flaming vehicle. Kabir thought he spotted what resembled the semi-crushed skull of a child underneath its wheels. He instantly looked away, the twisting knots in his gut making him want to puke.

How did we fail? All of us? He buried his head in his hands, overcome by agony and exhaustion, when his phone rang. It was an Indian number.

He picked up the call hesitantly, gathering himself.

'Kabir?'

'Sarah?' She sounded worried. Clamour and cries rang in the background. 'What are you doing here?'

'I was reporting on the crashes when a huge mob of men came charging in...'

Kabir could hear the tremors in her tone and the pandemonium around.

'They're carrying machetes and sickles, and they're on a rampage. It's crazy, there's bloodshed everywhere... would you be able to ge...'

An ear-splitting shriek rang through.

'Sarah?' His pitch rose. 'Where are you? I'll come get you...'

The line went dead.

Kabir screamed, suddenly punching the man who had stuck his arm in through the car window, to grab his collar.

'Get off!' he yelled, delirious. He screamed again.

'Fuck!' Bruce backed off, having barely ducked the punch that had come his way as he fell back on his seat in the airborne Xssault. 'All I was doing was checking on you. You sounded disturbed.'

Kabir sat up and stared around, blinking a couple of times. Cream interiors. Leather seats. Blue skies. Not India. No Taj. No riots. No bloodshed. No phone call from Sarah. At least not yet. *Two hours!* Exhaling a deep breath, he checked the time twice. 'We're still in the Xssault!'

'Where else would we be?'

Kabir glanced downwards. His shirt was drenched in a cold sweat and his forehead burnt. He had a fever. *That was disturbing!* He rubbed his eyelids, and he could sense a tear spring somewhere at the edge of his eye. *Haven't failed them—not yet!* Grabbing a bottle of water, he splashed some on his face and drank a few big gulps. 'Sorry, mate. I had the worst nightmare.'

'Must have been the morphine. Knocked you out, didn't it?' Bruce looked out of the window pensively. 'It's why I haven't been sleeping the past couple of days either. The nightmares were getting crazier. I have a family back home that I believe I will still meet, and I don't want anything shaking that belief!'

Allowing himself a short while to regain his composure, Kabir then asked, 'So where are we headed?'

'Take a guess.'

'Not Libya, obviously.' Kabir observed the terrain below. 'Flying over the Middle Eastern desert stretches?'

'Yup. Following the trail of the GPS on the nano-camera trackers.'

Suddenly and simultaneously, their mobile phones flashed with an incoming message from the taskforce on the ground. It was a series of coordinates: the latest location where the nano-camera tracker had come to a halt for longer than an hour.

Zooming in, they looked at each other, confused frowns on their faces.

'Tajikistan?'

'Why would the Murshid land in Tajikistan? When the Ikhwan barely has a couple of hours left for their momentous mission?'

They stared on in silence, the wheels in their heads spinning.

Tajikistan. It was an isolated country. An obscure mountainous landscape. No American military bases. And yet, strategically close enough to both, the Middle East and Europe...where most of the Ikhwan's bases were.

A second message flashed on their mobile screens.

'Tracker impaired. Nano-camera destroyed.'

A grim second later, they sighed in unison. 'That's the headquarters of the Ikhwan—Tajikistan!'

42

The World Forces Collude

As the Black Moth hovered around the skies in Tajikistan airspace, with a hawk-eyed view of the earth below, one grisly detail became glaringly obvious. The magnitude of evil they were dealing with!

For miles, they saw nothing but a range of ragged mountains and harsh ridges, with barely a spot of flatland below. And occupying one of the most enviable spots in this terrain, seamlessly tucked within the innards of a 5000-metre gritty mountain, was the colossal and yet tiny structure that housed the Ikhwan's headquarters. A befitting location for the nerve centre of the world's largest and most clandestine secret society.

They could fire shell after shell, missile after missile, and still not be able to blow up this cavity hidden deep inside. The Ikhwan had utilized the indestructible architecture of nature to build themselves a fortress. Ingenious!

At very short notice, various countries had managed to start setting up military camps in small sections of the flatlands, a few miles away. Jets were hovering, and rows of old armoured tanks flown in were steadily steering their way onto relatively smoother turfs. The entire scene gave one the impression of little ants on an anthill, easy pickings in front of the dominance of the Cove. By keeping themselves so secretive, the Ikhwan had left the world with little time to plan retaliation. And by engaging in a technological crusade, it had left no real means for a counterstrike. Cruise missiles and ordinance bombs had no power against the push of a button, it seemed. In this doomsday war, the Ikhwan had both the biggest fortress and the baddest ammunition. The rest of the world had only one remaining class of warfare to resort to—a warfare of wits!

On receiving the coordinates, the pilot began the descent, a short distance from the encampment, and the Black Moth was brought to a halt on a makeshift landing strip. The taskforce base camp was a large series of grey tents, set up a few miles away from the foot of the mountain range, all of which had turned into organized chaos. Rhythmic marching of military boots from battalions of the most elite soldiers. Constant drones of propellers from jets. Hum of the tankers' rubber tracks grating against rubble. Clacking of keys. Crackle of communicators. Yelling of commands. Above all, one uniform noise rang against the ears of all those who had gathered there; the sounds of everyone's adrenaline-fuelled pulse became almost audible as they joined the hardest battle to save lives that the earth was about to witness.

Getting off the jet, Kabir and Bruce swiftly descended the ramp. They stormed towards the communications tent in the base camp. The large tent was cramped with chairs, wires, maps and all sorts of hardware that the trio had to wade through before they could reach Vladimir's Russian colleagues.

Sitting on rickety seats, they were busy coordinating network and communication between the ground forces. With the region lying outside the range of most cell towers, satellite connectivity had been low. Resources from international satellite companies had been pooled in for additional coverage so as to effectively coordinate the operations.

'Hey, mates…'

'Hey, Vlad!'

'Didn't think we'd see you here.' They gestured at his heavily bandaged leg that was stretched out on a low step stool. 'How are you doing, by the way?'

'Nothing could have kept me away from this!' Vladimir fist-bumped his mates. 'You men look terrible. When did you last get some rest?'

'Don't know,' Bruce said, bobbing his head nonchalantly as he reached for a crate of Red Bulls sitting on the table. Helping himself to a can, he flicked open its lid and gulped the drink in one go.

Vladimir continued his conversation with the men in the camp, switching to Russian, trying to gather more vital facts, when Bruce interjected.

'So... what fresh information do you have for us?'

Vladimir drummed his palm on the wheelchair's arm-rest. 'We intercepted their comms a short while ago. Guess how many pilots are being dispatched for their...Holy mission?'

'Hundreds?'

'Three thousand one hundred and twenty-two volunteers!' Vladimir smirked. 'Around four fidayeens for each of the seven hundred and eight-six planes they intend to crash.'

'How many planes? God!' Kabir's jaw dropped. 'It is their holy number. Signifies Bismillah—in the name of God!'

The men were interrupted when they noticed a large group of high-ranking surveillance personnel, representing various nations, walk into the encampment and come to a halt at its centre.

Within minutes, a laptop was laid open and a larger projector screen set up opposite it. Commandos from the surrounding tents walked up to the spot and flocked around in groups, while the intelligence chiefs got ready to present their upcoming strategies to the select audience.

The first picture that came up on the screen was a spectacular 3D image of a cylindrical structure. An image comprising both external elevations and detailed floor-wise internal sections of the building.

'Is that the Cove?' gasped a few members from the audience. The name had finally emerged from numerous communication interceptions that had been coming in over the last few hours.

'Yes.' The surveillance officer waited for the crowd to fall silent before bringing his laser-pointer up to the skies. 'We managed to get the building plans from a few high-altitude drones we'd dispatched earlier today. An architectural advancement coming from Israeli labs, a new type of mixed radiation and gravitational analysis that can penetrate thousands of metres through solid rock was used for imaging. We have the outcome with us. Each wall inside the cove is now mapped down to an accuracy of 10 centimetres.' He circled his laser-pointer at a set of concentric circles in the centre of the image. 'This is the centrum. We believe this is the focal point or "head" of all their technical operations. If we have the slightest chance of being able to chop off the Brotherhood's tentacles, one by one, we need to take control of the centrum.'

'But "taking control" of the head in a heavily guarded fortress, sitting nearly 3,000 metres inside a mountain, is easier said than done!' quipped one of the commandos. 'They will have an advantageous position, multiplied many times over.'

'True! That said, however strong the fortification, it has to have entry and exit points. These are our biggest hopes, however bleak that might sound. Based on the imaging, we have assessed that there might be three access points in the building. Two of them haven't been located so far. But our satellite images picked this up...'

He changed the image on the projector to an external elevation of the Cove's mountain-face. The onlookers peered closer, but no oddity could be located on its rocky surface until the intelligence head flicked his laser pointer towards a small point at its very bottom. There was an outline in the rockery that resembled a tiny doorway. 'We suppose this might be a postern door—a concealed escape hatch that would allow the members to enter and exit the Cove during emergencies. It hasn't been used for a long, long time. And this is what will lead us in!'

'And is that the only tunnel in the mountain that our new

imaging technology could detect?' asked Kabir.

'No! There are around forty-five more...' the chief engineer sighed. 'But they are of no use to us. There is a network of natural arteries running through the body of the mountain, but most of them end up somewhere much higher than ground level. Lime-based arterial entrapments that got dissolved as the water percolated into the rock through ages.' He projected another image on the screen that showed a web of arteries criss-crossing the mountain from top to bottom.

'Doesn't sound very prudent,' added Bruce. 'Using the very path set up by the architects of this place. I'm sure they'll have set up all sorts of defence mechanisms to stop us.'

'We would have tried a more ingenious break-in, like drilling further into a close reaching artery,' the chief replied, 'but there's no time.'

The discussions were interrupted when the transmitter of the Russian intelligence team crackled with an incoming message. As the officer stepped aside to speak through his communicator, Kabir noticed the shift in Vladimir's expression.

'Shit!' The Siberian agent was exasperated. 'The Freeport strategic petroleum reserve in the US has been contaminated too.' He translated the messages as they continued to come in. 'Russia and the US have been cooperating on this contamination threat for the last two weeks. There have been repeated incidents in both countries. However, the experts are still unable to understand the real purpose behind such incidents. Most of them were detected on CCTV footage, with the culprit either disappearing or committing suicide.'

'What are they up to? It's not like they're contaminating a water supply. This fuel will ultimately go to refineries.' Kabir scratched his forehead. 'And the first news we got was a few months back. Nothing has happened so far...!'

'What else, man! They must be planning to blow them up, in the same orchestrated manner as the air strikes…massive explosions that would cause the earth's crust to shiver!' cried Bruce.

'Nah!' Kabir shook his head. 'There isn't sufficient oxygen down below to make that possible. It has to be something else.'

'And how can we be sure that the Ikhwan is behind this?' said Bruce.

'Just my gut feeling…!' Kabir's attention had slowly veered away from the proceedings as he took in the panorama. The entire world had come together to stop these airstrikes. Air strikes that everyone had presumed was the Ikhwan's fanatical retribution against the West. But what if these attacks were only a distraction? What if the Ikhwan's real vendetta was not violence, but something far more sinister? A slow takeover of the world's economy and thus power? *Oh God, save us!* His face blanched. *The air strikes are not the Ikhwan's holy mission. The air strikes are only a means to their end. Their holy mission is the establishment of a caliphate, in as many countries as they can seize.* And here, the world forces were too busy getting rid of flies to spot the army of locusts descending upon them!

43

The Countdown Begins

With arms behind his back, he surveyed the chaos unfolding thousands of metres below on the screens in front of him. It was like having a blueprint of the battle ploys of all his enemies being drawn out for him.

'Foolish people,' the young man said, smirking. 'Herding together to embrace death!' As supreme leader, the Sayyid had flown into the Cove for the grand day. When nine decades of hard work would bear fruition. And his legendary grandfather Hanif's dreams would come true. However, now he wouldn't be able to enjoy the official birth of the caliphate amidst the peaceful vista of snow-capped mountains as it should have been. Instead, he was forced to lead the crusade amidst the stress and the pandemonium of a global counterattack. 'Until a few months ago, hardly anyone had heard of the Ikhwan. And now,' he said, turning to the Murshid, his glare toughening, 'well, suffice to say, none of this would have happened had we decided to keep our timelines a secret as I had originally suggested...instead of bragging about them openly, Abu.'

'My apologies.' Abu Bakr swallowed hard, studying the Sayyid with a firm stare. Dressed in a spotless silk thwab of white and a matching shemagh headgear that accentuated his sharp features, the young man looked no less than royalty. There was barely a hint of the rumoured ill-health in his persona. If anything, he possessed a naturally domineering aura—one inherited from his legendary grandfather, no doubt.

That said, Fatih was decades younger. And far more inexperienced in leading such a large movement—glimpses of which he'd been seeing more and more of in the lead up to the grand day. However, none of the members of the Brotherhood—not even the governing council members sitting a few rooms away—would believe him if he said so. After all, Fatih was known to be extremely intelligent, ruthless and composed. And he exuded an aura of omnipresence despite the fact that he hardly travelled. However, Abu Bakr alone had seen what others couldn't. The young man was making a spate of rash decisions, despite being advised to the contrary. Unwilling to wait for the movement to follow its natural course of a hundred years, as Ghassan had originally intended it, Fatih wanted everything on his terms. Maybe because he was eager for a taste of success during his lifetime. So it felt ironical to be lectured about a careless moment from such a man—considering he was the Murshid, the architect of the movement, and more experienced of the two. These were those rare moments when he wished for the Shaytan to surface and make Fatih relent.

'Firstly,' he clarified, 'the taskforces were aware of the short timeline of the attacks already…as for what happened in the Libyan camp—I was surrounded, restrained and provoked…I needed something to keep my captors distracted until Khabib had the opportunity to save me…' He paused. 'Anyway, while the challenge has them all worked up, they have no idea of what's going to hit them! They will not be able to stop us…everything will go as planned…but, Fatih…' His eyes glimmered sharply. 'Do you not deem it unfair to blame me when I have often had to counsel you about not making hasty decisions? That rushing the grand day… that rescheduling it by a decade or two might lead to a crack…a leak of our plans?'

'They will not be able to stop us…everything will go as planned…isn't that what you just said?' Fatih cut the man off with an acidic smile. 'Anyway, how's your wound?' He indicated towards the bandages around the Murshid's waist that were bulking up his suit. 'I heard you were attacked by a bunch of crazy nomadic women.'

'D...doing better.' Abu Bakr nodded.

Fatih walked over to the intercom and buzzed the centrum. 'Let's show those men down there a few moves to keep them busy. We need to carry out the countdown in peace, don't we?'

'Yes, sir,' came a low voice.

44

The Earthquake

The tactical operations chief had rounded up a few select commandos to the front to begin apprising them of the strategy. The army stationed outside was to prepare for direct counterstrikes and assaults in case that was required. In the meanwhile, ten teams of the world's best stealth forces had been put together to breach the Cove—two of which would comprise counter terrorism technology experts. Each team would be led by a commando experienced in high-risk tactical warfare. With better insight about the Ikhwan's ways, Bruce and Kabir were asked to lead one each of those teams.

The directive was 'stealth'. 'You storm in from here...' The operations chief drew a trajectory using his laser pointer—from a set of designated hideouts in the mountain ridges towards the hatch. 'The plan is to take over the Cove section by section, capturing as many lead members of the Brotherhood alive as possible. Until the centrum is finally seized. We need eyes on the Sayyid, the Murshid and Khabib at all times.'

By the end of that hour, the camp was actively gearing up for their ploys to unravel. Bruce took a final peek at his family photo, slapped shut his wallet and handed it over to Vladimir. 'Take care of it for me.'

'Bruce!' Kabir grabbed the man's hand firmly. The jitters on the British agent's fingers were visibly bad now. 'What's going on? Are you sure you're up to this?' he whispered, after ensuring no one else around was listening in. 'Will you be able to pull the trigger with your fingers shaking that way? Maybe you need to just sit…take a breather for a few hours…some anti-anxiety medication may help!'

Bruce snapped his hand out of Kabir's grip. 'Speak for yourself! Would you honestly say you haven't been putting lives in jeopardy… leading the taskforce with one working shoulder?' He paused, his breath fast and shallow. 'We are soldiers. Can't sit back and watch those bastards take away everything that means something to us, can we?'

'Hey… hey…' Vladimir notified them of an approaching medic and the two teammates decided to drop the argument.

The medic ran up to Kabir and dropped his bag. Whipping out a clean syringe, he loaded it with the powerful drug that would numb the agony in the commando's rotator cuff for the next three hours. Then, he brought the needle to the Indian commando's arm and was about to begin enlightening him on the side-effects.

'Don't have time for all that now,' Kabir stopped him before he could start. 'Go on. Just shoot me with whatever you have!'

'Fine. As you say.' With a disapproving sigh, he inserted the needle into the muscle.

A few minutes later, Kabir slipped into his ballistic armour.

The teams crept towards the ridges, forming small groups, taking up positions behind rocks and crevices a few hundred metres from the hatch door. Timed and strategized to the last second, they lay in wait for the signal. The instant it came, their feet would fly off in the direction of the postern door.

'Here we go!' Pulling down his smoke mask, Kabir shut his eyes to mutter a prayer, his pulse pounding in anticipation. All of a sudden, his eyes opened to a thunderous echo. As if a heavy object had plunged down from the skies. 'What was that?' A brief stillness later, a strange groan rippled through the air. And he thought he saw a row of armoured vehicles parked on a flattish turf, jump an inch up and then fall down. A moment later, a few rows behind, the jets seemed to do the same.

'Bizarre! What's going on?'

'Is that a tremor?'

'An earthquake?' whispered the commandos.

In a few seconds, their doubts were silenced with an outlandish answer—the terrain upon which the bulk of the military transport stood began moving. Soon, the vehicles were riding on a crest of rocky stretches and were then flung back down. The vehicles smashed violently against each other, their metallic bodies cranking as they were torn apart by the forces of the seismic waves.

'That is not an earthquake.'

'Jesus Christ! Is that a seismic bomb?'

Hollers and shrieks reverberated across the valleys as the officers and civilians scrambled and scurried to get as far away from the unstable earth as they could. And then, the land mass at the epicentre of the quake began caving in. The fleet of armoured tankers—the jets, the tents, the weaponry—all sucked into the vortex of three craters, each half a mile wide, giving off waves of deafening explosions.

45

Something's Off!

'Yes!' Fatih stroked his jawline with pride as he surveyed the site of devastation. He had a privileged view through the screen wall. 'Spectacular! I've always wanted to see the Seismic in action!'

Abu Bakr shuddered at the thought of the alternative consequences the explosion might have brought about. Bringing the Cove crumbling down, for instance! Fatih was really brazen with his choices, taking a series of high-risk decisions. It terrified him to watch him play so ruthlessly with the organization he had built brick by brick. This decision, however, like the others was also turning out to be a productive one. With vehicles of all sizes and shapes parked on such an uneven expanse, most compact medium-range missiles they owned would not have been effective. The earthquake bomb had taken down a massive fleet of vehicles in one fell swoop. 'Risky, but ingenious!' he had to admit. Maybe Fatih had that knack for precision, a trait that ran through his lineage.

'No, something feels off,' Khabib murmured grimly, the lone voice to do so amongst the uproarious cheers ringing all around the Cove.

Fatih overheard the man's suspicions and was intrigued. He had always regarded Khabib's instincts highly. 'Why?' He turned around. 'What do you mean?'

'One moment, sir.' Khabib weighed the situation for a while before pressing down on the P2P communicator of his walkie-talkie, calling for a member of the surveillance team. 'Send me recent close-up footage of the scenes from the quake down below.'

Within ten seconds, the footage was delivered. Khabib pulled it up on one of the monitors of the suite.

He carefully flicked through the last sixty seconds of the chaotic images. By the end of it, his lanky face had stiffened. *'Just as I feared. No casualties! These kafirs are up to something.'*

46

Enter the Cove!

At their hideouts, the commandos were inundated by aftershocks of the quake, their ears still ringing.

The world powers had taken a massive hit. Hundreds of thousands of dollars of obsolete jets and old tankers had been sacrificed for the cause. Turned to scrap metal at the bottom of the earth. It was an elaborate decoy, but it had worked. The intelligence chiefs had summoned their combined assets, leading the Cove to believe they were surrounded. Parked a fleet right under their noses, to provoke them. Keeping the heavily guarded Cove distracted, so they would have no eyes on the postern door at the back—which was to be their main point of entry for breaching the Cove. Of course, they hadn't expected to be hit by an earthquake bomb! Regardless, they had used the diversion to send a mini-launcher in the air that had released the world's tiniest projectile. Guided by coordinates, the spike missile—its width no bigger than the size of a man's thumb—had lodged into the structure of the postern door, drilling into its armour. And it sat there, poised like an insect. Small! Quiet! But deadly when detonated!

Using the sounds of the explosion as a distraction, the spike was set off.

Boooom! The door blast open.

The guards standing behind the postern door had no idea what hit them, while the members of the Cove in the floors above were none the wiser.

'Go!' The command was given.

The commandos burst forth, past boulders and rocks that were still rumbling from mini-convulsions. The ten-team force had a very short window to breach the door and break in, before the might of the Cove's security came descending upon them.

The first team forged in with ballistic shields, forming a barricade in the corridor, thus allowing the rest of the team members to fall into the narrow passage safely.

47

The Armageddon Begins

Fatih watched the security monitor in the centrum, his attention brought to the breach at the basement by Khabib's update.

'Infidels!' Anger flashed in his eyes, then cooled. 'Khabib will deal with them.'

He walked to the core of the building. A group of engineers were flanking an extensive workstation at the centre, busy subjecting various components to rigorous tests. They stood on alert as soon as the supreme leader approached them.

'Sir?'

'Men, I am ready to give the orders.' He beamed.

The chief engineer exchanged a worried look with his colleagues. 'But, respected sir, there is still some time left for the countdown. Do you want us to override it all? Some of the carriers are yet to be airborne... In fact, a few of them may be on their previous trips, about to land.'

'Activate the prepone protocol! The software will reset the co-ordinates to other important buildings as per the current locations of those planes!'

Abu Bakr couldn't believe his ears. 'Fatih.' He stepped close to the leader. 'The mission was meant to be a coordinated terror attack. We've been planning it that way for a decade!'

'The Cove has been breached. I want the strikes to proceed now, leaving nothing to chance!'

'Those soldiers will be shredded to pieces by Khabib in no time.'

'I know what I am doing...' the leader's angry voice whipped across the room. 'Over 500 flights are already on their designated routes and our fidayeen pilots are there inside to take care of contingencies, aren't they? They can't override our remote navigation controls now. Neither do they know where our nodes are, nor do they have the technology to quash our programs. Even if they manage to reach here, it would be too late. The command would have rolled over to our worldwide node servers. By the end of today, all the planes will have crashed as scheduled.' He looked at the engineers. 'Go on, give the signal.'

The chief engineer stared at the sea of software controls and components spread out on the main desk. He then glanced up at the Murshid, then back at the Sayyid, once again. His numb hands reached for the panel, hovering over the two main buttons. This was a decisive moment. It would set off a series of events, from which there was no coming back.

'Go on!' Fatih slapped a palm on the table.

'Y... yes...' The engineer jittered and pressed one of the red buttons. He moved aside and his chief took his spot, typing in a password that no one else had access to—a complicated series of alphanumeric sequences.

'Password identified,' flashed the message on the screen.

It was time for the third and final step.

Picking up a biometric scanner, he held it up to the leader's face, like a hand mirror.

'Sir?' He waited for the man's permission.

Fatih nodded at him dismissively.

The engineer then connected one of its nodes to the skin at the bottom of the leader's neck, and clipped a second sensor around Fatih's finger. The sophisticated retinal scanner code would only respond if the body's vitals were within normal range. A safe wall to ensure that the person giving the orders was not doing so under duress.

'Confirmed,' the message beeped.

There was a quiet whirr as the internal processors responded to the commands. The coded messages were now whizzing through the invisible circuitry, traversing their way through networked nodes and simultaneously reaching 786 planes in various corners of the world. The game was on.

Very soon, the pilots in the cockpit of these 786 planes would lose control and the remote navigation software would take over. The site of crash coordinates had already been pre-fed. The nodal servers would ensure that even if the Cove was brought down, the planes would move along their programmed trajectories.

Fatih was now looking at the other red button, its activation implying a much deeper and longer-lasting impact on the world. It was the key to the world takeover which no external agency had figured out so far. Neither the Protettori, nor their smartass agents, not even their tactical chiefs.

'Activate the microcapsules too!'

'Yes, sir!'

The Armageddon had begun.

∽

A swarm of grey insects buzzed their way ahead of the taskforces as soon as the door was detonated open.

The way to the core of the mountain was a tunnel, several kilometres long and uphill. It would end at the encapsulated multi-storeyed structure in the stomach of the mountain, the Cove. And then there would be several floors of upward journey before they could reach the nerve centre located at the top floor. The taskforces knew there would be all forms of resistance to keep them at bay.

The retaliatory fire did not take much time. With Khabib having alerted the guards, hundreds of the Ikhwan's security personnel across all floors had braced themselves for a decisive fight. Chemical canisters came rolling down the dark corridors. LED light ropes were indented into circular notches, which outlined the circumference of the tunnel, every few metres. On a normal day, they would have made the tunnel look like a well-lit thrill ride. But today, it was pitch dark. Smoke bombs were a regular feature at every corner. And the gunfire was relentless, both from the guards and the strategic firing holes in the walls.

The grey dragonflies dodged their way past the bullets, staying just a few metres ahead of the forces, hovering around the next blind corner, passing on live footage of the activities ahead. The latest in counter-espionage, they were built out of G-202, the toughest and almost indestructible, alloy. With a clear view of the enemy's location, the damage to the forces was minimal, but the incessant rounds of bullets coming at them from the holes in the walls did bring casualties early on.

The heavy counterblows from the enemy were delaying the progress of the taskforces, far more than they had expected. However, they were the world's best stealth commandos and they swiftly learned to adapt to the lethal threats lurking around each corner. They stepped up the smoke cover, and using powerful long-range thermal imaging cameras, they tummy-crawled through the bullets above. Using clock code, each leader alerted his team of the enemy's presence and position. Once the enemy was taken down and the 'all clear' given, the rest of the team moved onwards.

They were halfway up the tunnel now.

Kabir looked at his watch. Thirty minutes to go! Would they be able to make it in time? Not at this speed! He would have to think of something. Some way they could forge ahead.

And then, something bizarre happened. He saw the scouts running back, shouting. 'Go back! Fire in the hole! Evacuate!'

He looked ahead but couldn't spot anything untoward.

And then, he saw it! It was a giant round boulder, right behind them, rolling down the tunnel. It fit the round section of the tunnel perfectly, leaving hardly any space for escape. And, it was gaining momentum.

There was no time to slither on the floor. Everyone got to their feet and started running, all the way back towards the exit. Kabir's mind was racing. He would have to do something. The bullets that were being fired from the holes in the walls had gained momentum. The ball was barely thirty metres ahead. Even if he placed something in its way, it would simply be dragged along the narrow path. He would need something strong enough to bear the momentum and weight of the giant rolling ball and it would have to be anchored firmly to the ground. But there was no time to call the engineering team or drill an anchor!

The scouts dashed past him, the lights on their helmets now on.

Suddenly, it hit him! There were hardly a few millimetres of clearance between the perfectly round boulder and the circular tunnel in which it was moving! He began tugging at an LED rope embedded in the wall. The rock was barely fifteen metres behind him now! He pulled out the portion of the lighting embedded in the floor and cast it aside. He could hear the rumble of the mammoth boulder, barely a few feet from him. He pulled out both his pistols, one with each hand and thrust them into the cavity on the floor created by the displaced LED rope. He stuck the muzzle and grip into the annular cavity. The two pistols now stood like puny V-shaped barriers in the path of the giant boulder.

Kabir had no time to run clear. The pistols would surely not be able to stand the onslaught. Maybe his body would provide a barrier to the close-fitting boulder. He wriggled back and closed his eyes.

The boulder hit the pistols hard, bending and dislodging one of them. But the other one did not give way. The second pistol bent under the impact, its holding stone notch unrelenting and the adamant boulder pushing its weight against it. And then, with a thud it got dislodged. The boulder began to roll ahead slowly as Kabir watched in horror, helpless. The dragonflies droned behind him, keeping safe distance.

The boulder rolled over the two pistols in slow motion, crushing them with its weight. And then it got locked into position! The crushed pistols had lifted it up sufficiently to fill the narrow clearance. The boulder was now trapped in the circular section of the rough tunnel walls.

'Good lord!' Kabir breathed a sigh of relief.

∽

'We're stuck!' The realization that the boulder had now totally stalled their progress dawned over Kabir in no time. *Twenty-seven minutes.* The engineers had already begun fixing the gelatine rods to blow up the boulder. Another team was laying the detonator cable.

'Stop!' Kabir's face lit up. He whispered something to the team leaders. And then, a squad of the best-built men lined up against the boulder, ready to push it back, while men with ballistic shields stood along both walls providing cover from the bullets coming from the concealed automatics.

The boulder now began rolling upwards, providing impenetrable cover while bulldozing its way forward. The gunfire from the other side had ceased as the enemy realized the futility of their resistance. The dragonfly drones were now leading the way again. The Ikhwan's security force could be seen retracting and soon the tunnel was completely evacuated.

They finally reached the iron door at the end of the tunnel, the entrance to the Cove!

The boulder was locked in position now by simply putting some guns beneath it and allowing it to roll back and get stuck. The gelatine explosive then blew it into pieces and the iron door was subjected to the same fate. The forces moved in, retaining the same formation, ballistic shields flanking the assault team.

Clean! Bruce gestured with a thumbs up after having checked the narrow slit behind the last set of doors.

The lead commandos responded with affirmative nods.

'Basement seized,' Kabir whispered through his communicator to the ground forces. 'No civilians or governing council members spotted. We've lost four soldiers. Moving up to the first level.'

While seeking an access path to the upper floors, the forces located a lift. It had been shut down. A subsequent search for an emergency exit led to none. But, a short while later, a locked access gate was found. It seemed to lead to a tunnel on an upward incline. Before long, the forces blasted it open and began making their way through.

The tunnel was a dark, narrow, lightless corridor with markers located at every ten metres or so—each equipped with surveillance cameras. *They're watching us!* Kabir knew instinctively, wondering what surprises Khabib had planned for them.

Switching on the emergency lights of their protective gear, they advanced upwards, scouring every inch of enemy ground as they did so. No sooner had they walked into an adjacent landing that led to the first floor, than they found themselves bombarded with shots. The crossfire went on for a solid three minutes, before the opposition was overcome. The forces were down by five more men. Eighteen Ikhwan guards had been killed as well, their bodies sprawled across the expansive first floor, occupied by security workstations, CCTV monitors and a library at its rear end.

'Where are all the civilians?' murmured one of the lead commandos. 'And the council members?'

'Probably hiding in a safe room somewhere!' Bruce suspected. 'No high-strength explosives used so far by the enemy?'

'You know why.' Kabir shrugged. 'For one, it will clog the exit paths and more importantly, it may destabilize the entire structure. Our masks are resistant to all kinds of gases. Doesn't leave them with many options other than manual combat.'

The second floor was a similar fortress—fifteen guards and a large storehouse for utilities, food and other supplies. They crept along. The third floor had a very high ceiling, almost ten metres and housed twenty guards, which the task force soon dealt with. The agents figured out the reason for the high roof. A very large portion of this floor housed the power generation section. It was a technological marvel: a self-sustaining hydrogen fuel-based system that could power the Cove for several months with no external contact with the world. They thought of deactivating the supply, but then decided against it. It would only make their task of reversal more difficult. Worse still, the whole place could blow up at the slightest mistake. Hydrogen-based systems were very dangerous at that.

The advance was gruelling for the teams, having to brave relentless clashes one floor after another. The number of casualties on their side was growing too. And there were still a few floors to go for the centrum!

However, when they walked into the landing of the fourth floor, things got quiet. Too quiet. No clashes. No gunfire. No enemy presence throughout the 20,000-square-foot office space. It was unusual, seeing how the repository of cabinets and computer desks implied that this floor was an important one.

∽

A floor above, Khabib, who had been watching the infiltrators from the monitors of the surveillance room, nodded at his deputies.

The lever was switched on.

∽

'Everyone's been evacuated,' Bruce said, pointing to the files and folders dropped on the floor in a hurry. This seemed to be their media section. Compiling news and intelligence from world over!

'But, to where?'

'To the upper floors probably. Or is there an escape hatch we don't know about?'

Three scouts began walking into the large hall for a further check. One of the men spun around, signalling to the remaining forces with a thumbs up. *Clean.*

Suddenly, a vaporous force came beaming through the walls. The soldier began screaming, and immediately, the floor was filled with the stench of burning flesh. A laser beam had sliced through both his legs like a surgeon's scalpel. The teams noticed a series of tiny holes in the wall. 'Motion sensors!' The floor was rigged with them.

The two other accompanying commandos immediately fell back into the landing, alongside the rest, having escaped the beam by a hair's breadth.

Staying as far back as possible, the task forces tried pulling the lacerated soldier aside, but it was too late. He was convulsing wildly from the shock brought on by acute blood loss. Within a minute, he was gone. The forces watched aghast as their fellow soldier was reduced to a sacrificial lamb by the laser beam.

It took them a short while to recoup from the horror before they laid his body to rest on one side.

'We need to find another way to get ourselves to the centrum!' said a lead commander after a few moments of silence.

Kabir pulled out an image of the Cove, which they pored over. Alas, there was no other way up. For any form of access to the floors above, they would have to walk right through the fourth floor hall.

'Could we crawl on the floor?' suggested a commando out of desperation.

'Nope! Even with a body like Catherine Zeta Jones we would never be able to repeat the feat she carried out in *Entrapment*.' Bruce pointed to one of the sensor holes that was barely an inch above the floor. 'Look!'

'Damn!' Kabir banged his fist against the wall as he glanced at his watch. *Twenty minutes!*

In the surveillance room, Khabib and his deputies bumped their fists, mocking the fretful expressions of the trapped men. Pushing the 'Rain' button on the panel in front of him, he then sent a message to the Sayyid.

'Situation contained!'

∽

'Perfect!' Fatih sighed, his eyes glued to the life-size screen in the centrum. The first newsflash had just rolled in at the bottom. An airplane had crashed into its first target.

The media reports were frantic, detailing news of a hijacked flight having collided with the tallest skyscraper in Seoul. The building was shown crumbling, level by level. The scenes being telecast by the news crews showed people screaming and running amok. The faces of the onlookers were painted with fresh dust and tears; the rubble was splattered with blood and many limbs were trapped in the stone.

The leader turned to his architect, an aura of achievement hovering over him. 'So, what do you think?'

Abu Bakr nodded, almost convinced. 'It's good. But there is still a long way to go.'

'And we will get there. Within the next hour, news channels will be driven to hysteria. They won't know what to report and what to leave out!'

The two men shared a short laugh.

∽

On the fourth floor, the commandos were pushed back into the tunnel as a fuming orange-yellow liquid started spraying from nozzles concealed on the roof of the landing. The liquid sizzled as it fell over their guns, dissolving the metal like cubes of sugar. Horrified, the commandos ran amok to avoid the killer fluid.

'Aqua regia!' hissed Kabir.

'What the fuck, man! Bloody primitives—trying to kill us with acid,' Bruce said, grinding his teeth.

'Not really! Had the tactical chief not been prudent enough to select these Teflon-coated Blackhawk coverall suits, the acid would have burned holes in our body too. Aqua regia dissolves everything, even platinum,' Kabir explained, shaking off the droplets from his suit. The showers were beginning to dwindle.

'Agent Agapov for Agent Rathore... come in...' A distress call suddenly erupted through his transmitter.

'Agent Rathore here.'

'First plane has struck. Target in Seoul hit. Thousands suspected dead already.'

Kabir slowly removed his smoke mask, his feet faltering, life seeping from his features. Bruce's expression mirrored his, as did the faces of several other commandos around them.

'Oh my god!' Kabir shuddered. 'It's happening! The air strikes have been rescheduled.' It was just like he'd feared. His nightmares were coming true! 'Have we failed?'

A crippling despair began holding the forces hostage.

Bruce quickly snapped his fingers at them. 'We have a mission on hand. Gotta keep going. The other teams are still hard at work, doing what they can. We have to continue too!'

'Yes.' Kabir blinked back the sweat that had been trickling down his brows. 'We must...'

He glared at the massive empty hall, watching its walls whose motion sensors were holding them back. Suddenly, it struck him. He noticed an abandoned ledger lying on the floor. He carefully stretched his gun forward and pulled it towards him. Picking it up, he flung it across the room. It went flapping across and fell on the floor. Nothing. The beams had not been triggered. He now needed something else to put his theory to test. Something warmer. A quick look around and his eyes halted on the dismembered leg of the dead soldier. Kabir touched the shoe. *Still warm.* He offered the dead soldier a quiet salute. *I am very sorry, buddy.*

Sliding the dead man's boot off, he flung it far. Three beams instantly came on from three different spots, smouldering the shoe to dust. 'Just as I thought. Sensors come on only when they sense a narrow range, within normal body temperature.'

'Which means,' another commando stood up, 'we need to make this hall very cold.'

'Or make it very very hot!' Kabir said.

The rest of the commandos guessed what he was thinking. He planned to set the hall aflame to deactivate the sensors.

Bruce looked down at the armour he had on. 'Our gear is not really fire-proof. How long will we last?'

Kabir shrugged, aware that the answer to this one was not going to be pleasant. 'A minute. A minute and a half, at best!' The door was about 700 metres away. It would take them at least two minutes to get to it, even at their fastest. But they had no other options.

Drawing in a deep breath, the commandos rolled the low-impact explosive along the wall, and then set it alight with the blowtorches. The furnishings and furniture were quick to catch fire. Within minutes, the hall was an inferno.

A few laser beams were immediately set off. But, before long, the sensor system was fizzing off, and ended up completely damaged. The smoke soon triggered the fire alarms in the building, activating the sprinkler system in the hall.

'Go! go!' ordered the lead commandos. Every second that they lingered in the red heat of the blaze, they risked being charred.

∽

'What are they doing?' yelled the deputy in the surveillance room above, slapping his forehead at the sight of the burning hall.

'Damn it!' hissed Khabib. 'They've confused the motion sensors. Destroyed them.'

'But, with all that fire...they wouldn't be able to make it through the heat!'

Khabib was not so convinced. Peering through the monitor, he took a closer look at the chief commando spearheading the mission. The man appeared to have a gritty streak and a determination about him. Through the visor of the smoke mask he noticed those familiar grey piercing eyes. He'd crossed paths with him twice before. 'The Indian commando!' he growled to himself. 'Bastard!'

Fatih, who had been awaiting news of the second airstrike in the centrum, glanced up at the ceiling. The sirens were still blaring. 'Oh, this smoke alarm is giving me a headache.'

He called Khabib. 'What's going on?' he demanded.

'A small hiccup, sir. That's all,' replied Khabib. 'I'll deal with it! In the meanwhile, I'd advise you and the Murshid to head to the secure suite, and stay locked within.'

'You said you had the situation contained, Khabib! You better not be lying to me!' He gritted his teeth, making his displeasure known as he stormed off towards the suite.

∽

Having left behind whatever explosives they were carrying, and following the brief clearings created by the water trickles from the sprinkler system, the teams had thundered out. Yet, the mad dash was not enough to stop some of the soldiers from suffering first- and second-degree burns. With a few more painful injuries endured, and several weapons lesser, they had reached an exit on the left wall.

Moving down the main level, they crept into the new floor cautiously, thus finally reaching the heart of the building, where they expected to face maximum resistance. They were now on the floor of the centrum. As it turned out, they were right! A few seconds, and they were confronting the might of the Cove's defence. Every inch was crawling with armed security, and they spared no violence in their attempt to take the infidels down, turning the business stations into full-fledged battlegrounds.

The Cove's engineers were scampering for their lives. Fluff, paper and foam from furniture flew through the room. Circuits crackled as wires were hit in the midst of combat. The floor was splattered with fragments of wood, shards of glass and pools of blood.

Taking a short breather from the rampage, Bruce took cover behind a desk to remove a splinter that had embedded itself in his leg. As he reloaded the magazine in his gun, he noticed that a part of a distant wall—about the size of a door—seemed to be of a slightly different colour from the rest.

'Rathore,' he said into his communicator, still catching up on his breath, 'I think I've spotted the safe room. Your ten o'clock!'

Kabir, who was hiding behind a cabinet, briefly glanced at the wall Bruce had called his attention to. 'You could be right. Inform the other teams—and our techies.'

'Roger that!'

Following instructions from Bruce, and under the cover provided by the forces, the engineer corps dashed towards the wall, and began scouring its surface for access. A thorough hunt revealed a panel hidden behind a light fixture. Unscrewing the panel fascia, they plugged a device into the connector. One click and the control panel was connected to an intelligence supercomputer that used brute force to crack the access code. Within minutes, the wall clicked open.

∽

Soon after Bruce's message, Kabir found himself embroiled in a fierce battle with two guards. Taking a split-second breather in a quiet corner, he removed a hidden revolver strapped to his ankle.

One... two... three... He counted, rolling out of his hiding spot and skidding onto the floor, startling both guards.

Bang! Bang!

He fired two simultaneous rounds at their heads, bringing them down. He cast a look around. Most of the Ikhwan's fighters and engineers were dead; the successful commandos were beginning to come out of their ambush. A few of the staff and engineers who had managed to escape the crossfire had been taken in custody by the commandos and were being escorted down the exits to the base camp.

The very next instant, a message echoed through his transmitter. 'Safe room cracked open. All governing members found. And restrained!'

Kabir celebrated briefly before making his way towards the centrum.

∽

He observed the arrangement of the concentric workstations, each of them segregated by smaller alleys. He scanned the room until he spotted the software controls and components spread out on what appeared to be the nerve centre of the operation.

'Gotcha!'

Suddenly, from nowhere, a kick knocked the gun off from his palm, while a death grip wriggled itself around his neck from behind. He instinctively reached for the blade in his pocket, about to jab it into the thigh of his attacker, but his wrist was stopped in mid-air.

'Arrrrggggh!'

He used raw force to claw at the clasp. But the fingers around his neck were like tentacles—they would not budge. Gasping for air, Kabir tried every trick he knew to free himself from the stranglehold. Elbowing the assailant's ribs. Poking at his eyeballs. Booting his nuts. But this attacker had a countermove for all of it, making it obvious that he was a seasoned fighter.

'It would take me a sec to shoot you down,' Khabib spat at his victim whose features were turning blue. 'But with you, Agent

Rathore,' Khabib continued, 'it's personal. I want to feel the breath leaving your body.'

Kabir was on the verge of losing consciousness when a loud shot clapped by his ear. A searing pain swept through his arm.

The death grip loosened, and with it, the blood and oxygen began to return to his head, sending him into a dizzy spell. It was then that Kabir realized that a bullet had chafed against—barely hurting him—before hitting the assailant behind him.

∽

Slumped on the floor, Kabir dragged himself to a safe corner. And the first thing he noticed when his vision cleared up, was the sight of Bruce showing off a Glock from the other end of the hall. *Now look who saved your life—with jittery hands and all!* Kabir caught his expression.

Staggering up to his feet, Kabir realized his assailant was not far. He promptly flung his blade at him. But despite the fact that Khabib was recouping from a bullet wound to his shoulder, he ducked in time, managing to escape the throw.

The two enemies exchanged a hard glare, both having spotted Khabib's gun from the corner of their eyes. In a flash, both men simultaneously dove for it. But Kabir now had the advantage of being closer, and got to it first. Spinning around on his spine, he took aim at Khabib. But the assassin was quicker than the speed of a bullet, it seemed. For, he had jerked off its path and disappeared within the blink of an eye. After all, it was his hometurf, and he knew every inch of it—every dark spot, every escape hole.

A team was put to task to track down the dangerous man and stop him from wreaking further havoc.

∽

'Thank you for having my back.' Kabir patted Bruce's shoulder in gratitude once they caught up.

'Anytime, buddy...' Bruce said, smirking.

The duo rushed towards the supercomputers block in the centrum, joined subsequently by the technical experts. In short order, the techies took over the command centre, connecting the master controller with the supercomputers of the international intelligence. The counterterrorism experts on ground now had access to the nerve centre of the Brotherhood's operations.

'Centrum's taken over.' Kabir had just finished relaying the message to the ground forces when fresh news suddenly flashed online.

Kabir and Bruce watched the breaking story on the large screen, adjacent to the command centre.

The cameras had zoomed into a new flight that had gone rogue. It was heading directly for the tallest skyscraper in Queensland. A residential one, 300 metres high—each floor packed with families and children. It was about thirty seconds away from the building with most of its residents still trapped inside. The fears and tears of those watching grew as each moment passed. Even members of the emergency crew seemed lost.

The duo glared at the screen, neither man in a position to utter a single word. With beats pounding heavily, they glared at their worst fears coming alive. 'No!' Kabir shut his eyelids. Bruce flinched, turning away as the flight went right towards the centre of the structure.

For a second, stillness prevailed.

Until duty reminded Kabir that he had to drag himself back to reality, and to what he could change. To the last part of his unfinished mission—the imminent pursuit of the Murshid, the Sayyid and Khabib.

Suddenly, a string of startled voices began springing up around the control desks.

'Wait...'

'What was that?'

'Wh…what is going on…?'

∽

'Wh…what is going on…?'

Inside one of the planes, the chief amongst the group of terrorist pilots was trying to switch the cockpit controls to manual. The airline pilots had been tied and locked inside the captain's cabin.

The rest of his fidayeen group dashed into the cockpit, amidst the dreadful screams and hollers coming from the passengers onboard. 'Has the remote navigation system failed?'

'Impossible!'

'Why has the path shifted sharply, then?'

'We don't know…' The chief fidayeen frantically worked his way through the various aircraft controls alongside his co-pilots, struggling to get the flight to return to its intended trajectory. They had less than ten seconds to revert to the original course, if they had to strike right through their target—the skyscraper that lay ahead. But the Air-Bee continued making an extremely sharp turn to its right.

They didn't know how, but an advanced datalink controller had seized full control of the craft's speed, altitude and direction. It was advanced enough to override the Ikhwan's improvised remote navigation and to overrule manual control. With the pilots completely pushed out of the loop, a fresh set of instructions from the datalink was now controlling the flight management system.

'H…how is this happening?'

∽

'H…how is this happening?' Kabir was utterly surprised.

Strangely, the rogue plane had taken a sharp ninety-degree turn. With the deviation having come just as the plane was about to collide, its tail fin ended up kissing the fascia of the building. Millions of onlookers gasped, as several windows were shattered into powder. A long crack ran through the fascia splitting open the surface of the building. Sparks soared, the tail fin soon catching fire.

However, the minor impact of the tail fin was not fatal to the stability of the skyscraper. The structure continued to stand. Thousands had been saved—in the blink of an eye!

'What in the world just happened?' Television viewers let out cries of joy.

∽

'What in the world just happened?'

An eerie stillness took over the duo, who had been watching the unexpected developments from the suite.

Fatih clenched his teeth. 'How is it possible?'

'I don't know!' The Murshid was breathing hard.

'What could have caused the flight to make that sharp turn?'

'Even if the pilots on board failed, the flight was being controlled by remote navigation technology...a modified and more advanced version of the original technology, at that!'

'How could so many fool proof measures not perform?'

'I...I...can't believe it!'

'After decades of planning...'

'After years of testing...'

'I'll get back to this...but we have to get out of here first...' The Sayyid pressed a button on his intercom. 'Get it ready...'

He then glared at the Murshid. 'Did I not warn you to move very cautiously, to not step out of the Cove at this crucial stage... if you hadn't made your fancy appearance at the Al-Kufra camps and spilled the beans, this might never have happened...'

'Stop it!'

'It gave them time...the forces were prepared...they came armed...'

'Fatih!'

'If the rest of the Ikhwan ask me what happened, I'll make

sure to let them know...' There was a hint of evil in Fatih's eyes.

'How dare you?' The Murshid grew further enraged. 'After everything I've done for the organization and for you...your impatience is what precipitated this mishap...had it not been Hanif's last wish that I follow you, I would never have allowed anyone to meddle in the Ikhwan's affairs, undo the original masterplan...' He rushed over and grabbed the young man's collar. 'You ruined everything!'

∽

'Buddy...God is kind...God is kind indeed!' Bruce threw an ecstatic punch in the air. 'We did it...I can't believe it worked, but we did it!'

Kabir remained stock-still with his palm glued to his mouth, experiencing a sense of relief that he could not put into words. Yes, they had done it! They hadn't failed the mission. They hadn't failed millions. At long last, the counterterrorism technical teams, in collaboration with the rescued Chinese engineers had managed to override the Cove's technology and taken control of the planes. If all went well, the remaining hijacked planes would be saved too.

'What about the teams of fidayeens inside the planes? They could still spell trouble...' Bruce thought aloud.

'With the distressed flights now getting priority landing clearance at the nearest landing strips, I don't think there is much the fidayeens can do,' quipped Kabir. 'Imagine how the passengers must be feeling! Like they were saved by some divine force...some kind of miracle!'

'Okay.' His expression changed. 'It's a little premature to celebrate yet...let's open our champagne bottles once we get hold of the Murshid and the Sayyid! Khabib has been missing too.' Kabir flipped through the channels on the surveillance monitor, but they all showed devastation scenes on the various other floors.

'Look for any hidden channels,' he said to an engineer, who set to work immediately.

'There...! Got it...!' Kabir stopped him as a mute channel

appeared on the screen. It streamed live footage of Abu Bakr and Fatih engrossed in conversation.

'A hidden suite! Look for a hidden door like the safe room where we found the board members...' Bruce commanded the taskforce members gathered around who fanned out in all directions. It was barely three minutes before a voice creaked over his walkie-talkie. 'It's at the farthest end, to our extreme left, sir... but it's rock solid!'

Within a few seconds the entire team was standing at the suite's door. Kabir turned to the techies who were busy with the main controls. 'Can you please hack into the access codes for this suite? ASAP!'

They observed the controls in front. 'I think we can, officer!'

'Good. Do it. Quick. We need to get in there before they leave.'

While the men got working at it right away, Kabir surveyed the security cameras of all other areas in the Cove, but he couldn't locate Khabib anywhere. He turned to Bruce. 'It is Khabib who holds the key to their escape—I am certain of it. Take three other teams, Bruce, and fan out...in pursuit of Khabib! I'll stay here, have my eyes on the Murshid and the Sayyid...'

'Roger that! Will cue you in on developments.' Bruce reloaded the magazines in his gun, signalling at the teams that had gathered behind the workstations, awaiting instructions. 'Come on...'

After the teams jogged out of the centrum, out in four different directions, Kabir reverted his glance to the systems in front. *Come on... come on...* His fingers restlessly drummed the desk, as he waited for the software experts to crack into the Cove's security to hack open the suite. Suddenly, from the corner of his eye he caught a shift in the scenes streaming in the surveillance video. 'What's going on?' He peered in. The two leaders were evidently having a heated exchange—a war of words. Compelled by a strange feeling, Kabir narrowed his eyes as he studied the young man, Fatih, whom he had never seen before.

48

You Are a Girl...

Fatima slumped onto the soft carpet of the hotel room. Benumbed, she sat that way, all by herself, for what felt like hours. Her BlackBerry messenger notifications were pinging away non-stop. But those were simply flippant messages. She knew she had no real friends to share her grief with—her stringent ways had alienated her. Nor did she have the company of cousins to seek comfort in. And now, it seemed she had no family either.

Fatih! A silent scream ripped through her lungs, as she hunched over from crushing grief. The lone twin was finally forced to face the fact that the only friend and playmate that she had had, the one person she could ever get herself to love, was no more! *Noooo!* She thrashed about, beat her palms against the wall, weeping until her cheeks were soggy and she had no tears to spare.

Over the months, she'd continued to cling onto the hope that her brother would recover—the sole member of her family to do so. Thereby, she'd urged her family to plan a trip to Mecca, in accordance with Fatih's wishes. And as if by Allah's calling, he'd breathed his last here, in the holy land, succumbing to his ailment.

Wearied from the sobbing, Fatima eventually raised her salt-stung eyes from the floor. To her right was a room from where her mother's aggrieved howls had not stopped echoing. A week later, the middle-aged woman would be back in the kitchen, cooking for her family. From another room came her father's sobs. He agonized over the future to an old relative—a confidante. She heard him clearly, saying, 'I've lost my bloodline, my heir and my dreams of seeing Fatih lead after me! My father's legacy has been shattered...'

When her father's wails would not stop, she picked herself off the floor and dragged her feet towards the doorway of the room he was seated in.

'Baba,' she whimpered.

'Get out. Leave me alone,' barked Zahur from within.

She stood there for a long while, listening to him pouring out his grievances.

'Baba.' She swallowed hard, her throat achingly sore. 'I shall join your movement. I shall fulfil your dreams!' She pushed back the damp locks of her hair. 'I'll help you accomplish the visions of my grandfather. I'll make you proud, I promise!'

'Fatima, you don't know what you speak. Go away. Let me mourn in peace.'

But even as a sixteen-year-old she was aware of what she was saying. Fatima was no child. She knew what she was committing to. What her father led. What the movement was. What it stood for. And it had always fascinated her—more than any of her subjects at school. Her father had noticed Fatih's dreams. Had he never noticed hers?

'Please, Baba,' she implored.

'Fatima, you are a girl! You cannot lead anything!'

That stung. Not that she was seen an inferior, but that she was a girl. Not that she was underappreciated as Fatima, but that she could never be Faith.

That night, when everyone was fast asleep, she opened a drawer and grabbed her mother's gold chains. Stuffing the jewellery into a bag, she snuck out of the hotel room with a packed bag.

It was the last her family ever saw or heard of Fatima.

49

A Face-off Between Titans

'Your impatience is what precipitated this mishap…and that's what led to the plans getting leaked!' He shook the young man's collar—back and forth until his grip loosened.

Fatih's headdress had come loose.

Abu Bakr's skin blanched. His trembling fingers let go. It was as if he had just seen a ghost.

'Ya Allah!' His feet faltered a few steps back, as he stared hard at the features of his adversary. 'Am I seeing things? H…how can you be Fatih?'

An ominous pause later, Fatih broke out into a vicious grin.

'Why can't I be Fatih? Can't I be the Sayyid? I earned the title as much as you did!'

'I must be hallucinating!'

'Ermmm… not really.' Fatih nodded mockingly.

'God, save us!' Abu Bakr heaved, the thoughts in his head taking a manic spin. His feet continued to stagger backwards. He was the great Murshid. He had orchestrated all forms of atrocities in his lifetime without so much as batting an eyelid. Braved all forms of absurdities throughout! But this was beyond anything he'd ever imagined.

'An impostor in the guise of our Sayyid? Wait, aren't you the agent? How did you manage to…' He spat, trying to cleanse the feeling from his mouth. 'You need to be dragged in front of the Ikhwan for this sacrilege. They'll hang you and skin you alive…

or stone you to a slow death. That's what you deserve for polluting our holy cause!'

Well aware of the thoughts flitting through his head, Fatih spoke in a steady tone, adjusting the headdress that had come loose, 'I am aware that you have done plenty for the Ikhwan, Abu Bakr. But I have done more. And I still have plenty more to do. I cannot let others know this secret. Not even Khabib.'

The Murshid reached for the gun in his suit.

Bang! Bang!

Fatih was twice as fast, having covertly reached for the concealed five-inch Smith & Wesson Shield tucked in a hidden pocket in the headgear. Two shots later, Fatih was watching the work of art that had been carved on the Murshid's head—two bullet holes where his pupils had been until a moment ago.

With a thud, the old man fell to the floor. Dead before he knew what had hit him.

With a glimmer of pride, Fatih slipped the pistol back into its slot, tied the headdress back on and gently tucked an imaginary curl behind the ear.

ౢ

Kabir froze in front of the screen.

Not because the footage showed that the Murshid had just been shot.

Not because he would no longer get an opportunity to interrogate the Murshid about the MH470 proclamation he had made at Nusrat's camps.

Not even because, another shocking truth had just come to light—that the Sayyid was, in fact, an impostor.

But because of whom the Sayyid reminded him of. The person appeared to have short spiky hair. But out of habit, tucked an imaginary curl behind his ear, as if he was used to wearing his hair much longer. And the characteristic manner in which he did it resembled the quirk of a particular woman he knew all too well.

'No. It can't be!' A hollow pit formed in his stomach. 'It's absurd! It can't be her... it cannot be!'

He would have to learn the truth.

He turned to the taskforce. 'I'll go in first. Alone.'

50

The Surreal Experience

It was deep into the night and most of the city was asleep. A week had passed since the crippling grief of having laid his son to rest. And it was the first day that he'd managed to catch a few hours of slumber, when he heard a knock on the door of his hotel room.

Wh... wh...? He woke up with a jump. *12.30 a.m.? Who could it be? At this time of the night?* Sliding out from under the sheets, he picked up the revolver from his dressing table and crept towards the door. 'Who are you?' he demanded, repeating himself a few times.

No answer came. But through the peephole, it was evident that there was someone standing outside. A youth in a keffiyeh. And even though he wouldn't ordinarily do so, something about this youth compelled him to open the door.

'Who are you?' he hissed through the slit in the door. The youth was frail, with a tight desert scarf masking his face and head. One feature stood out, however, even in the darkness. The pair of eyes underneath the scarf. They were dead, numbing.

'Speak up, boy,' he ordered.

'Allow me to step in and I'll explain!'

'No, speak up from where you are.'

'Please!'

The voice! Zahur gasped to himself. It was tugging at his heart, reminding him of someone very close to him. *Fatih?* Unable to refuse the youth much as he tried, he finally allowed him in.

'Who are you? What do you want?'

Once the boy walked into the suite, he removed his scarf to reveal a bald head. A second later, he moved in from the shadows into a beam of moonlight coming in from the windows.

No! It can't be... Zahur clutched the doorknob. His head spun. 'Fatih! Is that you?' He staggered close to the youth to hug him. But he was stopped a few inches away; the youth had stuck his palm up, halting his step.

'No, Baba...'

Baba? Baffled, Zahur observed the features of the intruder closely and recognized that they had a hint of femininity about them. 'W... w... wait... F... Fatima?'

The youth stayed tight-lipped.

Zahur turned and switched on the light. 'Fatima!' he screamed, 'Where have you been? Where did you go? We postponed our return to the States, because we've been so worried. We've looked for you everywhere. Why have you chopped your hair off? What have you done?'

There were so many things wrong with features. Her physique. So many oddities that made her seem different from the pretty girl she once was. The desperate father in him did what no good father would do. He stole a glimpse at her bosom. It was flat. Like a boys. 'What in Allah's name have you done?'

'Baba, I realized that,' she began, eventually confessing in a straight tone, 'Fatih, his dreams, and the movement, meant more to me than my own identity! Fulfilling my grandfather's vision—and my father's dream—is my dream too! As a girl, I wouldn't be allowed to follow the path. As Fatih, I would.'

'But h... how did you even?' He held his head in his palms, still wondering if this was all a nightmare of some sort.

Fatima thought it wise not to go into too much detail, lest her father would be mortified. For she had had to do unspeakable things to a rogue doctor to be able to get the surgeries she wanted. Surgeries that would make her less of a woman—and more of a man. Talking of the 'unspeakable', however, the doctor wasn't going to speak anything anyway. She'd made sure of that. The papers would soon be reporting the death of a Saudi doctor, found in his bedroom, with his clothes off and his neck snapped.

'Fatima... how could you do this to yourself?'

'Well, you have always blamed me for being very stubborn, haven't you, Baba?' She smiled grimly.

Too shocked to say anything else, Zahur sat on the couch, silent for a long time as Fatima waited, until a point when he recalled the prophetic words of his father during his last visit.

Fatih will live. Fatih will lead the movement.

It took him several hours of reflection thereafter to come around. But, once he did, there was no turning back. After all, no one could have sacrificed for the movement as much as she'd done. Not even his Fatih!

ട

'Fatih is cured. It's a blessing from God! The Holy Lands miraculously cured him.' That was the story everyone was told once they were back in America. If anyone asked about Fatima, they were told that she had decided to stay back in Saudi with her aunt, to finish her education. A year later, that narration was followed up with sad tales of how Fatima had decided to run off with a lover. And how she was dead to the family. The story was entirely Fatima's suggestion, of course.

It was a secret that thus lived on, where even those closest to the family knew nothing of the truth. And it was a secret that was taken to the grave, along with Zahur's passing.

Fatima sold off the family house soon after and disappeared. With the active role she intended to play in the society, she could no longer afford to be so traceable. She continued to lead the movement from the shadows, living a devious life of many names, faces and identities. She mastered the art of auto morphing, much like Proteus himself—transmogrifying her appearance in a Zelig-like swiftness. She was Fatih when dealing with the Brotherhood. Fatima, if she ever chose to be, when by herself. And at times, she donned the role of an American girl, especially when the need arose. For instance, when someone believably American had to infiltrate Air-Bee, to tap into its 'technological' secrets!

51

Keira Deciphered

The sounds of the helicopter's rotary blades echoed from a distance. Khabib would be here soon, to rescue his supreme leader.

Fatima rushed towards the wall at the far end and pressed a button. The hydraulic cylinders creaked into action, pushing the hatch outwards. A small fold along the mountain ridge split apart, and an eighteen-inch-thick door opened up.

She was about to walk into the adjoining cave that would lead towards the opening in the mountain when a familiar whisper brushed over her shoulders.

'Keira!'

A slow smile laced her lips. 'Kabir.' She gradually spun around to face the man. 'I see you've finally found me! I've missed you too. I did hope we would meet under better circumstances, but now that you're here, we must bid each other a proper farewell, don't you think?'

'Who are you?' A low growl escaped Kabir's throat as his eyes reviewed the person he stood facing. It was a twisted reality that could not have been in his weirdest nightmares. How different she appeared from the woman he knew. From the woman he had developed feelings for. And not because of her warped appearance, but because of what he saw behind her eyes. Pure malevolence! 'What are you?'

'Who am I?' she quizzed, inching towards him.

Kabir instantly reached for her headgear, and catching it, confiscated the concealed Smith & Wesson mini tucked into it. He unloaded its chamber before flinging it aside.

'Oh Kabir. I was only coming to give you a kiss.' She laughed teasingly, letting her breath caress his face. Running a lascivious look over his features, she then locked her lips on his. When he wouldn't submit to her overtures, she deepened the kiss by clutching his face and prying his lips apart with hers. Finally, a few seconds later, she came away, as if she'd just enjoyed the taste of her enemy on her tongue.

Bitch! The skin on his jaws flinched from rage. He wasn't going to spew monologues of the crippling moral dilemmas he'd suffered after Libya and give her additional reason to gloat. But the resentment on his face said it all.

'What happened? Now that I have no emerald eyes, no make-up, no long lashes, no cascading hair...and no breasts, you don't want to kiss me?'

'No, it's because you are ugly...from the inside!'

'Tch tch...' she said, 'if it is of any comfort to you, of all the people I have beguiled, you were one of the few men who made me feel guilty.'

His fingers itched to grab her fair neck. One squeeze and Kabir would get his much-deserved revenge. But he was far too sensible to let vindictive urges get the better of him. Removing his Glock from the holster, he pointed it at her chest. The shuffle of taskforce boots could be heard from the corridor outside the suite.

'Ugggggh!' An abrupt burst of pain had seized up his leg, leaving him floundering.

Keira had planned her countermove already. By striking her captor's hand in a deft manoeuvre that sent his arm flying, she'd swung down and jammed her heel against the sharpest spot of his shin.

Taking advantage of the split instant thereafter, she replaced her headdress, preparing to make a run for the platform. The helicopter was emerging on the horizon. Khabib had arrived, as planned. The cave connecting the suite to the face of the mountain opened on the hind side, flanked with equally tall peaks and a precipitous jagged terrain—out of immediate sight of the taskforce in the encampments below.

About to dash off, she reached across to wrestle the weapon off the injured man.

'Wh… what… what!' All of a sudden, her wrist would not move. 'What the hell!'

Kabir had slipped his handcuffs around her just as she'd leaned down to claim his Glock.

In all possibility, he had put his life on the line by doing so, but he had to do whatever he could to stop her from escaping. For, if Fatima and Khabib fled now, it would be almost impossible to track them down again. And it would only take a while for them to unleash havoc again.

Besides, the taskforce was right behind. And having the head of the Ikhwan as his hostage now could buy him some time. He stared over her shoulder at the helicopter hovering against the mountainous landscape, his eyes crossing paths with the deadly pilot sitting in it. And then back again at Keira, a defiant glare flashing across his eyes. 'Yup, it seems you are stuck with me!'

When he had recognized her a few minutes ago on the monitor in the centrum, watching her trying to tuck an imaginary curl behind her ear, one of the first thoughts that had struck him was that if she really was the Sayyid, what business did she have playing trivial games? Trying to win his trust by saving him on the streets of Kuala Lumpur! As an Air-Bee agent it probably made sense…she had been trying to acquire the amulet that contained incriminating evidence against Air-Bee. But as the Sayyid…really? It made no sense!

And then, slowly, it had started to dawn on him.

The Ikhwan's plan had already been progressing immaculately with the Murshid on to it. Becoming a confidante of the leader of the taskforce that posed the only real-time threat to them did make sense. Looking back at how it might have progressed, she had first won the confidence of Air-Bee…paved the way for Khabib to steal the remote navigation software from their control rooms the same night that the MH470 was being hijacked…then got into the Protettori through Air-Bee…won their trust and finally found a way to infiltrate the mission against her own organization. She had orchestrated Khabib's attack on him in the hospital, making Kabir run right into her trap. And then, she had infiltrated his heart in the same insidious way, clouding his judgement.

Thereafter, she had tried every subtle trick to foil the mission. Like trying to raise the alarm inside the Ikhwan and informing them of the Protettori's game plan, holding back the team at the old man's house, which eventually got the little girl killed. And then, parting from the team at the Al-Kufra camps and disappearing! She must have tried to get the message across to the Murshid without giving herself away. She had to conceal her real identity at all costs—as much from the outside world as within her own organization. Which she had deftly done.

He recalled the guard who had been rushing towards the stage inside the aviation centre when he and Olaf had made their first move on the Murshid. Her messenger! And then, she had gladly played hostage to the Murshid and Khabib twice to facilitate their escape. She had been the con woman all along.

'You bastard!' She frisked his pockets in a frenzy. 'Where are the keys?'

Even if she did manage to wrestle his gun off him and shoot him down, he would be tethered to her like deadweight. How was she meant to escape? *Come on… think… quick!* The taskforce was right at the suite entrance now! *Bloody hell—the hatch door, of course…*

She glanced up at the hatch. The men from the taskforce were spilling into the suite in droves, the muzzles of their rifles pointed at her. In a flash, she grappled her way past Kabir and before he could pin her down, she punched a flying fist into the panic button on the emergency hatch lock.

Thud!

The eighteen-inch-thick door clamped close as fast as lightning, shutting the taskforce inside the suite, and the two of them outside, stuck in the cave. Even the taskforce's best hackers would need time to get this one to open now.

52

The Final Skydive

The skirmish that followed in the cave was violent. Kabir wrapped his handcuffs around her neck in a chokehold, but as an equally well-trained agent, she knew her way out of every trap. Besides, she had an advantage too. *His weak point!*

With a few elbow strikes aimed at his ribs, she escaped his clutch. Deft as he was, Kabir defended the subsequent kicks that came at him. But those attacks were merely decoys. Her real target was his weak shoulder. When she had him distracted enough by her kicks, she summoned all the strength that she could into her fists, and punched his injured cuff.

He screamed. The pain was blinding. His head spun, his body about to drop to his knees. But he held on. And stayed up. Two shots escaped the muzzle of the Glock, as she tried to pry it off him, but his palms wouldn't let go.

'So you think you can stop us? Didn't the Murshid tell you about our subjugation plan? The one he talked about back at Nusrat's place. The powder we have contaminated the oil wells and Strategic Petroleum Reserves with…it is a microencapsulated radio wave-activated catalyst. While we talk, the oil around the world is getting polymerized to an unextractable gob. Except in the Middle East of course! Now, what will you fire your jets and tanks with? How will you endure the icy cold winters? How will you transport your supplies? You will be on your knees in no time!' Fatima blurted out, partly out of desperation, but mainly to divert his attention.

'Give yourself up, Keira. There's no road ahead. I speak not as your adversary, but as a well-wisher,' Kabir croaked in pain, diverting her attention as well as he could. His grip on the Glock would not loosen.

'Don't have time for this shit!' Allowing him no time to recuperate, she began yanking him towards the platform where the helicopter was still hovering in wait for her. All she had to do was get close enough, and Khabib would do the rest. He would shoot at both the handcuffs and Kabir.

Forcing himself out of his dizzy spell, he aimed the final bullet in his Glock right at her foot.

Bang!

'Allaena!' she grunted in anguish. But apparently, even a hole in her toe wouldn't stop her. Instead, she continued dragging his body like a rag across the cave till they reached the precipice.

He had another gun strapped to his foot, but with an injured shoulder on one side and a restraint on the other, he couldn't get to it fast enough.

And no sooner had they reached the edge than a loud echo reverberated.

Bang!

Through the open-door chopper, Khabib finished off in one clean shot what Fatima had been unable to do so far. He severed the links of the handcuff. In a trice, she leapt into the chopper.

'Sir!' Khabib stared at his supreme leader for an instant, wondering if there was something off about the man's aura today. He was about to conclude his grandfather's and Hanif's unfinished business. Once they escaped, the airstrike fiasco would hardly matter. Their final blow had already been rendered through the second button activated a short while ago. *No! Nothing should happen to Fatih. I shall let no one touch him! This man must live! He is our only hope!*

'Go on, Khabib. Quick, the taskforce is in the suite already!'

Fatih shook him out of his trance.

'But where is the Murshid?' Khabib quickly scanned the platform. 'And why is he not with you?'

Khabib had been working in close co-ordination with Abu after his father Bilal had passed away. He had expected that the Sayyid and the Murshid would come out together.

'That man shot him in the head,' she spewed, pointing at Kabir. 'Twice. Right through his eye sockets.'

'Bastard!' Khabib angled forward, about to fire a shot at Kabir's head, steering the helicopter for take-off while doing so.

No... no... no... Kabir darted his pupils around. With less than an instant to react, and no place to hide from the expert marksman, Kabir had only one avenue of escape.

He rolled off from the edge of the precipice.

'What? Where is he? Did he fall off?'

'Not sure...'

The two riders peeped from the sides of the chopper when they noticed the hatch of the suite opening. The taskforce team had managed to open the eighteen-inch-hatch door!

'Go... go... go... they're here!'

Just before the soldiers came storming into the platform, the chopper took off and away from the plains, where an entire army was waiting below to shoot them down.

∽

Aggggh!

Kabir was alone. Injured. And now, dangling off an armoured chopper that was riding higher up in the skies. Having rolled off the precipice, for a microsecond, his body had felt the profoundness of the 4000-metre drop, the force of gravity and the chill of the mountain air hitting him all at once. The sensations were mind-altering. Blood-curdling. But as a man of the skies, if there was anyone who knew what to do next, it was him. In the fraction of a pulse, he had grabbed onto the skid of the chopper.

With the 12,000-foot drop and the world's most dangerous terrorists sitting above, he had no option but to hold onto the bottom for as long as he could. But with every passing second, the crushing pressure was pulling apart every muscle in his body—the precarious position was probably the most gruelling demand ever placed on his limbs. Spasms of unimaginable pain were bolting through his shoulders despite the drugs. And it was his expertise alone that allowed him to withstand the breakneck forces, keeping him alert. Most other commandos in his place would have been rendered unconscious and tossed off from those altitudes by now.

∞

'Shit! I think he's still hanging off the chopper, sir!' Khabib could feel the additional weight while manoeuvring the lightweight chopper. It was the leanest in its category that could be parked snugly in a lead-lined crevice, invisible to satellites and radiation. 'What do you want me to do with him?'

'Keep flying. He's bound to fall off at some point.'

'Can't do that, sir. These men have some powerful trackers on them. That's how they located the Cove too. Have to stop him now before he pins a tracker onto our ride.' A minute later, he unbuckled his safety belt once the helicopter was in a steady path and stood up. 'Please take over the controls for a moment, I'll get rid of the bastard.'

Kabir's body was trembling from head to toe. The lack of oxygen was rendering him weaker by the second. In the absence of protective gear, with the air whipping past his face, his eyes were being squeezed shut, so hard that water had invariably misted his vision completely. He couldn't do this anymore. Using his chin, he pressed down on the transmitter tucked to his shoulder.

'Vladimir!' he screamed, his voice barely carrying through.

'Kabir?' came the response immediately. 'Where are you?'

'Under the chopper.'
'What?'
'Yes.'
'Which chopper?'
'The one the targets are getting away in. We're in your blind spot.'

'What the hell!' A burst of murmurs erupted in the ground camps.

'You have my coordinates. You know what has to be done. You have ten seconds.'

'No, wait!' Vladimir's worried voice crackled through. 'What about you? How are you going to…'

'Just do it, damn it!' yelled Kabir. 'Trust me.'

'All right,' his colleague relented with a sigh. After all, there was no argument there—the mission came before anything!

On the other hand, hanging off the handlebars, Khabib balanced himself on the helicopter skids with a loaded rifle, not a worry line on his face at the sight of the deadly drop below.

'You are one stubborn bugger!' he said, smiling as soon as he spotted the outline of the helpless commando hanging onto the chopper. The man's head was nearly convulsing from the effects of the monumental strain on his body now.

He pointed the rifle down, about to shoot. This would be child's play for him.

'Nine… eight… seven… six…' Kabir counted down. The ground force would need a few more seconds to use his trackers to align their coordinates for the helicopter. He would need to keep himself alive for a few more seconds.

'Mokhtar,' he blurted out in a loud tone to Khabib, trying to be heard over the chopper blades.

Khabib couldn't hear, but he read his grandfather's name on Kabir's lips.

'Wh…' The name stopped him in his tracks. It was a name

that was not often heard, the name of the one he admired the most—his grandfather.

'I can't believe how much you resemble him,' Kabir admitted. 'Lanky. Intelligent. Athletic. Determined. And you both died at the hands of the forces.'

At the next pulse, Kabir let go of the chopper skids, plunging down to jaw-dropping depths.

'What?' Khabib stared at the plummeting silhouette of the commando, still perplexed by why he had just given up. He glanced at the unfired rifle in his hand. But the next second that he looked down the conical warhead of a metallic guided missile was coming right at them.

'Wait...no! Sir!' he held out his hand to the Sayyid and yanked hard.

An instant or so thereafter, Kabir saw a huge blast erupt in the sky. The missile warhead had drilled right through the helicopter, rupturing its framework and sending it into a series of explosions. Shrapnel was hurled across the sky in all directions, some his way too. Arching his spine, he steered his limbs and began drifting sideways instead, operating at a drastic horizontal-to-vertical glide ratio, thus managing to get out of the way of the smouldering debris.

From the corner of his parched eyes he saw the remnants of the chopper come plunging down to the terrain below—the bodies of the world's deadliest killers trapped inside.

Kabir realized that he too was now trapped in the most dangerous aerial spot, plunging at an increased velocity, barely 3,000 metres above ground. Every second counted hereon. With a deep breath, he slipped a palm into his pocket and plucked one of the two pocket parachutes developed by RDOB. Soon, the emergency parachute opened up into a massive floater, instantaneously decelerating the freefall.

Kabir closed his eyes for a breather. 'Finally!'

It had barely been a second when he heard the whoosh of

something heavy approaching him. He looked up and through the skin-thin plastic umbrella, saw a two-foot-long shard falling directly on him. He tugged at the cords of the parachute, trying to steer clear.

Too late!

It cut right through the distended plastic and continued its manic freefall, missing Kabir's skewed body by a few inches. Kabir's mind raced for an escape plan; he was tangled in the thin plastic sheet and cords.

Oh God! He had managed to avoid the initial volley of slivers from the crashed copter, glided over towards plain land and kicked the parachute into action with immaculate timing. But alas! His time had come. He had no regrets. He had lived a full life.

He closed his eyes again, this time in prayer. There was a smile of contentment on his face. He wasn't leaving behind a grieving family, he had none! The most important mission in his life had just been accomplished. He had made sure the threat had been completely eliminated. And he had saved millions of lives!

53

Religion: a Convenient Vehicle

Brian Douglas Louis took one final look, pleased with himself at having aged so gracefully.

Broadcasting Tower, the headquarters of DDF News, had witnessed some of the most scintillating media trials over the century of its existence, but this would be by far the most important one. As their most popular news anchor, Brian had been given the responsibility of moderating a panel discussion between today's guests associated with the secret societies engaged in the recent debacle.

For the first time after the Seoul terrorist attack, there would be a speaker who had been in the eye of the storm, had interacted with both sides in person, face to face! With the news of the two secret societies—an Islamic one, the Ikhwan with its diabolical plan to crash 786 planes across the world on the one hand, and the taskforce appointed by another secret society, the Protettori, which circumvented the whole evil scheme on the other hand— occupying most of the airtime on news channels across the world, today's media trial would be a face-off. His mind was made up. He wouldn't be diplomatic in the slightest. He would expose the real culprits behind the wars, pain and misery in the world today.

He walked into the studio, aware that people around the world would have their eyes glued on to this media trial.

'Good evening, friends! Let's pay homage first to our departed heroes who sacrificed their lives to stall the disaster. Agent Kabir

Rathore, Agent Keira Brooks and Agent Olaf Adler, who as a part of a five-member taskforce, laid their lives down to save mankind from what could have been the biggest tragedy of modern times. An orchestrated terror attack at 786 critical locations across the world, aimed at creating terror ... and subjugation. The apparent convicts are obviously the secret organization called the Ikhwan-al-Jihadiya. The organization has been said to have stemmed from the Muslim Brotherhood. This brings us to our first guest today, Mr Mohammed Hadi, the supreme leader of the Brotherhood since 2010.

The camera turned towards the seventy-nine-year-old man. He leaned back on the sofa, pushing his thin-rimmed spectacle back up on his nose.

'Mr Hadie, your organization has outrightly denied any connection with the Ikhwan. But we all know that the Muslim Brotherhood is the mother of every fanatic Islamic outfit across the world today. You were there in Gaza, brought about the Islamic revolution in Iran, you fund and mentor most of the Muslim associations on foreign lands, including in the US! Do you realize... think for a moment...do you have the slightest idea what danger you could be putting our planet under by protecting the Ikhwan now?'

The camera went back to capture Hadi's expression. There was an incredulous smile on his face.

'Four days have passed and we have not been able to nab any of their top leaders. The men from the headquarters at the Cove— the officers, the civilians—they seem to know nothing about the organization's structure. With their leader, the Murshid, gone, it seems the Ikhwan is finished.' Brian paused for effect, letting his words sink in.

Then, turning to the camera, he continued. 'Or are they? Or is there a second line of leadership that has gone into hibernation and will strike again, stronger and more lethal this time?'

He turned towards Mr Hadi again. 'Even if your organization is not their parent organization and you are not their mentor, tell us whatever you know about them, sir. Our audience should know something about their modus operandi. Are their sleepers hiding amongst us? Who knows, some of our viewers' next-door neighbours could be Ikhwan assets!'

'Mr Brian,' Hadi began very calmly, 'the Muslim Brotherhood is a peaceful organization by its very nature. True, we are political, we fight for our rights, but we would never do something so gross. We too are taken aback that such a potent organization, which could conceive and accomplish a control centre as high tech as the Cove, could remain hidden from our eyes for so long.'

Brian shook his head in despair. 'You are so non-committal, Mr Hadi, just as expected.'

'Why, I only speak the truth. The intelligence agencies around the world must be at their jobs and they will unearth the assets sooner or later. What we should be discussing here is what spurred these people to form such an organization. If I go by what you are saying, thousands of men and women who work for this secret organization would be leading dual lives, hiding their intentions and their secret lives from their spouses, their children! What kind of pain must they have gone through to commit their lives to such a cause? Why don't we talk about that? About the oppression and meddling from the developed nations that the Arab world has suffered for decades.

'As a first step, we will need to curb that. Maybe that will be a good beginning towards saving our planet. You can't crush such movements with brutal force. See what happened in Iraq. In Afghanistan. It's the West's lust for oil and weapon deals that is responsible. The world must come together against such vested interests.'

'Ah, weapons!' Brian grinned. 'That reminds me of our second speaker today, Mr Spaniel Dackerson, one of the directors at Lockseed Perkin, the biggest weapons manufacturing company in the world. Mr Dackerson, your organization would have had high stakes in the Protettori. Very high! An organization with vested interests of arms manufacturers that leaves no stone unturned to fuel unrest in the world! An organization supported…or maybe, indirectly run…by governments whose economies depend largely on sales of weapons. Isn't Mr Hadi right when he says that you are the guys responsible, more than anyone else, for bringing mankind to this point?'

Mr Dackerson grinned. 'It's a naive supposition, Brian, to think that Lockseed Perkin would need a secret society to sell its products. And can you tell me your source when you present this society like demonic death mongers?' He paused to laugh. 'You rely on the Ikhwan's allegations, don't you? My informers tell me they are a government-supported organization who work *against* illegal arms trafficking. They infiltrate black markets and destroy them. And in that process, they often come across vital information. Information that has saved the day for mankind a number of times, including this recent incident. The agents you thanked just now! Who brought them together and put them on commission? Why should we be so thankless?'

'But the bigger point here is,' Dackerson continued, 'what makes you assume that weapons are responsible for the unrest in the world?'

'Well, what else? Do weapons bring about peace?' Brian smirked.

'Yes, of course! Remember history? Ambitious rulers used to trot around the globe with a jillion soldier to conquer nations. With swords, javelins, cannons and whatnot. Lakhs and thousands died in wars. Does that happen any longer? No! Then what do they do now? They negotiate! Even tiny countries like North Korea have the power to negotiate with world powers like America. The result? Minimal bloodshed. Weapons only give countries negotiating power. It is up to these countries whether to use them for that purpose or wield them against others. The world is a much more peaceful place, thanks to our modern weapons.'

Brian rubbed his forehead, his lips curled into an introspective smile. He had to admit there was merit in the logic. This was turning out to be more interesting and complicated than he had imagined.

'Just look at the wars fought around the world in the twenty-first century,' Akerson continued. 'Most of them have been fought between or with the participation of Islamic countries. Look at Libya, Yemen, Syria—can you deny that? Its Saudi against Iran, Turkey against Syria, Ethiopia against Somalia, Azerbaijan and Armenia, Iraq against the Kurds. The list goes on! Can you reason against statistics?'

Brian paused to consider, finally saying, 'While I do not endorse all of your reasoning, but we all agree on one thing after this attack. Islam, as it stands today, is not a peaceful religion. There is more resentment against Islam today than ever. Now that brings me to our third guest today, Mr Avijit Dongal, India's National Security Adviser. By his design, India successfully brought peace and prosperity to the state of Jammu and Kashmir, which had long been infested by Islamic militants. Tell me Mr Avijit, India has the second largest Muslim population in the world, and yet, it is one of the most peaceful countries. Do you agree with the fact that Islam is responsible for the precarious position mankind has landed into today? How does your country deal with that?'

'Brian, there is no denying the fact that Islamists have a domination plan. Many of their leaders, much like the Ikhwan, are still fascinated by the idea of re-establishing a caliphate across the world. Please observe here that India had a long history of Hindu-Muslim riots. It is only under the current government that complete peace has prevailed. Why? Because there is no more appeasement. People in power have to stop succumbing to the victim card played by such fanatics who want to establish Islam as the dominant religion.'

Dongal turned to face the camera, 'Liberalism is good when

dealing with a peaceful theology. Ours is a predominantly Hindu country, but a secular democracy at that. People from any religion are welcome to stay with us peacefully. But we don't tolerate people who live on our soil and spread hatred in the name of Islam. We sent out a clear message when a non-bailable warrant was issued against him. Or when Article 370 was abolished in Kashmir. Or when we put to death every single Pakistan-supported terrorist hiding out there. We have to stop being equivocal when it comes to peace and security.'

'I see where you are coming from, Mr Avijit,' Brian nodded in agreement. 'They call it polarization. And it's not happening just in India. Trump in America, Boris Johnson in Britain, Modi in India—all of them represent a sect of leaders who have been unequivocal. Many call them fascists. But the very fact that they came to power through the vote shows that people are no longer falling for pseudo-liberal reasoning. Islam is non-liberal by default. No one questions that. There is no guaranteeing the security of a non-Muslim in an Islamic country. So why is there such a hue and cry over isolated incidents of violence against them? I think it's a bit of tit-for-tat, an eye-for-an-eye kind of reaction the world is now resorting to. It's a balancing act.' He noticed that Mr Hadi had been waiting with his hand raised for quite some time, discomfited by his words. 'Yes, Mr Hadi...'

'You gentlemen seem to be concluding that Islam is responsible for all the fighting. But what about the US invasion of Iraq and Afghanistan? Was that an act of peace? Didn't it spread misery and resentment, which converted so many innocent people, who wanted to avenge their families' deaths, to suicide bombers? I am sorry, but you take advantage of being in the majority in this discussion today to declare us guilty.'

'Oh, but that's a wrong allegation, Mr Hadi.' Brian chuckled. 'Which brings us to our fourth guest today, Madam Nusrat. A very interesting discovery of the current debacle. She heads an all-women outfit that fights against terrorism in Libya. Berber Muslim women! Perhaps a reminder to the rest of the Muslims around the world that Islam can only be cleaned from the inside. I know you are a devout Muslim, Madam Nusrat, still I will ask you to answer that one. I hope your presence addresses Mr Hadi's resentment of being in the minority here.'

'Thanks, Brian. Mr Hadi has raised a very important point here. I agree with him that America has acted notoriously in invading these Muslim countries. But what is the Muslim world doing about it? If they are really so concerned about the well-being of the international Muslim fraternity, why don't they come together and offer resistance? Most of them are busy allying with America or earning its goodwill in some way or the other. Why did they not give up their petty fights and join hands to fight this evil force, the United States of America?

'Let me tell you why...' She continued, 'because there is no real enemy bigger than our own for Islam...because the current version of Islam being taught in madrasas advises people to pick up arms, to fight. All our leaders, whether kings or petty mullahs, they don't give a shit about the people. They just want to use Islam as a vehicle to legitimize their positions and wield power over the commoners. And so, the commoners fight! Fight till they die or kill a brother, if not an enemy.' Nusrat felt a lump rise in her throat as she choked on her words, her eyes watering.

The panel fell silent for a moment, chewing over the analysis just laid bare by Nusrat...and so did millions of Muslims around the world watching Brian's show.

Epilogue

Tajikistan…two days later

'Kabir.' The petite lady nudged closer to him, hiding her face from the shafts of morning sunlight that had started to filter in through the window next to their bed.

'Keira.' He withdrew, chuckling, both at being tickled in his side by her nose and being called by that name.

'Fatima, my love,' he whispered into her ear. 'I told you my real name is Zunaid!' He pulled her deftly on top, kissing her gently, feeling the warmth of her body over his. 'I'm so glad our scores are even.'

'Thanks for saving my life! I still can't believe that we both survived. But for you, I would be buried in the snow outside.' She remembered how she had fainted in the snow and then woken up in the warmth of his arms. She nuzzled closer. 'The best part is that you turned out to be one of our own!'

Memories of how death had eluded him just the day before flashed before Kabir. The parachute had saved him after all. He had closed his eyes to embrace death, entangled in the torn parachute, falling with staggering velocity. And then, he had felt a bone-jittering tug. The plastic strings splayed around his body like tentacles had gotten entangled in a pine tree. First, he felt the jerk, and then, he was thrown on the tree trunk, hitting it sideways with full force. The pain had been excruciating. But as it waned, and he lay there hanging in his cradle, he took in deep swigs of the fresh forest air, exhilarated that he was still alive.

'It is the end of a new beginning, as they say,' Zunaid said, turning to face her. 'Fatih, Keira and Kabir—are all dead to the world now. Their story is over! But here we are, making a new beginning!'

Fatima smiled. She couldn't get her own narrow escape out of her mind either. It had been miraculous.

She had realized the peril she had been in only when Khabib had pulled her out of the copter. During the free fall, she saw a missile heading for their copter, and the next second, they were swarmed by debris whizzing past them in every direction. Khabib was riding over her back, like a skydiving coach. She realized that he had, infact, been shielding her from the shrapnel when she felt his warm blood ooze down her body. They were gaining speed with each passing second. He steered them towards a valley between two mountains. She could see the white ground below them; it was like an ice-skating stadium in the wilderness of the mountains. They were headed towards its centre. She closed her eyes in horror as the icy wind whizzed past her ears. Suddenly their bodies flipped around and she heard a loud thud, followed by a spine-piercing chill. Khabib had turned his back to the ice cover, holding her body over his own as they hit the smooth hard ice. He cried aloud in pain as he took the impact…and then they were inside icy waters. It was a frozen lake and they were sinking to its bottom.

Khabib had kicked vehemently, holding her up, as if he had been through this many times before. And just as he had delivered her out of the opening in the ice, he had got a clear view of her face. With the wig, the turban and the make-up gone, he immediately recognized the person he had confronted several times over the last twenty-four hours. 'Allah!' He had given in to the spinning sensation in his head and the pain from the shattered spinal cord.

Fatima had plodded around the periphery of the lake till she found a path leading across a pass to the forest on the other side of the mountain. She had then walked for what felt like miles, far out on a desolate path in the forest. Only then had she noticed a man blissfully cradled along a pine trunk. She tried to cry for help, but the cold and exhaustion got the better of her and she collapsed.

Zunaid had climbed down the pine tree once the pain had ebbed and found her. Fortunately, he saw a deserted shack some distance away, and arranged a fire to retrieve her from the hypothermia.

After she had regained consciousness, he had revealed his real identity. He had told her how he had been brought up in a charitable orphanage run by a mosque, where he had been indoctrinated into radical Islam. At the age of six, a generous Hindu family had adopted him as their foster son and named him Kabir. Since their job involved a lot of travelling, he would stay back at the orphanage most of the times. But it wasn't till he got the chance to visit Egypt, at the age of fourteen, that he decided to dedicate his life to the Islamic cause. He retained his Hindu name and identity and went on to qualify the National Defence Academy exams, finally making it into Indian military intelligence. His secret life as a senior Ikhwan asset was known to none other than the Maulana, his mentor, who had arranged for the visit to Egypt and had died soon after.

Fatima had remembered how seriously he had performed the Salah with Tareq's men before the shoot-out at the old man's house and it had left no doubt in her mind.

'That day, when we were outside the Cove, I could see the hatred in your eyes, Zunaid, and you had me handcuffed. Why didn't you shoot me then? You had another gun on you, right?'

'Love, my love. Didn't I tell you?' he mumbled, still groggy from sleep. 'I have told you my story many times over since yesterday. I am an orphan. No one understands the value of parents more than I do. Who would have taken care of your old mother then?' he teased.

'Come on! I know you have had feelings for me, but that wasn't exactly on your mind right then. Don't play me,' she grumbled, planting a peck on his lips.

'You are a smart woman, darling. A deserving Sayyid! I was in Kabir's character then and I had to do justice to it! There were people watching us from the centrum monitors. I couldn't have given myself away. I have to admit I was shocked for a while when I recognized you from inside the suite through the large television screen in the centrum. But as reality sank in, I couldn't help but admire your mettle. Yet, I had to stop you. That was the most important purpose before me then. You would have ruined everything, the way you had rushed things. If our assets would have come out in the open, we could never have rebuilt that base. You know it took us eight long decades to put it together.'

'Hmmm.' She smiled. Her sizzle dampened by his icy-cold embrace. She found herself to be a calmer person in his arms.

'And now that we are together, we can work on it again, with a fool proof, well-timed plan.' He winked. 'Our assets—our greatest strength—are safe. With your acumen and my stratagem, we shall face no hurdles.'

'And what's the essence of the new plan?' She pulled his arm below her head, using it as a pillow, her breath washing over his face.

He turned towards her and whispered into her ear. Her face lit up, brighter with each word.

'Brilliant!' She turned to face him. There was no way this could go wrong. She gave in once more to his irresistible charm, taking him into her delicate embrace. They made passionate love, its culmination bringing her to unsurpassed ecstasy. A stark contrast to her last experience with the lecherous Arab doctor she had had to seduce.

'I have led a life of celibacy for almost two decades,' she admitted, smiling to herself, lying in his arms. 'My well-deserved bliss!' She cuddled Zunaid, who had dozed off soon after. Her body hurt too. It would take them a few more days to recover after the physical and mental ordeal they had been through.

Then Fatima sighed, whispering to herself. 'He is strong and capable. The Murshid is gone. I could do with a partner like him. Heaven sent! I would rather lie in his arms eternally, but alas!'

Saying this, she got up, stepped out of the bed and reached for his backpack lying on the side table.

∽

Something cold and hard pressed against her spine.

'Put your hands where I can see them!' She heard his voice and turned. She was at the working table, completing some important transactions on her laptop, which she had pulled out from his backpack.

'Good joke!' She smiled and began to get up.

'You really don't want to risk moving! I suggest you think twice.' Kabir's expression was playful.

'Wallah! My handsome killer. Go ahead, I'm all yours.' She got up and started to move towards him, certain this was foreplay before another lovemaking session.

But the next moment she saw him lower his gun and a throttled sound filled the room. She looked down to see her second foot bleeding, the one he had shot at earlier lovingly bandaged by him a few hours ago.

'Who are you?' a low growl escaped her throat.

A sly grin emerged on his lips. He was relishing every bit of this. 'Shaytan!'

'Wh…what?' Her jaw dropped. 'That's not possible!'

And then, the pieces started falling into place. Zunaid alias Kabir alias Shaytan. He was the Ikhwan asset who had turned rogue. While they kept thinking that the Shaytan was someone who had some personal or ideological enmity with them and wanted to kill their top leaders, he was, in fact, an insider who wanted to thwart the mistimed mission. Try as hard as he could, there was no way he could have handled the momentum alone. When the Protettori invited him for the counterstrike, he must have been more than happy to jump in. And now, he had turned greedy! Wanted to put her out of his way!

'Bastard!' she snarled. 'So you think you can run the Ikhwan alone!'

She saw a smile materialize on his face, hoping against hope that this was really a crazy joke. He broke into hysterical laughter.

She let out a relieved breath, taking a step forward. 'Are you mad—you really shot me!' She pointed towards her bleeding foot.

'Hold it!' He pointed the gun back at her. 'I can't believe you're such a fool, Fatima!'

'What!' she said, an uncertain expression clouding her face.

'You thought you were playing this game all along, didn't you?' Zunaid smirked and looked like a different person.

'Yes,' she snapped, losing all control, 'and you're just a lucky bastard!' She launched herself forward, her hands reaching out to claw at the flesh of his throat. But he moved aside swiftly, causing her to hit the wall, crashing head-on. She slumped to the floor, sitting with her back against the wall as he pointed the gun back at her.

'Lucky! You don't know how hard I tried,' Kabir continued, the gun still pointed right at her forehead, 'to reach you. I spied on the Murshid, made friends with his driver, Jameel, and finally broke into his house one day. After attending so many annual re-avowal meetings, I got the hunch that he was only a symbolic chief. The real powers rested elsewhere. When I took him captive that day in his house, I demanded to speak to you, but he wouldn't let me. He was willing to die instead. What was I supposed to do?

'So when you killed a faithful deputy like him in the Cove, I was shocked. But then you had to be cold-blooded…you couldn't leave behind a trail! You had kept your identity hidden from Abu and Khabib till that day and now Abu had seen you.'

'I was about to get Abu's call records and the other data at his house that day, when Khabib barged in and chased me across rooftops. I could have killed him right there, but I refrained. Bruce too had a clear shot on him from the CH-53 window, when he came riding the aerial hoverboard outside the copter. I stopped Bruce! Do you see now who was playing this game?'

'I still don't get it. You are the Shaytan, the rogue, who wants to replace me and carry out his own plan to bring on the caliphate? Why did you not kill me outside the Cove, once you knew I was the Sayyid? Why did you not eliminate Khabib at the first opportunity? It would have made your job a lot easier.'

'Because Khabib and Abu were the only persons who could have led me to you,' he continued. 'The poor guy didn't even know that I was the intelligence officer on the other side of the interrogation cell when he was taken captive in India. That day, too, I had asked him about your whereabouts, but he was one stubborn bastard. I got the smartass's sphincter torn instead, leaving his ass to smart every single second. To remind him of his limitations. To slow him down! But how could he? He was Mokhtar's blood, after all.'

'Son of a bitch!' she screamed, her eyes reflecting her anger ... and her fear. 'I still don't get you. If you just had to put me out of your way, why did you save me? What are we doing here? How does any of this help your plans for the Ikhwan?'

'Because there will be no Ikhwan hence. And no caliphate! Kabir alias Zunaid alias Shaytan, India's top military intelligence agent promises you this.'

'What!' Fatima's face turned pale. 'Didn't you just tell me that the Indian military intelligence thing was just a cover!'

'Yes, I did! Taqiyaa! Ever heard of it? The circumstances under which a true Muslim can resort to deception.'

'You're fricking crazy! Why would a Muslim use it against another?'

'It seems like you have forgotten your family history. Your grandfather's friend Mokhtar used it so often against his own, didn't he?'

'How do you know so much about Mokhtar?'

'From a journal I inherited from my grandfather. Adel Kamaal!'

'Adel!'

'Yes, it even has an old newspaper cutting with both their pictures side by side, the two estranged friends. Mokhtar had cold, lifeless eyes! I would be reminded of them each time I confronted Khabib.'

'So this is personal, right?' she roared. 'You're so much like your grandfather! A kafir, after all!'

'No, no... not at all! Nothing personal here! You've got it all wrong, Fatima. It's a long story,' he said, sniggering. 'I won't skip it; you have the right to know!'

'So this goes back to 1955, when Pandit Nehru, the Indian Prime Minister, visited Gamal Abdel Nasser, the President of free Egypt. They had started the Non-Aligned Movement together against the British after becoming free from British rule. It was then that Grandpa Adel met Rubina. She was with Nehru's delegation. Adel was Nasser's security chief. They took a liking to each other at first sight. Rubina shifted to Egypt a few years later and they got married. She was pregnant when Mokhtar killed Adel.'

'And then she had to move in with her parents in India, where she gave birth to my father. She belonged to a family of Indian intelligence officers, and so began our mission to counter the murky underground conspiracy brewing in Egypt. One that got my grandfather Adel killed! One on which my father's families in India and Egypt worked in communion for almost three decades. After which they realized that they had failed, miserably!'

'They needed someone inside the Ikhwan. But an asset's background check would run into several generations. So they planted me...as an orphan. It was a bold move, but very meticulously planned. With the support of Indian intelligence, my father and mother conned the identities of a Hindu family and adopted me from the orphanage. They imbued in me the true spirit of a global citizen. My name is Kabir for instance—a person who believes in both Islam and Hinduism. What is religion after all? Nothing but a way in which you choose to lead your life. Why shouldn't one taste the best of every religion? Be a Christian on Halloween, a Muslim on Eid, a Hindu on Diwali! Why be an atheist, why not be a heterotheist instead?'

'You are scum on the face of Islam. You won't stop us…ever!' Fatima's eyes were radiating repugnance. She screamed. 'Just pull the trigger, son of a bitch!'

'Not yet, my darling! Aren't you enjoying our tête-á-tête?' He walked closer, pressed a button on her laptop, making the screen that had gone into sleep mode come alive. Taking out his mobile with his other hand, he clicked a screenshot of the bank transaction page on display.

'We learnt this in Kashmir. If you really have to kill a terrorist outfit, cut off their spinal cord. Their funding! I tried to trace back the Ikhwan's account from the chit I got in Olaf's pocket, but the path was untraceable. Finally, now I have access to the ancient treasures of the Ikhwan. I will be the new Sayyid from now on.'

'Bastard! Why?'

'Didn't you just tell me that I can't ever stop the Ikhwan. But what if I become the Sayyid, tear down the Ikhwan-al-Jihadiya, shred by shred? Wipe out every single asset…till there is no trace left? Except this fund, sizeable enough to support counter terrorism operations across the globe for decades, maybe centuries.'

'Fuck you!' she spat.

'That you already have, several times over…and it was a pleasure, I must say!' he leered, pressing the trigger.

Acknowledgements

My first book *The Four Patriots* was met with more acceptance and love than I could have expected. The book went on to become a Rupa bestseller and even held its place as an Amazon #1 best-seller for a couple of days.

Now I have worked even harder for this second title—travelling the globe, meeting people of all faiths and delving deep into theology and politics; all to be able to do justice to the script. The subject, I believe, is sensitive but needs to be talked about more. If we are to understand the etiology of world-terror, we must engage with the past and trace its origins. That's what this story does—it ties the past and the future together.

I would like to thank my family for patiently supporting me in my adventures—be it business, writing, music or social work. COVID-19 has taught us so many lessons. It has nudged us towards living our lives to the fullest. Many of us have also realized the importance of giving back. I founded two NGOs last year— Savtik Roti Rolls and MLA Green Kanpur—and both of them have been doing well by God's grace. I urge my fellow industrialists in the country to come forward and carve out some time for social endeavours.

I would also like to thank my editor Shraddha P. who has worked tirelessly with me on this book and is currently in London. I pray she is safe. I would like to thank my friend and literary agent Suhail Mathur associated with The Book Bakers. Always cheerful and positive, he is backed with a formidable team who assist authors in their book pitch. I would like to thank Manpreet Kaur, the

Indian BookTuber, all my reviewers whose feedback has helped me enrich the book and several dignitaries who have endorsed my book through their testimonials. I would also like to thank Rupa Publications for bestowing faith and confidence in me. I would also like extend a bucket full of thanks to my readers, who give me a reason to carry on and do better.

A special thanks to my wife, Riya, for strongly standing by me, always.

And last but not the least, I would like to thank Bajrang Bali ji for his countless blessings.

Jai hind.